THE MISSING WIFE

SUE FORTIN

Storm
PUBLISHING

ALSO BY SUE FORTIN

The Dead Wife

Schoolgirl Missing

The Birthday Girl

Sister Sister

The Girl Who Lied

The Half Truth

Closing In

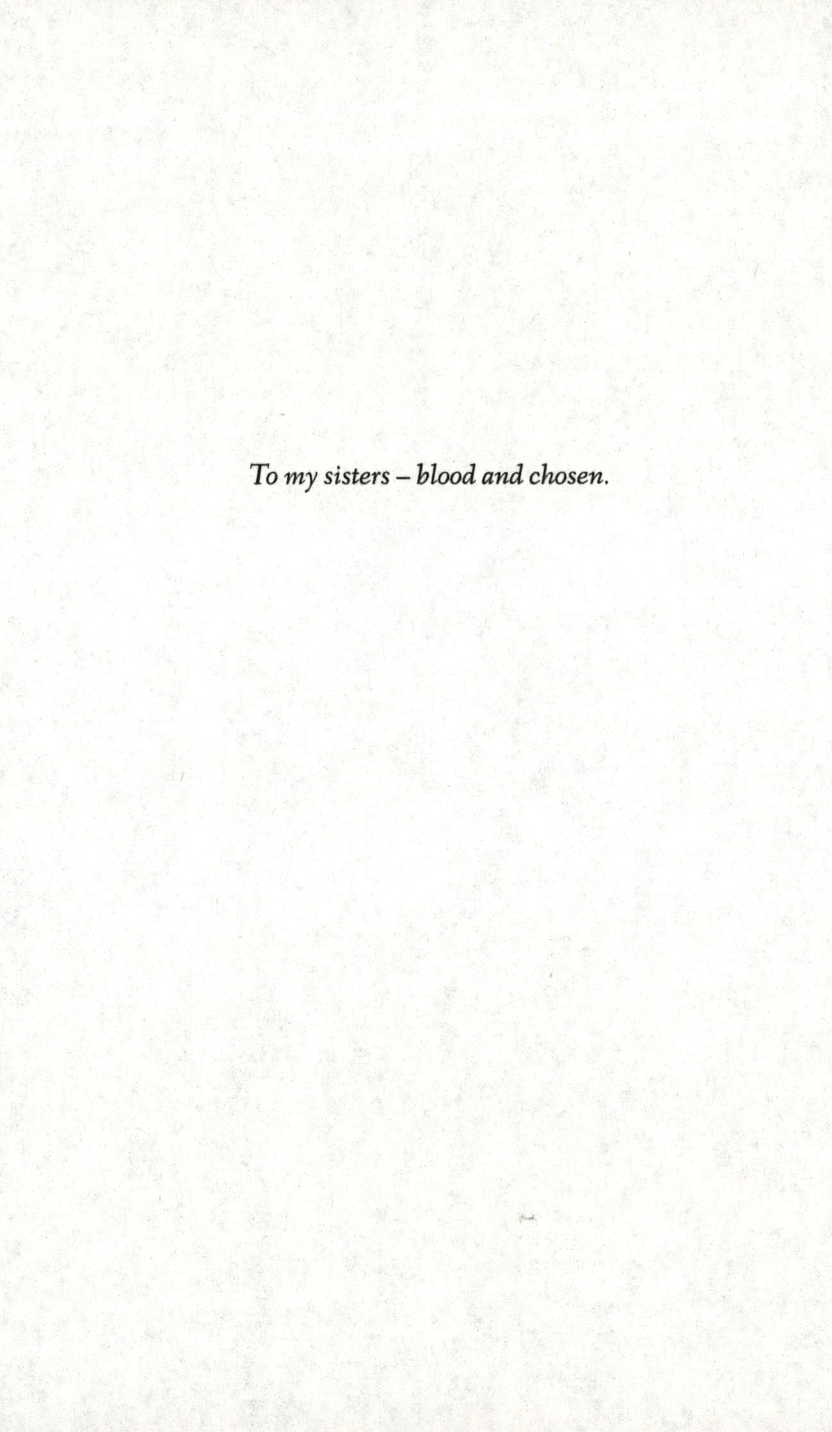

To my sisters – blood and chosen.

ONE

When I look back on that argument, I can't remember how it started. Who made the first comment to cause offence. At what point it went from a discussion to a debate, and then became a fight. Looking through the hazy window of time, six months seems like both yesterday and a lifetime ago. I can't remember the details. However, to a person, everyone in the little village on the west coast of Ireland – whether they were there or not – remembers how it finished.

'Sure, have you heard the news? Kathleen Regan – well, she's Kathleen Walsh now, but you know, the eldest Regan sister – she's gone missing.'

'Nooo, you're joking. What do you mean, missing?'

'Like, she never made it home.'

Of course, as interest grew in my sister's disappearance and the story was shared far and wide on social media, everyone had a theory as to what happened after the argument, or 'explosive row', as it was described.

'They had a fierce argument, the three of them. Right in the middle of the pub.'

'What was it about?'

'That's just it. No one really knows. It got all out of hand before anyone cottoned on.'

'That's terrible.'

Everyone who was at the pub that night, and everyone who wasn't, suddenly became armchair detectives, keyboard investigators who had all watched one too many episodes on the true crime channel – suddenly they were all experts in body language, speech pattern, eye contact and forensic evidence. Theories ranged from murder and drowning to witness protection and abduction by aliens.

'She's taken herself off. Probably got a fancy man somewhere.'

'But she wouldn't leave Kian. I know he's twenty an' all, but he's her baby.'

'If it's not a man, then I reckon the sisters know more than they're letting on. Did you see the way the youngest wouldn't look at the camera at the press conference?'

'Corin? No, she's the quiet one out of them. The baby of the three. She's distraught.'

'You know what they say – still waters and all that.'

And in the weeks that followed, as new evidence emerged, which the guards were not at that stage of their investigation able to share, the official line became that they believed Kathleen had left of her own free will.

Still, everyone had their theory. Thought they knew. And yet, no one knew a thing. My sister disappeared into the proverbial thin air. But for all the theories why Kathleen never made it home, everyone came back to the same one – I had ignored her late-night phone call begging for help.

'Apparently, Kathleen tried to call Siobhan that night, but Siobhan didn't pick up.'

'What?'

'I know. Ignored her sister. Can you believe that?'

'Ah, Jesus, imagine the guilt.'

And they were right. The millstone of guilt hung heavy around my neck.

From the window of my Brighton flat, I looked out at the sea where the waves were cresting and then lapping on the stony shoreline. Seagulls wheeled in the air before they swooped down to squabble angrily over the leftover chips strewn across the pavement. It reminded me of a time when me and my sisters were kids. I was about nine. Kathleen had been tasked with sharing a bar of chocolate between us. It was Easter and we'd had to give up chocolate for Lent, so it made the confectionary extra special and competition for the lion's share was strong. With only four years between the three of us, it was a hard-fought battle. As the eldest, Kathleen made sure she had two whole squares. Corin and I had to split the remaining three.

Kathleen was never far from my thoughts and my world tilted at her absence once again, rocking my foundations. I took a deep breath, exhaling slowly as I looked out at the greeny-blue south coast water, fixing my gaze on the horizon as I stabilised myself.

'Is that toast for me?' The voice of my fifteen-year-old daughter, Freya, broke my thoughts and I was grateful for the distraction.

Smile in place, I turned around. 'Sure. Help yourself.'

Freya was already jamming a slice of wholemeal into her mouth, standing at the worktop wearing an approximation of her school uniform. The skirt was rolled over one too many times, the sleeves of her blazer pushed up her forearms, and the tip of the tie definitely wasn't touching the fourth button of her blouse. I let it slide. I picked my battles, and uniform wasn't one of them. Neither was the laser-precision contouring of make-up which gave Freya's nose a thinner and slightly sharper look than I liked. And there was that blob of highlighter on the tip of her nose that I wanted to point out needed blending a bit more, but ultimately I didn't. Woe betide the mother who commented on her teenager's make-up.

'What lessons have you got today?' I opted for instead.

Freya reeled off her timetable. 'I've Textiles last and I should have the hat finished today.' She checked her reflection in the glass of the microwave that sat on top of the fridge. 'Does my hair look greasy?'

'No. Not at all.' The right answer. 'You look grand.'

Freya's phone pinged an alert. Whether it was a text, Snapchat, or something similar, I had no idea. I watched my daughter read the message; a frown crept across her face.

'Is everything all right?' I asked.

Freya shrugged and swallowed hard. 'It's nothing.'

'It doesn't look like nothing. What's the matter?' I placed my cup on the worktop.

Freya appeared to deliberate for a moment but then let out a sigh before speaking. 'Apparently, Sophie's mum saw Dad on the pier last night.'

'The pier?' I glanced towards the window where, if I craned my neck, I could just catch sight of the infamous Brighton Pier. 'What was he doing there?'

'He was at the bar with some friends.'

'Well, he's allowed to go out for a drink.' My mind instantly imagined some female draped over my husband. She'd be caught up by his soft Irish accent, which my English girlfriends told me was sexy. She'd probably be laughing at some wisecrack he'd made. I should know. That would have been me all those years ago.

'I don't think he's coming back,' said Freya. A single tear blobbed onto the worktop.

'Oh, Freya, come here.' I put my arms around my daughter, wanting to take away the pain inflicted by the slow disintegration of her parents' marriage. 'Me and your dad have a lot to talk about. It's...'

'Complicated,' said Freya, hijacking the end of my sentence. She pulled away from the embrace. 'I know. So you both keep saying.' She looked at her phone as another alert sounded. 'I've got to go. Sophie's here.' She gave me a quick peck on the cheek. 'Bye.'

With that she was gone. I went back to the window, like I always did when Freya left for school, and looked down on the street below. A few moments later, Freya emerged and greeted her friend with a hug like it had been weeks since they'd last seen each other, rather than less than twenty-four hours. Then both girls turned, looked up at the window, and waved. I waved back and watched them head down the street. I smiled at the sound of their indistinguishable high-pitched voices as they looked at Sophie's phone and shrieked with laughter, almost falling into each other in a bid to stay upright.

Freya was so like her dad, with her blonde hair and blue eyes. I always thought they would both make perfect extras for any Viking film. I wondered what Danny was doing right then. Was he standing at the window of his rented apartment, planning his weekend? Was he clicking his heels in delight at his newly found singledom? A night out with the lads. A curry? Sunday lunch at the pub? The female at the bar? Or was he, like me, wondering where fifteen years of marriage went and whether he'd made the right choice moving out last month? Our relationship was ultimately another casualty of the night Kathleen went missing.

My phone rang and vibrated its way across the worktop, making me jump and bringing me from my thoughts. Unknown caller. I accepted without a second thought, not being of the generation that would stare in horror and wait for the call to go to voicemail. No, I was ballsy Gen-X, if only squeezing in by a year. Besides, it might be a new job coming in. I'd been trying to rebuild my journalistic career since my split with Danny, especially if the trial separation was to become a permanent one. The thought sent a pain through my heart. I didn't want to be a single mum. I wanted to be a family. A happy family. I wanted to push back against my own childhood.

'Ah, good morning. Sorry to bother you, but can I speak to Siobhan, please?'

I could tell it was a west coast voice, an Irish accent not dissimilar to my own, except mine was less pronounced now after years of living in England.

'Hi, yes, that's me,' I replied.

'Oh, well, I found your purse. I was out walking my dog yesterday when I came across it.'

I frowned. I hadn't lost my purse. Or had I? With the phone still pressed to my ear, as the caller explained about the dog walk and how she'd found it on the ground, right by the gate, I rummaged in my bag. My purse was there.

'I'm sorry,' I said, interrupting the caller, who sounded like she was younger than me, possibly early twenties. 'There must be some mistake. I haven't lost my purse.'

'You haven't? Well, that's very strange altogether. You see, I have this purse and it has your name and number in it.'

I was confused. 'Where did you say you found it?'

'Up on The Banks.'

'The Banks? That's Dingle. County Kerry. Ireland.'

The caller gave a chuckle. 'Yes. That's right.'

I was finding it hard to make sense of the conversation. I hadn't been back to Dingle since Kathleen disappeared, so how she thought it was my purse was beyond me. I wondered if someone had my business card and that's how this woman had got in touch. 'Is there any ID in it other than my business card?'

'It's not your business card,' she said. 'It's a piece of paper: *If found please contact Siobhan.*' She reeled off my phone number. 'There's nothing else in it except a bus ticket and a train ticket.

No bank cards, no money – I want to make that clear, I haven't taken anything from the purse. It just has your name and number in it.'

I still wasn't any clearer. 'What does the purse look like?'

'Cream with black piping and a gold clasp.'

I swallowed hard. I'd bought Kathleen a purse matching that description for her fortieth birthday. The occasion we'd been out belatedly celebrating when she went missing. 'What else is inside it?' My heart was racing.

'Look, if it's not yours, maybe I should take it to the guards.'

'No!' I said, far sharper than I'd intended. I modified my delivery. 'No, don't do that. What else is in it? You said something about a train ticket.'

The woman hesitated and I thought for a moment she wasn't going to tell me anything, but eventually, she spoke. 'There's a train ticket dated last weekend. And a bus ticket from Tralee to Dingle.'

I still couldn't work out what was going on, but my gut instinct was to get the purse. 'Oh, it must be my sister's,' I said quickly. 'She lives on the outskirts of Dingle. Can you drop it to her? Or I could get her to come to you?'

'No, it's fine. I'll drop it.'

'That's great. I expect she'll be relieved it's not lost,' I prattled on, trying to contain the adrenaline charging through me. I relayed Corin's address and thanked the caller, reassuring her that the purse did belong to my sister. I just didn't tell her which sister.

TWO

'Don't freak out,' I said to Corin over the FaceTime call I made immediately after getting off the phone from the mystery caller. I went on to tell her about the woman who'd found Kathleen's purse.

'But that doesn't make sense,' said Corin. 'How has her purse only now been found? And why is there a train and bus ticket in it? And why your name and number?'

'I've no idea to any of that,' I replied honestly. 'I can barely think straight right now, but I needed to make sure she didn't hand the purse in. I want to see it first.'

'You're coming over?'

'Yes. Freya breaks up for half-term today. I'm going to see if she can stay with Danny, or she might want to come over herself.'

'It would be lovely to see you both, and you know you're welcome to stay here.'

'I will, thanks.'

'You want me to let Mam and Dad know?'

I let out a small sigh. 'Probably best. It's not like I can come over SAS style, in and out without being seen.'

'I'll tell them it was a last-minute, spur-of-the-moment social visit,' said Corin.

'Good idea. Look, as soon as I've arranged the flights, I'll let you know when I'll be there. Don't tell anyone about the purse. I want to see it first.'

'Of course.'

There was a small silence before Corin spoke again. Her voice was softer. More cautious. 'Do you think... you know... that Kathleen is alive?'

'God, I hope so,' I replied, looking up to the ceiling. I wasn't religious, but if there was a God up there, I prayed he was listening. 'We'll talk properly once I'm there.'

My next call was to Danny. I didn't know why this filled me with so much trepidation. Was it the knowledge that he'd been out last night, possibly with another woman? We may have been having a trial separation, but I wasn't sure that extended to shagging other people. I was pretty certain that wasn't discussed when we agreed this pause on our marriage.

I brought up his number and pressed call. He only went into the office three days a week and Friday was a work-from-home day. It went to voicemail.

'Danny, it's me. Look, something's come up and I've got to go...' I paused, swallowing back the word home. 'I've got to go to Ireland. I need you to have Freya for the half-term. Call me back as soon as you get this. Thanks.' Another pause, before I added, 'I hope you're OK.'

It had been Danny's idea to move out and I hadn't stopped him. I wondered now whether I had been too willing to agree to the separation and whether I should have fought a little harder for him to stay and work things out. I missed him. The fracture in our marriage had widened to a gap, but I didn't think it was at gulf-like proportions. He'd said things had changed after Kathleen's disappearance. I had changed. I'm not sure what he expected, but of course I was different now. Guilt, grief, loss, all held together by the fragile thread of hope. Yes, it had affected me, but had it changed me? The secrets and refusal on my part to be totally honest with Danny had brought a new element to our marriage. One of mistrust and hurt. I hadn't been honest with him and, although he knew what I'd done, I had refused to discuss it. That was a first for us. We'd never had secrets up until six months ago. So, maybe I had changed.

My phone rang. It was Danny.

'Siobhan. You OK?'

There was disquiet in his voice and my heart constricted at the concern levelled. A wave of emotion broke over me. I swallowed hard and blinked back tears that threatened. 'I'm fine,' I said, sounding far calmer than I felt. 'Are you able to have Freya next week? I've got to go over to see Corin.'

'Is everything all right?'

'Yes. Well, kind of. I can't really explain right now, but it's to do with Kathleen.'

'Kathleen?'

'Yes. Look, don't say anything, but someone's found her purse. I really want to speak to Corin, and maybe the guards.'

'And you can't do that over the phone?'

'No. I need to be there.'

'Siobhan, I'm not saying don't go, but do you really need to? If your sister's purse has been found, surely it's a matter for the guards.' I knew his words were said with kindness, but they irritated me all the same.

'I want to go. And I'm going,' I said. 'So, can Freya stay with you?'

'As it happens, she can't. I've got plans. I'm going to be away for a few days. Work stuff.'

He sounded shifty. 'Work stuff? Since when did you go away for work?' In my head I was really asking *Are you shagging that woman from the pier?*

'Since I got promoted two weeks ago.'

'You never said.'

A silence stretched down the phone and I knew we were both thinking he never said because that was the type of conversation you had with your partner when your relationship was solid, not when it was on the rocks. It was also a reminder that he had a career and I didn't. Not since I gave up my job as a journalist to become a stay-at-home mum. A pivot I'd gladly performed but, as Freya was getting older, the pull back into the working world was strong. Easier said than done when you've been out of the workplace for over fifteen years and heading into your forties.

'I could ask my mum if Freya can go and stay with her,' offered Danny. His parents had recently moved from Dingle to some remote place in Galway to be near his mother's sister. Freya would condemn me to purgatory for all eternity if I sent her there.

'No. It's fine. I'll take her with me. She can see her cousins and my parents.'

'She'll love that.'

'Not now, Danny.' We both knew Freya wouldn't relish seeing her grandparents, but at least in Dingle there'd be other distractions for her. However, I wasn't going to get into that with Danny. Those were conversations for married couples, not couples where the husband had moved out. The anger and frustration at the situation, neither of which I had any right to, rose to the surface, swamping the pain. 'I've to go. I have flights to organise.'

'Siobhan,' said Danny. 'Call me if you need me. If you want to talk. I know you think I've walked away, but I'm still here.'

The kindness in his voice quelled my anger immediately as I was reminded of the man I'd married and not the man who'd left. 'Thanks.' I cut the call before I burst into tears. I had no idea what he meant by that, but I didn't have time to dissect all the pain-riddled areas of our marriage. The irony that I was once again putting Kathleen ahead of everyone wasn't wasted on me.

Not only that, but there was a selfish thought lurking at the back of my mind, one that was hard to even acknowledge. What a newsworthy scoop it would be to solve the mystery of what happened to Kathleen Walsh. Newsworthy enough to relaunch my journalistic career. I batted it away, immediately feeling ashamed of myself.

Freya wasn't exactly enamoured with the idea of spending half-term in Ireland, but I'd already booked the flights by the time she came home and, as I pointed out, she was well overdue a visit.

'As long as you don't expect me to go to church with Nan and Granddad,' she said, folding her arms across her chest.

I held up my hands to placate her. 'Just so we're clear, you do NOT have to go to church. We're staying at Corin's anyway, so you won't have to say grace before you eat or prayers before you sleep. But if you go to their house, you will have to at least pretend to bless yourself with Holy Water.'

I was sure Freya muttered *for fuck's sake* under her breath, but that was another battle I wasn't going to get into. She stomped off to her room to underline her grievance at having to go. I couldn't blame her; it wasn't like I ever wanted to go back home. Far too many bad memories lay there, and that was before Kathleen went missing. Her disappearance only compounded the complicated feelings I had about Ireland.

We touched down at Shannon Airport, having got a flight from Gatwick on Sunday morning. Although Freya was born in England, having Irish parents meant she qualified for an Irish passport, and this made life easier getting through customs.

Corin was on the other side of the barrier waiting for us, along with her ten-year-old twin daughters, Erin and Sorcha. Freya was very sweet and made a fuss of them, which they delighted in.

'It's good to see you,' said Corin, giving me a hug. 'Just so you know, Mam said you're to come for tea this evening. Sorry. I tried to put it off until tomorrow.' Corin gave an apologetic smile.

'Sure, it's OK. We've time to talk before then.' I slipped my arm through my sister's, and we headed out to the car park with the girls following behind.

I watched the countryside roll along outside the window as we drove away from Shannon Airport heading towards Dingle – the harbour village on the Kerry peninsular that I'd called home for so many years.

An hour later, we were pulling up outside Corin's house. Her husband, Niall, was there to greet us.

'Good to see you, girl,' he said as he enveloped me in a hug. He was a giant of a man, but without a doubt the gentlest I'd ever met. Niall was the definition of laid-back. 'Shame Danny's not with you.'

'I know, but he has work,' I replied. Niall and Danny had hit it off straight away when they'd first met all those years ago, and it made visits back to Ireland much more bearable and enjoyable. Corin and Niall had even come over to England a few times for their holidays and stayed with us. I hadn't told them about mine and Danny's arrangement yet, but knew I'd have to broach the subject sooner rather than later as I couldn't expect Freya to make out all was fine at home.

'I thought I'd take the girls into town for ice cream,' said Niall.

'Ice cream!' cried both Erin and Sorcha.

I looked across at Freya, who didn't appear quite so

excited at the prospect, but she smiled and said she'd love some too. Bless her, she was such a sweetie to her little cousins.

'Thanks, Niall,' I said, smiling as he herded the girls into his truck.

After waving the quartet off down the road, Corin and I went inside. 'He's a good one,' I said, sitting at the kitchen table.

'Sure. I know.' Corin put the kettle on to boil. She went over to the dresser and, opening the drawer, took out the black-and-cream purse. 'It was on my doormat this morning. Whoever found it must have come late last night. They didn't knock. Well, I certainly didn't hear them. But I do have doorbell camera footage to look at.'

'You do?'

'Sure. I haven't had time to check yet. I didn't want Niall asking questions.' Corin placed the purse down on the table in front of me.

I studied the purse for a moment and braced myself to pick it up. 'Have you looked inside?' I asked.

Corin nodded. 'Don't get too excited.'

I opened the purse. It had a zip compartment in the centre for coins, and either side of that were four or five card holders. At the back of the purse a place for the notes. It was empty of both coins and notes.

'No money,' I said, looking up at Corin.

'My guess is whoever found it took the money. That's probably why they shoved it through the letter box and ran.'

I frowned. 'But if they've taken the money, why go to the trouble of returning it?'

Corin shrugged. 'I've no idea. Anyway, look inside the zip bit.'

I did as she said. Inside was a white piece of paper with my name and telephone number on it. 'It doesn't look like Kathleen's writing,' I said, taking it out and examining it. I placed it on the table and then looked in the card holder section, taking out the two tickets.

'The train ticket is from Cork to Tralee,' said Corin. 'And the bus ticket from Tralee to Dingle.'

'Someone has come from Cork to Dingle? That's quite a journey.'

'Where did you say the purse was found?'

'Up on The Banks.'

I put the tickets alongside the piece of paper with my name on it. 'Anything else in here?' The holder for a photograph or a pass of some sort was empty. 'Didn't Kathleen have a photo of Kian in here?'

'I can't honestly remember,' said Corin, putting two cups of tea on the table and sitting down adjacent to me.

'Strange that would be gone.'

'Let me get the doorbell footage up now,' said Corin, taking her phone from her bag.

I watched as she tapped away at the screen and then I shuffled around to her side of the table to look at the recording.

A figure appeared at the foot of the path leading up to Corin's front door.

'What time is this?' I asked.

Corin peered at the screen. 'Quarter to one in the morning. That would explain why I didn't hear anything.'

We continued to watch the figure make their way up the path, glance around, and then slide the purse through the letter box before hurrying away.

'It's a woman,' I said as Corin replayed it. 'She looks young. You've no idea who she is?'

Corin was frowning. She paused the footage as the person neared the door and their face could be seen square-on. 'I've watched this a few times and every time I feel like I recognise her,' she said. 'It's on the tip of tongue, like.'

'Must be someone in Dingle.'

'Yes, I've definitely seen her somewhere in town,' said Corin.

'School? The pub? Shops?' I suggested.

Corin's frown deepened. 'No. I can't remember. It's so frustrating.'

'She doesn't look that old,' I said. 'Younger than us, do you think?'

'Yeah, I think so. Maybe in her twenties.' Corin put the phone down and looked over at the purse. 'Do you think it's definitely Kathleen's?'

'It must be. I don't see how it can't be.' I squeezed my forefinger under the leather edge of the photo holder and peered in. 'There's something in here.'

Corin leaned over as I prised out another piece of paper. 'I must have missed that. What does it say?'

The paper was no bigger than a bank card, torn from the corner of what might have been an exercise book. Two words written in black marker filled the space.

HELP ME

'What the feck?' said Corin, echoing my thoughts. She snatched up the piece of paper as if she needed to touch it with her own hands to believe it was real. 'Is this someone's idea of a joke?'

'It's a sick one, if it is.' I took another look at the purse, checking every pocket and holder, but there was nothing else there.

'We should take it to the guards,' said Corin.

'I'm not sure what they'll do,' I replied, thinking how easily they had drawn their conclusion that she'd simply left John. In the immediate days, and even weeks, that followed, I'd been happy to agree with this but, as the weeks turned into months, a deep-rooted feeling of doubt had burrowed its way into the pit of my stomach.

'No, I'm not sure either,' said Corin. 'But we should still go down to the station.'

'Maybe they can check the CCTV on the buses or the trains. We can see if it's Kathleen.'

'Do you really think it's her?' asked Corin.

'I don't know what to think right now.'

'Don't say anything to Mam or Dad yet,' Corin said, getting up from the chair and picking up her handbag and jacket.

'Jesus, no. We don't want them getting all upset over this when it could be nothing.' I grabbed my jacket too and followed Corin out to her car.

'Maybe Finn Casey will be on duty,' said Corin, as she blipped the remote to unlock her car.

Finn was in the same class as Danny and me when we were at school. I wouldn't say the two men – or lads, as they were then – were the best of friends. They tolerated each other. The three of us were part of a wider friendship group that included Corin and some of her friends. Finn and I had gone out with each other when we were twenty. My first proper relationship, but it had only lasted six months. Two years on from that I started dating Danny. We had gone from zero to one hundred in a matter of months, and he was definitely my first love. My one true love. A little kick of sadness made me catch my breath at the thought we were now separated.

'I'd sooner speak to him than Rory Ahern,' I said, getting in beside her. 'I take it he hasn't retired yet?'

'No such luck. They'll have to take him out feet first.'

Twenty minutes later we were sitting in an interview room, across the table from Sergeant Rory Ahern. He was a friend of our father's and had been in the guards for what seemed like forever. We were all frightened of him when we were kids. Dingle was a small station manned by Ahern and two officers, one of them being Finn.

Ahern was now examining the purse. 'And you say someone called you to say this was found up on The Banks?'

'Yes, that's right. They were on a dog walk or something and came across it,' I replied.

'And you're sure this is your sister's purse?' he asked.

'As sure as we can be,' I said.

'There's nothing in it to confirm that though. No driving licence or... well, anything, really.'

'But my name and address are in it,' I said. 'And there's the other note.'

'It's very odd altogether,' remarked Ahern, checking the purse thoroughly.

'Can you not get the CCTV for the bus or the train station?' I asked, trying to rein in my frustration at any lack of urgency.

'Trouble is,' replied Ahern, 'we don't know which bus to look at. It runs every couple of hours during the day and more often during mornings and evenings. That's a lot of bus CCTV, and then the manpower to trawl all the way through it.'

'The CCTV from Tralee train station would be easier to look through,' I said. Ahern definitely wasn't giving me Scotland Yard vibes and appeared to have little or no interest in helping us.

'There's a lot of footfall. Again, it's time.'

'Can you at least put it to the Serious Crime Team?'

'I could, if a serious crime had been committed.'

I put my head in my hands and blew out a long breath to stop myself from losing it with Ahern. Jesus, he was testing my patience.

Corin spoke. 'Would you mind at least asking? It would mean a lot to our parents to know everything was being done to find Kathleen, even though it's six months down the line.'

Ahern looked at me and then at Corin, his face softening. 'Sure. I'll do that, seeing as I've known your parents for many years now.' He slid the purse and notes back across the table. 'I know it's hard to accept, but all our enquiries point to Kathleen having walked out on her marriage and her life here in Dingle.'

'So everyone keeps saying,' I said. 'But she's not contacted anyone in the last six months. Don't you think that's odd?'

Ahern nodded slowly. 'Sometimes the longer the time, the harder it is for people to contact their families.'

'But the purse, it could be Kathleen's way of trying to contact us,' said Corin.

Ahern let out a sympathetic sigh. A small silence enveloped the room until Ahern spoke again. 'I appreciate you both coming in. I'll be in touch as soon as I hear anything, but don't go getting your hopes up.'

'Thank you,' I replied, accepting the closure of the interview.

We left the station, and it wasn't until we were back in Corin's car that either of us spoke.

'He just wanted to get rid of us,' I said, fastening my seat belt.

'I got that feeling too. It's always the same. I don't know what we expected.' Corin pushed the key into the ignition. 'Maybe we would have been better speaking to Finn.'

FOUR

Rory Ahern sighs as, from the window, he watches the Regan sisters leave the station. He has no idea where that purse came from and can't help but wonder if it's going to cause problems. Or rather, if Siobhan is going to cause problems. She has always been more tenacious than her sisters, the one with a little bit more about her. She had ambitions. She was never going to be content with settling down in Dingle. She may have married a local lad, but their zest for life was what brought them together, and their desire to leave not only Dingle but Ireland were equally matched.

And now, after all that business with Kathleen, Siobhan is back, and he has the feeling she isn't going to take no for an answer. There was something behind her eyes that he can't articulate fully, but it tells him there is going to be trouble ahead.

He picks up his personal mobile from his briefcase. The burner phone that no one knows about. He opens the app that will record his conversation and, once he's certain that's running, he dials a number that is stored on his phone as The Conductor. Jesus was there ever a truer description?

The Conductor answers after three rings. 'Hello.'

Ahern doesn't bother introducing himself. It's unnecessary. 'Thought you should know: I've been paid a visit by Siobhan Regan.' Of course, Siobhan doesn't go by Regan anymore, but everyone here knows her as that.

'What did she want?'

'Someone sent her a purse that belonged to her sister, Kathleen. Siobhan is convinced it's a clue to finding her sister.'

There's a pause. 'And how likely is it that will happen?'

'She won't give up.'

'Maybe you need to dissuade her from poking around too much,' suggests The Conductor.

'I'll keep my eye on her.'

'That doesn't sound very reassuring.'

'Leave it with me.'

'I hope you're not going to let me down.'

'Whenever have I done that?' Ahern bites down on the tone of irritation creeping into his voice.

'You know it will be the end for both of us if she finds anything out?'

'I don't need reminding.'

'Good. Make sure you deal with her.'

The line goes dead, and Ahern is left looking at the mobile in his hand. He hates being spoken to like that. Like he's some worthless piece of shit. But he'll bide his time. He's a patient man.

He turns his thoughts back to Siobhan, tapping the mobile gently against his chin as he runs through various options open to him. He needs to be careful. He must be subtle. He's going to have to employ help, and he knows exactly who to ask.

He makes another phone call.

'Yeah,' comes the laconic reply.

Immediately, Ahern feels irritated at the lack of respect he's shown in that one word. 'I have a job for you,' he says, making a concerted effort not to be riled. Again, introductions and pleasantries are bypassed.

'Like what?'

'A bit of harmless fun, that's all. It will be right up your street. Causing chaos.'

'What's in it for me?'

'The usual. Some euros in your pocket and a blind eye to whatever else is in your pocket.'

'I'm upping my fee.'

Jesus, the kid's a cocky one, that's for sure, and it doesn't please Ahern. He's a mind to go over there and offer a clip around the ear as extra payment. That would put them in their place. 'I don't think you are,' he says. 'My rules. My terms and conditions. You'll do as I ask and be grateful you're getting paid. You're not indispensable.'

'Ah, sure, I was only having a laugh with you.' The voice is less confident now and Ahern feels a small sense of victory. Can't let these youngsters get too cocky with themselves.

'Good. Meet me at the usual place. Tonight. Eight thirty.' He ends the call and switches off the recording app.

FIVE

We drove in silence out of town along Slea Head Drive, passing the harbour with the fishing boats bobbing on the water as the waves sloshed against the stone walls. We went by the familiar row of terraced houses looking out to sea. They were all painted bright colours and, on a summer day, looked like a highly photo-shopped postcard. The holidaymakers loved it and, judging by the three coaches in the harbour car park, they were out in force today.

'Fancy an ice cream?' asked Corin. She pulled the car over without waiting for a response. 'Come on. You're a tourist these days. You have to try the Dingle ice cream.'

I didn't really want one, but I recognised Corin's need to lighten the mood after the visit to the guards.

A few minutes later, we were sitting on the harbour wall, me with my rum and raisin and Corin with mint chocolate chip – the favourites of our childhood on the rare occasion we were treated to such luxury.

'I expect Niall took the girls to Murphy's,' said Corin, refer-ring to the legendary Murphy's Ice Cream that originated from

Dingle but was now sold all over the country with its fancy flavours.

The town hadn't changed that much since we were kids; maybe a little more commercialised, but it brought in much-needed tourism as a boost to the local economy.

We finished our ice creams and were about to leave when a passing car came to a sudden halt just beyond us and reversed back.

Corin let out a groan. 'Shit. Look who it is.'

I followed her gaze. 'Father John himself,' I muttered, making the sign of the cross as our brother-in-law's car pulled up alongside us.

Kathleen's husband had been brought up in an even stricter Catholic family than ours and the fear of God had been engrained in him since he was a child. Over the years, and especially since his parents passed away, John had become more and more entrenched in his faith and the church. It had been a discreet stealth-like trajectory; something we'd joked about initially. I used to tease Kathleen that he'd leave her to become a priest at the rate he was going. The Father John nickname was our little in-joke. After a while the joke stopped being funny.

John buzzed down the window and leaned over from the driver's side. 'Corin. Siobhan,' he said with a nod to each of us.

'John,' I said, giving a cautious smile. To say relations with my brother-in-law were strained was something of an understatement. As the saying went, there was no love lost between us. I thought he was an overbearing bombastic hypocrite who'd have everyone believe he was a good man when, in reality, he was mean-spirited and a bully. Always trying to dictate to Kathleen what she should and shouldn't do, especially in the eyes of the Lord. I might as well have been Satan, as far as he was concerned. Apparently, I filled Kathleen's head with fancy notions about England and the freedom I enjoyed there. That was probably the only thing we agreed on.

'I heard you were here,' he said, looking at me.

'Didn't take long for word to get around,' I said. John was a well-known local businessman with more connections than a telephone exchange. He went to say something but stopped. It was probably going to be along the lines of bad news travels fast, but he was showing unusual restraint.

'When are you going back?' he asked.

Most people would ask someone how long they were staying, but not John. I wasn't on his wish list of visitors. 'I'm not sure yet,' I replied. 'How's Kian? I've got Freya with me. It might be nice for them to catch up.'

John gave a look that clearly said he didn't think that was a good idea. 'You'll have to speak to him yourself. I'd say you'd see him at Mass, but I don't suppose you'll be going.'

I resisted the urge to roll my eyes at the comment. 'It's not on the agenda,' I replied, knowing it would annoy him.

John gave me a look of disdain. 'Didn't think it would be.' He eyed me steadily. 'So, are you here to visit the family?'

'Partly,' I replied.

'And the other part?'

I was sure he knew but didn't want to say outright. I decided to save us both the bother of beating around the bush. 'Kathleen.'

There was no look of surprise on his face. In fact, his brows darted together angrily. 'Don't go around stirring things up,' he said. 'No one wants you here causing waves. And don't be putting any ideas into Kian's head. He's confused enough as it is.'

'How do you mean?'

John gave a snort. 'Do I really need to spell it out?' He shook his head. 'His mother going off like that. He doesn't understand and neither do I. What sort of wife and mother does that?'

'Aren't you at all interested in finding your wife?' I asked, the anger brewing in me.

'She walked out on us. We all know that. The guards even said she did.' John fixed his gaze on me and narrowed his eyes. 'And you know that as well, don't you, Siobhan.' With that he pulled away before I could reply.

'He's got a girlfriend,' said Corin, watching his car disappear up the road.

'What? You never said. Jesus, that didn't take him long. Do Mam and Dad know?'

'Yes, and Dad isn't too happy about it,' said Corin.

'I bet he isn't. What does Kian think about it?'

'He and John have fallen out over it all. Last I heard, they were barely on speaking terms.'

'What is wrong with our family? We're not exactly a walking advert for peace and harmony. Except you and Niall, of course.'

'And you and Danny,' added Corin. I didn't answer. I couldn't lie to her. She looked at me. 'Oh, Siobhan. Not you and Danny? Come on, not you two.'

'It's complicated,' I said, reminding myself of the conversation I'd had with Freya yesterday when I'd gone to use the same expression.

'Siobhan,' persisted Corin.

I pushed myself away from the wall. 'Not today, Corin.' We crossed the road to where she'd parked. 'We're working things out, but this trip isn't about that. It's about Kathleen.'

She looked at me across the roof of the car. 'OK, whenever you're ready.'

We got in and Corin started the engine. I was grateful for her easy acceptance of my reply. If Kathleen's disappearance had taught us anything, it was not to fall out with each other.

I took the cream-and-black purse from my bag, opening it

once again as if all the answers to all my questions would miraculously appear.

'Let's quickly drive over to the lighthouse where Kathleen's purse was found,' I said.

'Sure,' replied Corin.

She didn't ask why, and I don't think I could have explained it to her if she had. I wanted a sense of closeness to my older sister. I wasn't into all that mystical shit, but maybe I thought if she had been up there then I'd somehow know.

The wind whipped our hair around our faces as we stood next to the lighthouse that guarded the mouth of Dingle harbour. The whitewashed stone cottage next to the lighthouse had been empty for at least ten years now, but on the side was a mural of Fungie the bottle-nosed dolphin who had lived in and around Dingle harbour for nearly forty years. Another one for the tourists' tick-list.

Dingle town itself was a few kilometres walk along the clifftops, known locally as The Banks, and part of the larger Dingle Way trail.

'Has it ever got any easier for you?' Corin's voice was quiet, almost taken away on the wind.

I looked at her standing next to me. Her arms were wrapped around her body, keeping her jacket from flapping about. Her gaze was fixed on some distant point out across the ocean.

I knew what she meant without having to ask her to elaborate. I returned my gaze to the horizon. 'Not really. Maybe sometimes during the day when I'm busy and don't have time to remember that night. When I just think about Kathleen and wonder where she is or what happened to her, that's the easy part.'

'And the hard part is at night,' said Corin.

'Yes. When it's quiet and my mind has nothing else to occupy itself with,' I replied. I had found it even more so since

Danny had left. 'It's worse still when I'm asleep and the night-mares come.'

'You too, huh?' said Corin.

'Yeah. Me too.' We didn't often talk about Kathleen and that night for fear of upsetting each other. It was too painful. But up there, on the clifftop, our conversation felt freer and the desire to be honest overwhelming. I wiped a tear from my eye. I'd made a mistake that night and that feeling of guilt had never left me. It was in the pit of my stomach, gnawing away, eating me up from the inside. 'I've been over that night so many times. I've reworked it in my head as if, simply by thinking a different outcome, I can manifest it. One where we don't argue. One where I don't say all the things I did. One where I don't ignore the phone call.' Another tear leached from my eye; I let it fall.

Corin rummaged in her pocket and brought out a pack of tissues. She handed one to me and took one for herself, blowing her nose.

'Did you ever tell Danny what it was really about?' she asked through a sniff.

'No. Did you tell Niall?'

'No.'

'It has to stay that way.' I exchanged a look with my sister. 'We can't say anything.'

She nodded, returning her gaze to the ocean. 'I know.'

The edge of the cliff was fenced off by a few posts strung together with wire. A small gap, shouldered by two stone pillars, gave way to rudimentary stone steps that went down another thirty feet to a concrete platform. I had never known what it was for, but the braver tourists loved it for Instagram-worthy photo opportunities.

I turned my face to the wind and breathed in the salty sea air in a bid to cleanse my palate of the conversation.

'What was she doing up here?' asked Corin after a while.

'I wish I knew.'

I looked down at the jagged and unforgiving rocks of the cliff face below us. The choppy ocean crashing against the coastline, rising up and backflipping on itself. I shuddered as the unbidden image of Kathleen falling rushed to the fore of my mind.

'You don't think...' Corin didn't need to finish her sentence. The unspoken words might as well have been written in neon lights above her head.

'No. I don't think that at all,' I said firmly. I pushed my hands into the pockets of my jacket. 'Not Kathleen. She wouldn't do that.'

'I don't think so either, I was just checking what you thought.'

'I mean, why would she come back here to then... well, you know...' I nodded towards the edge. 'If she was going to do that, she would have done it when she disappeared. No. She's come back. I'm convinced of that. The more I think about it, the more I'm certain. She's back. She wants us to help her. We simply have to work out how.'

For the first time since I'd got the call about the purse, I felt a certainty in what I was doing. A purpose. Fuck the guards. Fuck John Walsh. And fuck anyone who told me different. Kathleen needed our help. I wasn't going to let her down this time.

SIX

THEN

'It's a shame you have to go back so soon,' said Kathleen. 'In fact, it's a shame you couldn't come three weeks ago when it was my actual birthday. It was such a fun night. You missed out on it, didn't she, Corin?'

'It was a great night,' agreed Corin. 'But it's nice just the three of us as well.'

'Danny's got a lot on at work,' I explained. 'As it is, I feel bad about leaving Freya.'

'Sure, she's a teenager now,' said Kathleen. 'She doesn't need you babysitting her.'

'I'm not babysitting her,' I protested. Kathleen worked at The Hub – the local community support centre. She loved her job, and it often brought her into contact with teenagers. And that, coupled with having her own teenage son, seemed to have made her an expert in parenting. Her advice was well-meant, but it annoyed me all the same. It wasn't like I had no idea how to raise a teenager, seeing as I had one of my own. I didn't think I was doing too bad a job at it either.

'As parents we're supposed to bring our kids up to be independent young adults so they can go out and make their own way in life,' continued Kathleen, pausing briefly to take another glug of her wine. It was her birthday celebration and we'd all had a bit too much to drink, but Kathleen, for some reason, was getting sanctimonious and it was pissing me off.

'Look, you work with kids, I get it,' I countered, going on the attack. 'But you can leave your work at work. I don't appreciate you imparting your wisdom on me.'

'We all parent differently,' chipped in Corin. 'And everyone's kids are different.'

I knew Corin was acting as peacemaker, and I might have left it there, but Kathleen was on a roll.

'I'm not imparting wisdom, as you put it,' said Kathleen. 'I'm talking to you in my capacity as a sister. As an aunty. As someone who wants the best for you. I don't know why you have to throw it back in my face.'

'I'm not throwing anything back in your face,' I retorted.

'Well, you are actually. Just like you always do,' snapped Kathleen, putting her now-empty glass down heavily on the table.

'What's that supposed to mean?' I demanded.

'Come on, you two, let's not get into an argument,' said Corin. 'This is supposed to be Kathleen's birthday celebrations.'

'Some celebration this is turning out to be,' muttered Kathleen.

'No, wait, I'm not done,' I said, feeling the rage ignite. 'I want to know what you mean about throwing it back in your face.'

Kathleen's eyes hardened as she glared at me. 'Trust me, Siobhan, you don't want me to answer that question.'

'As a matter of fact, I do.' I returned the glare with equal strength.

'Please...' began Corin, but Kathleen held her hand up to

silence her. Corin closed her mouth, her eyes darted between me and Kathleen.

'All my life I've looked after you two,' said Kathleen.

'I have not the first clue what you're talking about,' I said. 'I'm sorry you're the eldest sister and there's been some expectation of responsibility on you towards us, but that's not our fault. I feel the same about Corin. It's what you do when you're an older sibling – you look out for the younger one especially. You've got two younger siblings, but none of that is my fault. It's an accident of birth, that's all.'

'I'm not talking about that,' said Kathleen.

'Then what are you saying?' I downed the last drop of my wine.

'Are you prepared for the answer?' she asked.

I frowned and exchanged a look with Corin, who apparently had no idea either what was coming. I looked back at Kathleen. 'I'm ready. What about you, Corin?'

'Yeah. I'm ready.' Although her reply didn't hold the same confidence as mine.

Kathleen gave a covert glance around the pub and then leaned in towards us.

SEVEN

All too soon it was time to visit my parents. Corin and the twins were coming as well – for moral support. It would be easier with more of us there. More distractions for my parents, especially my dad. Although I knew it hurt my mother to see us all together when one of her daughters was missing.

'So, what's brought you here?' asked my dad.

We were now sitting around the kitchen table, and the girls had gone out the back to play. I looked at the three girls in the garden and it reminded me of me and my sisters.

I realised my dad was waiting for a reply. 'Half-term in England,' I said. 'Thought it was time to come over.' I picked up one of the cheese sandwiches Mam had put together and set out on the table, along with some bread pudding. The latter her signature dish. Something that she made every Sunday afternoon without fail.

'And you're here because you've nothing better to do,' replied my dad.

'It's lovely that you're here,' said Mam. 'How long are you staying?'

'Just the week,' I replied. 'We were going to try to see if Kian was about. Freya would like to see him.'

Dad made a huffing sort of noise. 'If you manage to pin him down then you've done a better job than us. I can't remember the last time we were graced with his presence.'

I resisted the urge to say if Dad wasn't such a grumpy git, then his one and only grandson might want to spend a bit more time in his company.

'I have his mobile number,' said Mam. She went out to the hall and retrieved her telephone and address book. The same book she'd had since the year dot. She'd never moved on to mobile phones or even saving someone's number on the landline phone memory. It was only in the past five years or so that she'd moved onto a cordless. I sometimes forgot my mam was only in her early sixties; although my father was ten years older, I used to think they had slipped through some wormhole and should really have been at least another twenty years older, from a bygone age.

I took out my mobile and copied the number into my contacts list. 'I'll send him a text.'

'You might want to remind him he's got two grandparents,' said Dad as he got up from the table.

'Where are you off to?' asked Mam.

'I've to go out now,' he replied. 'Promised Pat I'd see him for a pint.'

'But...' Mam waved her hand in my direction. 'Siobhan has come to see you.'

'I know. She can come again.' Dad looked at me. 'You will, won't you?'

'Sure,' I replied. 'Nice to see you, Dad.'

He held my gaze as if trying to work something out, but eventually gave a nod, before patting Corin's shoulder as he moved around her chair.

He crossed the kitchen and opened the back door. 'I'm away

now. Come and say goodbye,' he instructed the girls. He spoke with a gentler tone to his granddaughters, and the twins happily skipped over to give him a hug. Freya followed, although I could see she found this excruciatingly awkward. Her body was stiff as a board when Dad kissed her cheek.

As he went back through the house to leave, Mam followed him. I could hear their hushed tones as they exchanged words. I couldn't make out what they were saying though.

I looked out to the garden and smiled at Freya, who offered a rather diluted version in return.

'Teenagers. They're so awkward, aren't they?' said Corin.

'I guess. Also, Freya doesn't really know Dad that well. Not like Sorcha and Erin do.'

'He's a miserable bastard, for sure,' said Corin. 'I was always jealous of my friends whose dads were relaxed and not as strict.'

'Yeah. Me too. I don't know why he was like that with us.'

Before we could continue the conversation, Mam was coming back down the hallway.

'There we are,' she said. 'I'll make a fresh cup of tea.' She looked from me to Corin and back to me. 'You know your dad's not well. It's his diabetes. Makes him irritable. He's pleased to see you, really.'

I nodded and smiled, more to keep Mam happy than to accept the well-worn and often-trotted-out excuse for Dad's behaviour. 'A cup of tea would be great,' I said.

I was only halfway through my cup, chatting to Mam about Freya and school, when Corin looked at her watch and let out an unexpected gasp.

'What's wrong?' asked Mam.

'Oh, I'm really sorry, Mam. I promised Caroline Murphy that I'd bring Siobhan along to see her this afternoon.'

'You did?' I said, surprised. I was sure Corin hadn't mentioned this before.

'Yes,' said Corin, getting to her feet, the chair scraping on the tiled floor as she did so. She discreetly nudged my shoulder with her arm. 'Look, it won't take long. I know Caroline would be disappointed if she didn't see Siobhan. Can the kids stay with you for a while?'

I felt sorry for Mam; she looked disappointed. 'I promise we'll be back before you know it,' I said, getting up and giving her a squeeze around the shoulders. I didn't know what had got into Corin, but our long-unspoken sister code of conduct from when we were kids – *Don't ask, just do* – was coming into play.

'Dinner will be ready at five o'clock,' said Mam.

'Ah, sure, we'll be back long before then,' reassured Corin.

I went out to the garden where Freya was sitting on the bench, hunched over her phone, and Corin's girls were on the climbing frame.

Freya looked up with hopeful eyes. 'Are we going?'

'No. Sorry, love, but we're here for tea, remember?' I said, running my hand over her head. 'Look, me and Corin are popping out to see someone – an old friend of Kathleen's. We won't be long.'

'You're leaving me here?'

'Only for an hour.'

'Can't I come with you?'

'It will be boring.'

'Like it isn't here?' Freya let out a sigh. 'Sorry, Mum, I don't mean to be rude, but it is.'

'I know. I'm sorry, but please keep an eye on the girls for us. I promise we'll do something more interesting tomorrow. Maybe I can get Kian to come over and take you out.'

Freya's face lit up a fraction at this prospect. 'That would be good.'

I smiled at her and dropped a kiss on her head. 'Thanks, sweetie. I promise I'll be as quick as I can.'

I felt bad about ditching Freya, but at least she had Corin's kids there and my dad had gone out. He would be complaining they were being too loud or too messy or too anything.

I got into the car with Corin. 'So, where are we really going?' I asked, fastening my seat belt.

Corin grinned at me. 'I've remembered who the girl was on the doorbell footage.'

'You have! Who?'

'I'm not sure of her name, but I know I've seen her in Murphy's ice-cream shop, working behind the counter.'

'Brilliant. And I assume that is where we're off to now?'

'Of course.'

It only took a few minutes to drive into town and soon we had pulled up on Strand Street, managing to get a parking space a few shops down from Murphy's.

'I think that's her there,' said Corin, slowing down as we approached the ice-cream shop on foot.

Through the window, I could see a young woman who looked a good match for the person on the doorbell footage. 'I'll do the talking,' I said. 'Seeing as it was probably her who phoned me in the first place.'

We went into the shop and waited in line while the young woman served the couple in front of us. It gave me time to look at her properly and to hear her voice. It was hard to say if it was exactly the same as the person who had called me, but there was the familiar West Country lilt.

Close up, I estimated her to be in her early twenties at the most. She finished serving the couple and turned to us. There was absolutely no recognition on her face as she asked how she could help us.

'We'll take two plain vanilla cornets,' I said.

'Sure.' She picked up the first cone.

'This may sound an odd question...' I ventured, smiling over the counter at her.

'Oh, I get loads of those,' she said, not looking up. 'Everyone wants to know about the flavours and how we come about them and naming them.' She glanced up then and smiled.

'It's not the ice cream,' I said. 'My name's Siobhan. You telephoned me about the purse you found up The Banks.'

Immediately, her relaxed disposition vanished and a concerned look crossed her face. 'I'm sorry. I don't know what you're talking about,' she said.

'You found a purse up on The Banks,' I repeated. 'You phoned me, and I told you to drop it around to my sister's house.' I gestured towards Corin.

The girl shook her head. 'I didn't find a purse.'

'You did,' said Corin. 'And you put it through my letter box the other night. I've got it all on the doorbell video footage.'

The girl swallowed hard and placed the ice cream she'd been making into the holder on the counter. 'You must be mistaken.' She picked up another cone and leaned over to scoop from the tub.

'Do you want to see the footage?' asked Corin. 'It's you, all right. I can always take it to the guards and see what they make of it.'

She stopped mid-scoop. 'It's not illegal to return someone's property, you know.'

'So it was you, then?' I asked. 'Look, you're not in trouble or anything.' I tried to reassure her. 'We wanted to ask you a bit more about the purse, that's all.'

'What exactly?' She finished scooping the ice cream and plopped it onto the cone.

'When you found it, where was it?'

She looked a bit sheepish. 'Up on The Banks. I told you.'

'Where exactly?' I pressed.

The girl looked down at the ice-cream tubs. 'I don't know.'

'What do you mean?' I asked.

'Look, I didn't find it. Someone else did. I don't who they were. They asked me to put it through your letter box.'

'And you did that without asking any questions?' asked Corin.

The girl shrugged.

'Who asked you to drop the purse off?' It was frustrating, dragging every fragment of information from her, but I managed to keep my tone even.

'I don't know. Some girl. She knows my brother from The Hub. He volunteered me. I only met her the once.'

'Does the girl work at The Hub?' asked Corin.

'I don't know. I don't think so,' said the girl. 'She paid me. Gave me twenty euros. Like I said, I didn't do anything wrong.'

'No, you didn't,' I said. 'It's fine. Do you know the girl's name?'

She shook her head. 'No.'

'What does she look like?'

The girl sighed. 'I don't know. Blonde. Glasses.'

'Anything stand out?'

'She had on a bright yellow coat. Like the one you wear when it's raining. The sort your mam or granny would wear.'

I smiled at the idea. 'OK. Thank you.' I handed over a twenty-euro note. 'Keep the change. If you remember anything else, can you call me on this number?' I handed over one of my business cards.

'Look, you can't say anything. My brother will kill me if he knows I told you.'

'Who's your brother?' I asked. And then, when she didn't look like she was going to reply, I added, 'Just so I know to avoid dropping you in it if I speak to him.'

'Conor. Conor Doyle.'

'Thanks. What's your name?'

The girl looked warily at me. 'Shona.'

'Thanks, Shona.' I picked up the ice creams and, handing one to Corin, moved to leave the shop.

'You're her sister, aren't you?' said Shona.

I gave her a questioning look. 'Her sister?' I asked, nodding towards Corin.

'No. Kathleen Walsh's sister,' said Shona.

I nodded. 'That's right.'

'And I am too,' said Corin.

Shona nodded, momentarily flicking her gaze to Corin, before coming back to me. 'You're the one who didn't help your sister,' she said.

I was taken aback for a moment. I hadn't been expecting that. Corin spoke first. 'It wasn't like that.'

Shona's mouth turned down and she raised her eyebrows at the same time. An expression that said *If you say so*. 'That's what people say,' she said.

'You shouldn't believe everything you hear,' I said, surprised at how the comment stung.

'Is it true?' Shona asked.

I swear there was a hint of a smile. As if she was enjoying my discomfort. As if she was in some way getting revenge for me making her snitch on her brother. 'Thanks for telling us about your brother. I'll try to remember not to let him know it was you who told us.' I wasn't sure how I managed to get the whole sentence out without running out of breath. How could some kid from behind the ice-cream counter have that effect on me?

'I guess that's a yes, then,' called Shona. 'Yes, you didn't help your sister when she needed you. At least I helped my brother!'

'Shut the feck up,' I heard Corin snap at Shona, as I pushed the door open and rushed through.

As soon as I was outside, I took in a lungful of air. Fresh, clean air. Not the contaminated air in the shop. My chest was tight, and I fought to catch my breath. I wanted to get away. I don't know where, just away from that girl and her accusations. I couldn't think straight.

'Hey, Siobhan. It's OK.' Corin's voice was distant, like she was talking through a double-glazed window. I turned to look at her. Nothing was making sense. All I could see was her mouth moving and this faraway muffled sound, the words indistinct.

I shrugged her hand from my shoulder and ran down the path, dumping my ice cream into a bin as I went. I didn't know where I was going. I just needed to get away. I wasn't looking. Even my vision was blurry. I could feel tears streaking down my face. My heart was pounding against my breastbone.

And then I ran into something solid and unmoving.

'Ugh!' I let out a groan as my whole body was enveloped and constricted. I struggled. Tried to free myself.

'Siobhan! Siobhan! It's OK.'

All of a sudden my senses came rushing back to me in one big crashing wave of sensory overload. It took me a second or two to work out what was happening. I looked up and realised I had run into someone. A man. I recognised the face, but my brain wasn't calm enough to filter through the information.

'Siobhan. It's me. Finn,' he said, still holding me. 'Finn Casey.'

It took a couple of seconds to register, but then I was fully aware of everything. 'Oh Christ. Finn. I'm so sorry,' I stammered as I stopped fighting.

'Jesus, Siobhan.' It was Corin. 'Are you OK? You took off like Usain fecking Bolt.' My sister came to a halt, puffing beside me.

I held my head in my hands as fresh hot tears, this time of embarrassment, came. 'I'm so sorry,' I muttered again. Then Finn was pulling me in towards him, his arms around me, holding me tight.

'You're all right, girl,' he said. 'I don't know what's happened but, whatever it is, you're all right now.'

I took deep steadying breaths and finally I was back in some sort of control of my emotions. Then I became acutely aware of being comforted by my old schoolfriend and ex-boyfriend. I jumped back in alarm. 'Sorry.'

'You don't have to keep saying sorry,' said Finn, a smile playing at the corners of his mouth. 'What happened?'

I rubbed my eyes with my fingertips. 'I had a bit of a panic attack,' I said. That was the only way I could explain it. 'An explosion of pent-up emotion. Something like that anyway.' I smiled at Finn and then at Corin to reassure them both.

'I heard you were back,' said Finn.

'You too, huh?' I replied.

'I also heard you were asking around about Kathleen,' continued Finn. His smile had gone now.

'There's no law against that.' I sounded prickly, but I didn't care.

'No, there's not,' replied Finn. 'But you know what this place is like. Doesn't take much to upset anyone.'

'Have you had a complaint?' asked Corin.

'No,' said Finn. 'And I'd like to keep it that way.' He looked down the road, from where I'd sprinted.

'If you guards did your job properly, then we wouldn't have to go around asking questions,' I snapped, still feeling the sting of Shona's words and totally taking it out on the man in front of me.

Finn's posture remained relaxed and non-confrontational, but I could see the steely look in his eyes. I recognised it from years ago. 'We did everything we could,' he replied. 'I don't want to fall out with you, Siobhan, but you might want to be careful what you go around saying. Not everyone will be as generous as me with their understanding.'

'What's that supposed to mean?' I demanded. I knew I was being argumentative, but I couldn't help it. The shame of being called out by a teenager had transitioned into anger and Finn was getting the brunt of it.

'It's not meant as anything other than some friendly advice,' said Finn. He looked at Corin as if asking for her support.

To her credit, Corin shrugged and held her hands out palm up in a 'don't get me involved' gesture. I appreciated her solidarity.

'We should go,' I said. 'Freya will be wondering where I've got to.'

'Oh, you've your daughter with you,' said Finn. 'Is Danny here?'

'Why don't you consult your sources?' I said. 'They seem to know everything.'

Finn let out a sigh. 'Siobhan, let's not fight. I want to help you.'

I paused. 'You want to help?'

'Sure. I don't like to see you all upset like this. Let me help you.'

I looked at Corin, who gave a small nod. 'Why not?'

'How can you help us?' I asked. I was sure I was walking into some sort of trap that I couldn't see, but the offer of help was too tempting to pass up.

'I don't know exactly, maybe we can get a drink or have lunch or something.'

'OK. You have my number, I take it?'

'I can get it,' said Finn with a grin.

And there he was, back to the lad I knew as a teenager and the one I'd dated as a young adult. All the hostile thoughts and emotions slipped away. 'Thought as much,' I said. 'Call me tomorrow.'

I turned and walked back down the road with Corin to her car.

'That sounded remarkably like a date to me,' said Corin.

'Go away with that,' I said. 'That was not a date. And I don't care if it is, not if he can help us.'

EIGHT

Bingo! Freya has found her cousin Kian's number on WhatsApp. She doesn't want to wait for her mum to get back, besides the fact she is taking ages. She doesn't want to ask her nan either, because she doesn't want to have to explain what she's doing. Her nan would invite Kian around for tea and whatever the hell that stodgy fruit cake on the table is.

She messages her cousin.

> Hey Cuz! It's me, Freya. I'm here in Dingle for the week.

It's only a few minutes before she gets a reply.

> Hey back at ya Cuz. Didn't know you were coming. You staying with Corin? Do you want to meet up?

Freya has always got on well with Kian, despite their age difference of five years. He's always treated her like she was more grown-up and at the same time has looked out for her when she's been over. He came over to England a couple of times when he was younger. Their mums used to do what they called the kid exchange in the summer holidays, where Freya and Kian would be shuffled between Brighton and Dingle, three weeks in each place, giving their parents at least three weeks' free time to themselves. Freya thought their parents looked forward to it as much as she and Kian did.

> Meet up would be good. Not gonna lie I'm bored already. Love the twins but you know.

> Sure. I know. Will swing by at 12 tomorrow and pick you up.

> Cool. See you then.

Freya smiles to herself. That's something to look forward to. Her phone pings another message alert. She expects it to be Kian but is surprised to see it's her dad.

> Hi love. You OK?

> Hi Dad. Yeah. I'm fine. At Nan's house.

She adds an eye-roll emoji but then deletes it before pressing send.

> Ah, I expect that's fun for you.

Freya needn't have worried about deleting the emoji.

> Fun with a capital F.

This time she does add it and leaves it.

> Is your mum ok?

> Out with Corin. Gone to see a friend of Kathleen.

Who's that?

Can't remember. Carol. Caroline. Carolyn.
Something like that. What are you doing?

Just getting ready to go out.

Freya doesn't reply immediately. Her heart feels heavy. Is her dad going out to meet someone? A woman? She needs to remind him he has a family. He has a wife. He has a home, and he should be there.

Wish you were here. Can you come over?
Please.

Sorry, sweetheart. Work's very busy. I'll make it
up to you when you get home. Got to dash.
Love you lots.

Freya doesn't want her dad to make it up to her. She just wants him back. She's sure her mum does too.

I miss you. So does mum.

She waits for a reply, but it doesn't come.

NINE

'Ah, Kian. Great to see you,' I said, embracing my nephew as he came through the door. He smiled and, at nearly six feet tall, he had to bend to return the hug. He took after his father in stature and height.

Despite appearing pleased to see me, I could feel the tension in his shoulders and back. 'Good to see you,' Kian replied. 'Hey, Corin.'

'You all right, there, Kian?' greeted Corin. 'Do I get a hug too?' She gave me a wink.

Kian grinned. 'If you want one, but sure, I only saw you last week.' He went over and hugged Corin.

'Freya won't be a minute,' I said. 'How have you been?'

Kian nodded. 'Grand.'

'I take it that's your stock answer,' I replied. He may have been smiling and appearing cheerful, but his eyes betrayed him. Gone was the sparkle that lit up those green eyes of his. Now there was a dullness. 'How have you really been?'

He went to speak, probably to bat away my concern, but then he closed his mouth and looked up to the ceiling before returning his gaze to me. He shrugged. 'You know. It's not easy.'

I rested my hand on his arm. 'Of course it's not.'

'Dad said he'd seen you.' Kian shifted on his feet. 'He doesn't like talking about Mam.'

'You know you can talk to me anytime you want to,' said Corin.

'I don't know what to say, honestly,' said Kian. 'I used to think she was coming back, but now, I don't think so.'

Before anyone could say anything else, Freya made her entrance. 'Hiya,' she said, grinning at her cousin.

'Jesus, Freya, when did you get your glow up?' said Kian.

She pulled a face at him. 'Probably about the same time as you, I'd say.'

I smiled as the two cousins embraced; their easy familiarity with each other was there straight away.

'So where are you off to?' I asked.

Freya shrugged. 'Don't ask me, Kian's driving.'

'I thought we'd take a drive out somewhere and get a pub lunch.' Then, looking down at Freya's trainers, 'And seeing as Freya is in appropriate footwear, we might go for a walk after.'

'Sounds great,' said Corin. 'Lovely day for a walk.'

'That rain was shocking the other week,' said Kian. 'I got caught in it and was drenched.'

'There was something I wanted to ask you,' I said.

Kian's face grew serious. 'What's that?'

'Look, one of the reasons we're here this week is because someone found a purse that we think was your mum's,' I said carefully.

Kian's eyes widen. 'Does my dad know?'

'No. I'm not sure he really wants to speak to us,' I said. 'You know, it's tricky.'

Kian nodded. 'Where was the purse found? Can I see it?'

Corin took the purse from her bag and handed it over to Kian.

'We were asking around again,' I said. 'Trying to see if

anyone knows anything, has heard anything, or even knows how the purse got here.'

I watched Kian turn the purse over in his hands and then look inside. He pressed his lips together and swallowed hard. His thumbs grazed the stitching. 'It looks like Mam's purse,' he said finally. 'Do you really think she's here?' There was such sadness in his voice, but it was tinged with hope. I recognised that mix of emotions well.

'I don't know, sweetheart,' I said. 'That's what I'm trying to find out.'

He handed the purse back. 'When you're done, can I have it?'

'Of course you can,' I said.

'Have you found anything out yet?' he asked, injecting a more upbeat tone to his voice.

'Not really,' said Corin. 'Do you know a Conor Doyle? His sister, Shona, works in the ice-cream shop.'

'Conor Doyle. He's a bit of a dickhead at times,' said Kian. 'Oh, sorry. I mean, he's—'

I gave a laugh. 'It's OK. A dickhead is fine. We know where we stand with them.'

'He's a couple of years older than me. Fancies himself rotten when he's nothing to write home about at all. Why do you want to know?'

'Someone Conor Doyle knows at The Hub gave Shona the purse to put through Corin's door,' I explained. 'You don't know who that might be? Who does Conor Doyle hang out with?'

'I've no idea. I don't go down there. Not anymore,' said Kian. 'Mam was always down there.'

'Did you go down there with your mam at all?' I asked.

'Sometimes, but she was always busy trying to sort out someone else's problem,' said Kian. 'Always trying to fix something for someone. You know what she was like. I'd end up just sitting there, so I stopped going.'

'So, you don't know who Conor Doyle's friend might be?' asked Corin.

'Not really. I've seen him out and about a couple of times, but not with anyone in particular.'

'Have you finished questioning Kian now?' asked Freya. 'It's like watching an episode of *CIS*.'

'Sorry,' I said, acknowledging Freya had a point.

'No worries,' said Kian. 'Look if that's all, we'd better get going.'

'Sure. Have a good time. I'll see you later.'

Freya stopped on her way out and gave me a kiss on the cheek. 'See you later, DCI Martin.'

I smiled and watched the kids get into Kian's car and drive off. It was heart-warming seeing them together and I was glad Kian had stepped in to alleviate Freya's boredom.

'He's a good lad,' said Corin, as if reading my thoughts.

'He is indeed,' I replied. 'He takes after his mother, that's for sure.'

'Oh, I'd say so. Definitely not his father.'

Twenty minutes later, we had parked in the car park behind The Hub. The building had once been used as a nursery school but had been empty for twenty years or so before a group of volunteers got together and, with the help of local business funding, turned it into a youth club. Kathleen had been one of the founder committee members who had got the place up and running, her background as a social worker coming into play. She was in her element helping the local kids and within six months had expanded it to a parent-and-child centre and then opened their doors to the elderly members of the community to get together once a week for tea dances. She had been a driving force for expanding it.

'So what's our strategy?' asked Corin as we got to the main entrance.

'Not sure. We're winging it right now,' I said, sounding more confident than I felt.

We were greeted by a receptionist. It was very informal at The Hub – it wasn't the sort of place where you needed an appointment or were allowed in by invitation only – but nevertheless there was a woman sitting behind a desk in the entrance hall.

'Hello, ladies. How can I help?' she said, smiling at us. She was dressed casually in a long flowing dress, with her hair piled up on her head in a messy bun. I estimated her to be in her late forties.

'Hi, there,' I said. 'My name's Siobhan Martin and this is my sister Corin Foley. Our sister used to work here – Kathleen Walsh.'

The smile slipped from the woman's face for a moment. 'Oh, Kathleen. I used to work with her. Such a terrible business. I'm so sorry.' Her gaze rested on me for a moment. A look I'd come to recognise when someone suddenly remembers my role in Kathleen's disappearance. The look was there, albeit fleetingly, and then she was smiling again. 'How can I help you?'

Corin answered: 'It's coming up for six months since she disappeared and we're just speaking to people again, trying to jog memories in case anyone remembers something they didn't tell the guards.'

'Oh, I see. I remember the guards coming and speaking to us. Oh, my name's Sharon, by the way.'

I smiled. 'Hi, Sharon. Do you remember if Kathleen was worried about anything?'

Sharon let out a sigh. 'Nothing springs to mind. I told the guards that at the time. She had a strong sense of duty to the community, especially to anyone who was in trouble or needed help. She had such a good heart. Of course, you don't need me to tell you that.' Sharon laughed self-consciously. 'But I can't think of anything or anyone in particular.'

'Did she ever talk about Conor Doyle?' I asked.

Sharon's eyes widened a fraction. 'Conor Doyle?' she repeated, and I guessed she was stalling for time while she weighed up what exactly she should say. She fiddled with the crystal stone pendant hanging in her cleavage; the numerous bangles on her arm jangled as they slid about. 'Conor is the type of lad who always needs help,' she said eventually.

'Did Kathleen help him?' I pressed.

Sharon bit her lip, and I counted to ten to hide my impatience. 'Conor's high maintenance and he doesn't like to take no for an answer.'

'How do you mean?' asked Corin.

'I shouldn't really say this,' said Sharon, with every intention of saying whatever it was. 'He runs with a bad crowd. Gets involved with things on the wrong side of the law.'

'Drugs?' I asked.

'I can't say, but I'm not denying it,' said Sharon, her voice hushed. 'He's one of those lads who attracts trouble. Always up to no good. Your sister had words with him one day.'

'What was that about?'

Sharon looked back over her shoulder. 'He made inappropriate comments to one of the younger girls. Kathleen said she'd have to ban him and report him to the guards if he did anything like that again.'

'How did he react to that?' asked Corin before I could.

'Wasn't too happy. Called your sister a few names, but it was water off a duck's back to Kathleen. She just ignored him.'

'Did you tell the guards this?' I asked.

'I did, as a matter of fact,' said Sharon. 'But you know, for all Conor's big man act, he's not got the backbone for any of it. He's here today, actually.'

'He is? Can you point him out to us?'

At that moment the door to one of the rooms beyond opened and a young lad came out. He stopped in his tracks when he saw us, his eyes darting from one to the other.

'Oh, would you look at that. Here's Conor himself,' said Sharon. 'Conor, these two ladies were looking for you.'

Conor's brow knitted into a frown. 'What for?'

'We're Kathleen Walsh's sisters,' I said.

Conor gave a shrug. 'And?'

'Someone dropped a purse around to my house,' said Corin. 'It was Kathleen's purse. Do you know who that was?'

'Sure, I've no idea,' said Conor. 'Why would I?'

'You all right, Conor?' came a female voice from the room behind him.

I saw a flash of yellow before Conor darted back through the door and slammed it shut.

I rushed forward and tried to open the door, but it was being held from the other side. 'Open the door, Conor!' I called.

Sharon darted over. 'I told you he was trouble.' She hammered on the door. 'Conor, let go of the door.'

'Is there another way in?' I asked.

'Around the back. This room goes through to the kitchen and there's a back door there.'

I gave the door another shove and it suddenly flew open. I nearly fell flat on my face as I stumbled forward from the momentum. I looked around the room and through the open serving hatch, caught a glimpse of the unmistakable yellow coat rush by. I was about to give chase when Conor stepped in front of me.

We bashed into each other.

'Get out of the way,' I said, trying to shove him to one side while I sidestepped the other way.

'What's the hurry?' said Conor, not budging. He was a good few inches taller than me and solid as a house.

Corin went to move around him and he stepped into her

path. There was no way he could block both of us and I took my opportunity to get past him. Unfortunately, I didn't foresee him putting his foot out and tripping me over. This time I did go flying, right into a table where some other kids were sitting.

'Hey, watch it!' one of them said.

'Yeah, watch where you're going,' said another.

'Sorry. Sorry,' I said, pushing myself up from the table and then promptly wincing in pain as I put weight on my foot, where Conor had caught me.

'Oh, you haven't hurt yourself, have you?' said Conor, feigning innocence.

Nothing would have given me greater pleasure than to swipe the smirk from his face. 'Who was that?' I asked, pointing towards the kitchen.

Conor shrugged and held his hands out. 'I've no idea.'

'Yes you do,' I snapped. I turned back to the kids at the table. 'Who was that in the yellow coat?'

The silence was deafening, only broken by Conor's laugh. 'No one knows who that was.'

I looked around for a member of staff. 'Who's monitoring this room?'

With impeccable timing, a woman wearing the same blue-and-white lanyard as Sharon walked purposefully into the room. The receptionist trailed in her wake. I felt I recognised the woman but couldn't put a name to the face.

'Is everything all right?' she asked, taking in the scene before her.

'Everything is fine,' said Corin before I could say anything.

'They're Kathleen Walsh's sisters,' supplied Sharon.

Enlightenment settled on the other woman's face. 'Oh, I see.' She held out her hand. 'Aisling Denvers. Councillor here in Dingle for the Fianna Fáil party.'

'Siobhan Martin,' I said, accepting the handshake.

Corin nodded. 'Hello, Aisling.'

'Hello, Corin.'

'They were wanting to ask about Kathleen,' continued Sharon. 'It's been, what, six months now since Kathleen disappeared?'

'Of course,' said Aisling. She frowned at me. 'Are you all right?' She nodded towards my foot that I was gently resting on the floor to avoid putting weight on it.

'I twisted my ankle,' I said. 'Got caught on the leg of a chair. Wasn't looking where I was going.' I suspected making a big deal out of what had really happened wouldn't benefit me. 'Actually, you might be able to help,' I said. 'The girl wearing the yellow jacket, she was in here just now. What's her name?'

Before Aisling could answer, Conor got in first. 'You can't tell her. You're not allowed to. Confidential information, and all that.'

Aisling looked apologetically at me. 'He's right, I'm afraid. It wouldn't be ethical of me to divulge that information. I'm sorry. Why do you want to know?'

I exchanged a look with Corin, who gave a small shake of her head. I looked back at the local councillor. 'Doesn't matter. We'd better get going. Sorry to disturb you all.' I walked tenderly out of the room, followed by Corin and Sharon.

'Sorry about that,' said Sharon. 'I told you he was trouble.' She picked up a pen from her desk and scribbled something on a Post-it note.

'Thanks anyway,' I said. I leaned on the desk and rotated my ankle. The initial pain had already subsided.

'Is your ankle OK?' asked Corin.

'It's fine now. I'll walk it off.'

'Here, let me help you,' insisted Sharon.

'I'm fine, honestly,' I really didn't need a fuss made, but Sharon wasn't taking no for an answer. She grabbed my elbow and then held on to my hand in order to escort me to the door. 'I can walk, I promise. It's not even hurting now.' It wasn't quite the truth, but I certainly didn't need any help.

'Hope you find out what happened to Kathleen,' she said. As she let go of my hand, I realised Sharon had pressed the Post-it note into my palm.

I glanced down at the note and then back at Sharon. Before I could say anything, Aisling Denvers came out into the reception area.

'I hope your foot is OK,' she said. 'Look, I'm sorry I can't help you.'

'It's all right,' I said. 'I understand. Thanks anyway.'

We left the building under Aisling's watchful eye and went around to the car park.

'What's Aisling Denvers doing at The Hub?' I asked.

'Oh, she's there all the bloody time. It's her pet project,' said Corin. 'Earning brownie points to keep the locals sweet in the hope that she gets elected again next time.' She looked at the blue note in my hand. 'What you got there?'

I unfolded the Post-it Sharon had given me. On it was a name:

Nicole Elleford

TEN

'That's the girl who asked Shona to drop the purse to you,' I said. 'You don't recognise the name, do you?'

Corin looked at the piece of paper. 'No. And I don't know anyone in Dingle with the name of Elleford.'

'It's a start,' I said, getting into Corin's car. I fastened the seat belt as Corin pulled out of the car park. Something made me look up towards the wall at the back. I was sure I caught a glimpse of that yellow coat again. I spun around in my seat to get a better view, but there was no one there.

'You all right?' asked Corin.

'Stop the car!'

'What the feck?' Corin hit the brakes and we lurched forward.

I was out of the door and sprinting towards the three-foot-high brick wall at the back of the car park, ignoring the twinge in my ankle. The girl was nowhere to be seen, but she couldn't be that far away. I vaulted the wall, using my hands as springboards, landing on the other side on both feet, even though my ankle protested at the jolt. The footpath ran parallel to the row of buildings but branched off to the left a few feet along. I raced along the track, my feet skidding on the loose dust as I took the corner at speed. I lost grip and slipped as I tried to regain my balance. I caught another flash of yellow as the girl vanished from my line of sight.

'Nicole!' I shouted as I tried to gain on her. 'I just want to talk!'

I kept myself in good condition and was a regular visitor to the gym, but my fitness was no match for hers. She had the benefit of youth on her side. My legs were protesting at the sudden and brutal expectation of high performance.

The footpath twisted its way through the back of the shops, and as I rounded the next bend and exited into a garage compound, the girl was nowhere to be seen. I spun around looking for any trace of her, but she was gone. I was panting so hard, I had to bend double for a moment to catch my breath.

As I straightened up to walk back, Corin appeared from the footpath.

'Jesus, Siobhan, are you trying to give me a heart attack? Whatever got into you? I can't be chasing after you every fecking day, you know.'

'Sorry. I saw the yellow-coat girl – Nicole Elleford,' I said, checking out my ankle for any further damage. It seemed OK, thankfully. 'Thought I could get her to talk to me, but she left me in the wind.'

'You shouldn't be running around like that. You're pushing forty, for God's sake.' She turned and began to walk back down the footpath.

'I'm thirty-eight!' I shouted indignantly and then jogged to catch up with her. 'I've got a bloody stitch now,' I grumbled as we made our way back.

'Don't complain to me if you can't walk tomorrow,' said Corin. I was getting zero sympathy from my sister, and I followed on in silence, mentally assessing the worth of my gym membership if this was the result.

As we hopped over the wall of the car park, we stopped dead and gawped at Corin's car.

'What the hell happened?' I said, stunned by the sight of the smashed-in back window. 'That wasn't like this when you left it just now, was it?' In hindsight, a stupid question, as Corin issued a string of curses.

'Of course it wasn't,' she snapped. 'That's happened in the few minutes I took off after you.'

We approached the car and stood, staring at the damage.

'Looks like you're going to need to get that repaired,' came a voice from over the other side of the car park.

It was Conor Doyle and a couple of other kids from The Hub.

'What the feck do you know about this?' demanded Corin, storming towards them.

I wanted to tell her not to go over, but she was practically there so, despite my aching legs, I jogged over to her. 'Don't let them wind you up,' I said under my breath.

Conor held his hands up in surrender. 'Don't know anything. We came out here and saw it like that.'

We were standing in front of them now. I cast my gaze around and spotted a camera on the side of the shop. 'Don't worry, we can check the CCTV footage and that will show us exactly who did it.'

Conor gave a laugh. 'You really think that old thing works? Sure, ya man only keeps that up there for show. A deterrent, like.'

I wouldn't have been surprised if Conor himself hadn't wrecked the camera, but I wasn't giving him the satisfaction of my frustrations. 'Come on, Corin. We'll take some photos and report it to the guards. You lot won't mind if we give the guards your name, will you? Just in case you might have seen something.' I smiled sweetly at them.

'You won't be giving my name to the guards,' said one of the other lads.

'Nor mine,' said another.

'It's OK, I'll give them Conor Doyle's name,' I said, feeling a sense of triumph at the look on Conor's face, who clearly didn't realise I knew his name.

'Do what you like,' he said, full of bravado. 'I haven't done nothing, and no one can prove I have. Anyway, why would I want to smash the window of your shitty car?'

'Oh, get lost, the lot of you,' said Corin and then marched away.

I glared at each of the youngsters in turn before following my sister.

'I'm not going to the guards,' said Corin once we were at the car. 'They won't be interested.'

'Won't you need a crime reference number for the insurance?'

'No. Niall will get it done. I don't want to go through the insurers. It will cost me a fortune in the long run.' She looked at the back seat, now smothered in tiny fragments of glass. 'Did you have anything important in here?'

'No. Fortunately, my tablet's in my bag.'

'Get in,' said Corin. 'I don't want to give that lot any more satisfaction than they have already.'

I climbed in the passenger side. 'Do you think it was Conor Doyle?' I asked.

'I'm sure it was, or at least one of that lot,' said Corin. 'You're certainly stirring up the locals.'

I wasn't sure if that was a dig or not, but I didn't challenge it. Corin had enough on her plate right now without me stoking the flames of her anger.

We pulled out of the car park and headed out of town towards Corin's place.

'What were you planning on doing if you'd caught up with

that girl? Nicole Elleford, if that's who it was,' asked Corin, breaking the silence.

'I'm not sure, really. I guess ask her what she knows about the purse. Who put her up to it.'

'Sounds a bit vague.'

'It was impulsive, I know,' I admitted. 'But I get the feeling she was waiting for us.'

'I don't think she was there because she wanted to talk to you, otherwise she wouldn't have run.'

I looked out of the window as we whizzed past the harbour. The boats were bobbing on the incoming tide and the clouds were trying to make way for the sun.

'It's like she's taunting us,' I said. 'Otherwise, like you say, why would she run?'

'My guess is, the kind of people who hang out with Conor Doyle have a natural aversion to talking to anyone who might be remotely interested in what they're getting up to, because, I can guarantee you, they'd be up to no good.'

The sound of a text message alert had me diving in my bag for my phone. I realised I was hoping it was Danny and was disappointed when it was a text message from a mobile number I didn't recognise. I steeled myself, wondering if John Walsh had a new number or if Sharon from The Hub had been found out and they were about to reprimand me.

'Aren't you going to open it?' asked Corin, side-eyeing my phone.

I tapped at the screen and scanned the message. 'It's Finn Casey.'

'Didn't take him long,' observed Corin.

I read the message out loud. '*Hi, Siobhan. Hope you're OK after bumping into me yesterday. Do you fancy meeting for a drink tonight? We can grab something to eat, if you like. We can chat about Kathleen.*' I looked at Corin, who stole a glance at me, the corners of her mouth twitching. I let out a sigh. 'He's an old friend and, in case you'd forgotten, I'm a married woman.'

'Now seems a good time to tell me what's going on with you and Danny,' said Corin.

Another sigh escaped my mouth, deeper and heavier this time. 'We've not split up,' I said. 'Not officially, but we're having a bit of space.'

'Space?' Corin accelerated out of Dingle. 'That doesn't sound good. Just how much space are we talking?'

'He's taken a three-month tenancy on a flat in Brighton,' I said. There was no point playing it down. I needed someone to talk to, and who better than my sister?

'Oh, Siobhan, I am sorry,' said Corin, with genuine sympathy in her voice. 'I thought you and Danny were solid. You've been together for years. You're the fairy tale of childhood sweethearts – well, almost, but you know...'

'Yeah, I do know.' Unexpected tears came to my eyes, and I blinked hard to stop them from falling. 'I've not been myself since Kathleen disappeared. I know that, but I can't help it. I feel I want to grieve, but to grieve means I've given up on her. Jesus, Corin, you must know what it's like.'

She nodded. 'I understand perfectly. It's hard to carry on as normal. All the time, the thought of her is there. What happened to her? Why didn't she get in touch?'

I couldn't answer that because it would mean I'd have to either lie or admit to a lie.

ELEVEN

Freya breathes in a lungful of air, grateful she is away from the annexe and having to make small talk with the adults and let the twins restyle her hair goodness knows how many times.

'Don't get me wrong, I love them to bits,' she tells Kian, who is driving the car taking them away from Dingle. 'But they won't leave me alone – or rather, won't leave my hair alone.' She smooths down her hair that isn't out of place. She has it in two French braids this afternoon as it could have done with a wash, but she couldn't be bothered with drying it.

Kian gives a laugh. 'Fortunately, I don't have that problem. Not that I see a great deal of them.'

'Why is that?' asks Freya, looking absently out of the window at the rugged coastline to her left. It's sunny today but the wind is up, and the water looks choppy. It reminds Freya of home and her dad. She's lost count of the number of times she's wished he was here.

'Oh, you know, adult stuff. My dad doesn't really get on with the Regan side of the family.' Kian steers the car around a tight corner, causing Freya to grab onto the door handle to stop herself from falling into her cousin.

'Why's that? Is it since your mum went missing?'

'Nope. It's always been a bit strained, but since Mam has been gone, it's been worse. He's been worse.'

Freya looks across at Kian, not knowing what to say. She might be pissed off at her parents at the moment because they can't sort their own shit out without separating, but she can't imagine what it must feel like to have your mum go missing.

There's an awkward silence in the car and Freya has the need to fill it. Words exit her mouth before her brain has had time to apply a filter.

'Do you miss your mum?' She inwardly groans at the stupid question, but it's too late now.

'What do you think?' Kian shakes his head. She deserves that.

'I'm sorry. I didn't mean... what I meant was... Oh, fuck it. I don't know what I meant.' God, why can't she just shut up?

'It's OK. Forget it.' The silence is heavy again. 'Hey, Freya. Honestly, forget it. For the record, yes, I do miss my mam, but I don't blame her for leaving.'

The weight lifts in the space between them and Freya is relieved Kian appears to want to talk now. 'Why's that? Because of your dad?'

'Yeah. They were always arguing. I don't know how they stuck it out for so long.' Kian pulls off the road into a car park and cuts the engine. They are overlooking the Atlantic Ocean and the white crests of the waves are rising higher than before. Kian's hands remain gripped to the steering wheel and he drops his head down to rest on them.

Freya wants to say something but she's no idea what. She reaches out and puts her hand on his shoulder. 'I'm sorry. I didn't mean to...' Again, she wishes she could just shut up. She doesn't know how to comfort him.

Kian's shoulders heave as he sucks in a breath. He is still bent forward. And then he sobs. One long sob that sounds like a roar but it's not one of anger. It's one of pain. And then his shoulders shake violently as more sobs follow.

Freya moves her hand across his shoulder blades and gently rubs his back up and down. Sometimes it's good to cry, to let it all out, and she guesses it's not something Kian does very often. She unclips her seat belt and leans closer to her cousin, resting her head on his shoulder.

'I'm sorry,' mumbles Kian, sitting up and running his hands down his face. He sniffs heavily and squeezes the snot from his nose. Freya rummages in her bag and finds a tissue which she hands to Kian without saying anything. His face is red and blotchy, and his eyes are still puddles of unspent tears.

'You don't have to be sorry,' says Freya quietly.

Kian rests his head back. 'You know, sometimes I hate her,' he says, wiping his nose again. 'Like really hate her for going off like that. But then I get it. I mean, my dad can be a bastard at times. But why go off and not tell anyone? That's the bit I don't get.'

'Parents can be selfish,' says Freya. 'They get wrapped up in their own dramas and forget about us. We're supposed to just go along with it all.'

'I know, right. Even when we're adults, we're not allowed to question anything.' Kian rolls down the window, coughs and then spits on the ground to clear his throat. 'And you know what the worst thing is?' he asks, but continues without waiting for a reply. 'I feel guilty for feeling like that. Imagine that. I feel guilty. I'm not the one who's done anything. It's them pair.'

'What's your dad been like?' Freya has heard her parents moan about John Walsh in the past. Bits and pieces here and there, mostly when they think she's out of earshot or too engrossed in her phone to register their conversations, but she's heard them. What was it her dad called him? Oh, that's it – a Bible-bashing bully. And her mum once said something about him being a hypocritical twat. Freya smiles to herself but thinks better of relaying this information to Kian.

'My dad? I don't know,' admits Kian. 'I don't speak to him much if I can help it. If I mention Mam, he gets all weird. Agitated, like. Told me the other day not to say her name. He calls her "that woman" now.'

Freya thinks about her parents and, even though they are living apart, she can't imagine her dad saying that about her mum. Ever. 'Do you think she'll come back?'

Kian takes a deep breath and swallows. His Adam's apple bobs in his throat. 'Not if she's got any sense. Not to him at any rate.' He takes another breath, and Freya senses he's trying to put on a brave face now. The tears are back in his eyes, but he blinks hard and turns his head to look out of the window. 'It had been getting really bad. I don't know what it was all about, but it was different the last few months before she went.'

Freya senses Kian wants to talk. She guesses he's not been able to talk about it before now. 'In what way?'

'Usually they'd argue about nothing. You know, the sort of things your parents fight about. Not putting the plates in the dishwasher. Whose turn it was to walk the dog or water the garden or some other mundane boring shit like that.'

Freya gives a small laugh in solidarity. 'Tell me about it.'

'Well, it was different. It was like something was causing them to argue all the time. The same thing. Over and over again.'

'And you don't know what that was?'

'No.' Kian sniffs, wipes his nose, and screws the tissue up into a ball which he stuffs in the pocket of the door. 'It was always in whispers and, when they realised I was about, they'd stop and then make little digs at each other or not talk.' Kian lets out a long sigh. 'I swear I'm never getting married. If that's what happens to ye, then no fecking way, thank you.'

Freya smiles at her cousin. 'Ditto to that.' Her mind turns to her dad and the unanswered message that still sits on her phone. She thought about messaging him again, but in the end decided not to. What was the point?

'So, what do you get up to in Brighton?' asks Kian, switching the conversation to her. He's done talking about his mum now.

'Not much.' And that's the truth, thinks Freya. She doesn't do a great deal, not anything that sounds cool or that Kian would be interested in, at any rate.

'Do you still do that cheerleading stuff?' He holds imaginary pom-poms and shakes his hands. 'Give us an F. F! Give us an R. R!'

Freya can feel herself blush and whacks her cousin on his arm. 'That's sideline cheerleading, not competition. And, yes, I still do that.'

Kian is grinning. 'Sure, I'm only teasing you. But, seriously, what do you do? There must be loads to do in Brighton.'

'To be honest, it's not much different to here,' says Freya. 'The beach. Loads of tourists. In Brighton we get the killer seagulls that swoop down and steal your food or shit on your head. If you're really unlucky, both.'

'I suppose you're too old for building sandcastles and too young for nightclubs.'

'There's not much in-between stuff. Tell me there's stuff going on here. What do you do?'

It's Kian's turn to shrug. 'Not a lot, if I'm honest. There's Hillgrove nightclub – that's been about for years – and there are a few good bars, but that's about it. Nothing that I can take you to.'

'Guess I'll be spending my evening playing hairdressers with the twins again.'

Kian taps the steering wheel with his fingers. 'There is actually a party Friday night that I've been invited to.'

Freya sits up, alert now at the prospect of a party. 'Where's that?'

'Here in Dingle. Do you want to come?'

'Now that is a stupid question,' says Freya, buoyed by the prospect of something to do at last. 'Who's having the party?'

'A girl I went to school with.'

'Oh, do I know her?' Over the years Freya has met a lot of Kian's friends.

'I don't think so. It's Mia Denvers.'

'I don't think I know her but, yeah, cool. That's something to look forward to.' She grins to herself at the prospect of a party.

TWELVE

'You're going on a date,' declared Freya.

'I am not going on a date,' I insisted for the fourth time that evening. 'I'm meeting a friend who is a guard and he's going to talk to me about Kathleen.'

'At the pub and you're putting on your nice clothes,' said Freya. 'That's a date.'

'Oh, will you stop it,' I replied, closing my laptop on the document I'd been working on earlier. 'This is work. This is how I'd get ready for any work-related interview.'

'Except it's not work,' said Freya. She tapped the closed laptop. 'That's work.'

'Just because it's my sister, it doesn't mean it's not work.' I was uncomfortable at Freya's suggestion it was a date with Finn, and I certainly didn't want her telling Danny anything like that. Although, part of me did wonder whether it would make him jealous, but in a good way. That he'd come to his senses and want to come back home. Ultimately, though, it wasn't a good game plan to put my marriage back together. 'Now, what are you up to this evening?'

'Kian is coming over. We're going down the beach with some of his friends. One of them has a kayak.'

'Be careful out on the water.' I knew Freya wasn't stupid when it came to open water. She'd lived all her life on the south coast of England; water awareness was second nature to her. I was also confident for the same reasons about Kian's judgement when it came to the sea. 'I don't want you out late.'

Freya rolled her eyes. 'I'll be fine, and I won't be late.'

'Eleven o'clock and no later. I'll tell Kian the same.'

Freya gave another eye roll, but she didn't answer. The eleven o'clock curfew was later than she got at home, but I trusted her cousin with her and giving her some more flexibility would, I hoped, incline her to comply. Freya wasn't a bad kid anyway. She rarely argued about anything and went along with what Danny and I expected of her, so giving her a bit more freedom felt like a reward. A sign of mutual respect and trust.

The sound of a car pulling up on the drive had us both looking out of the window. It was Finn in his BMW. Freya gave me a sideways look. 'You know what Dad says about BMW drivers being dickheads?'

I sighed. 'Well, you don't have to repeat it – and you know there are exceptions to the rule.' I picked up my phone and dropped it into my bag, before giving Freya a peck on the cheek. 'See you later.'

'Back by eleven o'clock,' she replied.

'Yes. No later,' I said, pausing at the front door.

'I meant you.'

I opened my mouth to say something but couldn't help laughing instead. 'Bye, Freya.' I went out, shaking my head in mock despair.

'I heard what happened to Corin's car,' said Finn as I got into his BMW. 'Did you report it?'

'No. She didn't want to.' I fastened my seat belt. 'I'll pass on the advice though.'

Finn nodded. 'Right, where do you want to go?'

'The Harp,' I said. I'd already thought about this earlier. It was one of the pubs that Kathleen and John often went to; their local, if you like. I might see some of her old friends or people who knew her, which could, in turn, give me the opportunity to talk to them, ask a few questions. Admittedly, questions that had been asked six months ago, but as a journalist, I was aware people remembered things over time and think they're not important.

'The Harp?' repeated Finn. 'You sure?'

'Positive.'

'OK, it's your shout,' he said. 'We can always go on somewhere else if you want to.'

'The Harp will be fine. I just want a quiet drink,' I insisted.

The Harp wasn't especially busy. It wasn't a popular pub with the youngsters in the town, but it had a loyal fan base, so I wasn't surprised when I recognised a couple of faces in there who acknowledged me with a nod and a 'how ya doing, girl?' It still didn't prevent some of the conversations coming to a halt as people looked up and clocked me and Finn.

'If you were planning on making an entrance, I think you've achieved that,' muttered Finn as we got to the bar. 'What you having to drink?'

'Glass of white wine, please.' I leaned against the bar and waited while Finn was served. I felt the presence of someone close to my side and turned. The smile dropped from my face. It was Kathleen's husband. 'John,' I said, wondering how I hadn't noticed him when I came in.

'Look what the cat dragged in,' said John, who clearly hadn't just arrived at the pub. He was holding a near-empty pint of Guinness in his hand.

'Charming way to greet your sister-in-law,' I said.

'What the feck you doing here?' He downed the last of his drink and placed the glass on the bar.

'We don't want any trouble,' said Finn. 'We're only here for a quiet drink.'

John's gaze went to Finn. 'You should know better than to bring her here.'

I jumped in before Finn could reply. 'I asked him to bring me here. If I want to come into the pub, I can. Now why don't you just leave us alone?'

'Hey, John. What can I get you?' It was the barman, who'd walked over from the other side of the bar as soon as it was apparent there could be a situation. 'A pint of Guinness? Anything for Anne?'

Anne? Who the hell was that? I immediately spun around and saw a young woman with long blonde hair sitting in the corner. She held my gaze as she flicked a bouncy curl over her shoulder and gave me a satisfied smile. Smug, to be exact.

'Yeah, a gin and tonic,' replied John.

'Who's your friend?' I couldn't help myself asking.

John gave me a long look of contempt before answering. 'She's the woman who makes me happy,' he said purposefully. 'Since your sister fecked off, I haven't been happier.'

'You're a bastard.' My words came out like a snarl, which only served to amuse my brother-in-law. I heard Finn softly say my name as a warning not to go too far. I was a professional, I could usually keep my emotions reined in, but it was so hard when it came to Kathleen. The guilt, the need to atone and the need to protect her were a big whirlpool of fervour. 'It didn't take you long to move on from your wife of twenty years.'

John made a scoffing noise and then leaned in closer to me. 'For a start, it's none of your fecking business. You've not been home for so many years, you've no idea what went on with me and your sister. Secondly, you think your sister was a saint, then think again. And finally, Anne knows how to treat a man, which is more than I can say for your sister who I only married because she was pregnant. Now, feck off back to England. No one wants you here and, more importantly, no one fecking cares about her.'

'Siobhan, let's go somewhere else,' said Finn, his voice soft in my ear and his hand resting on my arm.

I held firm as I locked eyes with John. He was goading me. Trying to get a rise out of me, probably so he could get me thrown out of the pub. I wasn't that stupid, but my God, did I have to use every ounce of self-control not to punch him. I took a deep breath and, with my eyes still fixed on John, I replied to Finn. 'No, you're all right, Finn, I'm happy to stay here.' I turned away from John and picked up the drink the barmaid had placed on the bar. I could sense all eyes were on us. 'Cheers, Finn,' I said, holding up my glass before taking a sip. Finn took a sip of his pint and, although trying to look relaxed, I could see the tension in his shoulders.

'Shall we sit down?' asked Finn.

'Sure.' I looked back over my shoulder to where John was still standing. 'Did you want something? No. I didn't think so.'

Without waiting for a response, I turned away and followed Finn over to a table on the other side of the bar. Finn took a sip of his pint and placed it on the table, before sitting back and eyeing me expectantly like a headteacher who'd called a naughty pupil to be admonished.

'He started it,' I said, fully aware I sounded exactly like a petulant child.

Finn smiled. 'You're not ten years old.'

I looked around the pub at the familiar and not so familiar faces. My gaze travelled the room to where John was sitting. He stared back at me. I was unnerving him simply by being here, and I liked the sense of empowerment that knowledge gave me. Maybe I'd come every day, purely to annoy him. I turned back at Finn. 'Do you know who Nicole Elleford is?'

Finn looked thoughtful for a moment before answering.

'Yeah, the name rings a bell. I think she might be known to the guards.'

'In what way?'

'I can't say exactly.'

I resisted the urge to roll my eyes as I wondered what sort of help Finn thought he was going to give me. 'OK, so you can't tell me any details but, off the record, what sort of girl is she?'

'Why do you want to know?'

'I've been trying to talk to her but she's proving elusive. You don't know where she lives, do you?'

'What do you want to talk to her for?' Finn supped his pint.

'She was the one who found Kathleen's purse. I've got no other leads to go on, so it makes sense to start with her.'

Finn took another sip of his drink before replying. 'Nicole is in and out of trouble all the time. Not really bad stuff – petty things.'

I ignored the fact that Finn had made out he only had a vague recollection of her. 'She hangs around at The Hub with Conor Doyle,' I said.

'My, you have been busy.'

'What do you expect? It's a case of getting things done. I saw her earlier today, but she ran off. Where does she live?' I might as well be direct. Being subtle wasn't getting me very far.

'I can't divulge that info and, yeah, I know it's frustrating, but leave it with me and I'll go and speak to her.'

My frustration levels were going through the roof. 'When will that be?'

'As soon as I can. Maybe tomorrow.'

'I don't have much time here. Freya's back at school next week so I'll have to go back to England.' I finished my wine, the exasperation at the lack of forward motion really getting to me. 'I'm having another drink. You want one?'

'I'll get them.'

'No. It's fine. I want to.' I got to my feet.

I went up to the bar, which was busier now. It was the longest wait ever and I was aware of someone else standing next to me. I glanced up at the mirror behind the optics and saw the reflection of one of the men who'd been sitting with John. He was standing far too close. I moved to the left a fraction and he moved too. Definitely too close to me.

'What can I get you, Kevin?' asked the barmaid.

'Sorry, but I've been waiting for ages,' I said.

'I'll come to you next,' said the barmaid.

'I was before him.'

'What's your problem?' asked the man. 'You'll get served, but locals before strangers.'

The barmaid brought over the drinks and lined them up on the bar, taking the money Kevin handed over. From the corner of my eye, I could see him pick up the pint of Coke he'd ordered.

The next thing I knew, the back of my neck was drenched in ice-cold soda. I gasped as the ice and liquid cascaded over my shoulder, soaking both my front and back.

'What the hell?' I cried, prising my blouse from my body.

'Oh, I'm sorry,' said Kevin.

The smile on his face clearly said he wasn't sorry in the slightest.

'You did that on purpose,' I snapped.

'It was an accident,' insisted Kevin.

By now Finn was at the bar. He procured a towelling beer cloth from somewhere, went to dab at my blouse and then thought better of it.

'Come on, Siobhan. Let's go and get you cleaned up,' said Finn.

'Yeah, Siobhan, you'd better leave now,' said Kevin. He picked up his tray of drinks. 'Leave now. Like properly leave,' he added, before walking away.

I looked across the pub at John Walsh, who was grinning

broadly at me and then pulled a mock sad face. 'Tut. Tut. Tut,' he called out. 'Kevin, you're so clumsy.'

I stormed out of the pub with as much grace and dignity as I could muster in the circumstances. I knew Finn was right behind me.

'And that was your idea of a quiet drink,' he said. He released the lock and held the car door open for me.

'I perhaps underestimated how much I'm loathed around here,' I said, getting in. Finn walked around the front of the car and got in behind the wheel.

'Only loathed by those not worth worrying about,' he said gently. He twisted in his seat. 'Not by those who matter. Those who really know you.'

With that small drop of sympathy, my resolve crashed spectacularly, and I sobbed into his chest as he held me to him. It had been a long time since I'd felt this kind of human comfort and it made me feel both cared for and vulnerable.

'I'm sorry,' I said, finally pulling away. 'I'm a complete mess and I've blubbed all over your shirt.'

'Sure, it can be washed,' said Finn. He sat back in his seat. 'Are you OK, Siobhan? I mean, really, OK?'

I rummaged for a tissue in my handbag and blew my nose. 'I am,' I assured him, inspecting my soggy blouse that clung to me, revealing the lace of my bra underneath. 'I should go home and get cleaned up.'

We drove in silence back to the annexe.

Finn got out of the car and walked me to the door.

'Thanks for tonight,' I said. 'Sorry I wasn't much fun.'

'Honestly, don't give it a second thought.' He reached over and softly grazed my cheek with the back of his fingers. 'It was nice to have your company.' He slid his hand away and down my arm, finding my hand.

We stood in silence, and I was very aware of the charged

energy passing between us. His thumb caressed the back of my knuckles, and I squeezed his hand.

A small gesture, but a huge green light.

Finn moved his other hand up to my shoulder and slipped it around the back of my neck.

'You can trust me,' he whispered.

I don't know which one of us moved in first but the next thing I knew, his lips were on mine, and I was responding. A small flutter of a kiss, before a longer, more pressing one. He tasted of Guinness and minty toothpaste. And, for a few seconds, I was lost in the moment.

It was only seconds though. Thoughts of Danny leaped from my subconscious, and I pulled back from Finn.

'Finn, I don't know…' I began.

'You don't have to know anything.' His voice was soft in my ear. 'Not yet. It's OK. Just know, I'm here for you. And for whatever you want me for.' He kissed the top of my head. 'I should go,' he said.

I nodded. 'Yeah. Goodnight, Finn.'

He paused before getting into his car and turned to look at me. 'Danny's a very lucky man.'

I went inside, closing the door. Guilt raged through me. I had willingly kissed Finn and I had enjoyed it. Or rather my ego had. My heart, however, felt an utter traitor to Danny, to our marriage, and to our daughter.

THIRTEEN

The following morning the guilt was still strong, but I tried to console myself that it had stopped before anything else had happened. Never had I been more grateful for my conscience popping up just at the right moment.

I opened my laptop, the welcome screen greeting me with a picture of Danny, Freya, and me, taken at a wedding we went to in Brighton last year. The ceremony was more pagan than Christian, with wildflowers, coir mats, yurts and straw bales, conducted in the middle of a field on the Downs. It had been a lovely day and all the wedding photos had been taken with a dozen or so disposable cameras the bride and groom had left out for guests to use. I loved this photo. I was leaning into Danny, who had his arm around me, and Freya had photobombed us at the last minute, almost diving across our laps. We were all laughing, wide-mouthed, heads thrown back. This had been Danny's old work laptop which I had inherited, and it was he who had chosen this screen saver. It was such a wonderful photo; I'd never wanted to change it. There was so much joy and love oozing out of the screen.

I decided I'd call him that night, just to speak to him, to see how he was. I longed to have him home again, but I knew there were conditions, and I wasn't in a position to agree to those conditions yet. I hated keeping secrets from him. All I had to do was tell him the truth, but I couldn't, not until I knew Kathleen was all right.

I opened a Word doc and forced myself to think about Kathleen and everything I'd found out or that had happened since I got here. I needed it in some form of order so I could think straight. I needed to approach this as a journalist putting together a story. I mean, that's what I was doing, wasn't it? I was trying to get to the truth so I could tell the truth. And in so doing, hoping it would save my marriage and my career. Without the truth, I'd have nothing.

Half an hour later, I was done. Everything logged in order. Known facts typed in black; assumptions in green; hypotheses in blue; and questions that still needed answers typed below in red.

At this point there was a lot of red on the page, but I felt happier now I could see it all at a glance. This was how I worked, and if I could keep thinking of it as that, and manage to suppress my personal feelings, then I'd stand a much better chance of succeeding.

I poked my head around Freya's bedroom door. She was sound asleep. I decided I'd go into town and get some pastries. Freya loved the pain au chocolat from our local French bakery back home in Brighton.

I went over to the main house and, walking around the back, I waved to Corin who was in the kitchen. She beckoned me in.

'You OK?' she asked.

'Yeah. I was about to nip into town to get some pastries.'

'Oh, here's the local troublemaker,' said Niall, coming into the kitchen.

'Don't. I'm so sorry about the car window, Niall,' I said.

'Ah, sure, it's only a piece of glass. I'm getting it fixed later this afternoon,' he replied nonchalantly as he flicked the kettle on to boil. 'Did I hear someone say pastries?'

'I'm going into town; do you want any?' I asked.

Niall looked at Corin, a smile tipping the corners of his mouth. 'Did you hear that? Your sister's asking if I want any pastries. What a stupid question.'

'In that case, I'll take it as a no,' I said. Niall was well known for his sweet tooth.

'For the life of me I don't know how you're not diabetic,' sighed Corin. 'Or how you don't put on any weight.'

Niall picked up his car key from the counter. 'Here,' he said, gesturing with the key and then tossing it to me. 'Take my car, but please, for the love of God, bring it back in one piece.'

I caught the key. 'You sure?'

'Of course. You can't be walking down there now,' said Corin.

'And I'll have a cinnamon swirl and a croissant,' added Niall.

'I'll get a good selection for everyone,' I said. 'See you soon.'

Niall was an absolute darling. I didn't think I'd ever known such a laid-back person as him. Danny was pretty easy-going, but Niall took it to a whole new level.

It was a nice steady drive into town, and I had the window down to let in the fresh salty sea air. The sun was out, and dazzling rays bounced off the water. Of course, there was the Atlantic breeze, but even that didn't feel very strong.

As I drove down Main Street towards the bakery, I nearly crashed the car gawping at the sight of John Walsh standing on the pavement talking to Nicole Elleford in her now familiar yellow coat. They didn't look to be having a friendly chat. He was standing over her and she was backed up against the wall.

I slowed the car, looking for somewhere to park, but as I passed them, Nicole looked up; her eyes widened as she recognised me. John turned around and, once he saw it was me, his face folded in anger. A car behind tooted me because I was now crawling along. I looked in my rear-view mirror and held up my hand to say sorry. As I looked back at Nicole and John, I could see her making a hasty exit from the street into the church grounds.

I wasn't stupid enough to think she was going to confession. I accelerated and went as fast as I dared along the street, taking the next right, which was a narrow road between two rows of shops that came out onto what essentially was wasteland at the back of the church.

I pulled the car over onto the grass verge where it was partially hidden by the branches of an oak tree. If my hunch was right, any minute now Nicole would appear through the gate at the back of the churchyard. I crouched down behind the wall and, running bent over, I scurried parallel with the wall, stopping at the corner.

I heard the latch of the gate click, the hinges protested with a squeak as the gate was opened and then clanged shut.

One. Two. Three.

I jumped up from behind the wall, straight into the path of Nicole Elleford.

She let out a squeal of surprise.

The look of shock on her face was quickly replaced by anguish as she took a moment to realise it was me standing in front of her.

'I just want to talk,' I said quickly.

She started to back away. 'I can't speak to you.'

'Nicole, please.'

She hesitated. 'How do you know my name?'

'It doesn't matter, but you know what Dingle's like. It's a small town. I only had to ask.'

She turned and began walking. 'Then you don't need to ask me, you can ask someone else.'

Shit.

I jogged after her, cutting in front, and walking backwards. 'What was John Walsh talking to you about?'

She stopped walking. 'Nothing.'

'It didn't look like nothing to me,' I continued. 'He didn't look very happy and neither did you.'

'What's it to you anyway?' Nicole glanced around. We were still alone out the back of the church.

'I don't like bullies,' I said.

Her shoulders dropped a fraction, and the confrontation left her eyes. 'What do you want to speak to me for?'

I mentally sighed with relief at the small headway I had made. I didn't fancy having to sprint after her again. 'I know it was you who had the purse put through my sister's door.'

'You've got the purse back. I don't know what the big deal is.'

'Something happened to my sister, to Kathleen, and no one seems to care.'

'That's rich, coming from you.'

The words stung as another person levied the accusation at me. 'It wasn't quite how it looks. I promise you I care very much about Kathleen.'

She looked down at the ground. 'That's not true.' She looked up at me. 'About no one caring. I care.' There was a vulnerability in Nicole's voice that I hadn't expected.

'You care?' I replied. 'You knew Kathleen from The Hub, is that right?'

'Yeah. She was nice. She wasn't like the others.'

My chest tightened and I blinked away tears. It was good to hear someone speak so fondly of Kathleen. 'She loved her job at The Hub,' I said. 'She cared too.'

Nicole looked up to the sky. She blew out a long breath and then met my gaze. 'She found something out, but it put her in danger. That's why she left.'

'I know. She told me, but she needed a bit of time before it all came out,' I said, trying to make out I knew more details in the hope that Nicole would open up. 'I need to know who exactly is involved so I can try to find what's happened to her.'

'You think something bad has happened, don't you?' There was genuine fear in her eyes.

'I don't know,' I replied honestly. 'Whatever has happened, I just need to know.'

'You're a journalist, aren't you?'

'That's right.'

'Kathleen told me. Said you could help her.'

I didn't know my heart could feel any more pain over Kathleen. We may not have always seen eye to eye, but our sisterhood, our bond, our blood ties, kept us close. 'I didn't know that,' I said, feeling an immense sense of pride that she believed in me so much that she told someone else. 'You can trust me. I promise.'

Nicole looked at me for the longest time. The sound of voices from the churchyard behind drifted over us. 'I can't talk here,' said Nicole. 'I'll contact you when I can.'

'Take my number.' I dove into my bag and pulled out the wallet containing my business cards. 'My number's on there. Text or WhatsApp me.'

She took the card. 'Did Kathleen ever tell you about Dervla Collins?'

I shook my head. 'Not that I recall. Why's that? Who's she?'

'You're the journalist.' She started to walk away.

'Who gave you the purse?' I called out. Nicole stopped in her tracks and slowly turned to face me. I walked towards her. 'Please, I can't work this out on my own. I need help. Who gave you Kathleen's purse?'

'No one,' said Nicole, her voice a whisper. 'No one. I had the purse all along.'

I heard a gasp and realised it was me. 'I don't understand,' I said, my voice was faint. I could hardly hear my own words. 'What about Conor Doyle? He said...'

'I asked him to get someone to drop the purse off,' said Nicole. 'Wanted to see if you were really serious about looking for Kathleen.'

I raised my eyebrows. 'You were testing me?'

'If that's what you want to call it.'

'And have I passed the test?'

'I guess so.'

'So, how come you had Kathleen's purse in the first place?' I asked, recovering my composure. The voices in the churchyard grew louder, cutting through the stillness of the waste ground we were standing in.

Nicole looked beyond me towards the church. 'I've got to go.'

Before I could say anything, she was gone, scurrying away down the track and out of sight.

I went back to the car in a state of shock. Nicole had Kathleen's purse? How? Why? I was baffled. None of it made sense. I was in the dark with dots that I couldn't join up. I must have sat in the car for several minutes trying to work it out, but it was no use.

I put this to one side, focusing instead on the small solid piece of information I did have: the name. I googled Dervla Collins but only came up with a few suggestions on Facebook; none of those seemed to have any connection with Dingle or anyone I knew. I debated what to do and, in the end, sent Finn a text message asking him if the name meant anything to him.

In the meantime, I'd do a bit more digging when I got back to Corin's. Maybe she'd know who Dervla Collins was. I spun the car around and went off in search of pastries.

Fifteen minutes later, I was back in Corin's kitchen, sitting at the table having a cup of tea and eating a croissant.

I didn't want to say anything in front of Niall about talking to Nicole, so had to patiently wait for him to eat his pastries before heading off to work.

'Come on, then. Out with it,' said Corin as soon as Niall had driven away.

'Out with what?'

Corin gave me a sceptical look. 'I know you better than you know yourself,' she said. 'There's something you're wanting to tell me or ask me, but you didn't want to in front of Niall.'

I held my hands up. 'Guilty as charged.'

'The girls are in the other room watching the telly, so it's now or never,' said Corin, eyeing me across the rim of her mug.

'OK. Long story short – I saw Nicole Elleford in town, talking to John Walsh.'

Corin raised her eyebrows. 'Go on.'

'When I say talking, what I mean is, he was standing over her and looked like he was taking her to task about something. When she saw me, she legged it. Ran off through the church.'

'What did you do?'

'Drove around the back and waited for her.'

'You ambushed her?'

'If that's what you want to call it,' I said. I went on to give the abridged version of my conversation with Nicole. 'Anyway, before she went, I asked her about the purse again.'

'And?' prompted Corin.

'And it turns out, it was Nicole who got the purse from Kathleen. She said she asked Conor to drop it off to you or get someone else to drop it off.'

'Wait, she got the purse from Kathleen?' asked Corin, as if she didn't quite believe what she was hearing.

'Yes. I know. I don't get it either,' I replied. 'But Nicole's going to message me and arrange for us to meet somewhere safer. She'll tell me then.'

'And you believe her?'

'I do, actually.'

Corin sat back in her chair. 'I can't understand why that Nicole girl would have Kathleen's purse.'

'I'm glad it's not just me, then,' I said. 'There was something else.'

'I'm all ears.'

'Nicole gave me a name: Dervla Collins. She's from The Hub. Do you know her? I tried a Google search but nothing.'

'I don't remember Kathleen mentioning her. Whenever she spoke about The Hub, she didn't name names. Confidentiality thing, you know.'

'I've asked Finn, but not heard back from him yet,' I said.

'I'm sure he'll know,' said Corin, getting up and putting her cup in the dishwasher. 'What have you got planned today?'

'I'm hoping Nicole will message me soon, but in the meantime I thought I might pay the lovely Conor Doyle a visit.'

'You're wasting your time there,' said Corin. 'He won't speak to you.'

'I'll see if I can make it worth his while.' I rubbed my thumb against my forefinger.

'Bribery?'

'Recompense,' I corrected.

'Good luck with that. I hope you have deep pockets.' Corin glanced up at the clock. 'The girls have a friend coming over today so I'm a bit tied up, but let me know if you find anything out and don't go getting yourself into any kind of trouble. Oh, and before I forget, Mam wants us all to go for tea this evening.'

'She never said.'

'No, she's left that to me. So, make sure you and Freya are ready at four o'clock. Don't let me down, otherwise I'll never hear the end of it.'

'Sure.' I knew I should look forward to it more than I did. Any other person who went for months without seeing their parents would be delighted, but I always found it stressful. No, that wasn't the right word. It put a strain on me, and I felt guilty even acknowledging that to myself.

I left Corin to get the girls ready for their friend and went back over to the annexe where Freya was sitting on the sofa, eating the pain au chocolat in a shower of flaky pastry.

'I know. I'll clean it up once I'm done,' she said.

'We have tea tonight at Nan and Grandad's,' I said.

'I'm out with Kian today,' said Freya.

'That's fine, but make sure you're back by four.' I got my laptop and sat at the table with it, trying to see if I could have some luck finding out who Dervla Collins was.

'OK,' said Freya, picking up her phone and poking her tongue out at the camera to take a selfie.

'Gorgeous,' I said with a wink.

'I know, right,' said Freya. 'It's only Sophie.'

A knock came at the door. 'Must be Kian,' I said.

'I'll get it.' Freya jumped up, adjusting the shorts of her PJs, which in my opinion couldn't possibly be shorter and were barely bigger than a pair of pants. She opened the door. I had time enough to register it wasn't Kian but someone else, in a leather jacket, jeans and wearing a crash helmet. It seemed to happen in slow motion as he threw a bottle at her, dousing Freya in some kind of liquid.

Freya screamed in terror, throwing her hands to her face to try to protect herself.

'Hey!' I shouted, leaping up from my chair. I dashed across the room. My immediate thought was it was an acid attack. 'Fuck off!' I yelled.

I was aware the perpetrator had turned and fled from the doorstep. I could hear the sound of an engine, but I wasn't focusing on that. All I could think about was Freya and what to do in the event of an acid attack.

Was it water? Milk? Shit. I couldn't think straight.

'Mum!' wailed Freya, taking her hands away and looking down at her.

'It's OK. Come indoors,' I said quickly, my brain still stumbling over what to do. Milk. It had to be milk. I was sure of that.

'It's piss,' cried Freya. 'Someone's thrown fucking piss all over me.'

FOURTEEN

As much as I was relieved Freya hadn't been the victim of an acid attack, I was repulsed at what had actually been thrown on her. I strongly suspected I had been the intended victim.

Freya had spent a good twenty minutes in the shower, scrubbing herself clean and washing her hair several times. She had insisted the PJs be thrown in the bin as there was no way on this planet she was ever going to wear them again.

She emerged from her bedroom an hour after the incident, her hair done, make-up on, wearing her jeans and a T-shirt.

'Are you all right?' I asked as she busily tapped away on her phone. I doubted very much this incident was going to make an Instagram story.

She gave a shrug without looking up. 'Suppose so.'

'I spoke to Finn, while you were in the shower. He said he'd come over tomorrow and take a statement.'

'I don't want to give a statement,' said Freya, pushing her phone into her back pocket before sitting down to tie the laces on her Converse high tops. 'I don't even want to think about it.'

'I know, but it needs to be reported. I told Corin and she was appalled.'

'Great. Everyone knows I've been covered in someone's piss.'

'Freya, please,' I admonished.

'It's not exactly swearing. Maybe in your day.'

I took the jibe on the chin. She was angry and embarrassed. Who could blame her? I felt desperately sorry for her. 'I know it's horrible, but it needed reporting.'

'I wish I'd never come here,' she said, getting to her feet, her shoes now fastened. She checked her reflection in the mirror over the mantelpiece. 'It's all because you're poking around and stirring everyone up.'

'I know and I am sorry,' I said. 'Look, I think you should cancel going out with Kian today.'

Freya looked at me as if I'd suggested she retire to a convent for the rest of her life. 'Are you serious?' she said once she'd deemed the look of contempt had had its desired effect. 'I am not staying here. I need to get out of this place.'

'But I'm worried about you,' I said, treading carefully along the balance beam of concern and outright fear for her safety. 'I'm worried that whoever threw that bottle of... well, you know... I'm worried they're out there and might do it again.'

'It clearly wasn't meant for me,' said Freya. 'You're the one who should be worrying.'

She had a point. One I couldn't argue with. 'I'm still worried about you though. We could do something nice together instead.'

Before I had time to come up with anything remotely interesting to a fifteen-year-old stuck in a small town in Ireland, Freya was already holding up her hand for me to stop.

'No. Don't even go there,' she said. 'I'm going out with Kian. I'll be fine with him.'

The sound of an engine made us both start. I realised it was a car engine rather than a motorbike. I looked through the blinds at the window, relieved to see it was my nephew. 'That's Kian now.'

'Don't say anything,' warned Freya. 'Please.'

'OK. I promise.' I opened the door to welcome Kian in, but for some reason he stayed in the car.

Freya bustled past me. 'See you later, Mum.' She paused briefly to give me a peck on the cheek.

I didn't want her to go, but I couldn't exactly hold her hostage. 'Ring me if you need me.'

She rolled her eyes. 'I'll be fine.'

'Remember, tea at Nan's this evening, so back by four.'

'I know.'

I looked over towards the car, waiting for Kian to look up, but he kept his head turned away. What was it with kids these days? I went over to the car and tapped on the window. Kian turned his head a fraction and smiled at me. I gestured for him to buzz the window down and with an obvious reluctance, he did so.

'You all right, Kian?' I asked. I looked across at Freya, who was now in the passenger seat, and I could see the anxiety on her face. 'Kian?' I asked again.

'Show her,' said Freya.

Kian slowly turned his head towards me. I let out a gasp as I saw the bruise on his cheekbone.

'What on earth happened? Who have you been rucking with?' Kian wasn't known for getting into fights. As far as I knew, he wasn't even particularly aggressive or argumentative.

'It's nothing,' he said.

'You're not answering my question,' I said, trying not to sound like an old fuddy-duddy. I was sure Kathleen would want me to look out for her son, twenty years old or not.

'If you don't say, I will,' said Freya when Kian didn't reply.

'You know about this already?' I asked my daughter.

'He texted me right before he got here,' said Freya.

'So, one of you needs to tell me what's happened,' I said. 'I don't want to have to go and ask your father.'

I regretted the empty threat as soon as it had left my mouth. Kian's eyes narrowed. 'He won't care. He was the one who did it.'

I was momentarily stunned. 'Your dad did this to you?'

'Yes,' said Freya.

'He can't go around hitting you,' I said, the outrage ramping up. Kathleen would be horrified if she knew this had happened. 'Why did he do that to you?'

'We had an argument.'

'Well, yes. But what did you argue about?' I asked.

Freya nudged Kian. 'You might as well tell her. She'll find out anyway. And if you don't tell her, then I will.'

Kian's gaze moved to the steering wheel.

'It's OK, Kian,' I said. 'I'll spare you the agony. It was me, wasn't it?'

'Kind of. He didn't want me hanging around with Freya or you. Said you'd talk shit about him. That you shouldn't be here. That sort of stuff.'

'I can imagine,' I said. 'But he shouldn't have laid a finger on you. He had no right to do that. And if you argued back out of any sense of loyalty to us, then, thank you but I wish with all my heart you hadn't, not if this was the outcome.'

I wanted to cry at the thought of John punching his own son. Kathleen's son. My nephew. It made me furious, and I already knew I would be having words with that git.

I leaned through the open window and gave Kian a hug. 'I'm really sorry.'

'It's not your fault. He's a miserable bastard anyway. If I could afford to move out, then I would. I hate living with him,' said Kian, returning the hug which, on the whole, was rather awkward through the car window, but we managed it somehow.

'Why don't you come for tea at Nan and Grandad's this

afternoon?' I suggested. Anything would surely be better than going back to his dad's. 'I know it's maybe not top of your wish list, but you and Freya can keep each other company and it will earn me some brownie points with them.'

'Oh, say yes,' pleaded Freya. 'Please, Kian.'

Kian sighed but then smiled. 'No pressure or anything, like.'

'Is that a yes?' asked Freya.

'It's good enough,' I said. 'Now off you both go. See you back here at four. And be careful. Both of you.'

I stood on the drive and watched the car disappear down the road. What a morning it was turning out to be.

As I went back inside, my phone was ringing. Danny's name was on the screen and my heart gave a little flip of excitement.

I managed to answer the call just before it went to voicemail.

'Hi,' I said.

'Siobhan. It's me. Danny.'

His voice didn't hold the same tenderness it once did. There was a more brittle, businesslike sound to it. 'Hi, Danny,' I said. 'You OK?'

'Not really.'

Shit. This wasn't going to be the kind of call I'd hoped for where he asked me how I was and would explain he was ringing me because he missed me and had been thinking about me. No, definitely not one of those. 'What's wrong?' I asked, wondering if he'd got bad news about his parents or something had gone wrong at work.

'I had a text from Freya earlier. I've only just seen it. I've tried to ring her, but she said she can't talk right now.'

My heart bumped out of time for a couple of beats as I wondered what Freya had told him. 'She's out with Kian,' I said.

'She's OK, then?'

'Yeah.'

'What the fuck was the message I had about someone throwing a bottle of piss over her?'

I could hear music in the background, and I wondered where he was. 'Are you at home?' I couldn't help myself from asking.

'Err, no. I'm not as it happens, but that's by the by. I want to know what happened to Freya.'

'You're in a pub?'

'Fuck's sake, Siobhan. What does it matter?' He was almost shouting now. 'Tell me what happened to Freya.' He ground the words out for a second time.

'She's all right and I don't really know what it was about,' I said. 'There was a knock at the door and Freya answered, thinking it was Kian. The next thing, someone threw liquid all over her. I was so scared. I thought it was acid at first.' I had to stop as my voice cracked a fraction. I swallowed down a sob. There was a deadly silence on the other end, so I continued. 'It was someone on a motorbike. They rode off. Freya had a shower and I've reported it to the guards... Danny? Did you hear what I said?'

'Of course I did.' I knew his tone well enough to know he was doing everything to control his anger. Danny, the laid-back lad from Kerry... well, he was to a point, but get him angry and it was like a wild animal had been unleashed. 'What the fuck is going on over there, Siobhan?'

'It was meant for me, I'm sure,' I said. 'Freya's OK. I wish I'd opened the door.'

'It's because you're asking questions about Kathleen. You do know that, don't you?'

'Of course I know that.'

'Then you need to stop. Get the next flight back to England and away from all that. I don't want my daughter there. Not if she's in danger.'

'She's not in danger. As I said, it wasn't meant for her and

I'm not going to stop,' I retorted. I hadn't actually had that conscious thought until that point, but I realised nothing was going to stop me finding out about Kathleen's disappearance. 'Whatever happened, I'm getting close. I'm frightening people. So no way am I going to stop now.'

'You've no right to carry on. Now come home.'

Come home. The words spiked my heart. He didn't mean come home to him, simply back to England. I might have been persuaded if he'd meant the former. 'I'm staying here,' I said, quietly but firmly.

I could hear him take a breath before he replied. 'That's the single most selfish thing you've ever done.' His words were ice-cold.

There was a silence for a long moment. Then I spoke. 'No, it's not, Danny. You're wrong there.'

I ended the call and slumped into the chair, feeling more broken than ever before about my relationship with my husband. I held my head in my hands, wondering how long I was prepared to put my marriage on hold or even forfeit it completely. It wasn't a question. I knew the answer. I'd risk everything to find out what happened to Kathleen. I'd come this far, carrying the weight of my secret, I wasn't going to stop now.

My phone rang, breaking my thoughts, and I snatched it up, expecting to see Danny's name on the screen. He'd calmed down now and was phoning to say sorry. It wasn't Danny. It was Finn.

I took the call.

'Hey, how are you?' asked Finn. 'How's Freya?'

'OK and OK,' I replied.

'I'm going to guess that's the official line. How about the unofficial line? The real one.'

'Sort of OK and totally fucked off, not OK,' I replied, surprised that I suddenly felt like crying at the concern levelled at me. I brushed away an unexpected tear. This wasn't like me at all. I wasn't a crier. 'Freya's gone out with Kian. She's…' I stopped myself from saying pissed off, it felt an inappropriate phrase given the circumstances. 'She's upset and angry at what happened and at me.'

'It's not your fault,' said Finn gently. 'Don't be beating yourself up about it now.'

I didn't want to argue that it was my fault. His concern was touching and the total opposite reaction to Danny's. 'It's upsetting when you see your daughter attacked like that.'

'Sure. Do you want me to come over?'

I hesitated. I wanted to say yes, but I knew I shouldn't. 'Probably best not to.'

'You're not answering the question. Do you want me to come over?'

I closed my eyes for a moment before answering. 'Not right now, but thank you.'

'Sure. You know you only have to say if you change your mind,' said Finn.

'I know.'

He cleared his throat. 'I did actually want to talk to you,' he said in a more businesslike manner. 'You messaged me about Dervla Collins.'

'Yes, that's right. Do you know her?' Glad the conversation had shifted territory.

'I don't know her, but I am aware of the name. Why do you want to know?'

'I remember Kathleen mentioning her. I wondered what the connection was.' For some reason, I didn't want to say I'd spoken to Nicole. 'I'd forgotten all about the conversation, to be honest, but you know what it's like. I was lying in bed and suddenly it popped into my mind from nowhere.'

'Hmm,' said Finn. 'So, Dervla Collins used to live in Dingle. She would hang out at The Hub. Wasn't known to the guards in that way, but we knew a lot of the kids there. She was on the periphery.'

'You're saying "was". Why the past tense?'

'She moved on. To Cork, I think.'

'Cork?'

'Yeah. I think that's where,' replied Finn.

'And that's it?'

'That's it. What were you expecting?'

I don't know why, but I had the feeling Finn wasn't telling me everything. Call it my journalistic nose, but there was more to Dervla Collins than that. And going to Cork. That in itself wasn't unusual. It was a few hours by road. Big city and all that, but I thought of the tickets in Kathleen's purse. Was it a coincidence? 'She was a local girl, then?' I asked.

'That's right and if you're going to ask me her address, don't. I can't give you that.'

'I wasn't.' That was the truth. I'd find out another way. 'OK, thanks, Finn. I thought I'd mention it, that's all. I'm sure if there was any connection someone would have said by now.'

'She went off to Cork a while ago,' said Finn. 'I'm positive there's no connection.'

'OK, thanks.' It was hard to hide my disappointment. Why had Nicole mentioned her? Why didn't she just tell me what had happened?

'So, what are you up to now?' asked Finn.

'I'm hanging out with Corin today and then later going over to my parents.'

'Well, good luck with that,' he replied.

'Thanks. I'll need it.'

We ended the call with Finn saying he'd drop by tomorrow to take a statement from Freya.

I had no intention of hanging out with Corin and the girls, but it gave me some breathing space. Feeling now I had something positive to do, I felt emotionally stronger. I thought of

Kian and his black eye and what I needed to do, not only as Kian's aunt but as Kathleen's sister. She wasn't here to look out for her boy, but I was.

Ten minutes later, I was standing on John Walsh's doorstep, waiting for him to answer.

'What are you doing here?' he demanded when he finally opened the door. He looked at me like I was something nasty on the bottom of his shoe.

'I've just had Kian at my house, and I saw what you did to him,' I began. I had rehearsed this on the way over. I was going to say what I wanted to and get out of there. I wasn't getting into a discussion with him. 'I don't care what it was you argued about, you don't put your hands on my nephew. That's assault. You're nothing but a bully and if you ever lay a finger on him again, I will make sure the whole of Dingle knows what you're really like. See how that sits with all your bigwig friends on the council, on the school board and whatever other pie you've got your grubby fingers in.'

I glared at him and then spun on my heel. As I marched back to the car, I could hear him shouting after me.

'You don't get to come around to my house and tell me what I can and cannot do!'

I could hear his feet stomping on the path behind me. I spun around. 'You watch yourself,' I yelled, with more confidence than I felt. I stood my ground. He wouldn't dare hit me, would he? I could feel my fingers tingle as adrenaline coursed through me.

John was right up in my face, towering over me. 'Don't you tell me about what's right and what's wrong. You're as bad as your sister when it comes to morals.'

'What is that supposed to mean?'

'Dirty fecking whores, the pair of you.' He took a step back and spat on the ground, inches from my feet. 'Both of you open your legs and trap the first decent man that comes along. Poor

Danny. No wonder he left you.' He gave a derisory laugh. 'Oh, don't look so surprised. Everyone knows he's come to his senses. I should have done that years ago with your sister. Now feck off out of here before I call the guards. Silly fecking bitch.'

I was so stunned by the foul-mouthed verbal attack from John, I just stood there staring at his back. He got to his doorstep and turned around. 'You still here? Go on, feck off!' He flung his arm towards the gate. 'Now!'

I gave him one last look before turning and walking down the driveway and out onto the road. His words played on repeat in my head as I walked back towards Corin's house on autopilot.

FIFTEEN

I felt momentarily better for confronting John, but at the same time a whole lot worse. His parting comment rattled around in my head like a noisy tenant.

I drove out of Dingle and along the narrow road of Slea Head Drive – or Slí Cheann Sléibhe, as the local Gaelic sign informed drivers – towards Fahan, passing the beautiful Ventry beach on my left as I went. I remembered many a trip down to the beach in the summer when I was over, and Freya was young. A glorious sandy horseshoe-shaped beach, where it was relatively safe to swim, watched over in the summer by lifeguards. To my right was the patchwork of fields and several derelict stone cottages, abandoned during the Great Famine. The vista was as beautiful as it was brutal, in both its looks and history.

It wasn't until I saw the sign for Beehive Forts parking that I realised I'd driven so far. It was only twenty minutes or so, but I was well out of town now. I wasn't driving especially fast and became aware of a white van behind me. It was getting quite close, hurrying me along. A local, no doubt, trying to get from one place to another and cursing like mad at being held up by tourist drivers, because that's essentially what I was driving like.

The road was too narrow to pull to one side to let him pass but there was a place a little way ahead. He'd have to wait until then. I checked my rear-view mirror, and the bloody van was right up behind me now. If I hit my brakes, he'd crash into me. What an idiot. I accelerated to let him know I was trying to get out of his way, but he matched my speed.

The road twisted its way along the coastline, but I was too preoccupied with the tailgater to take in the views anymore. The pull-in was around the next bend and although I slowed, I veered off into the space faster than I would have wanted. The van whizzed past me and then came to a sudden halt at the end of the lay-by.

I sat in my car, wondering what the hell was going to happen next. It was just my luck that there wasn't a single other car in the lay-by. Then the van began to reverse towards me. Instinctively, I hit the central-locking button on the door, reassured only slightly by the clunk of the locks falling into place.

I tried to look in the nearside wing mirror of the van, to get a look at the driver, but it was the wrong angle. Fumbling with my phone, I opened the camera. My hands trembled as I went to take a photo of the number plate and realised the digits had been masked with black tape.

I'd been in the odd tricky situation in the past, and some deep-seated journalistic instinct had me on high alert. I felt vulnerable out here on my own. I switched the setting to video and began recording, in case I got a look at the driver, and then I began making conscious visual notes of the appearance of the vehicle.

White but dirty.

A dent in the nearside rear panel.

A scratch on the rear bumper.

No wheel hub on the nearside front wheel.

Rear number plate covered with black tape.

The corner of the van was almost level now with the offside front wing of the car. God, Niall wouldn't be happy if I brought another of his cars home wrecked.

But the van stopped a few inches away.

My heart was thumping. I glanced in the rear-view mirror but there was no sign of any other vehicle.

I gauged the gap between the van and wall, wondering if I'd be able to zip past without damaging the car. I put the car into first gear, ready to make a break for it, all the time listening for the van door to open.

My hands were sweating, and I swiped at the leg of my jeans with one and then the other, passing the phone across as I did so.

The longest moment stretched out.

Then I heard the sound of an engine. A motorbike.

I thought of this morning's unwelcome visit.

Fuck.

I rammed the gear stick into reverse. I needed to get out of there. There wasn't enough time to do a three-point turn, but I could get around the offside of the van and then floor it. Fahan was only a little way ahead and it had a lamb-petting visitor attraction. There were bound to be tourists there.

I was about to pull out around the van when it suddenly sped off.

I hit the brakes, not knowing if it was just going to block my way. The motorbike was nearing. I could see it in my wing mirror, leaning over as it came around the bend.

I looked up ahead of me and the van was disappearing out of sight.

The motorbike zoomed by. I held my breath, expecting it to stop, for them to try to do something to me, but they didn't. They too were gone in a matter of seconds, away up the road.

I dropped my phone into my lap and, holding on to the top

of the steering wheel, I rested my forehead, letting out a long sigh of relief. I didn't know if my imagination was getting the better of me or not. But the van, surely that was menacing? Otherwise, why would it drive up close like that and then reverse towards me? And then there was the obscured number plate. No, I wasn't being paranoid – someone was definitely trying to unnerve me.

I decided to head back to Corin's and not take any more chances out there on the deserted road.

The weather was changeable on the west coast and the earlier bright skies over Dingle had faded, replaced by grey clouds and the ominous threat of rain.

However, as I got to Corin's house, I had an unexplained desire to visit The Hub. I had no idea what I was looking for, but my gut was telling me to go there. I had nothing to go on with Kathleen's disappearance. The only clue was Dervla Collins, and yet that had drawn a blank. I wondered if anyone at The Hub would speak about her.

Before I had time to talk myself out of it, I had driven into Dingle, parked the car – this time on the roadside, where I was lucky enough to find a space – and I was pushing open the door to The Hub.

'Oh, hello,' said Sharon. 'I wasn't expecting to see you again so soon.'

'Hi,' I said, making sure my smile was warm and genuine-looking. 'I know. I thought I'd come back sooner rather than later – bit like falling off a horse, best to get back in the saddle as quickly as possible.'

Sharon looked a little bemused. 'OK,' she said, probably more out of politeness than anything else. 'What can I help you with today?'

'Is Aisling Denvers about?' I asked.

'Aisling? Erm, well, she'll be here this evening. She runs a drop-in surgery. Do you want me to make you an appointment?' Sharon sounded hesitant.

'She's not about now?' I asked. 'I thought I saw her car in the car park.' I had not seen her car at all and, in fact, had no idea what car she had, but I was hedging my bets.

Sharon gave an uncomfortable-looking smile. 'I'll buzz through to her.' She picked up the phone, pressed a button and waited a moment for the call to be answered. 'Oh, hi, Aisling. I have Siobhan Martin here, wanting to speak to you... Yes, that's right... she was here... yes. OK.' Sharon put down the phone. 'Aisling won't be a moment.' She twiddled with the biro in her hands. 'I probably shouldn't say this,' she began.

I looked at her and smiled. 'Don't stop on my account,' I said.

'Aisling wasn't very happy you were here yesterday. Some of the youngsters complained about you.'

I raised my eyebrows. 'Did they? Now, why doesn't that surprise me? I expect Conor Doyle was heading that up.'

'Just be careful,' she said.

The door off the entrance hall opened and Aisling Denvers walked through. 'Miss Martin,' she said.

I cut her off. 'Mrs. It's Mrs Martin.'

'Of course, Mrs Martin. How can I help you?'

'I wondered if I could have a word in private?'

Aisling exchanged a quick glance with Sharon before addressing me. 'Come this way. I have an appointment in five minutes, so I hope that's enough time.'

'Thanks,' I said, following her through the double doors. 'I hope so too.'

Aisling's office was the second door on the left of the corridor. It was sparsely furnished, more reminiscent of a police interview room than an office for a local councillor. She gestured for me to sit on the blue office chair.

'This isn't my everyday office,' she said, as if reading my mind. 'This is the one I use when I'm here. I have another office at the town hall. Anyway, what can I do for you? I assume it's to do with your sister, Kathleen? That's why you were here before?'

I liked that Aisling Denvers got straight to the point and was obviously an intelligent woman who didn't need things spelled out to her. 'That's right,' I said. My phone began to ring before I had a chance to say anything, and I quickly whipped it out of my pocket. It was an unknown number.

'Please answer it, if you need to,' said Aisling.

'No. It's fine. They can leave a voice message.' I switched it to silent, aware I only had a few minutes with Aisling. 'Someone mentioned the name Dervla Collins and that she had a connection to The Hub and to my sister. I wondered if the name meant anything to you?'

Aisling sat back in her chair and pursed her lips. 'Why are you asking me?'

'You're involved with The Hub. It's your baby, if you like, and you seem the sort of person who doesn't miss much.'

'I'll take that as a compliment,' she replied evenly. 'Who gave you the name Dervla Collins?' There was nothing in her tone to suggest whether the name stirred good or bad emotions.

'I'd rather not say,' I replied.

She studied me for a moment as if weighing me up. 'I am familiar with the name,' she said at last. 'I didn't know the girl well but, if it's who I'm thinking of, then yes, she did come to The Hub, but for what, I don't know. We have lots of people, youngsters especially, drop in on a very ad hoc basis. We don't ask questions, that's part of the deal. It's a safe place for them. We're not here to judge, only to support, if they want it. If they ask for it.'

I nodded. 'I know. Kathleen was very proud of her work here and all that The Hub does for the community.'

Aisling smiled, rather like a parent on sports day whose child had won a race. A smile of satisfaction and tempered glory. 'I believe Dervla moved away, but that's all I know, I'm afraid.'

'Did Kathleen ever speak to you about any of the youngsters, like Dervla? Did she ever say she was worried?'

'I'm sorry, I really can't say. Confidentiality. I know it's important, but I can't bend the rules for anyone, otherwise we lose the trust of the community and then what is the point of this place?' She spread her hands as an indicator to underline her words.

'Do you have an address or any contact details for Dervla?' I already knew the answer but asked it anyway.

Aisling gave me a sympathetic smile. 'I'm sorry.'

I nodded. 'Yeah, I know. Thanks anyway.' I got to my feet and shook hands with Aisling, thanking her again, before going to leave. I paused in the doorway. 'Does Dervla's family still live in Dingle?'

Not for the first time, Aisling appraised me before answering. 'I suppose saying her mother still lives in Dingle isn't giving away confidential information. It's not like I'm giving you the actual address.'

I patted the doorframe with my hand as I pushed myself away. 'Thanks.'

'You're welcome.'

I left The Hub through the main entrance, giving a small wave to Sharon, who was on the phone. As I stepped out onto the street, I took in a lungful of fresh air. The sky was greyer than it had been before, and it matched the frustration I was feeling about the lack of progress. That, coupled with the impending evening meal at my parents where I knew my dad would probably wind me up about something and Freya would be sending me begging eyes across the room as soon as the meal was over to leave.

I looked in my bag for my phone, wanting to text Freya to remind her not to be late. My dad hated lateness. It had always been a thing with him. Woe betide us kids if we were late for anything. I remembered being late home for dinner once and finding my dinner in the bin. I was so hungry, but I wasn't allowed to have anything. I was made to sit at the table and watch everyone eat their meal. Later that evening, Kathleen had sneaked some food up to me. A cold sausage and an apple.

I tutted impatiently at not being able to find my phone and checked my pockets, but they were empty. Then I remembered I'd taken it out when I'd got that call in Aisling's office. I'd absent-mindedly put it down on the desk and forgotten to pick it up.

I nipped back into The Hub. Sharon had disappeared from the reception desk, so I went through the double doors and down the corridor to Aisling's office. The door was open, and I could hear her voice. It took a moment for me to tune into her conversation.

'It needs to be stopped,' she was saying. 'You need to deal with this.'

I slowed my pace, the carpet-tiled hallway dulling the sound of my trainers on the floor. There was a pause in the conversation, and I assumed she must be on the phone.

'Make sure you do,' she snapped, her tone one of irritation. 'Wait a minute.'

My heart jumped and I resumed a normal walking pace. 'Hello! Anyone there?' I called out innocently as I approached the office door.

Aisling appeared in front of me, and I pretended to jump in surprise. 'Oh, sorry. I wasn't sure if you were still here,' I said, throwing in a broad smile. 'I forgot my phone. I think I left it on your desk.'

Aisling held her own phone to her shoulder, and she looked back towards her desk. 'So you have. I didn't notice it.'

'Sorry,' I said, nodding towards the mobile in her hand as I slipped by and scooped up mine. 'Bye and thanks again,' I said in a hushed voice.

I could feel her gaze on my back as I headed out of the hall, through the double doors and exited the building.

SIXTEEN

Freya and Kian arrived back at the annexe with five minutes to spare. I had forced myself not to text either of them with a time check, so was relieved when Kian's car pulled up on the driveway.

I went out to them. 'I'm going to hop in the car with Corin. Why don't you drive and then if you need to leave a bit earlier, you can?'

Freya didn't even try to hide her enthusiasm for this suggestion. 'Great idea. It's not like you're going to be able to drink at Nan and Grandad's.'

'No, that's true,' said Kian resignedly.

'But it doesn't mean you can leave straight after dinner, though,' I warned. 'You have to stay for at least forty-five minutes after that.' I looked at their faces. 'That's the deal, otherwise the three of us will get a taxi.' I withheld the chuckle of amusement as they both rapidly assured me they would be fine making their own way and, of course, they wouldn't shoot straight off.

Corin, Niall and the kids came out of the house, and I climbed into their car. 'Freya and Kian are going to follow us down,' I said, squashing up next to Sorcha on the rear seat, with Erin on the other side.

Ten minutes later we were all bustling into my parents' whitewashed stone cottage. The twins headed straight for the garden; the older two went to follow, but Kian's battered appearance, naturally, was cause for delay and discussion.

'Ah, Kian,' Mam cried. 'What's happened to you? Séamus, have you seen this boy's face?' She had hold of Kian's shoulder with one hand and his chin with the other. She turned his head to face my dad.

'Where did you get that from?' asked Dad.

I was sure we were all holding our breath as we waited for Kian to answer.

My nephew shrugged. 'Messing around with the lads,' he said simply. 'I didn't duck quick enough.'

My mother tutted and released her grandson. 'You shouldn't be fighting, even if it is play-fighting,' she scolded.

'Next time, you make sure you get in first,' said Dad.

'Come on,' said Freya. 'Let's go and keep an eye on the twins in the garden.'

I gave Freya a small smile of appreciation as she hurried her cousin out of the questioning line.

'You shouldn't encourage him to fight,' said Mam.

'He may be a Walsh by name, but he's got Regan blood in him, and no Regan man is going to end up worse off than their opponent,' said Dad.

'Ah, Séamus,' said Niall, interrupting the conversation. 'I've got some photos of that old car my friend's restoring. Let me show you them.'

Niall was an absolute darling, distracting Dad like that. 'Let us help you in the kitchen,' I said to Mam, and Corin and I followed her down the hall.

'Nice that Kian came,' commented Mam as she turned

down the gas for the potatoes that were violently bubbling away on the stove, threatening to overflow.

'He's good company for Freya,' I replied, going over to the dresser and getting the plates down while Corin began setting out the place mats.

'Oh, you need to put out an extra place,' said Mum.

'We've got another guest?' I asked, exchanging a quizzical look with my sister, who shrugged.

There was a knock at the door. 'Oh, that will be him,' said Mam. 'Your dad asked him to come.' She wiped her hands on her apron and patted her hair, which didn't need patting into place due to the copious amounts of hairspray applied. The smell of the lacquer was one I always associated with my mother. 'I'll get it!' she called out needlessly. Mam always got the door, even when my dad might be closer.

Corin and I listened as she greeted the caller. 'Ah, Rory, come on in. The girls have just got here.'

I exchanged a look with Corin. It was Rory Ahern, the sergeant at Dingle Garda Station.

'What's he doing here?' I whispered to Corin.

'No idea. Mam never said he was coming.'

The tall and broad figure of Rory Ahern filled the doorway to the kitchen. 'Hello there, Corin. Siobhan. Good to see you,' he said, with a smile and a nod to each of us. 'I hope you don't mind me gate crashing the family meal?'

'No, not at all,' replied Corin.

'Yeah, it's a nice surprise,' I added. I wasn't sure how I felt about Ahern being there. As kids, we'd feared him when he was a regular guard and he used to stop to talk to us in the street, which wasn't always cool with our friends. He kept the teenagers in the town in order and employed rather more traditional policing tactics, where a clip around the ear was a perfectly acceptable form of punishment, along with dragging someone back to apologise for whatever misdemeanour they had committed.

He didn't appear to be letting on that he'd already seen me and my sister at the station, which I appreciated. Although, I did wonder how much he and Finn had discussed about my being here and Kathleen's purse turning up.

'You're here for the school holidays?' Ahern asked Freya, as we all sat down to eat half an hour later at the same kitchen table my parents had had since forever.

'Yes,' said Freya in the way only an awkward fifteen-year-old could, avoiding eye contact as much as possible.

Rory forked a roast potato into his mouth, almost swallowing it whole. 'And where's your dad?' he asked. 'He couldn't make it, no?'

Freya shook her head.

I intervened. 'He has work. This was a spur-of-the-moment visit.'

'Yes, Finn Casey was telling me he'd seen you a few times,' said Ahern. 'Which, of course, is all well and good, but I've had to remind him not to get distracted by a pretty face.'

There was another awkward silence for a few seconds and then Niall laughed, rather enthusiastically, before saying. 'Don't be telling Siobhan that, it will go to her head, like.' He threw me a wink.

'Sure, her head will get too big to fit through that door,' Corin chipped in.

There was a small ripple of laughter, and I appreciated Niall and Corin's attempt at making light of the comment. It was, to say the least, uncomfortable.

My discomfort was compounded further when, after dinner, I was in the kitchen making everyone a cup of tea.

Rory had got up to use the toilet and, on his way back down the hall, came into the kitchen.

'I didn't mean to embarrass you back then,' he said.

'Oh, you didn't,' I lied.

'It's just Finn, he's a good lad. A good guard. He's a nice fella but you know he's always had a soft spot for you.'

'We've known each other since we were kids,' I said, dropping the teabags into the pot. Dad hated tea made in the cup. I wasn't sure he'd be able to tell the difference, but I wasn't going to risk it. Avoiding his wrath was a hard habit to shake off.

'You know what I mean,' said Ahern. 'But you went off and married Danny Martin instead. Sure, the boy was heartbroken.'

I wasn't sure if that was an accurate account of events, but I didn't argue. 'Do you have sugar?' I asked, trying to deflect the remark. I picked up another teabag.

'Two.' Ahern stepped further into the kitchen, pushing the door closed behind him. 'What I'm trying to say is, don't mistake Finn's willingness to help you for anything more than him still having a thing about you.'

'Have you spoken to the Serious Crime Team?' I asked.

'I'm waiting for someone to get back to me.'

I wasn't sure I believed him. 'Maybe you could chase them? I don't have much time before I have to go back to England.'

Ahern looked thoughtful for a moment. 'I shouldn't really be telling you this,' he said. 'There are certain things about the investigation that haven't been revealed to anyone. That includes yourself.'

'What sort of things?'

'There was a possible sighting of Kathleen in Tralee a couple of days after she went missing.'

A flutter of panic whirled in my stomach. 'There was? Did you follow it up?'

'We did. We had a long hard look at CCTV footage in the area.'

'And you found nothing?' My voice wobbled as I spoke.

Ahern put his hand on my shoulder. 'I know it's hard to accept, I honestly do, but your sister wouldn't be the first person to walk away from an unhappy marriage. Maybe it was the menopause, midlife crisis or something. Not being rude, but that sort of thing can send a woman a bit... you know...'

'I don't know, actually,' I said, my jaw tensing at the ignorant insult. This man definitely needed to retire. No wonder he was friends with my dad. They were both stuck in the 1980s. 'Look, whether Kathleen was in Tralee or not doesn't matter. She went missing and no one has seen or heard from her since until her purse turned up. Now that surely needs taking seriously.'

'Someone is messing with you, that's all,' said Rory. 'You'd be wise to ignore it. Don't go stirring up trouble for no reason, you won't be thanked for it.'

'I'm not put off that easily,' I replied.

Ahern took his hand away and drummed his fingers on the counter. 'You know, when we looked at the CCTV in Tralee, we didn't see Kathleen at all,' he began.

'So you said,' I replied, pouring the now boiling water into the pot.

'We saw someone who we thought was her but on closer inspection realised it wasn't.'

He paused as if what he said was significant enough. 'So, she wasn't there,' I said. My hand shook and I slopped hot water onto the countertop.

Ahern let out a sigh. 'I'm sure it was pure coincidence that there was a potential sighting of your sister in Tralee, and you just happened to use a cashpoint at Lower Castle Street, Tralee, that same day.'

The flutter of nerves turned into a swarm. This had never been mentioned before. I had no idea the guards knew about this. 'Why haven't you brought this up before?' I asked, acutely aware of the nerves showing themselves in my voice.

Ahern tipped his head to one side and then the other. 'There was no need as far as I could see. It would only muddy the waters. Probably cause more trouble with all the speculation that was going on. All the theories about what happened. I thought your parents had enough to deal with. I passed it by. I was doing you a favour.'

'Not sure how you work that one out,' I said. I wasn't about to be held to ransom over me using the cashpoint in Tralee. 'It has nothing to do with Kathleen. Besides, I'm not worried about ruffling a few Dingle feathers.'

'Well, maybe you don't care what happens, but I don't want to be breaking the news to your parents that another one of their daughters...' He didn't finish his sentence.

'One of their daughters what?'

Ahern's face folded into a deep frown. 'I don't want to tell them that there's been any trouble,' he said.

'Why doesn't anyone want me to find out what happened to Kathleen?' I said, turning away, swilling the teapot around.

'Because there's nothing to find out and it's upsetting people,' said Ahern. 'I don't know why you've a sudden interest now it suits you. You didn't seem that concerned six months ago.'

The accusation cut deep, and I felt a flush of blood to my face – a declaration of both my guilt and my shame. I couldn't argue with it. I didn't push hard enough back then. Hindsight is a wonderful thing, they say. If I had that time again, and knew then what I later knew, I would most certainly do things differently. 'I... I thought she'd come back,' I said, looking down at the cups. 'I thought she'd be back by now.'

'Siobhan,' began Ahern, 'you have to remember, you're an outsider these days. You haven't lived here in such a long time; no one trusts you. You need to drop trying to find your sister. As a friend of your father's, I'm asking you to leave well alone.'

'And if I don't?'

He took a moment before answering. 'I can't guarantee your safety.'

I looked sharply up at him. 'Can't or won't?'

He raised his eyebrows as if that was a ridiculous question. 'You need to take some responsibility for your own actions,' he said, without taking his gaze from mine.

'Sounds like you're trying to blame me.' I was irritated now. Unrepentant as he tried to lay the blame at my feet.

'I don't want to lock horns with you, girl,' said Ahern. 'I've known you all your life, so this is friendly advice. Don't be making trouble for yourself or your parents.'

Something made me look beyond Ahern and I almost jumped when I saw Corin standing in the doorway to the kitchen. I hadn't noticed her open the door. I wondered how long she had been standing there and how much she'd heard.

Next thing, Mam bustled in. 'I came to see what was keeping you,' she said. 'I hope you haven't roped Rory into helping you – he's our guest.'

'We were just catching up,' said Rory. 'I was asking how Danny was. Good to hear he's doing well.'

'Right, well, sit yourself back down with Séamus, and we'll bring the drinks in.'

I wasn't sure how I managed to carry the tray through to the living room without spilling the tea. Ahern knew I'd been in Tralee using the cashpoint a few days after Kathleen disappeared. He might not be Scotland Yard, but he'd worked out what I was doing there. And he was trying to use that as a bargaining chip – a threat to make me stop asking questions. Trouble was, he had underestimated me.

To their credit, Freya and Kian stayed a good hour after dinner before making their excuses to go. Dad had made a comment about them going to Mass at some point, but once again Niall had diverted the conversation, telling Dad about the latest fishing exploit he had been on.

'You owe your Uncle Niall a thank you,' I whispered to Freya as I saw them to the door.

'Buy him extra pastries tomorrow,' Freya whispered back before hotfooting it after Kian.

It was another sixty minutes before Corin made a move and I was able to go with them.

'That wasn't so bad, was it?' said Corin as we pulled away, smiling and waving to our parents.

'No, it was OK, to be fair,' I said. I leaned forward and patted Niall on the shoulder. 'You were a star in there.'

Niall reached over and squeezed my hand. 'I'm well practised.'

I sank back in the seat and closed my eyes. I always felt exhausted after being at my parents. I could never fully relax there and the elephant in the room was always Kathleen. I don't think they would ever forgive me for what happened that night.

We were back at Corin's in a few minutes, and I declined the offer of a coffee.

'I'm fine,' I said. 'I'm really tired. I'll have an early night.' I also had a mind to give Danny a call to try to clear the air after our conversation earlier about Freya.

'I'll see you in the morning,' said Corin, giving me a hug. 'Well done for this afternoon.'

'Thanks,' I said, returning the hug.

I was glad of the peace and quiet in the annexe. I needed time to restore my equilibrium. The frustration at the lack of support was weighing me down and I was missing Danny. I just wanted to be held by my husband and for him to tell me everything was going to be all right.

I picked up my phone and brought up his contact details on the screen. My thumb hovered over the call button. What if he didn't want to speak to me? What if he was out? Was I ready for the disappointment?

What was wrong with me? I was never usually indecisive.

My confidence hadn't been shattered since Danny left, but it was under attack. I didn't like this lack of self-belief. It was a new concept and alien to me.

However, the decision was taken out of my hands as the sound of a car pulling up outside had me at the window. That was another thing I disliked. The anxiety I was now experiencing every time a vehicle pulled up. It was only Kian and Freya.

I opened the door to let them in. Immediately, I could see the serious looks on their faces.

'What's happened?' I asked before they'd even sat down. I closed the front door and turned to face them as they both stood in the middle of the room. Kian was clutching a carrier bag in one hand.

'Dad said you had been up to the house today,' said Kian hesitantly.

'Yes, that's right,' I replied. 'When did he tell you that?'

'He phoned me,' said Kian.

'I take it he wasn't very happy,' I replied. When I'd gone up there to confront John, I hadn't considered Kian. I hoped I hadn't made things worse.

Kian gave a dismissive shrug. 'I'm staying out of his way for now.'

'I'm sorry,' I said.

'It doesn't matter,' replied Kian. He held out the bag to me. I was intrigued as to what was inside. At first I thought it was an e-reader, but when I took it out and opened the case, I realised it was a tablet. 'The tablet, that was Mum's. Dad didn't know she had it.'

'What?'

'She kept it hidden from him,' said Kian. 'I came home early from school one day. Dad was at work and Mum was in the kitchen. She didn't hear me come in, and when I walked in, she nearly fell off the stool. She was properly flustered and shut the tablet quickly. I didn't realise at first and was like, oh I didn't know you had a tablet. She was like, it's not mine. It's Corin's. I only borrowed it. I asked her why she didn't use the laptop and she made up some random excuse about wanting to book a holiday as a surprise for Dad, so I wasn't to say anything.'

'And did she book a holiday?' I asked.

'No. It was never mentioned again but she went upstairs, and I heard her go into the spare room,' explained Kian. 'Later, when I was home alone, I went up there and found it. She'd hidden it at the back of the wardrobe in a shoe box. It was underneath some tissue paper. She definitely didn't want anyone to find it.'

'So how come you've got it now?' I asked.

'After she went missing, I went and got it. I didn't tell my dad. Whatever was on there, she didn't want him to know.'

'And what was on there?'

'I don't know. It's password protected. I've tried to google how to unlock it, but you need some special software. I didn't want to ask anyone in case they got suspicious and said something to me, Dad or the guards.'

'I said Dad would know how to unlock it,' said Freya.

Kian had obviously consulted with Freya before coming to me, and I was glad he felt he could confide in someone. The burden was weighing heavy on his young shoulders.

'I'll ask Danny,' I said. 'Have you told anyone about this?'

Kian shook his head. 'No one.'

'Good. We must keep this quiet until we know what's on here,' I said. I picked up my phone. 'I'll ring Danny now.'

Danny was clearly still sulking with me and wouldn't pick up or return my messages. Freya tried but she too got no response. I was a bit peeved he wouldn't even reply to Freya, which made me wonder where he was. As per usual, my thoughts went to all the places that would keep me awake at night, fuelling my anxiety over my marriage.

I had invited Kian to stay the night on the sofa, but he had declined and said he'd go home; his dad would be OK now he'd had a chance to calm down. I was reluctant to let him go, but I couldn't exactly hold him hostage. I got the feeling that maybe this wasn't the first time John had lashed out at his son. Lashed out. Who was I kidding? I scolded myself for using language that played the attack down, because that's what it was: a physical assault.

When I went to bed, my mind was ravaged by thoughts of Kathleen and the argument we'd had that night. Of everything she had told us and the knock-on effect our actions had caused. If she knew her son would be sporting a black eye from John because she wasn't there, then I was sure she would have done things differently.

SEVENTEEN

THEN

I stared in disbelief at what Kathleen had just said. Was this some kind of joke, albeit in the worst taste? I could feel my chest tighten as her words replayed themselves. I blinked hard and studied the face of my sister. She wasn't joking. There was no curve to her mouth. No mischief in her eyes. No lightness to her features.

'You were groomed?' I said, as much to check I was hearing right as to question what had been said.

'That's right,' she replied, her gaze holding mine. 'I was groomed from when I was about fourteen. I just didn't know it at the time.'

'Who was it?' I hardly dared ask.

'It doesn't matter.'

'It fucking well does,' I retorted. 'Who was it?'

'You can ask all you like, but I'm not saying,' replied Kathleen. 'Not yet anyway.'

Corin put her hand on my arm to stop me from replying.

'Why not yet?' she asked, her tone more one of concern than anger like mine.

'I need to sort a few things out first,' said Kathleen. She looked up at me. 'It wasn't as seedy as it sounds.'

I went to reply that I begged to differ, and how could it not be seedy, but again, my younger sister's gentle touch on my arm had me biting down on my words. 'What happened?' I asked instead.

'It started out as a friendship. I was very taken with him. He showed kindness. It wasn't something we got at home, as you know. He made me feel better about myself, and when I was upset about something, he listened. He showed real concern and care.'

'That's how it all starts,' I said.

'I know that,' said Kathleen. 'I know that now, but not then. Basically, I lapped up the attention, the kindness and the love. It was everything I wanted and everything I had never experienced.'

I thought of our dad, and I knew exactly what she meant. She didn't need to spell it out but, despite all the strict and religious rules we had to abide by as children, I knew our parents loved us.

Corin spoke ahead of me. 'You were looking for something you thought you were missing at home,' she said gently.

Kathleen nodded. 'Yes. I fell in love with this man, but for all the wrong reasons.'

'He took advantage of you,' I said, although I didn't think Kathleen needed telling. As I was labouring over how to phrase the next question I wanted to ask, Kathleen saved me the trouble.

'It wasn't sexual, at first,' she said. 'In fact, I'd got to sixteen and thought there must be something wrong with me. Why hadn't he tried to seduce me? I actively encouraged him, to the point I was almost begging him to sleep with me.' She closed her eyes and took a deep breath. 'I look back and I feel so embarrassed.'

'You have nothing to feel embarrassed about,' I said firmly. 'Nothing. It's all part of the long game people like that play.'

She gave me a grateful smile, but I don't think she was convinced. 'It finally happened when I was seventeen,' she said. 'So, technically, it was legal.' Her fingers fiddled with the stem of the wine glass, twisting it one way and then the other. She spoke again and it was almost a whisper.

'I... I don't know what to say,' I began and then shook my head. I reached across and touched her hand. 'I had no idea. I'm so sorry.'

'Why would you have any idea? We kept it a secret. He said he needed time to get some money together and then he'd leave his wife. That we'd go off and start a new life of our own.'

'What a twisted bastard,' I said, as I thought back to when Kathleen was eighteen. Were there signs there that I had missed at the time? And then it struck me: Kathleen was with John Walsh when she was seventeen. 'What about John? How does he fit into this, if you were having a relationship with the married man?'

Kathleen took a sip of her wine. 'He, the married man, encouraged me to get a boyfriend. He said it would stop people getting suspicious.'

'He had it all worked out,' I said.

'Around that time, he started giving me money,' continued Kathleen. 'And you know how poor we were. He told me I needed to get myself a boyfriend, which meant I needed to start looking more attractive.'

'Jesus, this just gets more and more twisted,' I said.

'So, I actively went searching for a boyfriend and, well... that's how I was with John. I knew him from school and church.'

'I always wondered what the attraction was,' I said. 'Now I realise John was a decoy, it makes more sense.'

'I know,' said Kathleen. 'It gets worse. He encouraged me to sleep with John.'

'What the actual fuck?' I looked in horror at my sister. 'He wanted you to have sex with another man?'

'Yeah. And I did.'

'And he didn't care?' asked Corin, who seemed equally shocked by the idea.

Kathleen looked down at her wine glass. 'No. I think he liked it. He'd get me to tell him about it and then he'd make love to me and ask me who was best.'

'Jesus Christ,' gasped Corin.

'That's awful,' I whispered.

'I knew there was a bad side to him, but I didn't want to see it,' said Kathleen. 'I was besotted with him, and I would have done anything he asked. Absolutely anything, without a moment's hesitation. By the time I realised that it was all wrong and kind of sick, it was too late.'

'Kind of sick?' I scoffed, shaking my head as I took it all in. 'When you realised it was wrong, didn't you try to break it off?'

'Don't judge me,' said Kathleen.

'I'm not. I'm trying to understand it, that's all. I am not judging you, I promise.' Although, if I was totally honest, maybe I was a little. It was unfair of me. I had no idea how I'd react in that situation.

'I did try to finish it at one point,' said Kathleen. She eyed me and Corin carefully. Neither of us said anything as we waited for her to continue. 'He said, "Oh, if you did that, I'd be heartbroken. I suppose I could see if one of your sisters would want any of the gifts or money instead."'

'Oh, dear God,' I whispered.

Corin inhaled deeply. She pushed her chair back and got to her feet. 'We need another drink.'

I watched Corin go up to the bar and then lean across the table. 'Why didn't you say anything before?'

'What was the point? It wouldn't have changed anything.' There was a note of bitterness to Kathleen's voice.

'But we could have helped you. Done something. Spoken out.' I didn't know what, but there must have been something we could have done.

'I told you, it wouldn't have changed anything,' snapped Kathleen again. 'I didn't want you to know. I didn't want Corin to know. I was trying to protect you both but at the same time I was being selfish. I didn't want either of you two to have the things he gave me. We always had to share stuff when we were kids and, for the first time in my life, I didn't have to do that. So, you see, I had my own reasons not to say anything. Don't try to make me feel guilty for not telling you.'

'I'm not trying to do that,' I said. 'Not at all.'

Corin arrived back at the table with a bottle of wine and filled up our glasses. None of us spoke and we all gulped our drinks down. Corin refilled them straight away. 'You should have said something.'

'Not you as well,' said Kathleen. 'For feck's sake. I wish I'd never told you at all.'

'Then why did you?' An irrational surge of injustice swept up through me. 'Why did you tell us?'

'Because you think you have it all sussed with your happy successful lives. You especially, Siobhan.'

'Kathleen, what happened was awful. Truly awful and I can't even begin to get my head around it,' I said. 'But all we're saying is, we wish we'd known so we could have helped you. Jesus, it's quite a revelation, what you've just said. By our ignorance we feel guilty. Of course we do, but you have to give us time to process it all.'

'And there you go, bringing it all back around to yourself again, like you always do,' said Kathleen.

'That's not fair,' said Corin, raising her voice.

'Why are you telling us this now?' I asked again, trying to ignore the barbed comment.

'I don't know,' said Kathleen. 'Well, that's a lie, actually. I do know why.'

'Are you going to share that with us?' I asked.

'I can't. Not yet,' said Kathleen. 'I don't care about myself. What's happened has happened. For me, it's over. But for others it's not.'

I sat back in my chair, feeling mentally exhausted trying to keep up with the conversation. I had nothing but admiration for my sister. She'd been a victim of grooming and carried that secret around with her, but it also explained why she was passionate about her work at The Hub. It made so much sense now; why my reserved, sometimes starchy, sister wanted to help others. She was a contradiction up until that point – the two sides of her had seemed at odds, but now it all clicked. She wanted to look after and care for vulnerable people in the community because of what she had experienced as a minor.

Corin leaned in, her voice quieter. 'How did it all end?'

Kathleen glanced around the pub as if to make sure no one was paying us any attention before she answered. 'When I got pregnant with Kian. John was there for me. He did the right thing by me.'

'And John is Kian's father?' I asked, sitting forward in my seat again. 'If you were sleeping with both of them... I mean, what sort of contraception did you use?'

'Condoms, but I also had unprotected sex with John,' said Kathleen. 'Once the married man found out I was pregnant, he didn't want to know me. I guess I didn't fit his criteria anymore.'

'I don't know how you can stay around here with all those memories,' I said.

'It's because of those memories I do. They are my fuel. They are what drive me on. I knew one day there would be a reckoning for it all, and that day is just around the corner. I'm not a child anymore. I'm a grown woman who understands it all now and I can help others who find themselves in the same situation. I couldn't save me, but I can save them.'

'You're so brave,' said Corin.

Kathleen shook her head. 'It's not bravery. It's atonement.'

'You've nothing to atone for,' I said.

'I look back and wish I hadn't been scared, and wish I could have stood up for myself. So now I'm standing up for others.'

'At The Hub?' asked Corin. 'Is something going on there now?'

'I can't talk about it,' said Kathleen. 'But I'm on the brink of something massive.'

'When you say on the brink, how close to that brink are you actually? Are you safe?' I asked.

'I'm teetering on the edge,' said Kathleen. 'I need to get some advice. I need to make sure my next move is watertight.'

'And then what?' asked Corin.

'And then there's going to be a major fucking shitstorm,' said Kathleen. 'And I mean major.'

'Should you go to the guards?' Much as I admired Kathleen for what she was doing, I didn't think she should be on some personal mission to save the town. Not on her own.

'No. It's too dangerous.'

'Look, Kathleen,' I began. 'You can't go on some sort of vigilante crusade. Especially if it's dangerous. In fact, what you need to do is let the authorities deal with this. Is it the same thing that happened to you?'

Kathleen gave a derisory laugh. 'The same thing that happened to me. Can't you bring yourself to say the correct term? Is it too unsavoury for you to say child abuse?'

Corin made a shushing sound. 'You'll have the whole pub knowing at this rate.'

'Oh, that won't do, will it?' said Kathleen. She swayed in her seat as she brought her wine glass to her mouth and sloshed some down her top before she made it to the desired destination.

Corin and I said nothing as we watched her down the contents of the glass. She grabbed at the wine bottle and went to pour another. I reached across, putting my hand on the bottle and lowering it to the table. 'Maybe we should go back to the annexe and talk there,' I suggested.

'There's nothing more to say,' said Kathleen.

'You can't say that,' I protested. 'You've dropped this bombshell on us and we have so many questions.'

'Always about yourself, isn't it, Siobhan?' Kathleen plonked her glass down.

'It's about all of us,' I insisted. 'You've shared this with us. We love you and we need to try to understand this. We want to help you.'

Kathleen laughed out loud. A few heads in the pub turned in our direction but this didn't deter Kathleen. 'Why don't you go back to England and your cosy life in Brighton and forget I ever said anything.'

'I know you're hurting,' I said. 'But we're sisters. We're always here for each other.'

'I wish we weren't,' said Kathleen. 'I wish you two had never been born.'

'Oh, feck off,' said Corin. 'That's a terrible thing to say.'

'It's true though. If you two weren't my sisters then I would never have had to stay with that man. I only did because I was protecting you, and what have you ever done for me in return?'

'Don't even answer that. She's pissed out of her head,' said Corin.

It wasn't like Corin to get annoyed, but even she was beginning to tire of Kathleen's irrational thought process.

'You've no right to blame us,' I said.

'You don't get it, do you?' said Kathleen, her voice loud now. 'It's still about you when it's nothing to do with you.'

The hum of conversation in the pub receded. Kathleen was now on her feet. 'My wonderful smart sister who sold out to England with her perfect life. You know what, Siobhan, you feck off back to Brighton. We don't need you here. Or want you, for that matter.'

Corin jumped to her feet. 'Kathleen, that's enough now. Let's get you home.' She moved around the table and took our sister's arm.

'Oh, go away. I don't need your help. Typical of you to side with her. You always have been as thick as thieves, you two.' She pushed Corin away.

I don't know what came over me, but I was on my feet and grabbing at Kathleen. Telling her to leave Corin alone. I'm not sure if I was shouting at that point. And then chaos descended as the three of us started yelling at each other.

'You always take her side!'

'You're drunk!'

'No. I'm not.'

'Get off me.'

'I never want to see you again.'

'Typical of you, being the martyr.'

I don't even know who was saying what. It was a cacophony of disjointed words and voices. Accusations and verbal assaults followed by counterclaims and denials.

And then we were being pulled apart by Finn Casey and a couple of his mates who were drinking in The Harp that night. They were telling us to calm down and how silly it all was, that it was getting out of hand. Someone pointed out that when our dad heard about it, there'd be trouble.

I shrugged Finn's hand off my arm and straightened my blouse as if I'd been in some sort of brawl. 'It's OK,' I said. 'I'm leaving anyway.'

'Thank the lord,' muttered Kathleen.

'Someone take her home,' I said, turning away from my older sister. I didn't even want to look at her at that point.

'I'll take her,' said Finn. 'Come on, Kathleen.'

'I'm perfectly capable of taking myself home,' she snapped. And then turned to Corin. 'Hadn't you better run along with that one?' She jerked her head in my direction.

I could see the hurt in Corin's eyes. She was the most sensitive one out of us all and I knew she felt her loyalties split, but the sneer on Kathleen's face enraged me again.

'Oh, fuck off, Kathleen.' I stepped forward and, by taking Corin's hand, was effectively taking the decision from her. 'Come on, Corin. Let's go.'

EIGHTEEN

When I woke the morning after having tea with my parents, I felt groggy, like I'd been on a heavy night out, and groaned when I remembered Finn was supposed to be taking a statement from Freya today.

I messaged Finn to see what time he'd be over, so I didn't have to wake Freya up any earlier than necessary, and then I went to take a shower. By the time I'd finished in the bathroom, had dried my hair and got dressed, Finn had pinged back a message.

> Really sorry. Something's come up at work. Will phone you later.

I didn't suppose Freya would be that bothered. She had grumbled about having to make a statement as she went to bed, reiterating that she just wanted to forget about it.

I checked my phone for any reply from Danny but there was still radio silence from Brighton.

There was nothing from Nicole either. I couldn't help worrying she'd got cold feet and decided not to make contact after all.

I was fast discovering I didn't have the patience I thought I possessed. I was restless. I needed to do something. Anything. Sitting in the annexe thinking about all the things that frustrated me wasn't helping. I didn't have many more days here in Dingle before I'd have to go back home.

Dervla Collins still bothered me. There was obviously a reason why Nicole gave me her name. Since no one was telling me anything, I wondered if I should try her mother. First, I needed to find out where she lived.

I went on Facebook and found the local community page for Dingle. It wasn't a private group, so I didn't need to be approved to join and was able to see all the posts. I typed the name Collins into the search bar for the group. It was times like this when it would be handy if someone had an unusual surname. There was a whole list of contributors to the group with that name. I began looking at each post or comment, dismissing anyone who was male or looked too young to be Dervla's mother. The comments were what I'd expect from a community page. They ranged from anyone able to recommend a plumber to my dog is missing to who stole the hanging basket from outside the laundrette and who the feck had been singing 'Delaney Had a Donkey' at two o'clock in the morning on John Street?

I was about to give up when the profile picture of an Orla Collins caught my attention. A woman, around my age, with dark hair, holding a drink up towards the camera with one hand and her arm wrapped around a younger woman. Young enough to be her daughter. I clicked on her profile and was able to see all the contributions she'd made to the group. Finally, I found what I was looking for. Someone else had moaned about the smell from the new fish and chip shop on Main Street and how bad it was, especially on a Friday evening. Orla had commented: 'You should try living above the place.' Some comedian had replied to her comment with

'Don't you mean above the plaice?' adding a series of laughing emojis.

Excellent. I finally had something to do. Something positive.

It all sounded very quiet at Corin's house, and I was going to ask Niall if I could borrow his car again, but it wasn't on the drive, so I assumed he'd already left for work. Corin's wasn't back from the garage yet, so I'd just have to walk into town.

I hesitated about leaving Freya alone, the events of yesterday still playing on my mind, but rather than wake her and drag her with me, I decided not to disturb her. I'd leave the spare key on the worktop, along with a note telling her I'd be back soon, and then lock the door behind me.

It didn't take long to walk into town and twenty-five minutes later I was standing outside the fish and chip shop on Main Street. There was a door to the shop and another door next to it, which I assumed went up to the flat above. I pressed the bell.

It was on the third buzz that I heard the sash window above the shop open.

'Can I help you?' came a voice.

I looked up and there was Orla Collins. I'd probably got her out of bed by the look of her bleary eyes and unbrushed hair.

'Hi, there,' I said. 'Orla Collins?'

'That's right.'

'Are you Dervla's mum?'

Orla looked taken aback by my question and when she answered there wasn't the earlier gruffness to her tone. 'Yes. Why are you asking?'

I looked around and, although it wasn't yet ten o'clock, the street was getting busy. 'My name's Siobhan Martin. Can I talk to you, please?' Her eyes were wary. I tried again. 'It's important. It's to do with your daughter and my sister, Kathleen Walsh.'

'Kathleen's sister, you say?'

'That's right.' I felt a glimmer of hope. I got the impression she knew Kathleen personally rather than just as the woman who disappeared.

'I'll come and let you in,' she said.

I waited out by the front door and a few minutes later, Orla appeared. This time her hair was brushed, and she was wearing a T-shirt and three-quarter-length trousers. 'Come on up. I haven't cleaned so don't be looking at all the mess.'

'Doesn't bother me,' I said. The smell of stale cigarette smoke and mature curry hit me as soon as I walked into the flat.

'Straight ahead,' said Orla, standing to one side of the hall. I caught a glimpse of the kitchen on my left. I could see several dirty plates stacked by the sink, together with cups and glasses scattered across the work surface. 'Haven't had time to wash up this morning,' she said, closing the door on the chaos.

'Don't worry, I'm not here on behalf of booking dot com,' I said, trying to make a joke.

She gave a small snort of laughter. 'Just as well.'

The living room was tidier than I expected, and Orla moved a couple of piles of washing to one side so I could sit in the armchair, while she took a seat on the sofa. There was a dining table in the window and a sideboard next to it. You could barely see the top of the sideboard for an impressive array of framed photographs.

'That's Dervla,' said Orla, nodding towards the picture gallery. 'There's a photo for every birthday. And of other special occasions. First Holy Communion. Her prom the year before last.' She lit a cigarette and drew on it.

'She's very pretty,' I said. 'She looks gorgeous in her prom dress.' I mentally did the maths, if that was her prom two years ago, she'd have been about sixteen, so she'd be eighteen now. I looked back at Orla to confirm this, but realised she was crying. 'Oh, are you OK?' I asked. Always a stupid question when someone is crying, and I wanted to face-palm myself. I went over to sit beside her. 'Can I get you anything? Water? A tea?'

Orla pulled a tissue from the box on the coffee table and dabbed at her eyes. 'Sorry. It gets to me sometimes.'

'Gets to you?' I asked, not sure what she meant.

'She moved away. To Cork. I miss her.' Orla sucked hard on her cigarette. She inhaled deeply, held the smoke for a few seconds and then blew it out. 'Why are you here?'

There was a tension in her voice, which I guessed was a tool for keeping her emotions at bay. However, the bleak and empty look in her eyes betrayed her.

'I'm trying to find out what happened to my sister, Kathleen,' I began. 'She knew Dervla from The Hub, is that right?'

'Yes. She talked about Kathleen a lot. To be honest, it got on my nerves.' Orla gave me a sideways look. 'Kathleen this and Kathleen that. Kathleen was like a fecking saint.' She leaned forward and flicked the ash into a cup half-full of cold tea. There was an ashtray on the table, but I resisted the urge to slide it closer to her.

'Kathleen likes to help people,' I said. 'So, Dervla, she moved to Cork?'

'Yes. That's right. Got a live-in job at a pub. She didn't stay there long,' said Orla, dragging on her cigarette. She held the smoke in her lungs before blowing it into the air. 'Said she couldn't settle. I thought she was going to come back home.'

'What did she do instead?' I remembered Finn being a bit vague, as if he didn't think it was important.

'She went travelling.' There was no joy in Orla's voice.

'Lots of people her age go travelling,' I said. 'I expect she's having a great time. Do you hear from her much?'

'Not really. I don't think she'll be coming back here again any time soon. Last I heard, she was in Australia.'

'When was that?'

'A couple of months ago.'

I wasn't sure if I'd be so nonchalant about it if it were Freya. In fact, I know I wouldn't be. A week's silence and I'd be climbing the walls. 'Does Dervla have a social media account? Instagram?'

'I don't know.' Orla picked up her phone from the coffee table and slipped it into her pocket. 'If she has, she's not told me. Kids. You do your best for them, and they repay you by sodding off to the other side of the world and forgetting all about you.'

I wanted to offer reassurances that Dervla was probably no different to any other young person her age, who were all a bit hedonistic and didn't think us parents would be worrying about them 24/7, not to mention missing them constantly. 'I'm sure she'll be in touch soon,' was the best I could come up with.

'Look, I've got things to do,' she said.

'Of course. Just quickly before I go, do you mind if I take a look in Dervla's room?'

Orla hesitated, her cigarette halfway to her mouth. 'What, are you the police or something?'

'I just want to get a feel for who Dervla was. She was close to Kathleen; it will make me feel close too.' It was a bit of a wishy-washy statement.

Orla made a scoffing noise and went back to dragging on her cigarette. 'Second door on the left,' she said.

I was pleased Orla didn't follow me in. I certainly wasn't here for any spiritual connection. I was looking for a diary or a journal or something that might help me.

The room was surprisingly tidy, unlike the rest of the flat. The bed was made, with several cushions propped up against the headboard and a white throw draped across the end. There was a white dressing table and mirror on the opposite wall, with several photographs stuck around the edge.

I went over and took a closer look. They were of Dervla with some other girls her own age. They looked like more prom photos. There was a strip of four taken in a photo booth. Again, of Dervla and her girlfriends. I couldn't help wondering where they were now and if she'd confided in any of them or kept in touch.

I gently pulled open the single drawer on the dressing table. It had a few pens and pencils, a make-up brush, paperclips, face wipes – all the kind of stuff Freya had in her own dressing table. I closed the drawer and moved around to the wardrobe. There were a few items of clothing hanging up and the shelving on the side still had several jumpers and T-shirts folded neatly.

I wondered if Dervla had been planning on coming back or whether she'd only had limited space in her luggage when she'd left.

The only other piece of furniture was the bedside table. I perched on the edge of the bed and slid open the drawer. Again, it contained much the same as I'd expect to see in any teenager's drawer. I picked up a white disposable lighter and absently flicked it into life before releasing the tab and shutting down the flame. It had a gold outline of an elephant on the side and lettering underneath which had partially worn away. A promotional freebie for a restaurant, maybe? I put the lighter back and pushed the drawer closed.

I didn't know what I was expecting to find, but there was nothing in Dervla's room that gave me any indication as to what she had confided in Kathleen about.

'Did you find anything of interest?' asked Orla, looking up from her phone as I went back into the living room.

'It's a nice room,' I said.

'Yeah, well, she doesn't take after me, that's for sure,' said Orla. 'She's the opposite. Doesn't drink. Doesn't smoke. Doesn't make a mess.' Orla turned her gaze to the window.

'She doesn't smoke?' I asked.

Orla looked at me. 'No. She's got more sense than that.' Orla coughed as if to underline her own bad choices. 'You look like you don't believe me.'

There was an accusation in her voice. 'Oh, it's not that,' I said quickly. 'I noticed a lighter in her room, that's all.'

'In her drawer, you mean?'

I gave an apologetic look. There was no point denying it. 'Yeah.'

Orla shrugged her indifference. 'Her boyfriend gave her that. Odd present, but she liked to light her candles with it.'

'Who's the boyfriend?' I tried to make my voice sound casual as I could feel a bubble of excitement building in my chest.

'Oh, I don't know who he was. She never said.' Orla was back to looking out of the window.

I wanted to press her for more information, but I had probably asked enough questions and I thought she was being honest that she didn't know who the boyfriend was. 'I should be off,' I said.

'Yeah. I've got things to do myself,' said Orla. She stayed seated. 'I hope you find your sister, or at least what happened to her.'

'Thanks,' I said. I took a business card from my bag. 'If you think of anything else Dervla might have said that could help, perhaps you wouldn't mind calling me. Or if by any chance she does get in touch, maybe ask if she can contact me?' I held the card out and when Orla didn't so much as look my way, I placed the card on the coffee table. 'Bye, then.'

'Yeah. Bye.'

I let myself out and was glad of the fresh air. I liked Orla Collins. There was an honesty about her in a take-me-as-you-find-me sort of way. And yet, when she said she didn't have much contact with Dervla, I couldn't help sensing the honesty was absent.

I walked along Main Street, my mind still occupied with thoughts of Kathleen and Dervla. I was proud of my sister, the way people felt they could trust her with their problems despite being unaware of all the things Kathleen had been through herself. Maybe that's why the young people at The Hub gravitated to her. Maybe it was a subconscious pull of invisible but strong ley lines of empathy.

I was lost in thought as I waited to cross the road when, as I glanced to my right to check the traffic, I half-registered someone heading straight for me from the side. I instantly turned my body, moving my shoulder out of the way and at the last second, they sidestepped around me. Or so I assumed.

The next moment, I felt a sudden and hard jolt to my back as their shoulder collided with mine. The impact forced me to lose my balance and I stumbled forward into the road and into the path of an approaching car. I gave a yell of combined shock and fear and just managed to regain my balance as the VW Golf swerved to avoid hitting me. The driver gave a long blast on the horn to display his lack of appreciation for the near miss.

A hand took hold of my upper arm. 'Ah, Siobhan, you'll get yourself killed if you're not careful.'

I turned to see a guard at my side. It was Sergeant Rory Ahern. 'Someone barged into me,' I said, looking down the road at a figure in a hoodie, striding away with their hands in their pockets. I tried to match the image up with the fleeting impression I'd seen right before I was shoulder-charged.

'These pavements are wretched,' said Rory. 'Easy to lose your balance.'

'But I was shoved,' I said, reiterating my previous statement.

'What you doing up here?' he asked, not even acknowledging my claim. He looked up the street towards Orla's flat and back at me.

'I was having a walk,' I said, not wanting to tell him where I'd been for some reason. 'Reminiscing. That type of thing.'

'Do you want a lift anywhere? Back to your sister's?'

'No. I'm fine, thanks,' I said. 'I'll get off.'

'Mind how you go. Don't want you getting run over, now, do we?'

He looked me in the eye as he spoke. I hesitated before answering. 'No. Definitely not,' I said.

'Good. Glad we got that straight.' He smiled.

I crossed the road, this time without incident, and when I turned to look back, Ahern was still standing on the other side, watching me. He gave a nod and another smile. To anyone watching, it was a warm exchange. To me, it felt chilling.

NINETEEN

Freya is bored. She takes a picture of herself lying in bed and captions it with *B.O.R.E.D. Bored AF* and sends a Snapchat to Sophie.

There's a note on the side from her mum, saying she'd popped out and didn't want to wake her. Freya debates what would be more boring. Sitting here on her own or going into town with her mum, who's probably only gone to get pastries or something. Freya remembers the incident with the bottle of piss and finds herself wishing she wasn't alone. She checks the door to make sure it's locked.

Kian has had to go into work today, so she's been left to amuse herself. God, how did her mum ever put up with living here? No wonder she moved to England as soon as she could. The only thing keeping Freya from going out of her mind is the party on Friday night that Kian is taking her to.

She takes a shower, washing her hair, not that it needs washing but it still feels dirty when she thinks of what happened.

An hour and a half later, her hair is straightened, her make-up completed, her face contoured with precision accuracy, and she's bored once again. The annexe is cute but it's even smaller than her flat in Brighton. Freya feels hemmed in. She could go across to Corin, but she doesn't feel like being sociable, not in real life, anyway.

She takes another photo of her standing at the door and sends it as a Snapchat to Sophie.

Jailbreak!

The weather isn't so good today as it has been since she got here, and Freya thinks she should grab her jacket, but she really can't be bothered to go back into the annexe. She might get spotted by Corin and made to go and sit in the house. Freya has promised to help the twins bake cakes this afternoon. She is actually looking forward to that, but for now, she wants some time away from them. They're a riot, and she loves them, but she also loves a bit of space. As an only child, Freya is used to a quiet home, and Sorcha and Erin are very full-on, bless them.

There's no footpath along this part of the road and Freya can't remember if she's supposed to walk on the left or the right. She sticks to the left – at least that way she can dive into the grass verge – but it does mean having to check behind her every so often when she hears a vehicle approaching. Maybe she was supposed to walk on the right?

A van is heading away from the town on the other side of the road. It slows as it nears her. Freya doesn't pay any attention to it at first, but it slows right down and is now level with her. She looks up but the van has passed and then accelerates, continuing on its way.

That was weird. She could go back to the annexe but she's enjoying the fresh air and the walk if she's honest. The rumble of an engine coming from behind her has her stepping onto the verge. The grass needs a cut and is up to her shins, making her jeans damp.

She looks back and realises it's the white van again. She can see a dent in the side of it, which is hardly surprising for around here with the narrow roads. The van slows right down.

The van is level with her now, and the driver buzzes down the nearside window. He's young with dark blonde hair that, with its loose waves, gives him a surfer-type look, thinks Freya. He smiles at her.

'Hey, there,' he says. 'Sorry, to bother you, but you're Kian Walsh's cousin, aren't you?'

Freya relaxes a little at the suggestion he knows Kian. 'That's right,' she says. Just answer the questions and then he'll get on his way.

'I thought it was you. I saw you on the beach the other night.'

Freya takes a closer look at him. His green eyes have a glittery look to them. She'd remember them, she's sure, and yet she can't recall seeing him on the beach. Will he be offended if she doesn't remember him? She decides to play it safe. 'Oh yeah,' she says, hoping that sounds the right sort of answer.

'Was a good night, right?'

Again, she doesn't want to sound rude, not to one of Kian's friends. The evening on the beach was OK but it wasn't anything wild. 'Yeah. It was nice,' she replies. He's really good-looking and Freya wishes she could remember him.

'It's Freya, isn't it? You going into town?' he asks.

'Yeah.' God, why can't she think of anything better to say than yeah all the time? He'll think she's a right idiot.

'Want a lift?'

Freya hesitates. She looks back up the road and wonders why he turned around. Was it because he recognised her from the beach? 'It's all right, I'll walk,' she says.

He gives her an amused look. 'I'm not a murdering axeman, if that's what you're worried about.'

Freya gives a forced laugh. 'Never thought you were,' she says.

'Then you won't mind jumping in,' he says. 'Come on, you'll be there in a few minutes. Kian would kill me if I was to let you walk along this road on your own. You're taking your life into your hands. It's fecking dangerous.'

Right on cue, a car tears around the bend in the road and then has to anchor up and swerve to avoid hitting the van. 'See what I mean?' says the lad. 'Jump in before someone rear-ends me and then I'll be for it. I'm only borrowing the van.'

Freya wants to say no but feels she can't. He's being insistent and she doesn't think he will give up. She hesitates, her hand on the door handle. It doesn't feel right. But he knows Kian. He knows her name. He was at the beach. He's urging her to hurry up so Freya opens the door and climbs up into the passenger seat.

'Thanks,' she says, fastening her seat belt. As he pulls away, she is regretting her decision already.

'No worries,' he says. 'Where in town do you want dropping?'

'By the harbour,' says Freya. Maybe she was overreacting. He's already talking about dropping her off. She wishes she could remember his name. Or remember him at all. But it would be awkward to ask. He's chatting away about the weather and how it looks good for surfing. That he might go down to a nearby cove and take his board out.

He's driving fast and takes the next bend at speed, sending the detritus of used paper coffee cups, receipts and a notebook flying across the dash. Freya puts her hand out to stop everything from falling but she can't catch it all and the book shoots off, hitting the floor.

'Oh, shit. Sorry about all that,' he says.

She wedges it all back on the dash and reaches down to pick

up the notebook. 'Oh, better not lose that,' he says. 'That's got all my jobs in it. The boss makes us write everything down.'

'Who's your boss?'

'Funnily enough, it's someone you know,' he said. 'Your uncle.'

'Niall?'

'No. John Walsh.'

She feels reassured further because now this lad also knows her uncle. 'I didn't realise he had someone working for him.'

'Just when he needs me.' He reaches for the book.

As Freya hands it over, she notices his name on the cover. Conor Doyle. At least now she knows who he is. 'You working for him today, then?'

'Yeah. Doing a delivery for him.'

Freya sits back in the seat, feeling much more relaxed now. Of course, everyone here knows everyone else. She has nothing to worry about.

They reach the harbour and, to her relief, Conor pulls over. 'There you go,' he says cheerfully.

'Thanks very much,' says Freya.

'Look, if you're free tomorrow, we could go out again,' suggests Conor. 'The beach, maybe? I'll bring my board.'

'I can't surfboard,' says Freya.

'I can teach you.' He grins at her, and Freya can't help the butterflies going off in her stomach as she once again acknowledges how good-looking he is.

'OK. Why not,' she says.

'Great. I'll pick you up in the morning. Let me have your phone number.'

They exchange numbers. 'I'll text you when I'm outside. There is one thing though.'

'Yeah?'

'Best not mention it to your mam, or anyone,' he says.

'Why's that?'

'Well, for a start, they might not like you going out with someone who's a bit older,' says Conor. 'But also, I work for your uncle and your mam might not like that either. Nor will Kian, for that matter. Best keep it to yourself.'

It sounds reasonable to Freya. She's no doubt her mum would give her the third degree about who she's going with and the possibility that she'll be grounded is strong. She doesn't want to come across as a baby. 'OK. I won't say anything,' she agrees.

'That's grand. I'll see ye tomorrow.'

Freya gets out of the van; aware she has a silly smile on her face. God, she's embarrassing herself, but she can't help it. Especially when Conor winks at her before driving off.

TWENTY

I rubbed my arm where Rory had held on to it rather too tightly and wondered what he had been doing on Main Street. It wasn't like he walked the beat. Usually, he was behind the desk at the station, orchestrating from there.

The sound of a message coming through on my phone distracted me.

It was from a number I didn't recognise. With a certain amount of trepidation, I read the message.

> Be at Hussy's Folly in half an hour. N.

I paused in the street, moving to one side as I considered it. It had to be from Nicole.

I checked my watch: it was ten fifteen. Hussy's Folly was a semi-derelict stone tower up on the clifftops roughly halfway between Dingle town and the lighthouse.

From the town to the tower it was about a thirty-minute walk, mostly across the fields that ran to the edge of the cliffs. There was a small car park at the end of a track, but I didn't want to take a taxi as this was a clandestine meeting and I didn't want to put Nicole in any sort of danger.

After sending a text message to Freya to say I had been held up and I'd be back by lunchtime, I set off on foot towards Hussy's Folly.

The tower had been built during the Great Famine to give jobs to a few of the locals, but it served no real purpose. The doorway and windows had long since been bricked up and, unless you were an experienced rock climber, there was no way you'd be getting in through the higher openings. The tower was just a landmark and the opportunity for some beautiful photographs of the harbour mouth beyond.

Twenty-five minutes later, I trudged up the grassy hill towards the folly. The yellow gorse that dotted the ground was in full flower and, every now and again, I caught its coconut scent dispersed by the offshore breeze.

I couldn't see anyone at the folly from my approach, but as I reached the tower and walked around to the side that was hidden from view, there was Nicole in her yellow waterproof coat.

'Wasn't sure if you'd come,' she said.

'Wasn't sure if you'd be here,' I replied, puffing slightly from my exertions.

It was more blowy this side of the tower and the sky was a dappled grey and white, with darker patches further out to sea.

'You didn't tell anyone you were coming, did you?' she asked.

'No. I came straight here. I was in town,' I replied, leaning against the building. 'I went to see Orla Collins.' I watched for a reaction.

Nicole turned to look at me. 'And she told you about Dervla?'

'What she knew, which wasn't much. Only that Dervla had confided in Kathleen about something, and Kathleen got her sorted with a job and somewhere to live in Cork. She said Dervla was backpacking in Australia now.'

A small smile came to Nicole's mouth. 'Good. I'm glad she got away.'

'What did she get away from?' I asked.

'Everything. Everyone,' replied Nicole.

'Please, can you tell me what it was?' I wanted to shake some answers from Nicole, but I managed to keep my frustrations locked down. 'I'm assuming you want to tell me something, otherwise why get me to meet you?' The wind lifted strands of my hair and I coiled my fingers around them, wishing I'd brought a hair band with me.

'I don't know everything,' said Nicole.

'Just tell me what you do know. Like, how come you had Kathleen's purse for a start?' There was no point waiting for Nicole to tell me, I had to get her talking.

'I took it from her bag one day at The Hub,' said Nicole. There was no shame or embarrassment in her voice or in her expression. 'I needed money. I was trying to save up so I could get away from this place too.'

'Did Kathleen know you took her purse?'

'I don't think so. If she did suspect me, she never said anything.' Nicole bit her lip. 'I was going to give it back once I'd got the cash, but there was never the chance and then she went missing anyway. After that, I was too scared. Thought I might get in trouble. That someone would go to the guards.'

'Do you have any idea what Dervla was trying to get away from?' I asked, sensing Nicole wanted to tell me but was scared. 'If I know, then it might help me find my sister or what happened to her.' And there it was again, the acknowledgement that Kathleen might not still be alive. The idea that had lurked in the darkest recesses of my mind, stalking my subconscious and then stealthily slipping into thoughts I could voice. It hurt. A lot.

Nicole walked closer to the cliff edge, which made me nervous. It wasn't a sheer drop below, but the rocky cliff face that sprawled out into the sea would not be forgiving on the body. I pushed myself away from the folly wall and went to stand beside her. The waves below surged and crashed against the boulders before rebounding back. It was like the ocean had its own lungs and was breathing in and out, in and out. It was hypnotic.

'Dervla had been having an affair with a married man,' said Nicole, her voice snapping me from my trance.

'Who was the married man?' I asked.

'She didn't say, but he was older than her. She said she loved him, and he was going to leave his wife. All that usual crap you hear about.'

'I'm guessing he had no intention of leaving his wife.'

'No, and Dervla wasn't happy at all. Said she was going to out him at first, but when that didn't work, she asked for money.'

'And this is what Dervla told Kathleen?' I put my hands in my jacket pockets and, as if by magic, found a hairband.

'Yeah. Kathleen was going to sort things out for her. Speak to him, apparently,' said Nicole. 'Before that though, Dervla started getting threats.'

'What kind of threats?' I asked as I tied my hair back into a ponytail. 'And who from?'

'She was followed home one night. They didn't do anything, but it frightened her. Then someone put a note through her door saying something like "Be careful walking home. Don't want anything happening to you." She also had some nasty phone calls from a withheld number. I think there was one that said something about her mum getting arrested for drug dealing.'

I raised my eyebrows. 'They were really going for it then?'

'Dervla was scared. Her mum used to have a bit of a drug

problem. She's all clean now, but Dervla didn't want her getting into trouble.'

'So had the relationship with this older man ended?' I asked.

Nicole scuffed the ground with her foot. 'That's the strange thing; he said he had to end it, not that he wanted to. He was sad and upset.'

'So who was threatening her?' I asked, trying to work out what exactly had gone on.

'Dervla thought it was him, but he denied it,' said Nicole. 'So, it must have been someone else, but she didn't know who. He swore blind his wife didn't know.'

'And you've no idea who the man might be?'

'She wouldn't say.' Nicole gave a shrug. 'She said he had a lot of influence and knew important people.'

'So it wasn't in his interest for the affair to be common knowledge,' I said.

'That's the impression I got. He wasn't happy when Dervla asked for money. He accused her of blackmail.'

I thought about it for a moment as I committed what had been said so far to memory. 'She told Kathleen about the threats and Kathleen helped her move away,' I said, trying to get it all straight in my head. 'So why did you want me involved? And why go to all this trouble of pretending it wasn't you?'

'I think I'm in danger from knowing all this. I know you said Dervla's in Australia, but do we know that for a fact? Has anyone heard from her? She hasn't posted anything on social media. It's like she's disappeared. Just like your sister.'

A chill ran down my spine and it wasn't from the blustery weather. 'It is a coincidence, I admit, but it could be just that.'

'But what if someone is protecting this man and they wanted to get rid of Kathleen because she knew too much? That means I'm in danger too. I couldn't let anyone think I had got you back here to investigate it.'

'But you got Conor Doyle to lie for you about the purse,' I said.

She shrugged. 'It was no big deal. I asked a favour and he did it. We look out for each other. It's how we survive.'

'And the tickets in the purse?'

Nicole nodded. 'That was me. I found them chucked down at the bus station. People throw them away. I wanted to make it seem like your sister was here, using the bus and train.'

'So I'd have to come,' I said.

I felt embarrassed that I had been sucked in so easily over it all. Enough that I'd dropped everything and got the first flight over, but then I suppose Nicole was banking on that. It wouldn't take a genius to work out that Kathleen's disappearance was my Achilles' heel and I'd do anything if I thought it would mean finding her. I didn't want to be angry with Nicole, but it was hard not to feel resentment that she had got my hopes up and for nothing. There really wasn't any trace of Kathleen. She hadn't been back to Dingle. There was no proof. No wonder there were no sightings of her. I had been duped. What sort of a journalist was I? Maybe I wasn't quite the hotshot I thought I was.

'What do you think happened to Kathleen?' I asked after a long silence.

Nicole looked down at the ground before looking back at the water. 'I think she knew too much, and someone made sure she wasn't going to talk.'

Tears filled my eyes at the bluntness of the observation. Again, this was a spoken acknowledgement that my sister was probably dead. I had to find out the truth. I couldn't leave this now. Whatever the truth was, however much pain it caused, I needed to know.

'We need to know who the married man was,' I said.

'There is something I haven't told you,' said Nicole.

'What's that?' Again, my impatience was rearing up.

'I overheard your sister and her husband having a big argument at The Hub once.'

I wasn't especially surprised by the fact Kathleen and John were arguing, but I always got the impression it was behind closed doors. 'What were they arguing about?'

'I don't know exactly. I was in the storeroom off the kitchen, and they were in the actual kitchen.'

'They didn't know you were there?'

Nicole shook her head. 'I was getting some food. I wasn't supposed to be in there, but needs must.'

'OK, well, I don't really care what you were doing, so don't worry about that. What did Kathleen and John argue over?'

'They came in arguing, so I don't know how it started, but John was accusing Kathleen of having an affair. She said he was ridiculous. He was like, "So what were you doing skulking around meeting up with him in secret and not telling me?" She said it was about work at The Hub and that he was being paranoid. She said it wasn't as if he was actually jealous; he was more put out that someone might see and that would ruin his image.'

From what I knew, I could imagine this argument taking place. Father John was all about what people thought of him and what God would think of everyone else. Nicole's account sounded authentic enough. 'Did they say who Kathleen had been talking to?'

'No, but at one point John said, "He needs to stop fecking hanging around here,"' said Nicole. 'Kathleen was like, "I can't tell a grown man what he can and can't do. Besides, his wife works here."'

'Who would that be?' I asked.

Nicole shrugged. 'Your guess is as good as mine. Sharon, the receptionist. Maureen Ahern? She used to be one of the counsellors.'

'Maureen Ahern, as in Rory Ahern's wife?'

'Yeah, that's her. All the busybodies work or have worked there.' She gave a guilty look. 'I'm not saying your sister was a busybody, but some of them were. Especially that Aisling Denvers, but then she's always poking her nose into stuff. That's what politicians do, don't they?'

Nicole had a point. 'Anyone else?'

'There's Anne. I don't know her surname, but she comes in and helps Caroline in the café.'

'And their husbands visit The Hub?' Nicole was bringing up a lot of familiar names.

'I don't know. I'm not there all the time. I know it probably seems like it.'

'So, going back to John and Kathleen arguing in the kitchen, what else did they say?'

Nicole blew out a breath. 'Kathleen was like, "Stop being so paranoid. Anyway, if you think I'd have an affair with him, then you really don't know me. I'd want someone who was totally the opposite to you. I'd want someone kind and caring. Someone who loved me and someone who I'd love back." She was sort of shouting in a whisper, if you know what I mean.'

I was surprised to hear Kathleen goading John like that, but if she'd finally come to her senses and had enough of him, perhaps she hadn't cared what she said. 'What was John's reaction to that?'

'He wasn't happy.'

'What do you mean by that?' I asked, certain I wasn't going to like the answer.

Nicole didn't meet my gaze. 'There was a cracking sort of noise and Kathleen cried out. She said, "Feck you" and walked out.'

'He hit her?' I wondered if Kathleen had thought she was safe talking to him like that out of the house. Clearly she wasn't, and maybe his violence was getting worse.

'I didn't see it so I can't swear to it, but that's what it sounded like.'

'What happened next?'

'They left. Or I thought they had. I came out of the store-room and the kitchen was empty, but when I went to leave the kitchen, John was standing in the hallway making a phone call. He looked surprised to see me. I kinda froze on the spot and I'm sure he knew I'd heard everything that went on in there.'

'He didn't say anything to you, though?'

'No. I hurried past him and out of the building.' She moved away from the edge of the cliff back to the wall of the folly. 'There's someone coming. I have to go.'

I looked beyond Nicole and could see a man and a woman making their way up the hill, with their dog running back and forth in front of them. 'Wait. Is there anyone who'd know who Dervla was seeing and who John thought Kathleen was seeing? Are they the same person?'

'I've no idea. John Walsh could answer one of those questions, but I guess he won't want to speak to you.'

'No, you guess right.'

'I need to go.'

'Call me if you think of anything else. I can meet you any time. I just need to find out those names. Thank you, Nicole. I appreciate it. I really do.'

She paused and looked at me. I thought she was going to say something, but then she was off down the hill. I stayed out of sight at the back of the folly and waited a while until the couple with the dog had passed by.

I had a good forty-five minutes' walk ahead of me back to the annexe, and it would give me time to digest everything Nicole had said. I took out my phone and quickly dictated a note to myself, covering the conversation while it was still fresh in my mind.

Then I texted Freya, telling her I was on my way home and I'd murder a cup of tea when I got back.

I wasn't particularly concerned that she hadn't replied by the time I was walking up the drive of Corin's house. Freya had probably just rolled out of bed or was even still in it.

When I went into the annexe I called out to her, but there was no reply. Even as a baby, Freya had always slept well. Danny and I could have friends over for dinner and she wouldn't be disturbed. I tapped on the bedroom door and, when I got no response, I looked inside.

The bed was made, but no sign of Freya.

I went back through to the kitchen and put the kettle on, before nipping over to Corin's to see if Freya was there.

'I've not seen her all morning,' said Niall's mother, who was on babysitting duty. 'Maybe she's gone for a walk.'

'Yeah, could be that. Or Kian had a change of plans and took her out.'

I went back over to the annexe and tried to call Freya's number. It went to voicemail. I didn't bother leaving a message as I knew Freya never checked her phone for voice messages. Instead, I rang Kian's number and that too went to voicemail. They must be together somewhere.

When my phone did ring, I assumed it was one of them, so was surprised to see it was Finn.

'Hey, Siobhan. Sorry about letting you down this morning. Been really busy at work,' he said.

'Oh, it's OK. No worries. I've had a productive morning anyway.'

'I was wondering, would now be a good time to pop round and take a statement from Freya?'

'She's not here at the moment.'

'Oh, right. When would be good?' he asked.

'Shall I give you a call when she's back and then, if you're not busy, you could come over or we can arrange a better time?'

'Sounds good to me,' he replied. 'So, what are you up to now?'

'I'm home alone twiddling my thumbs,' I said, flicking the kettle on for the second time. 'I've been out this morning.'

'I heard you bumped into Ahern.'

'Not exactly. Did he tell you someone shoved me into the road? I was up on Main Street. It was Ahern who pulled me back onto the path.' I dropped a teabag into the cup and took the milk from the fridge.

'What were you doing up there?'

'I went to speak to Dervla Collins's mum,' I said, unable to hide the triumph from my voice.

'Orla Collins? What did you learn?'

'I think I should be a guard, not you. I've found out quite a bit, actually.'

'Look, I've some free time; shall I pop over and you can tell me all about it?' I hesitated a moment. Was this a good idea? 'Or I don't have to, if you're busy,' added Finn.

'No. Come over,' I said, deciding I might be able to glean some more information from Finn or give him something to find out. It wouldn't do any harm.

'See you in ten.'

I tried Freya's phone and Kian's phone one more time, but still no answer. Why didn't kids answer their bloody phones?

As I flopped down on the sofa once again, I couldn't help being reminded of my own actions six months ago when I didn't answer Kathleen's call.

TWENTY-ONE

I was still fuming when I got back to Corin's house after leaving the pub. I was staying in the annexe, and we were now standing together in the driveway.

'Try to get some sleep now,' Corin said. 'We've all had a bit to drink tonight and maybe said stuff we wouldn't normally say.'

'I'm sober. I wasn't drunk,' I said, folding my arms. It was an April evening and we'd had especially nice weather that weekend, so I hadn't brought a coat with me. We'd got a taxi back from the pub in town and had travelled in silence, not wanting to share our thoughts with the taxi driver. It would be all around the town in a matter of hours if we did. Now I was feeling the chill of the night air.

'What do you think about what Kathleen said?' asked Corin. 'I don't know what to think.'

'Exactly what part of the conversation are you referring to? Kathleen certainly unpacked a lot back there.'

'The stuff about being groomed.'

I let out a sigh. 'It's terrible. And I don't care what Kathleen says, I wish she'd told us sooner.'

'But she thought she was protecting us.'

I nodded. 'She's obviously not dealt with it all properly. I mean, how could she if she's never told anyone? But I felt she was angry at us, resentful that she'd had to carry that burden all by herself or that we should have been grateful instead of questioning her.'

'I don't know what to think,' admitted Corin.

'No, neither do I.'

'I'm shocked by it,' said Corin. 'I feel so... so... I don't know how to explain it.'

'So sad?' I suggested. Corin nodded. I continued. 'It's heartbreaking, finding this out and realising all those years we had no idea whatsoever.'

'She won't let us comfort her.'

'No, because for all this time, she's dealt with it on her own. Kept it locked away,' I said. I might have been angry with my sister for what was said, but it didn't mean I didn't love her. I knew Kathleen was frightened to let her emotions show, to confront head-on what she had gone through. She had it all locked away, too scared to open the box. I wondered what she'd think in the morning. Would she regret having told us? Would she be frightened she had? Frightened that now she couldn't keep it locked away?

'Do you think we should call her to make sure she's back home all right?' asked Corin. She already had her phone in her hand.

'Finn will make sure she's OK.'

'I'd sooner check.'

'Go on then. I'll wait while you do.'

I watched Corin tap at her phone. She held it to her ear, but I could hear it ringing. It went to voicemail. Corin tried a second time and again it went to voicemail. 'Should I ring John?'

'It's late. He'll probably be in bed.'

'I'll send a message.'

I waited while Corin tapped at the screen again. 'There. I just said, *Are you home OK? We can talk tomorrow.* Hopefully she'll let us know.'

I gave Corin a hug. 'Don't be worrying now. Kathleen will be fine. You know what she's like. We'll all sit down and talk tomorrow once we have a clear head. Trust me.'

Corin smiled and returned the hug. 'Night, Siobhan.'

I let myself into the annexe and locked the door behind me. It was only then that I allowed myself to indulge in the tears that I had bottled up since Kathleen's revelation and the ensuing argument. My legs buckled under me and I staggered to the sofa, falling into the soft leather seat. I buried my face in one of the cushions to muffle the scream that erupted from deep inside me.

It wasn't until a few minutes later that I realised I was mumbling my sister's name over and over again. 'Kathleen. Kathleen.' The pain in my heart was like a bereavement. I was grieving for the sister I thought I had. My wonderful, strong, determined older sister Kathleen. I would never be able to look at her the same, not now I knew her vulnerability. What had shaped her into the woman she was. Her strength hadn't come from a good place, it had come from a deep well of darkness. It wasn't something to be admired, it was something to be heart-broken over.

I looked at the cushion cover and swore. My mascara had smudged all over the oatmeal-coloured fabric.

I was surprised to see I had been in for over half an hour. I needed a drink of water. Wine was appealing, but getting totally wrecked to block out the pain of my sister wasn't the way to go. I had to flush the alcohol from my system. Whatever the next day had in store, I needed a clear head.

Two things had been at play in our argument, and I thought they were somehow connected, but I was too emotional – maybe too close to the situation – to work it out. First there was what happened to Kathleen, and secondly there was this resentment towards me and Corin – me especially. I didn't know if that came from the first issue or whether it was separate. Did they coexist? Could one exist without the other? It was impossible to tell, and my brain wasn't in the game.

I felt an overwhelming tiredness descend on me as I stood at the sink, forcing myself to drink a whole glass of water. I needed to go to bed.

I washed my face in the bathroom with good old soap, not bothering to spend fifteen minutes on my night-time cleanse, tone, moisturise routine. As I was brushing my teeth, my phone pinged in a text message. I went out to the living room and, after rummaging around in my bag, found my phone.

There was an earlier text from Danny.

> Hope you had a good evening and you're not too pissed. No wait, forget that. Hope you had a good evening and you're hanging. The Regan girls are back in town, eh? Night babe.

I smiled at my husband's text message and then felt tears spring to my eyes. I had a sudden urge to be back home in Brighton with him. To be in his arms. He'd hold me tight. Kiss the top of my head and tell me everything would be all right. I longed to phone him and hear his voice, but it was far too late, and he'd only worry if I was to call him in a near-drunken mess. There was more to his forward-facing easy-going manner than most people saw. I was lucky enough to see the compassionate, kind and loving man as well. I'd text him in the morning.

There was also a message from Freya, telling me she'd been

out shopping with Sophie. Dad had got them a takeaway and she was missing me.

More love for my chosen family swelled in my heart. I was so looking forward to being back home in a couple of days.

There was another alert informing me that fifteen minutes ago, I had missed a call and there was a voicemail message. It must have been when I was in the bathroom. I dialled into the voice messages. One missed call. It was from Kathleen and was only two words long.

Help me.

What the fuck did that mean? Help her? Help her do what? And why was she sending me cryptic messages at gone midnight when we'd just had a blazing row? Was it even meant for me?

I quickly texted Corin to see if she'd heard from Kathleen. She messaged straight back saying she'd got a reply and Kathleen was at home.

I listened to Kathleen's message again, trying to figure out whether calling or messaging her at this time of night was a good idea. Probably not, I reasoned after several minutes. I didn't want to get into another argument with her until I was completely sober and had a clear head. Besides, amongst all that sorrow and pain, I was still angry with Kathleen and, rightly or wrongly, most probably the latter, I wasn't in the mood for reconciliation right then. No, she could sweat it a bit, think about what she'd said, and we'd sit down tomorrow with Corin and talk about it like sensible adults, not drunken sisters.

Ten minutes later I was in bed, relishing the soft mattress and cosy duvet with the duck down feather pillows. I must have gone to sleep fairly quickly because the next thing I was aware of was some sort of tapping noise.

I groped in the dark for my phone. It was two fifteen in the morning. There were no more messages from Kathleen and I flopped my head back down on the pillow, vaguely wondering what the tapping noise was that had woken me.

Then it started again. This time it was louder.

Tap. Tap. Tap-tap. Pause. Tap. Tap. Tap-tap.

No. It couldn't be. I recognised that pattern. I was wide awake now. I listened again.

Tap. Tap. Tap-tap. Pause. Tap. Tap. Tap-tap.

I went to switch on the bedside light but stopped. It could just be a coincidence.

My heart was ramping up its rhythm, clearly not at its resting rate.

When the tapping came again, I nearly jumped out of my bloody skin. It was on the bedroom window. I managed to hold back the cry of alarm. When it came a second time, I went over to the window, glad the curtain was drawn and took a minute to prepare myself before opening it.

Then I heard a voice.

'Siobhan. It's me. Let me in.'

I pulled the curtain back and, even though I was expecting to see Kathleen there, I still jumped at her face pressed up against the glass.

I opened the window. 'Jesus Christ, Kathleen, you nearly gave me a heart attack.'

'I need to talk.'

'It's gone two o'clock in the morning. I thought you were home.'

'Clearly I'm not. Do you know how ridiculous this is?' snapped Kathleen. 'Speaking to me out the window like you're the fecking ice-cream man. I'm freezing my tits off out here, just let me in.'

I closed the window and half debated leaving her there, but in all honesty, I couldn't.

A minute later, Kathleen was sitting on the sofa of the annexe. 'Have you got something to drink?'

'No. It'll have to be coffee.'

'That's what I meant. Jesus, Siobhan, I'm not a raging alcoholic.'

I put the kettle on and eyed my sister while she looked intently at her phone. Her hair was the darkest out of the three of us and it was styled in a long-layered bob, framing her petite chiselled features.

I took the hot drinks over and put them on the coffee table, taking the seat opposite. 'So, what did you want to talk about?' I asked. 'What's with the *Help Me* message?'

'My phone died practically as soon as I began to leave a message,' said Kathleen. 'Anyway, you didn't reply to me, did you?'

I felt a ripple of guilt and embarrassment at having been called out on that. 'I was still mad with you,' I said. 'Still am, if truth be told.'

Kathleen let out a long sigh. 'If truth be told,' she said. 'Now there's a statement.'

'Can you get to the point?' I asked, my earlier anger downgrading to irritation. 'It's late. I'm tired. I need to get to sleep, and I dare say you do too. Can't any of this wait until the morning?'

Kathleen didn't reply straight away, and I felt the atmosphere in the room change. She rubbed her face with her hands and let out a long breath. 'I need your help. I need you to do something for me.'

'Like what?' Again, I was filled with such conflicts of emotion. Irritation. Intrigue. Guilt. Sorrow.

'I'm going to tell you something,' she said. 'Something you can't repeat. Something you can't talk about. Something dangerous.'

Whatever we'd said to each other earlier, whatever accusations we'd made about who did what, was insignificant now. All my journalistic instincts were telling me I was on the edge of finding out something big. And all my sisterly instincts were telling me I wasn't going to like it.

Kathleen sat forward in her seat. 'OK,' she said. 'I've found something out. Someone has told me something that will put a lot of important people in line for a long jail sentence.'

'How important are we talking?' I asked.

'Oh, the very top. I can't name names. It's more than one person.' Kathleen ran her hands through her hair. 'The trouble is I need to get some legal advice. Out of county. I can't risk anyone in Kerry knowing.'

'In all of Kerry or just Dingle?'

'All of Kerry.'

'Wow. That sounds serious,' I said.

'Once I've spoken to a solicitor about my legal position, I'm going to report it to the guards in Cork.'

I frowned. 'Can't you tell me what's going on?'

'Not yet. Not until I know it's safe,' replied Kathleen. 'Now, listen up. I'll be away for a while. You're the only person who knows this.'

'Oh, come on, Kathleen. This is ridiculous. You can't up and away without telling anyone. What will I say to John? He'll have the whole bloody town out looking for you.'

'There's something else,' said Kathleen. 'I need out of my marriage and there's no way he'd let me leave.'

'You're not doing this whole *Sleeping with the Enemy* shit, are you?' I looked at my sister. 'Oh, no, Kathleen, you can't disappear off the face of the earth. Everyone will be distraught. Think about Mam and Dad. What about Kian?'

'It's got to be this way. I need to leave John and I need to sort out the other stuff too. It's giving me the perfect opportunity to do both. But I'm coming back. I promise you. It's just I don't know when. I'll let you know.'

'You basically want me to lie for you.'

'Yes. I do.' There was no remorse on her face. 'You have to help me.'

'I thought you were...' I searched for the word. 'Settled. I thought you and John were settled. Why wait until now to leave him?'

'I married John because I thought no one else would want me.' Kathleen looked down at her hands.

My heart went out to her. 'You didn't think you were good enough?' Yesterday, I would have wondered how my strong, older sister could feel so inadequate, but today, armed with the knowledge of her grooming, it was all so clear. Her sense of self-worth had been taken away from her.

She nodded. 'I was dirty.'

'No!' The word leaped from my mouth. 'No. You were not. You were never that, Kathleen Regan. Never.' I moved swiftly to her side, putting my arm around her shoulder. I kept it there despite feeling her tense under my touch. 'You were never dirty. That's how you were made to feel. There's a difference. That man – that married man – did that to you.'

'I know that, really,' said Kathleen, swallowing down a sob. She looked up at me and tears streamed down her face. 'I know that now. And that's exactly what I would say to anyone else in the same position. But at the time...' She reached for a tissue from the table and blew her nose. 'At the time, I was only a kid. I didn't know that. So when John paid attention to me, I was flattered that someone else would want me.'

'And then you got pregnant.'

'And then I got pregnant.' She let out a sigh and blew her nose again. 'And John married me out of duty. Again, I didn't care. I simply wanted to be loved, or what I thought was love. I know he didn't love me. Still doesn't, but then again, there's no love lost between us.'

'I knew things weren't great, but I didn't realise it was that bad.'

She gave me a wry smile. 'That's because you were never here. You and Danny had the right idea and got out of this place when you could.'

I tamped down the little spike of irritation this comment ignited. 'I did nothing wrong by moving away.'

'Sure. I know, but what I'm saying is, by not being here, you escaped all the shit.'

I couldn't help feeling Kathleen was jealous that I'd moved to England and resented the fact that she'd had to stay. She got to her feet and went over to the fireplace, her finger running around the edge of the mantelpiece. 'I don't blame you. I just wish I could have done it myself.' She turned around to face me. 'But I'm going to do it now and I need you to cover for me. And if things go wrong, I need someone to know the truth.'

'You're scaring me.'

'Don't be scared, that's purely worst-case scenario,' reassured Kathleen. 'If all goes to plan, which it should, in a couple of months you'll have the scoop of Western Ireland and be able to get that job on a big paper you've always wanted.'

She sounded so confident, I think I believed her and bought into her crazy idea.

'There is one more thing I need to tell you, though. And you can't breathe a word to another living soul.'

TWENTY-TWO

When Finn arrived, he was in uniform. The new style of a polo shirt rather than a shirt and tie and a two-tone jacket, together with navy blue utility trousers. He took off his peaked cap as he exited his car. I had to admit, he looked pretty good in uniform. I batted the thought away. This was not the time to revisit a crush on an ex-boyfriend.

I made Finn a coffee and we sat down on the sofa.

'I'm glad you're on your own,' said Finn. 'I've found out some information that I'd rather not say in front of Freya.'

'OK. What's that?'

'I don't think you're going to like this, but I did a bit of digging and...' He hesitated.

'What is it?'

'Kathleen was on a warning at The Hub,' he said.

'What?'

'I'm sorry, Siobhan. I shouldn't really be telling you, but it gives a better picture of what was happening in Kathleen's life.'

'What had she done?'

He reached over and held my hand. 'Some money had gone missing from the petty cash at The Hub.'

'Right.' I drew the word out to underline my thoughts that if this was going where I thought it was, then it was ridiculous. I waited for Finn to continue, and he obliged.

'It was when Kathleen had access to the money.'

'How much are we talking about?'

'It happened over a period of time and amounted to about a hundred euros,' said Finn.

A bubble of laughter finally forced its way free from me. 'You're telling me that Kathleen took a hundred euros from the petty cash? That she stole money? Honestly, Finn, that's the single most ridiculous thing I've heard.'

Finn gave me a sympathetic smile. I went to move my hand from his, but he held firm. 'Look, I know it's hard to accept,' he said. 'No one wants to believe someone in their family would do that, but if I had a euro every time a family member said their son, daughter, brother, father – whatever – would never do what they've been accused of, then I would be a very rich man.'

'I get what you're saying,' I snapped, snatching my hand away successfully this time. 'But I'm telling you, Kathleen was not a thief.' I briefly caught myself referring to her in the past tense again, but I was too angry to correct myself. 'Anyway, why would she do that? It wasn't like she was short of money.'

Again, there was that pitiful look from Finn – the one I wanted to slap right off his face. I balled my fingers into fists but kept them firmly in my lap.

'Look at it this way,' said Finn. 'Kathleen was planning on leaving John. She needed money for her squirrel fund. Cash is always the best option as no one can trace you, unlike a footprint of digital transactions. Squirrelling money away is what people do. I've seen it before. Taking a few euros here and a few there means there's less chance of it being missed or, if it is, then it can be written off as an anomaly.'

'You're not listening to me,' I said. 'Kathleen wasn't short of money. She had her own account. She had a job. Besides, she just wouldn't do that. Not to The Hub.'

'But after she left, she'd need money. Untraceable money.' Finn held my gaze. I wanted to look away but couldn't. Had Ahern told him about me being spotted at a cashpoint in Tralee?

My mouth was dry as I spoke. 'I hate to say it, but it's more likely to be someone who uses The Hub than an employee.'

'They're not all bad people who visit the place,' said Finn. 'You're making assumptions and, to be honest, I'm surprised at you.'

The superior tone in his voice really pissed me off. 'I'm making observations. There's a difference,' I said. There was a heavy silence in the room. Suddenly, I didn't want him there. His very presence was infuriating me. 'Was that all you wanted to tell me?' I asked.

'More or less. I can leave if you want me to,' said Finn. He got to his feet.

I wanted to yank the door open and tell him to fuck off, but my professional head was telling me not to burn bridges. Finn could still help me. He could still be a source of information. It was always useful to know what was being said amongst locals and what the latest rumours were. These were often the sparks that ignited potential bombshells. I had a ridiculous fleeting image of Marlon Brando in *The Godfather* – keep your enemies closer.

'I don't want to fall out with you,' I said, standing up. It was the truth. Despite our difference of opinion, I didn't want to argue with an old friend. 'Don't leave on a bad note.'

He took my hand, lifting it to his mouth, and his lips grazed my knuckles. 'How could I resist?' he asked. His eyes never once left mine and for a moment I thought he was going to kiss me, but then he broke into a broad grin. He let go of my hand before sitting back down on the sofa. I sat down next to him but a suitable distance away. I wasn't sure what was going on between us or if indeed anything actually was, and it was simply the imagination of a spurned wife looking for validation as a desirable woman. I internally cringed at my pathetic neediness.

'All I'm getting at,' Finn began, 'is Kathleen may have been planning to leave John for quite some time.'

'Why the "help" message?' I challenged, wanting to know what his thoughts were behind this. I knew the truth, of course, but I wanted to know what the guards really thought. The version they might not necessarily have shared with the public.

'My hypothesis is this,' replied Finn. 'Kathleen had finally had enough, wanted to go off, either on her own or with someone else.' He held up a hand to silence me before I had time to protest about the idea that Kathleen was having an affair. 'She wanted you to either: (a) lend her money; (b) give her a lift to the station or someplace; or (c) cover for her.'

I gave a small intake of breath. Did Finn know the truth, or was this a guess? I was on the brink of telling him what had happened, but something was stopping me. I don't know what exactly, but I bit down on my lip. Was it because I didn't trust Finn? He hadn't given me any real leads or insight into what happened to Kathleen, and I couldn't make up my mind if his offer to help was genuine or whether he was keeping an eye on me. Had he been told to steer me in a certain direction? What it boiled down to was I didn't trust him. Not yet.

'I guess Kathleen is the only person who can answer that,' I said, looking down at my hands.

'Siobhan,' said Finn gently. 'Do you know anything else? Something, for whatever reason, you didn't tell the guards about that night? Anything that you've remembered since then?'

I shook my head. 'No. Nothing. I was hoping you'd be able to help on that score.' I was acutely aware of his nearness and got to my feet.

'What are you going to do now?' he asked.

'Stir a few people up, I guess.' I adjusted the position of the vase on the mantelpiece for no reason whatsoever other than something to do with my hands.

'What's that going to achieve, other than aggro?'

I turned to face him, folding my arms across my chest. 'Sooner or later, someone is going to feel the pressure and slip up,' I said defiantly.

My phone rang and I was somewhat relieved to see it was Kian. However, my relief was short-lived.

'I'm doing some work for my dad today,' he said, when I asked him if Freya was with him.

'Are you OK?' I asked. I was surprised he was having anything to do with his dad after John hit him.

'Don't worry about me. I'm grand,' said Kian. The way he said it sounded so much like the way Kathleen would have spoken. Breezy, nothing-to-see-here kind of attitude. Of course, victims of domestic abuse, whatever type of abuse, were experts at covering it up too.

'Why don't you call over later?' I suggested. 'Drop by for something to eat.'

'Sure. I'd like that. So, Freya, where do you think she's gone?' he asked.

'For a walk, maybe,' I replied, sounding unconvinced even to my own ears. 'I'm sure she'll be back soon. I was ruling out alternatives. If you hear from her, get her to call me.'

'OK. I've got to go. See you later.'

'Bye, Kian.' I ended the call and immediately tried to get hold of Freya again, but still no luck. I sent a text message. It went through as green.

'Problem?' asked Finn.

'I can't get hold of Freya. My message has gone through as a text rather than an iMessage.'

'Probably the signal,' said Finn. 'I've got to go now but I'll keep an eye out for her. She's probably having a coffee or an ice cream and forgotten the time. Don't be worrying, now.'

I forced a smile as memories of the bottle of urine being thrown at her came to the fore. The only consolation I took was that I was certain it had been meant for me and not her. 'Thanks. I might take a walk out myself if she's not back soon.'

'She can't be getting lost here. Not exactly a busy metropolitan city.' He gave me a wink. 'Catch you later.'

'Thanks, Finn.'

As Finn was leaving, Niall's mother was getting the girls into her car. 'I'm off to the park with them,' she called.

I smiled and waved at my nieces as they left with their grandma. It was nice they had a good relationship with Niall's mother, and what seemed a reasonable one with my parents. I had a little attack of guilt that, by moving to England and bringing up our child there, Danny and I had, essentially, deprived our daughter of that closeness with either set of grandparents.

For the first time, I was questioning my wisdom at readily moving away from Dingle. It was me who had driven the move. Danny hadn't been bothered one way or the other, but I had wanted to leave the tourist hotspot, leaving everyone I knew, including my family.

If I'd stayed, maybe Kathleen would have confided in me. I might have been able to help her through whatever problems she was facing. Her words of that last night when we'd argued in the pub came back as clear as if she was standing in front of me saying them, there and then. 'I just wanted to be loved.'

'Oh, Kathleen,' I said out loud to the empty driveway, to the fall of the land out to the coast and the sea beyond that. 'You were so loved. Still are. I'm not giving up on you.'

. . .

With still no word from Freya ten minutes later, my irritation at her being irresponsible and not getting in touch was beginning to sway into low-level anxiety. Where the hell was she and why hadn't she returned any of my messages or calls? She knew better than to not contact me.

I didn't want to alarm anyone yet, but I was clock-watching and checking my phone for messages or a missed call every few minutes.

An hour later and I was grabbing my jacket to go out and look for her myself when the front door opened and in came Freya with Kian.

'Where the hell have you been?' I demanded. 'I've been trying to get hold of you all afternoon. I was about to go and look for you.'

I knew my anger came from a place of love and relief, but I couldn't stop myself. She looked like she couldn't give a fuck that I'd been worried sick about her.

'All right, calm down,' said Freya. 'I'm sorry. I was out and forgot about the time.'

'But didn't you see my messages? Missed calls?'

'My phone was on silent,' she said.

'And you never looked at your phone?'

'No. I didn't, actually.'

'You didn't take photos or Snapchat pictures?'

'No, because I don't have any internet while I'm out. Couldn't get my phone to work earlier.' Freya scowled at me and then turned to Kian, who had been standing in the doorway. 'See what I have to put up with?'

'Freya—' began Kian.

'It's true,' snapped Freya. 'Always on my case. Treating me like I'm twelve. God, it's stifling.'

'Let's not have this argument in front of Kian,' I said, suddenly feeling guilty for my outburst. He'd probably had enough of this sort of stuff at home.

Freya huffed. 'Dad was right,' she said.

Instantly, I was on high alert. 'What do you mean? What did Dad say?'

'That you're stressy all the time. I bet if I lived with Dad, he wouldn't be like this.'

It was a low punch, and I felt every word of it. I saw a moment of regret on Freya's face, but it was too late; the damage was done, and it hurt. I wanted to cry but blinked away the tears. Freya was just lashing out at the injustice of her home life – and who could blame her? I didn't want to be the villain, but that was the label she'd clearly applied to me. There was no point arguing; it would only reinforce her accusation. If I did nothing, I was condoning what she'd said. I was in a no-win situation.

I looked from my daughter to Kian, who was painfully uncomfortable at this point. I took a deep breath before speaking. 'I'm not being stressy, just worried. You're back now so that's all good. Where did you go, anyway?'

Freya shrugged. 'About.'

Never before had I levelled so much self-control. 'Dingle?'

'Yeah, the beach. That was all.'

'I thought you were working for your dad?' I said to Kian, trying to work out why he was now here when earlier he said he was busy.

'I finished what I was doing and went for a drive to see if I could find her,' said Kian.

'And, hey-presto, he did,' said Freya.

'I should be getting off now,' said Kian, edging towards the door.

'Of course. Mind how you go,' I said. 'Thank you for bringing Freya back. I didn't mean to worry anyone.'

'Sure, it's no trouble,' said Kian. 'I'll be seeing you, Freya.'

'Yeah. Sure. Bye,' was all my grumpy teenager could bring herself to say.

I walked to the door with Kian and waited while he got in his car and gave a toot of the horn as he drove out onto the road. By that time, Freya was in her bedroom with the door shut.

I sighed. I didn't want to get into an argument with her. I'd leave her alone until we were both calmer.

It was getting late, but I wasn't tired. I didn't want to think about Danny and the stressy comment. I tried to dismiss it. Worrying where my daughter was wasn't overreacting. It was being a concerned parent, and there was nothing wrong with that. Still, I was aware the catty remark had left a claw mark which stung.

Instead, I thought of Kathleen. Whatever was happening between Danny and me would have to wait. I had limited time here and a sense of urgency was setting in.

I sat down with a cup of coffee and closed my eyes. It was hard to sift through all the snippets of information I'd gathered so far. I was sure I was missing something. I made a conscious effort to relax and let everything filter through. The thought that was playing on my mind was bound to find its way to the front of my mind sooner or later.

And it wasn't long before I struck gold. Dervla was having an affair with a married man. I'd been told that, and I'd even said finding who that was would be a key piece of information. But I hadn't done anything about it. I'd got sidetracked. Nicole thought she was in danger because Dervla had confided in her about the affair. It was coming back to me now.

I sat up, feeling invigorated. What I needed to do was to find out who the married man was. Kathleen, Nicole and Dervla all had one thing in common. The Hub. In fact, the more I thought about it, the more people I could connect with the place. Ahern. Aisling Denvers. Conor Doyle.

The Hub held the answers, I was sure.

TWENTY-THREE

'There you go, dotes,' says Rory, placing the supper he's prepared for his wife, Maureen, on the table. He sits down beside her. 'Do you want me to help you?'

'No. I'll do it myself,' replies Maureen. Her hand trembles as she attempts to pick up her cutlery. Even lifting her arms is an effort for her.

Ahern resists the urge to grab the knife and fork and wrap her fingers around the wooden handles. It breaks his heart to see her trying to feed herself. She's not having a good day today.

ME is a bastard and it's robbed his wife of her life and him of his wife. There's no treatment according to the doctors here in Ireland. It makes Ahern mad. He's seen articles online about new treatments in the US. He's researched it and even taken it to their own doctor, but he's told no every time. It's not been medically proven to help and there's no money in the system for it.

'Let me help you,' says Ahern.

'No. I can do it. I want to do it,' she says.

Maureen does her best, God love her. He knows he should encourage her to be as independent as possible, but it's hard for a man such as himself. He was brought up the old-fashioned way. He's the provider and he's the fixer. Always has been. That's why he became a guard – to make sure everything happened as it should. And that's why it's so frustrating he cannot fix his wife. What sort of man is he?

He gets up from the table and leaves Maureen to eat her supper. She'll call him if she needs him. The stairs creak under his weight as he goes up to the box room at the back of the house. When they'd first moved here all those years ago – when they were newlyweds, when Maureen was well – they'd earmarked this room as a nursery. They had been so excited at the thought of starting a family, but, alas, it wasn't to be. God must have had other plans for them, Maureen said. He was fecked if he knew what those plans were. If it was Maureen getting ill with a virus ten years ago that left her a shell of the person she once was, then he didn't understand God at all.

In the box room, he reaches up to the top shelf and lifts down the locked tin. He twiddles the combination dials and the lock springs open.

From his pocket he takes the brown envelope he'd been given earlier and withdraws the used notes. Five hundred euros. He slips it into the tin alongside the many other bundles. He keeps a card in the tin with the running total and he marks it up to include the latest deposit.

He's not far off his total now. Once he's hit the magic number, he can take Maureen to America – Chicago, to be exact – and the private clinic where she can take part in the trials of the new drug to cure her ME.

It's a bittersweet tin. On the one hand it could be the cure he and Maureen have dreamed of for the past ten years. On the other hand, the money is tainted. Corrupt, like him.

He hates himself for what he's done to get this money. Foregoing his beliefs and morals, his duty as an officer of the law, and compromising his integrity. But what choice does he have?

The end justifies the means. If Maureen is cured or has something of her life back, then it's a price he's willing to pay.

Ahern locks the tin and replaces it on the shelf.

He could do with a smoke and heads out to the garden, checking in on Maureen as he does so. She's still eating. It's a slow and painful process and it breaks his heart to see. He feels guilty to be standing out in the garden while she's struggling, but she doesn't want him there. He knows that's out of embarrassment.

He takes a cigarette from the packet and fishes around in his pocket for his lighter. The gold elephant print has all but worn off, and it takes a few flicks with his thumb to get the thing to work. He makes a mental note to get a new one before it runs out completely.

As he draws on his cigarette, his mobile phone rings. The ringtone tells him it's his burner phone and he knows exactly who it is.

'Hello,' he says as he answers it.

'I thought you had a handle on our little problem?'

'And I do,' he responds, his skin prickling at the tone taken with him as if he's a child who needs reprimanding.

'Well, our little problem is still here and still being a problem.'

'As I said, I'm dealing with it.'

'Deal with it more effectively, then.' The line goes dead.

Rory closes his eyes for a moment to maintain his composure. What he'd like to do is throw the fecking phone across the garden. He's so had enough of all this. He rues the day he ever got involved. It had started with a favour for an old friend, turning a blind eye here or there. But gradually over the years, step by step, he's moved through the murky waters of right and wrong and somehow ended in the deep end. He inhales through his nose, blows out a long slow breath, and consoles himself with the fact that soon it will be over.

TWENTY-FOUR

When I woke the following morning, Freya was already up.

'Sorry about yesterday,' she said.

'That's OK,' I replied with a smile. 'I know it's boring for you here. I was just worried, that's all. Shall we walk into town and grab some breakfast?'

'Yeah, sure, that will be nice.'

The key was finding out who Dervla was having an affair with. I was sure of it. If Nicole felt in danger from supposedly knowing, then it was logical to assume that Kathleen had been in danger too. My stomach churned and I felt a wave of sickness wash over me at the thought someone had harmed Kathleen because she knew too much about Dervla's affair. If this was right, then whoever harmed her – it was too horrific to say killed – had a lot to lose.

I grabbed a bottle of water from the fridge and took several gulps, forcing myself to remain calm. I had to distance myself emotionally from Kathleen otherwise I'd fall apart and I'd never find out the truth.

I felt a renewed sense of purpose. I had something I could do today.

. . .

Sharon greeted us in the reception hall of The Hub. 'Hello. I didn't expect to see you here again so soon. Everything all right?'

'Hi, Sharon,' I said, smiling warmly. 'Just wanted to show my daughter The Hub. I was telling her about it. This is Freya.'

'Hi, Freya,' said Sharon. Although she was welcoming, I could tell she was wondering why a fifteen-year-old would be interested in the place.

Freya politely said hello but didn't offer any explanation.

'Is the café open today?' I asked.

'Yes. It opens in...' Sharon glanced at her watch, '... five minutes.'

'Perfect. We'll go get ourselves a coffee and bite to eat,' I said.

'Great,' muttered Freya as she followed me through to the main hall.

The shutters weren't up at the counter yet, but I could hear voices and the clinking of crockery from behind the screen. There was a young woman with her toddler over in the area sectioned off for under 5s, according to the sign taped to the back of one of the plastic chairs. It was probably a toddler group morning or something. I seemed to remember Kathleen mentioning once that they were fundraising for some play equipment.

Apart from that, the hall was empty. I guessed it was too early for Conor and his crew to show up. I didn't know how often they came, but I got the impression they were regulars to The Hub.

We sat down in a soft seating area, which had various different, probably donated, chairs and a sofa, with a coffee table in the middle. Freya slumped down in the couch and immediately took out her phone. She was no doubt taking pictures and sending them to Sophie with captions: *Look at this dive my mum has brought me to* or *Can't tell you how bored I am right now.*

She had mentioned a party Kian was taking her to the following evening and, although I wasn't exactly keen on the idea, I did trust her and Kian. Freya, on the whole, was a good kid who hadn't given Danny and me any real trouble. As a rule, she was happy and easy-going, but I had noticed the change in her in recent weeks and I could only put that down to the separation. Again, I promised myself that I'd get things sorted out one way or another with Danny so then at least Freya wouldn't feel in limbo. This temporary arrangement wasn't working for either of us.

There was a noticeboard on the wall beside one of the armchairs and I wandered over to it.

There were the usual safety notices about a fire drill and assembly point. Another notice about treating staff and others with respect. Violence would not be tolerated. But it was the photographs that drew my attention.

There were some more of the fifth anniversary celebrations. Most of them appeared to be the ones I'd seen on social media, but a couple I didn't remember seeing before. I looked closely but none of them stood out for any reason, and I almost missed it at first. I looked again at the last picture.

'That was a good night,' came a voice from behind me.

I looked around and a woman was standing there with a double buggy. She knelt to undo the straps to allow a toddler out. 'Off you go over to Maggie,' said the woman to her child. The little boy of about two sprinted across the room, clearly familiar with where he was going. The woman stood up and came over to me. 'You're Kathleen Walsh's sister, right?'

'Yeah, that's right. My notoriety precedes me,' I said.

The woman eyed me. 'Something like that,' she said. 'I'm Ellen Dougherty. I often chatted to your sister here.'

'Pleased to meet you,' I said. 'Kathleen loved working here.'

'She was a good woman.'

'Thank you, I appreciate that.' Another person who appreciated my sister. It touched my heart to know she was well thought of.

Ellen looked around and then took a step closer to me. 'You know your sister was upset at that party?'

'Was she?'

'I went outside for a smoke. Round the back of the building, like. I wasn't supposed to be smoking, you see,' explained Ellen. 'And she was there. She didn't see me at first. Too busy looking at her phone, but she was crying.'

'Was she all right?' It was a stupid question because clearly she wasn't, and Ellen looked at me as if to say much the same. 'I mean, did you speak to her? Did she tell you what was wrong?'

'Of course, I asked her.' Ellen gave another look as if to say that was my second stupid question. 'She didn't really say. Just she'd had an argument with someone, but it was OK and she was overreacting.'

I felt my frustrations rise again. All these snippets of information that didn't make any sense. 'And this was at the party?'

'Yeah. The week before she disappeared. I did tell the guards.'

'And what was their response? Who did you speak to?' If it was Finn, he sure hadn't mentioned it.

'They just thanked me and said if they needed anything else, they'd be in touch. It was Sergeant Ahern.'

There was Ahern's name cropping up again. Surely it was a coincidence. 'And you've no idea what it was about?'

'No, but...' Ellen paused for dramatic effect. 'When I was on my way out for a smoke, before I saw your sister, as I was going out the door at the back of the building, Fergus Denvers was on his way in. He was in a right old hurry. Nearly knocked me flying. He barely stopped to say sorry. Stormed right off down the corridor and into his wife's office. I remember because he slammed the door as he went.'

'Do you think he had been talking to Kathleen?'

Ellen shrugged. 'I wouldn't swear to it but, you know. And before you ask, yes I did tell Ahern about that too.'

I gave Ellen a smile. 'Thanks. I don't know what that means, but thank you for telling me,' I said. 'So, Denvers, does he hang around The Hub much?'

'He's always here. I don't like him, but he doesn't bother with me. I'm not his type.'

'His type?'

'You know, young and pretty.' She gave a dramatic shudder. 'Gives me the creeps, but everyone likes him; after all, he's Aisling Denvers's husband and Aisling Denvers holds the purse strings for this place.'

Before I could ask any more questions, the baby in the pushchair started crying. 'Better see to his lordship,' Ellen said. 'Nice meeting you.'

'Yeah, and you,' I said, watching Ellen go over to the buggy and wheel it across the room to the toddler area.

I could feel the cogs whirring in my head as titbits of information began to evolve into fully-fledged thoughts.

'Can we go somewhere else for food?' asked Freya, eyeing the cold counter and the uninspiring sandwiches. 'Somewhere for proper breakfast.'

I smiled at her. 'Yeah. Sure. There's a café just along from here.'

Ten minutes later, we were sitting outside the Harbour Tearooms, having ordered bacon sandwiches.

'I know it's not been great for you this week,' I said. 'But I'm glad you came.'

'I didn't have a lot of choice.'

'True. But I'm still glad you're here. I'm sorry it's been boring.'

'It's not that bad, Mum,' said Freya. 'It would be worse if Kian wasn't about.'

'I'm glad you two get on,' I said. 'Kathleen would be so pleased.'

'I miss Kathleen being here,' said Freya.

A simple statement, yet it prised open my heart like a tin opener. 'I do too,' I said, reaching over and squeezing my daughter's hand. 'I do too.'

I dabbed at my eyes with my napkin, not wanting to cause a scene in the café. I was well aware that the locals who knew me and my family were surreptitiously monitoring me, assessing me and passing judgement on what I did or didn't do in the past and what I was or wasn't doing now. The unwelcome feeling silently extended itself further around me each day.

As I finished eating, my phone began to ring. 'It's Corin,' I said, looking at the screen and accepting the call. 'Hey, Corin.'

'Where are you?' she asked without any preamble.

I could tell straight away something was wrong.

TWENTY-FIVE

I looked at Freya, who instantly picked up on my tension. 'Down at the Harbour Tearooms with Freya. What's up?'

'Stay there. I'll come and get you.'

'What's going on?'

'I'll explain properly when I get there but it's Mum and Dad. Someone has sprayed graffiti all over the front of their house.'

'What the fuck!' I scrabbled in my purse for my card and gave it to Freya. 'Go and pay.'

Freya didn't argue and immediately went over to the counter. I was aware of some looks I was getting from the other early-morning diners.

'I'll be there in five minutes,' said Corin.

'Wait.' I got up and went outside, away from the satellite ears. 'What does the graffiti say?'

'Rory and Finn are there,' said Corin. 'Finn sent me a photo. I'll forward it to you. Look, I'm getting in the car now. See you in a minute. Wait outside.'

The line went dead.

Freya came out of the café. 'What's going on?'

'I'm not sure,' I said, checking my phone for Corin to send the picture through. An alert sounded, but it wasn't from Corin. It was a text message from an unknown number. My hand shook as I opened the message.

> See what your meddling does. Wouldn't be warned.

Then Corin's message came through with a picture of the graffiti. Freya looked over my shoulder. She gave a sharp intake of breath.

'Bloody hell,' she said.

'This is all your fault!' my father shouted, before my feet had even touched the driveway. He was standing in front of the garage with a bucket of soapy water at his feet and a sponge in his hand, which he dumped into the suds. 'You should be doing this.' With that he stomped into the house, leaving my mother standing in the doorway. She looked at me with a combination of disappointment, anger and sadness. It was amazing how she could convey all those emotions with just one look.

'Don't worry,' said Niall, getting out of the car. 'I've got some graffiti remover gel. We'll soon have all that off.'

I wanted to hug Niall. In his usual quiet way, he was smoothing things over with the Regan family. He really should be nominated for the Nobel Peace Prize.

'Thanks, Niall,' I said, surveying the bright red wording on the garage door. The message was crystal clear.

SEND THE BITCH BACK TO ENGLAND

'Someone sure does love you,' muttered Freya, who had got out of the car to come to stand beside me. Niall and Corin had dropped the girls with Niall's mother before coming to get us on the way here.

'Yes, I think we can safely assume that message refers to me,' I said.

'You don't say,' came a voice from the house.

I looked up and saw Rory Ahern stepping out of the house, with Finn following. The two men came over.

'All right, Siobhan?' asked Finn.

'Yeah. Great.' I knew he wasn't really asking after my well-being, and I regretted being snappy with him. I pushed my personal emotions aside, engaging my journalistic brain. 'When did this happen?'

'Sometime overnight,' said Finn. 'One of the neighbours saw it first and came over to tell your parents.'

'Anyone got any CCTV footage or doorbell camera?' I asked.

'We're about to ask around,' said Ahern. 'Leave the investigation to us.'

'Yes, of course,' cut in Corin, no doubt anticipating a scathing comment from me. She put her hand on my arm. 'Let's go inside. Niall will have this cleaned up in no time.'

'If I told you someone is targeting me, would you do anything about it?' I asked Ahern.

'We can take a statement if you've something to report,' he replied.

'Would you investigate it, though?'

'We have to look at the evidence and make a decision then.' Rory frowned. 'At the moment, I'm keen to chat to some of the neighbours. Maybe you should go and apologise to your parents. Bringing all this trouble to their door again. Your mother is very upset, and as for your father...' He left the sentence unfinished before striding off down the drive, calling to Finn to hurry up.

'Ignore him,' said Finn. 'You know what he's like. I'll call you later and let you know if we find anything out.'

'Thanks, Finn,' I said.

As he trotted off to catch up with his boss, I could see Freya scowling after him. I put my arm around her shoulders. 'Come on. I need you for moral support.'

'Are you happy now?' Dad asked as I went into the living room.

'Of course not,' I said. 'I'm sorry.'

'Rory says you're asking questions about Kathleen. Going around making accusations. Upsetting everyone.' Dad glared at me. 'What you want to be doing that for? Hasn't there been enough pain and upset?'

'Rory said something about Kathleen's purse,' said Mam. She twiddled the wedding ring on her finger. 'You never told us.'

'I didn't want to worry you,' I said. 'In case it was nothing.'

'And it is nothing,' insisted Dad. 'Someone found her purse, but that doesn't prove anything. Besides, it might not even be hers. It might be someone messing with you.'

I looked from one parent to the other and wondered how they could be so dismissive. 'Don't you want to find out what happened to your own daughter?'

'Siobhan,' Corin said softly.

I wasn't in the mood for listening. 'Surely, you want every lead followed up and looked at?'

'That's for the guards to do, not you,' said Dad. 'Rory is the investigating officer. Leave it to the professionals. Just because you once worked for some sort of newspaper, doesn't mean you're above the law and can go off conducting your own enquiries.'

'But they're not interested,' I retorted, ignoring his dismissive comment about my journalistic career – one he'd never approved of. 'I've been to the guards, but they don't care. They think Kathleen left of her own accord.'

'Siobhan, please,' urged Mam.

'Do you honestly believe that's what happened?' I asked. My chest was getting tighter with every word that came out of my mouth. I gulped in a lungful of air.

There was a silence in the room as everyone waited for my dad to speak.

He let out a sigh and sat down in his chair by the side of the fireplace. He glanced at Freya. 'This is not the right time for this conversation.'

'Oh, but it is,' I replied. My voice wobbled but it wasn't from fear; it was from rage. I could feel the temperature of my mood rising. It was a wonder I didn't spontaneously combust. 'Don't worry about Freya, she knows exactly how I feel about all this.'

'Sit down,' said Mam.

'I'm fine standing,' I replied, not taking my eyes from my dad. 'I'll ask again. Do you believe Kathleen simply upped and left everything and everyone, including her son?'

'As a matter of fact, I do,' Dad retaliated. He stood up, his six-foot frame filling the space. His presence compressed the air in the room.

I felt like a child again, when I was being told off and was scared because I'd upset him. I refused to succumb to those memories of intimidation and fear. I was grown. He could hardly send me to my room. I was also acutely aware that Freya was there. I wanted my child to grow up to be a strong, independent woman, never kowtowing to anyone. I stood my ground and was aware of Corin coming to stand by my side, our shoulders touching. I felt her hand find mine.

'Dad,' she began.

'Don't you start,' he said, cutting her off. He took a step towards us, his finger pointing at me. 'Kathleen was having an affair.' I heard my mother gasp. My father looked over at her. 'Sorry, Marie, I didn't want you to know, but seeing as Siobhan here has forced my hand, I've no choice in the matter.'

'How do you know she was?' I asked, the belligerence in me growing parallel with my anger.

'John told me,' said Dad. 'He came to see me a few days before she left. Told me he'd found out about it and confronted her. Said Kathleen had told him she wanted a divorce.'

'So, why did she disappear?' I challenged. 'If it was out in the open and she wanted to divorce, she had no reason to leave without a trace.'

'Because John didn't want that. He's a good man who believes in the sanctity of marriage. He believes in his vows. He wanted to try to make their marriage work. He was prepared to forgive her indiscretion. But Kathleen refused. Said it was over.'

'That's not true,' I said.

'You're clutching at straws,' said Dad. 'Now, I'm not asking, I'm telling you. Stop all this nonsense. Accept that she left – in the most selfish way possible, I might add. She doesn't care about us, you, Corin, her husband, her son, any of us. She's done what she wanted to and started a new life somewhere else.'

'Who was she having an affair with?' I asked.

'John wouldn't say, but he suspected it was someone she'd met at one of her work dos. It wasn't like she was gallivanting much elsewhere.'

'And you're happy to believe that?' I looked at Mam and then back at Dad. 'That's what you want to believe.'

'Yes. I won't discuss it anymore. Now, like I said, you're to stop all this nonsense. Go back to England and get on with your life and leave us to get on with ours. I'm going out in the garden to water the roses and when I come back, I don't expect you to still be here.'

I was lost for words as he walked past us and out of the room. I stood in a stunned silence. I heard him go into the kitchen and put on his boots, before opening the back door and gently closing it behind him.

He'd kicked me out in such a calm manner: it was more

unnerving than had he done it in a temper. That was my cool, calm and collected father, telling me I wasn't welcome. Maybe I'd asked for it. Maybe I'd overstepped the mark. I knew I had stood up to him like I'd never done before, but where had it got me?

'You'd better go,' said Mam. 'He's cross now, but he'll calm down.'

I nodded. 'Yeah. OK.'

Mam stepped forward and we looked at each other for a moment. I could see the pain in her eyes and how conflicted she felt. I didn't want to make things worse for her, but at the same time it hurt to think my dad could just turn his back on me.

'I'll call you later,' Corin said to Mam. Still holding my hand, she led me out of the house, with Freya following.

Niall was scrubbing away at the garage door. 'I'll get the pressure washer on this and then it will be all gone,' he said. He stopped when he registered the look on our faces.

'Dad wants us to go,' said Corin.

'He wants me to go,' I said, touched by the solidarity of my sister. I could see Finn across the road, standing on the doorstep of a neighbour's house. Ahern was sitting in the police car, writing something in his notebook. He looked up at me for a moment, before returning to his jottings. No doubt he was happy to see me leaving.

'I'll run Siobhan and Freya home and then come back for you,' said Corin to Niall. She went over to him and gave him a quick kiss. 'Thanks for doing this.'

'No worries,' said Niall. He looked over at me. 'It will be all right, girl.'

I smiled at my brother-in-law and felt grateful for his kind heart and the obvious love he had for my sister. At least one of the Regan girls had got it right.

. . .

'I'm going out this afternoon,' announced Freya as soon as Corin had dropped us back at the annexe.

'I thought Kian was busy,' I said.

Freya shrugged. 'Maybe he's not now.'

'OK. That will be nice.' I couldn't pretend I wasn't disappointed. I was feeling pretty low about the graffiti and the argument with my dad. The thought of hanging out with Freya and maybe doing something nice together had been appealing. I didn't want to stop her fun, though.

Freya came over to me and put her arms around me. 'You look like you need a hug,' she said. 'Don't be sad, Mum. I love you.'

And those three sweet words from my darling daughter were enough to break me. I couldn't quell the sob that launched itself from my throat as I promptly burst into tears.

'I'm sorry,' I said after a moment. I was the parent; I should be the supportive one. I shouldn't be putting my emotions on display for a fifteen-year-old to carry.

'Don't be sorry. It's all right,' said Freya. 'I'm sure Grandad didn't mean what he said.'

I pulled away and gave something close to a smile. 'He probably did, but that's because he doesn't know how to show any emotion other than anger. That's his default. It doesn't mean he doesn't care; it's just how it manifests itself.'

Freya plucked a couple of tissues from the box on the coffee table and handed them to me. 'You're making your mascara run.'

I dabbed under my eyes. 'Grandad is old-fashioned, that's all.' I realised I was making excuses for Dad, in much the same way Mam would have when we were younger. Words I was now echoing. I was sure Dad loved us all, but he had never been one to show affection.

'Do you think Kathleen had an affair?' asked Freya. 'I mean,

I know you said that didn't happen, but do you think it could have?'

I blew my nose. 'I don't know what to think sometimes.'

'Kian doesn't believe it.'

'Why's that?' I hadn't realised Freya and Kian had spoken about Kathleen.

'Just said it didn't add up and it's not the sort of thing his mum would do.'

We sat in silence for a moment and I gave Freya a reassuring hug. 'I'm OK now. Sorry about that.'

'Are you going to be all right this afternoon? I can cancel going out if you want me to stay,' she said.

I was touched by the offer. 'That's very sweet of you, but I'll be OK,' I said. 'I might have a walk. Get some fresh air.'

'Have you heard from Dad at all?' asked Freya, going over to the sink and running the tap for a glass of water.

'No. Have you?'

'He messaged last night.'

'Is he all right?' I tamped down the disappointment that he hadn't returned my call.

'Yeah.'

'What did he say?' I felt Freya was waiting for me to ask, otherwise why bring it up in the first place?

'Just wanted to see if I was OK. He asked if you were too.'

The flutter of joy in my stomach was disproportionate to what that little snippet justified, but it gave me a glimmer of hope that he wasn't still pissed off with me. 'What did you say to him?'

'I said we were fine. He wanted to know when we were coming home.'

'Did you tell him Sunday?'

'Yeah. He said he could pick us up from the airport if I let him know what time.'

'Oh, that will be good. I'll give him a call later,' I said. 'I need to ask him about unlocking Kathleen's tablet anyway. Unless you mentioned it?'

'No. I thought you'd best speak to him about that.' Freya's eyes were now fixed on her phone. 'What's for lunch? I'm hungry.'

'I'll do us some sandwiches now,' I said, getting up.

While I was preparing lunch, Corin and Niall returned. Corin came over.

'The garage door is all clean now. Looks as good as new,' she said.

'Thank goodness. How are Mam and Dad? Is Dad still really angry with me?' I shouldn't be still seeking my dad's approval at my age, but there was that part of me that didn't want to disappoint.

'He's still angry,' confirmed Corin. 'But you know what he's like. He hates the thought that we are once again the talk of the town.'

I gave an eye roll and my need to be forgiven promptly disappeared. 'God forbid we should be worried about Kathleen.'

Corin gave me a sympathetic smile. 'I'm taking the girls to Ventry beach this afternoon. They've a party there. You're welcome to come.'

'That's kind of you, but I might give it a miss today,' I said. 'Freya is out with Kian later. I'm planning to have a couple of hours to myself to recharge. I feel... I don't know... so lost. Confused. Maybe I shouldn't have come, after all.'

'Stop that, now,' said Corin. 'What were you going to do? Sit at home and never find anything out after that purse turning up? I don't think so. No one in their right mind would ignore it. You did and are doing the right thing. Just because it's upset Dad, don't let that make you doubt yourself. I know I've not been much help the last couple of days, but I'm with you all the way on this.'

It was the pep talk I needed. It felt reassuring to hear

someone say those words. 'Thanks, Corin,' I said, giving her a brief hug. 'You're the best.'

'You hear that, Freya?' Corin asked. 'Your mum has finally admitted I'm the best. Praise be to God.'

Freya briefly looked up from her phone and gave a pitiful smile.

After Corin had left, I went out into the small garden at the side of the annexe to try to call Danny. I wanted to ask him about the iPad, but my overriding desire was to hear his voice. I was buoyed by the fact he'd asked after me.

After several rings, he answered. 'Siobhan. Everything OK? Is Freya all right?'

'Hi. Everything is fine,' I said.

'Oh. Right. I was worried something else had happened.' His voice was lacking the warmth I had been expecting but I put it down to that awkward feeling you have after a disagreement, when you're guarded yet, at the same time, not wanting a confrontation and unsure how to progress the conversation.

'I'm sorry we argued the other day,' I said, taking the lead.

'I don't like arguing with you,' he said.

The absence of an apology stung a little, but I ploughed on. 'So, we all good?' I asked.

'Yeah, as long as Freya is OK, then I am,' he replied. 'I'll be happy once Sunday comes and she's back here.'

And me! I wanted to say. 'She said something about you offering to pick us up from the airport?'

'Send me the flight number and I'll be there.'

'Thanks, I really appreciate that,' I said. 'How are you?' I was enjoying listening to his voice. I'd never gone so long without hearing it as I had recently, and I missed it. I missed him.

'I'm fine.' There was a short but noticeable silence before Danny spoke again. 'So, what did you want? I'm assuming you called for a reason.'

'I need to get into Kathleen's iPad, but I don't know the password,' I said, trying to pretend I didn't care that he hadn't asked after me. 'Can you tell me how to do it, please?'

'Why do you need to do that?'

'It's locked.' I tried not to sound impatient. This was supposed to be a friendly phone call, one where we didn't end up arguing.

'I appreciate that, but what's on the iPad that's so important?'

'I don't know. It might be nothing. Kian gave it to me,' I said. 'John doesn't know about the iPad, and I want to see if Kathleen had anything on there that might help.'

'Jesus, Siobhan, I was hoping you'd stopped all that.'

'All what?'

'Amateur detective crap.'

'It's not crap. I'm a journalist, remember?' I retorted. 'Anyway, I don't want to argue about it – can you please just tell me how to log in to it?'

'No.'

I looked up as the sound of an engine idling in the road on the other side of the hedge registered. I stood up to get a better look. It was a white transit van. My heart did a flip. I couldn't see over the hedge clearly, so couldn't tell if it was the same one that had pulled up alongside me. I heard a car door bang and then the van pulled away.

'Did you hear what I said?' Danny's voice brought me back to the conversation.

'Sorry, what?'

'I'm not helping you log in to the iPad.'

'What?' I asked, even though I recognised the stubbornness in his voice.

'Take it to the guards and let them do it. This is not for you, Siobhan.'

'I'm not taking it to the guards. I need to see what's on there first. If it's something important then I will, but I need to look first.' I paced across the patio and back again, trying to walk the frustration out of me.

'No, you don't,' he said. 'You don't need to do any of this.'

'Danny, please, help me,' I said, exasperated.

'Don't ask me again. I'm not telling you.' He paused before speaking again. 'I have to go. See you on Sunday.'

Before I could get another word in, he was gone.

I let out an irritated groan. He was being bloody-minded for the sake of it.

I went back inside, wondering if Kian knew anyone who was a computer geek and might be able to help. If not, I'd try to google it. I knew there was software on my laptop from when Danny used it for work, but I had not the first clue about using it.

When I went back into the annexe, Freya had already gone.

I huffed in yet more frustration that I'd missed Kian. I'd just have to ask him when they came back later.

TWENTY-SIX

Freya's in her bedroom putting the finishing touches to her make-up when her phone pings through a message.

Am outside. Chop. Chop.

He'd messaged her earlier, asking what she was doing and did she want to go out for a spin. She's bored in the annexe and needs to do something. She feels a bit guilty for not correcting her mum, who assumed it was Kian she was going out with, but Conor had said not to say anything to her as she wouldn't like it, seeing as he worked for John. It's all very complicated, and Freya doesn't know why they are making it difficult. Adults were supposed to be the mature grown-up ones and yet, here they were, not speaking to each other, not wanting their kids to speak to each other. It's all bullshit as far as she can tell.

'I'm going now,' she says, coming through to the living room, but her mum isn't there. She can hear her mum's voice through the open kitchen window, and it sounds like she's on the phone to her dad. Freya smiles. She hopes they will sort things out. She misses her dad not being at home and she knows it's making her mum sad. And her dad, for that matter. That's another adult confusing thing. Her mum and dad love each other and miss each other but can't live together. It's doing Freya's head in and sometimes she feels really angry at them. It's not fair that they are making it so difficult. Can't they see that all three of them are hurting?

She gets into the van, which Conor has stopped down the road.

'All right?' he asks as she climbs in.

'I'm good. You?'

He puts the van into gear and pulls away. 'I am now.'

Freya fastens her seat belt and can feel herself blush a little at his compliment. She embarrasses herself sometimes. She needs to act a bit cooler, like she's used to all this. She doesn't want Conor to think she's some immature kid.

'So, where are we going?' she asks.

'Just for a drive,' he says. 'I've got to drop something off for John and then we can do what we like for a couple of hours.'

Freya's phone pings through a text message. It's from her mum.

> I didn't realise you'd gone. Be back by six for tea. Say hi to Kian for me. Tell him he's welcome to come to tea.

Freya crafts a carefully worded reply.

> Sorry. I did call out. Sure. See you later. Love you. Xx

She kind of feels guilty for letting her mum think she's out with Kian but it's too late to do anything about it.

> Love you too. xx

Conor drives into town and pulls to a stop in the harbour car park.

'I've got to make a delivery,' he says. 'Won't be long.' He hops out of the van and Freya hears the side door sliding open. She looks in her wing mirror and sees Conor lift out a shoebox-sized parcel. He heads off across the road to one of the shops.

Freya passively people-watches. It's easy to spot the tourists from the locals. The former always in groups, usually two couples or families, sometimes a young couple on their own. They mill in and out of the shops and cafés looking all around, taking photos with cameras and smartphones. Whereas the locals walk with purpose, not paying attention to the pretty coloured houses or the harbour view or the selection of ice cream, fudge and cakes strategically placed in the windows of the cafés to tempt trade.

A knock at the window makes her jump. There's a man, maybe in his fifties, smiling at her. His dark hair is flecked with silver and his beard is cut short. He's wearing sunglasses and a suit.

He gestures for her to roll down the window.

Freya looks towards the shop that Conor went in but there's no sign of him. She inches down the window a fraction.

'Hi there,' says the man, removing his sunglasses to reveal sea-green coloured eyes. 'Sorry, I didn't mean to frighten you.'

'It's OK,' mutters Freya. It's not, but what else is she supposed to say?

'I'm looking for Conor,' says the man. 'This is his van, right?'

Freya nods. 'Yes. He's in the shop over there. The yellow one.'

The man doesn't look back at the shops but continues to smile at her. 'Are you riding shotgun for Conor today?'

Freya doesn't know what he means and gives an awkward laugh. 'He won't be long,' she says. The man doesn't take the cue to leave. He doesn't say anything and is practically staring at her with that stupid smile on his face. She looks away and then back again. She glances up towards the shops and is relieved to see Conor jogging across the road towards the van. 'Oh, here he is now.'

The man turns. 'All right there, Conor?' he says.

'Mr Denvers,' says Conor as he reaches the van. 'Everything OK?'

'Sure. I was just talking to the young lady.' He looks back at Freya.

Freya sees an uncertain look cross Conor's face. 'She's Kian Walsh's cousin. Freya.'

Mr Denvers raises an eyebrow. 'Kian Walsh's cousin. Oh, I see. You're Siobhan Regan's daughter, is that right?'

Freya nods. 'Siobhan Martin,' she corrects.

'Of course. Sorry, us Dingle folk we still call everyone by their childhood names,' says Mr Denvers. 'But you're right to correct me. Siobhan and Danny Martin's daughter.' He takes a packet of cigarettes from his pocket and offers one to Freya.

Freya shakes her head. 'I don't smoke.'

Mr Denvers smiles. 'You're a good girl.'

Freya hates the way his gaze lingers on her for a second too long. He offers Conor a cigarette with obvious reluctance, but Conor doesn't read the subtext and is happy to take one.

'Thanks very much, Mr Denvers.' He pops it into his mouth and then pats down his pockets. 'You don't happen to have a light, do ye?'

Mr Denvers produces a lighter from his pocket. Freya's surprised it's not something more fancy than a cheap throwaway one. Conor lights his cigarette and then offers the lighter back to Mr Denvers.

Denvers shakes his head. 'Keep it. Consider it a gift.' He smirks at Freya.

'Oh, thanks very much, Mr Denvers,' says Conor. 'We were just heading off now.'

'Don't let me hold you up,' replies Mr Denvers. 'I'll see you at Mia's party, no doubt.'

'That's right,' replies Conor.

'And Freya?' He turns to her. 'You're more than welcome to come. It's my daughter's birthday party.'

'Kian already said about it,' Freya replies. Then adds, 'Thank you.'

'That's good. Right, I'll be seeing you both soon, then.'

Freya watches with relief as Mr Denvers walks off towards a Mercedes parked nearby.

Conor gets in the van. 'Sorry about that.' He starts the engine. 'You're OK, aren't you?'

'Yeah, why wouldn't I be?' She's not about to admit that Mr Denvers gave her the creeps.

'Just checking. Denvers is a bit... actually, never mind.' Conor steers the car out of the car park and onto the road, heading out of town. 'Let's get out of Dingle. I'll take you to this place where we hang out sometimes.'

They drive out of the town, passing Corin's house, and heading out along the Slea Head Drive. The wind has picked up today and the clouds are being swiftly blown through the sky. It looks like it might rain, and Freya is glad she put her jacket on before she left.

After about ten minutes driving along the narrow coast road, Conor pulls off onto a dirt track. They pass two stone beehive huts, as they are known. So called because of their shape, although Freya has always thought they look more like stone igloos.

'When I was younger, my mum and aunty used to take us to this petting farm,' she tells Conor. 'You could stroke the lambs and then walk around the stone houses.'

'That will be along the road here at Fahan,' says Conor. 'It's a bit of a tourist thing. Sorry, no lambs here.'

Further up the track is an old stone farmhouse and Conor parks the van around the back.

'What's this place?' asks Freya. It looks deserted and the windows at the front are boarded up.

'This is Skerries Cottage. It's the hang-out place,' says Conor. 'Surely you've been up here before?'

'I don't think so. Why do you say that?'

'John Walsh owns it,' says Conor. He gives her a quizzical look. 'Have you never been here? Kian's not brought ye?'

Freya shakes her head. 'No. Never. I'd remember if I had.'

Conor hops out of the van, taking a rucksack and crowbar from behind the seat, and Freya joins him at the back door to the old building. 'I don't know why John doesn't sell this place,' says Conor. 'Or do something with it. Could make a good few euros from the tourists. The Yanks would love it. I think his mother used to live here.'

'Is it safe to go in?' asks Freya as she watches Conor prise the board away from the back door with the crowbar.

'Yeah, we go in all the time. I haven't been for a while, admittedly, but it's cool.'

Conor eases the door open, and it scrapes the step. Freya tentatively follows him inside. It's dark downstairs, with only shafts of light finding their way through the gaps in the boarded-up windows. There's a damp, musty smell and faint whiff of urine as they pass a downstairs toilet. The door is hanging on by one hinge.

They scuff through some newspapers and unopened envelopes that litter the flagstone hallway. There is a room to the left which still has a dresser against the wall. Empty beer cans, Coke bottles and endless cigarette butts taking the place of dinner plates, cups and teapots. It reminds Freya of her nan's kitchen – stuck in a time warp from forty years ago.

'How long since anyone lived here?' she asks.

'Years. Maybe fifteen years. I don't know.'

Conor is at the foot of the stairs now, his hand on the newel post.

'Are we going upstairs?' asks Freya, appraising the wooden staircase with apprehension. She looks towards the room on the other side, which was once the living room. The door is ajar, and she can see a brown floral armchair which is covered in dust and cobwebs. A tattered curtain hangs at the window and the matching half is bundled up on the floor.

'It's better upstairs,' says Conor.

She hesitates. 'I don't like it here. What if someone comes?'

Conor gives a chuckle. 'Sure, no one is going to come here. They never do.' He begins to climb the staircase, which creaks in protest. 'Look, do you want me to take you home?'

'I don't know,' says Freya. She really wants to say yes, take me home right now, but she feels embarrassed.

'Don't be a baby – come upstairs,' said Conor.

She's not a baby and doesn't want to be treated like one. With more reluctance than she felt possible, she puts one foot in front of the other and forces herself to follow Conor to the first floor.

TWENTY-SEVEN

Kathleen hadn't planned on telling Siobhan the secret she's concealed from everyone for all this time. And she meant absolutely everyone, bar one person. But they didn't count, and they weren't going to say anything. They'd already made that perfectly clear.

And now she's about to share her secret with someone else. The only person she could share it with. Siobhan.

'There's something I need to tell you,' she says.

Siobhan frowns. 'OK,' she says slowly.

Kathleen bites her lip. She could still change her mind. Think of something else to say, but no, she realises she is too far along the line. Besides, if someone else knows – and who better than her sister? – then it is some kind of insurance policy.

'There's two things, actually.'

Siobhan nods. 'Kathleen, whatever it is, I won't be shocked or judge you or anything.'

Kathleen offers a ghost of a smile. 'The first thing isn't as bad,' she begins, realising she's stalling. Her usual confidence and ability to confront matters isn't at the front where it usually is. Now it is lagging behind like a reluctant toddler. She reminds herself she's a grown woman and she's dealt with this for the past twenty-plus years, she can deal with it now. 'John has become quite controlling. He's always liked his own way about things. I used to think he was protective. You know, didn't want me to get a job. Wanted me to be a stay-at-home mum. All that type of thing.'

'Yes, I know,' says Siobhan. 'But you were happy about it all, from what I can remember.'

'I was. I felt loved. I felt cherished. Valued,' replies Kathleen. 'But over time – and I'm talking years – it changed. Or I did. I realised him not wanting me to work was so I wouldn't be out of the house, meeting new people, having opinions that weren't necessarily in line with his.'

'John's always liked things his way.'

'Totally. And if I disagree too robustly, we end up in an argument,' says Kathleen. She lets out a sigh. 'I don't know when it happened, I think it was a gradual thing, but I began to push back against it. I matured and realised that John's love was too overbearing. And when I pushed back too much one night, he'd been out drinking and got really angry. He... he got physical.'

'Oh my God, Kathleen. I had no idea.'

'Good. I didn't want anyone to know. I felt embarrassed.'

'You should never have felt that.'

'I know. And that's what they tell you and that's what I tell anyone who comes to The Hub in a similar situation, but when it's you, when it's happening to you, it's very hard to change how you feel.'

'Was it only the once? I mean, how bad was it?'

'The first time it was only a shove.'

'The first time... there were others?'

Kathleen looks at her sister, trying not to resurrect those old feelings of embarrassment. 'It escalated over time. It was a couple of years before he hit me properly.'

'No. No, Kathleen. Not properly. There's no grey area. He hit you, no matter how soft or hard. It's still a physical attack.'

'When I told him I was getting a job at The Hub, we had a furious argument. He forbade it.'

'Unbelievable. Forbidding you to do something. Jesus, that man. Or rather, that excuse for a man.'

'I know.' Kathleen feels ashamed and weirdly a little guilty, almost like she's betraying John for sharing details of their marriage.

'Good for you for standing your ground.'

'Well, that was strange. We had this fight and he went off. Came back a couple of hours later and was a different person. Said he thought it was a good idea to work there if I was insisting on working.'

Siobhan frowns. 'Why would he say that?'

'I didn't know at the time, but Rory Ahern apparently said it would be good and pacified John with promises of being able to keep an eye on me there.'

'For God's sake. Ahern said that?' Siobhan pulls a face at the mention of the sergeant.

'I know. At the time, I thought Rory was only saying that to calm him down. Like, side with me but make John feel like it was a good idea.'

'Why would he do that?'

'Because he's another control freak,' Kathleen explains patiently. 'Why do you think he's a guard?'

'I don't get it.'

Kathleen sighs. 'He was going to report back to John on what I was doing. He also wanted me to tell him anything I was told by people at The Hub, whether it was in confidence or not.'

'He wanted you to be a grass.'

'Pretty much.'

'Did you agree?' Siobhan clearly can't believe what she's hearing.

'More or less, but that was only so I could get some freedom.'

'Oh, Kathleen, this sounds terrible. I had no idea it was that bad.'

'I had the situation under control, believe it or not. I let them think I was oblivious to their scheming, but all this time I've been planning my escape.'

'Does Kian know about any of this? You know, the domestic abuse?' Siobhan asks.

Kathleen winces. She hates that expression when she applies it to her situation. It makes her feel like a victim, but she also knows it's because she is desensitised to the treatment by her husband. The emotional and physical abuse has become part of her marriage. 'Kian's never witnessed any violence, not as far as I know,' she says. 'He's not daft though. He understands the emotional abuse.'

'But Kian's never been on the receiving end?'

'He's been shouted at and told what to do, but John's never laid a finger on him.' Of that Kathleen is certain. There is no way she would tolerate that.

'That's something at least.'

'No. I would have gone long before now if that had happened. And I'd have taken Kian with me. Where, I've no idea, but I would have done something.'

'You could have come to me any time you wanted,' says Siobhan.

'I know,' replies Kathleen, even though she would never have done so. Siobhan had got away from Dingle: why would Kathleen bring it all to her door? 'Look, don't be upset. It wasn't all bad. Just bad at times.'

'You're only saying that to make me feel better,' says Siobhan. 'Did you love John?'

Kathleen lets out a big sigh. 'I thought I did. I tried to and I think I even managed to convince myself for a while. But it's hard to love someone who doesn't love you back. I'm not sure he really loved me; he only married me because I was pregnant.'

'I suppose there is that,' says Siobhan.

'Well, you see, that leads me on to the second thing I need to tell you.' Her words might sound lightweight but the wobble in her voice betrays her. 'It's a bit of a bombshell.'

Siobhan studies Kathleen's expression silently for a moment. She reaches over and holds Kathleen's hand. 'Go on.'

Kathleen can feel the tears gathering in her eyes. She doesn't want to cry. She's not a crier, for God's sake. She blinks hard and swallows before managing to speak. 'John is not Kian's father.'

Siobhan takes an audible gasp of breath. She looks at Kathleen for confirmation.

Kathleen nods.

'Fuck,' whispers Siobhan after a few moments.

Kathleen watches her sister processing this information. No doubt doing the math in her head. She saves Siobhan the trouble. 'The married man I had an affair with is Kian's biological father.' With that, Kathleen can't hold the sobs back any longer.

Twenty years of keeping that knowledge to herself has battered her heart like an Atlantic storm against the cliffs of the Dingle Peninsular. Now, after all that time, in just a single sentence, her defences have been swamped and she feels both liberated and defenceless, all at the same time.

Siobhan cradles her in her arms. Holding her close as she gently rocks and pats Kathleen's back while making soothing noises. Eventually, Kathleen is able to get her crying under control. She pulls away, tugging several tissues from the box.

'That was some bombshell,' says Siobhan after more silence. She sits up straighter and wriggles her shoulders as if shrugging off the shock.

'I'm sorry to burden you with the secret now,' says Kathleen. 'But I wanted someone to know and you're my sister. You're the one I can trust.'

'I take it Corin doesn't know.'

'No. I didn't want her to have to carry on around Mam and Dad, Kian, John, everyone, and pretend she didn't know. You can, you don't live here. You don't have to see them every day.'

'Does the married man know about Kian?' asks Siobhan.

'He does. But he doesn't want anything to do with him,' says Kathleen. 'And now I'm stuck in this lie. How can I tell Kian that John isn't his father, and this other man is?'

'Can you keep it a secret forever, though?' Siobhan asks. 'What if Kian finds out? What if John does?'

'They won't. If they do, it won't be because of me.' Kathleen gets to her feet. 'Look, I have to go.'

'Are you sure about this?'

'Positive. Remember what you've promised me. It's only for a short time, that's all. Once I've been to the guards, got legal advice and sorted something else out, I'll be back.'

Siobhan stands and Kathleen hugs her younger sister. She wants to say she loves her, but it isn't something they'd ever say to each other. She hopes Siobhan knows. Kathleen might not always have been a demonstrative sister – not a hugger, not one for sweet little sentiments – but she loves her sister dearly. Both her sisters. She just needs to do this one thing and then she could be free. And when she's free, she'll be able to set others free too. She owes this to her younger self. She couldn't help her then, but she can now.

'Please be careful, whatever you're doing,' begs Siobhan.

'Sure. I'll be grand,' replies Kathleen. 'I'm not going to be a victim anymore and I'll not stand by and let anyone else be either. I need to be true to myself.'

TWENTY-EIGHT

Freya follows Conor up the staircase. The carpet is worn in places and has come away from the edge. It's sticky and heavily stained; it's hard to see where the pattern ends and the marks begin.

There's more light upstairs as the windows haven't been boarded up and Freya squints as her eyes adjust to the brightness. There's a bathroom at the top of the stairs with a once pink carpet which is now covered in mouldy patches. She catches a glimpse of the toilet bowl and wants to gag at the brown marks but is thankful it at least doesn't have anything in it.

Conor goes into the bedroom at the front of the house, and she is surprised to see a wrought-iron bed frame with a mattress. There's a blanket on the floor and he spreads it out on the mattress and sits down, patting the bed next to him. 'Here,' he says.

Freya feels sick. What happens if she sits on the bed next to him? Is he expecting her to do something? Panic wells up inside her. She does not want to be here. She wants to be home. She is regretting leaving without telling her mum what she's really doing. No one knows she's here.

She feels for her phone in her pocket and wonders if she can call someone? She doesn't know how to phone the police in Ireland. What even is the emergency number?

She takes a step back towards the door, wondering how far she can get before Conor catches her. Will she make it to the back door? She tries to remember if they closed it behind them. It opened out. She should be able to bolt straight through it.

'You don't have to be scared of me,' says Conor. 'I'm not a weirdo or anything. I'm not going to do anything to ye.'

'I just don't want to sit on there,' she says. Her eyes scan the room, and she notices several empty plastic bottles of water piled in the corner next to a bucket which has a piece of wood over it. She can see the sash window has been nailed shut.

'It's not that bad,' says Conor, surveying the bed. 'That's why I put the blanket down.' He brushes it with his hand as if that will make a difference.

'No. You're all right,' she says. 'Still don't want to sit on it.'

He pulls a face. 'Are you always this fussy? Prissy English girl.'

'No.' Freya is on edge and out of her depth. She doesn't know if he's being serious or not. She feels vulnerable and scared. Why the hell did she agree to come up here? She inches towards the door.

Conor bursts out laughing. 'Jesus, I'm only fecking joking. You should have seen your face. What did you think I was gonna do to you?' He falls back on the bed and laughs out loud again, before sitting back up. 'No, seriously, I wouldn't do anything like that. You're safe with me.'

Freya offers a weak smile. She hopes he's telling the truth, but she's not going to let her guard down.

'Can we go somewhere else?' she asks, trying to sound more confident than she feels.

'Sure,' says Conor. 'But tell me something, first.'

'What's that?' Again, her nerves prickle. Conor is unpredictable and she has no idea what he's going to say or do next.

'What's your mam found out about her sister since she's been here this week?'

The question takes Freya by surprise. 'Not a lot,' she replies.

'She must have found out something. Otherwise, why don't people like her being here?'

'She hasn't told me much,' says Freya. She's at the door now and hopes Conor will get up and follow her. She wants to get out of this house as quick as possible.

'But she's found out something?' insists Conor. 'What does she think happened to Kathleen?'

Freya tries to think what she's overheard her mum say to Corin. 'She doesn't think Kathleen left John. She doesn't believe she had an affair.'

'What about that guard, Finn Casey? What's he doing sniffing around your mam?'

Freya isn't sure she likes the turn of phrase but, equally, she doesn't want to object in case it makes Conor angry. He seems very uptight, especially when asking about her mum.

'He likes my mum,' says Freya. 'My mum likes him, but only as a friend. Finn said he'd help her find stuff out. But that's all I know. She hasn't told me much. It's just what I've overheard.' Freya thinks she is going to have to make something up if Conor persists with his questioning. Anything to shut him up.

'Has she said anything else? Anything about anyone else?'

'No. She doesn't tell me stuff.'

Conor gets to his feet and walks over to her. 'I like you a lot, Freya,' he says. He cups the side of her face with his hand. 'I need you to find out what your mam knows. Ask her and then tell me.'

'OK,' she answers, her voice wavering. She wants to swipe his hand away but she daren't. He has a strange look in his eyes.

He's staring at her and then his gaze tours her body from top to toe and back again.

'Yes, find out for me, Freya,' he whispers. 'And when you come to the party tomorrow night, you can tell me everything you know. You'll do that, won't you?'

She nods. 'Yes.'

'There's a good girl. Don't forget, will you?'

'No.'

'Promise?'

'I promise.' She wants to cry but she's also angry at him for making her feel like this. She's angry at herself too.

'Don't break promises or I might have to come and find you,' he pauses. 'Or your mam. Understand?'

'Yes.' Her voice is barely a whisper.

Then he takes a step away and is grinning at her. 'Let's get out of here. It's a shithole, really.'

Freya can't get out of the house quick enough and thanks God, or whoever it is looking out for her, that she will never have to go back there again.

As Conor drives them back to Dingle, he whistles an Abba tune. 'Money, Money, Money'. Freya wants him to stop. It's unbearable. It's weird. He's weird and it's all her fault for getting herself into this situation.

Finally, he pulls up along the road from Corin's house.

'Thanks for the lift,' says Freya quickly, snatching at the door handle to the van. She feels Conor grab her arm and she looks around at him.

'Don't forget,' he says. 'Find out everything your mam knows and tell me tomorrow. Make sure it's everything.'

'Yeah. I will.'

He lets go of her and Freya hops out of the van and hurries back to the annexe. She wants to cry with relief.

'Is everything all right?' her mum asks as she walks through the door.

'Yes. Fine. I need the loo.' Freya scuttles past her mum and into the toilet before she's intercepted. She locks the door and, resting her hands on the sink, she takes deep breaths and manages to keep the tears from falling.

That was sketchy in the derelict house with Conor. She berates herself for going there alone with him. And why does he want to know what her mum's found out about Kathleen? That's weird.

Freya looks up at her reflection in the bathroom mirror. She needs to get a grip on herself. She can't have her mum asking questions, otherwise she won't let her go to the party.

All she has to do is ask her mum a bit about Kathleen and then she can tell Conor and he'll leave her alone after that. Yes. That's a good plan. That's what she'll do.

She flushes the toilet and then washes her hands before going back out to her mum.

'Kian not with you?' asks her mum.

'No,' replies Freya, remembering her mum messaged about asking him for tea. 'I forgot to tell him, but he'll be by again tomorrow. You know I'm going to that party, right?'

Her mum frowns. 'I haven't said a definite yes, yet.'

Freya withholds a huff of annoyance. That will only make her mum dig her heels in. She's got to keep on the right side of her. She goes for a change of tactic.

'How are you getting on with finding stuff out about Kathleen?' she asks.

The frown lifts from her mum's face. 'It's slow going,' she admits. 'There's a girl, Nicole, from The Hub where Kathleen worked, who I've been speaking to.'

'What did she say?'

'She's given me a name of someone Kathleen was trying to help. I've spoken to the girl's mother, and she backs up the story.'

'Do the police know who graffitied the garage?' Maybe Freya can give a name to Conor to get him off her back.

'Not yet. I wouldn't put it past one of the kids from The Hub,' replies her mum. She's looking at her phone. 'But I don't think the kids there are behind it all. I think there's someone else – an adult – involved. I just don't know who yet. Not for certain, anyway.'

'You should get a job as a detective,' says Freya. 'Who do you think the adult is?'

Her mum looks up and Freya recognises the look on her face. She's making an on-the-spot decision whether something is a good idea or not. Freya waits and is eventually rewarded with a reply.

'I'm not sure. Now you can't go saying anything to anyone,' says her mum. 'But I don't trust that guard who came to tea at Nan and Grandad's. You know, Sergeant Rory Ahern? I don't think he's interested in investigating Kathleen's disappearance properly and I think someone else is applying pressure on him.'

Freya's eyes widen. 'Wow. Sounds like some sort of police drama on the telly.'

'I know, right. Anyway, don't be worrying about it all,' says her mum. 'Now, tell me, what did you get up to today?'

Freya looks at her phone. 'Oh, hang on. It's Sophie. I need to speak to her.' She darts off into her bedroom, closing the door behind her. Sophie isn't on the phone at all, but it was a good excuse for Freya not to have to lie to her mum about what she did today.

Instead, she sends a text message to Conor.

> I asked my mum. She says the sergeant is involved.

It doesn't look like much information. She adds a couple more sentences.

And a girl called Nicole from The Hub has been secretly helping my mum. My mum thinks it's all to do with the adults at The Hub. My mum also spoke to the mum of some girl at The Hub my aunt was helping.

There, that should satisfy him. She presses send.

TWENTY-NINE

I was surprised, not to mention pleased, when I got a phone call from Danny the following morning.

'Is everything OK?' I asked immediately, wondering if something had happened at home.

'All good,' he replied. 'Erm... Siobhan...'

It wasn't like him to sound uncertain, and my heart expanded as a surge of love for this man surfaced. I might only have been gone a week, and I might not be living with him, but I was missing him. Maybe being back in Ireland and all the uncertainty the week was bringing was making me feel vulnerable. I don't know, but right then, all I wanted was my husband.

'Yes?' I prompted gently.

'Do you still need to get into Kathleen's iPad?' The uncertainty was gone from his voice now and I couldn't help wondering if he was going to say something else but changed his mind at the last moment. Still, if he was about to offer to help with unlocking the iPad, then I wasn't going to pass up the chance.

'I do. I've got that software on my laptop that you installed when you were using it for work,' I said. 'I was going to see if I could work it out or ask Kian if he had a computer geek for a mate.'

'Ah, well, you know I am the best computer geek around, so I'm at your service.'

There was humour in his voice, and it evoked another resurgence of love for him. Danny the Geek was a little nickname I'd given him a long time ago and it was a joke we hadn't shared for a long time. It brought a smile to my face.

'Danny the Geek is back?' I queried.

'At your service,' he replied with another of our old quips. They were lame jokes, but we had enjoyed them all the same.

'Right, give me a minute. I charged the iPad up the other day. I'll grab it.'

'FaceTime me back,' he said.

'Sure. That will be nice,' I replied. I couldn't remember the last time we'd FaceTimed. It would be nice to see him, and I felt a flutter of excited nerves. I ended the call and grabbed the iPad, setting it all up ready. I was about to FaceTime him back when I suddenly remembered that I hadn't even brushed my hair that morning.

I rushed through to the bathroom and freshened up, before nipping into the bedroom and applying an ever-so-light touch of make-up. Of course, Danny had seen me in all states and conditions, but I wanted him to see me looking presentable. It was vain, but I didn't care. I even added a dash of perfume, ridiculous as it was, but it made me feel more confident in some weird way. It turned out I had insecurities I was unaware of or maybe they had surfaced since he'd moved out.

My phone rang and I let it ring twice before answering.

Danny's face appeared on the screen and my heart somersaulted like a teenager's on a first date with the high school It Boy.

'Hi,' I said, aware the smile across my face was way ahead of my conscious thoughts.

'Hey, there,' replied Danny. 'You OK?'

'I'm good. You?'

'Yeah,' he nodded. 'I'm pretty good, thanks. Freya OK?'

'She's over at Corin's. Promised Sorcha and Erin she'd braid their hair for them this morning.'

He looks disappointed for a moment. 'Ah, not to worry. Right, have you got the laptop and the iPad on?'

'Yes, both right here.' I angle the phone briefly to show him.

'So, go to the laptop and click on the ColdPen logo. That will open up the software to allow us remote access.'

I did as Danny instructed and then proceeded to follow further directions. It was relatively straightforward, but then Danny was an expert and I was just the average user.

'Done all that,' I said as I completed the last sequence.

'Great. Now, double click on Accept and you should be able to see on your screen everything that's on the iPad.'

I watched as the cog icon rotated 360 degrees and then the screen came to life. 'I'm in!' I cried, excited.

'Now you can download everything and that is that.'

'Oh, you're brilliant, Danny! Thanks so much.'

'Right, well, I'll leave you to it. Hope you find whatever it is you're looking for.'

I was disappointed Danny was going already, but at the same time I was so excited now to have full access to Kathleen's iPad. 'Thank you.'

'And, Siobhan…'

I looked away from the screen towards my phone. 'Yeah?' I could see from the look on his face he wanted to say something. 'What is it?'

'I'm sorry I was such a dick over not helping you when you asked me yesterday.'

'That's fine. Don't worry about it,' I said. 'You've helped me now. I'm sorry we argued but I'm glad we're OK.' I wanted to tell him I missed him but didn't want to go in too fast. In fact, I wanted to tell him to come home, and we could stop all this nonsense, but I knew it was too soon. If and when we had that conversation, it needed to be face-to-face.

'Whatever you're doing, please be careful,' he said.

'I will. I promise.'

'And look after Freya. If anything happens to her... well, I don't know what I'd do.'

'Don't worry. Nothing is going to happen. I promise. Trust me.'

'Yeah. Sure.'

'I'll give you a call tonight and let you know how I get on.'

'Oh, not tonight. I'm out,' he said. 'Text me anyway. I've got to go.'

'OK. And thanks again for helping me. I really appreciate it, Danny,' I said.

And then he was saying goodbye and I felt a numbing sensation creeping up on me. He was going out and didn't want to tell me where.

While I was home alone, I turned my attention back to the contents of the iPad and started the *Download all files* mode Danny had told me to implement.

One by one, the files began to ping onto my laptop. I was tempted to start opening them but waited patiently until it was complete, so I didn't interrupt the process.

I had thought about asking Kian to be here – after all, it was his mum – but changed my mind in case I found something he shouldn't see. I thought of my last conversation with Kathleen and the shocking news about John not being Kian's father. I had no idea how Kian would react. As far as he was concerned, John was his dad. Would Kian become curious about his real father and try to find him? And as for John, I've no idea what he'd think of the news. I could only imagine he wouldn't take it well. It would be a complete cluster-fuck going off. The whole thing was just another part of the secret Kathleen had carried for all those years and one which I had inherited.

A message appeared on the screen, breaking into my thoughts. *Download complete.* I was surprised there were only five files altogether. For some reason I'd expected more, and it made me go back into the system to check on the iPad, but that was all that was there. Five files numbered, unimaginatively, one through to five.

I clicked on file 1. It contained JPEG images, and I began to open them. They were all taken in and around The Hub. I had seen some of these on social media and on the noticeboard at the centre. There was another folder within this folder, marked 1a. I double-clicked and there were three more JPEGS within that.

Picture 1 was Rory Ahern talking to Dervla Collins. They were in The Hub sitting at one of the café tables. Ahern was in uniform. Neither looked particularly happy and the picture was obviously taken without their knowledge, probably on a phone.

Picture 2 looked like to be a still from CCTV. Taken within The Hub, it showed someone – a man with his back to the camera – heading down the corridor to where Aisling Denvers' offices were.

Picture 3 was another CCTV still shot, but this time the figure was coming out of Aisling's office. It was Rory Ahern. The clothing, hair and build of both figures were the same. It was safe to assume that picture 2 was also of Rory.

I wasn't sure what the images proved or disproved, but that was all there was.

I went to the second folder.

As before, there were photographs of events at The Hub, but it was the sub-folder I was interested in. I opened it and there was just one JPEG in it this time.

It was of Rory Ahern outside a shop. I looked closer. It was the fish and chip shop or, rather, the side door to the flat above the premises. It looked like he was about to enter and was checking the street before he did so.

Folder 3 followed the same format as the previous two. The JPEGs were of Aisling Denvers talking to Dervla in the car park outside The Hub. It was looking down on them, so maybe from an upstairs window. It must be storage up there, as The Hub appeared to be one level. I made a note to try to find out. The second photo was taken from a distance and on a mobile phone. It was grainy and hard to make out the image. It looked like three people, possibly Aisling and Fergus Denvers with someone else who I couldn't make out, walking into a farmhouse of some description. It looked like it had been raining or was raining, the way they were hunched forward slightly. The house could be any house on the Dingle Peninsular. Stone-built, slate roof with nothing but fields around it. Maybe they were going to a party or to someone's house for dinner.

I sighed at my inability to decipher the relevance of the photos. They meant something important to Kathleen, otherwise why would she have gone to the trouble of keeping them on her secret tablet and hidden within other files? If only there was a Word doc explaining it all. Of course, that would be far too simple.

I opened the next folder without paying too much attention to the photos that came up immediately; they were of what looked like Kian's birthday. A couple taken around the table and him grinning with a chocolate birthday cake in front of him. No doubt made by Kathleen.

As expected, there was another folder further down the screen. It took me a moment to realise what I was looking at. The greens, yellows, blues, purples and browns looked like abstract art, but as my brain made sense of them, I wanted to cry. The canvas to the swirls and splurges of colour was skin. Kathleen's skin, with an array of bruises.

'Oh God, Kathleen,' I said, shocked at the savagery of the horror show in front of me.

Bruises inflicted by John on parts of her body that wouldn't show. He knew exactly what he was doing. An upper arm. A thigh. One taken in the mirror of her back. Five photos in all. I wanted to be sick. I wanted to scream. I wanted to inflict the same sort of injuries on John.

The tears poured from my eyes. I'd reported on acts of violence before, but to see the callous brutality inflicted on my sister by the man who was supposed to love and protect her was beyond shocking.

What she must have suffered and never told anyone was beyond me. I wished she had been able to confide in someone. If I had stayed in Ireland, I could have been there for her. Not for the first time, guilt at leaving Dingle battered my heart.

I closed the images. My hand was shaking as I clicked on the final folder. I was expecting to see much the same format as I had for the other files, but this one contained a voice note.

I clicked the play button and waited a few seconds while the recording buffered and then began.

As I listened, my heart raced. It was a conversation between Kathleen and a man. The quality wasn't great, and I had to assume she had recorded this without the other person's knowledge. The more I listened, the more amazed I became.

It only lasted a couple of minutes, but it was most definitely bombshell worthy. I sat back in the chair. I needed to hear it again.

In fact, I listened to it twice more. Just to be certain what I was hearing. There was no way I could risk losing this file or it being damaged in some way, so I quickly sent a copy to my email address and saved a duplicate file to a memory stick I had in my bag. Finally, I opened a Word doc and began to create a transcript of the conversation. It was a laborious task of pressing play, listening, pausing the recording, and then typing up that sentence before starting the cycle all over again for the next part.

Eventually, I had a full transcript of the conversation, which I saved to my laptop, to the memory stick and emailed myself a copy.

I then read the whole document, to cement it in my mind. Reading was a different experience to listening and I didn't want to miss a thing.

THIRTY

TRANSCRIPT

Kathleen
Come in.

Male
What is all this about? All this cloak and dagger. I haven't got long, so get on with it.

Kathleen
You mean you can't guess what it's about?

Male
No. As a matter of fact, I can't.

Kathleen
Do you want tea?

Male
No I fecking don't. This is not some tea party. What do you want?

Kathleen
OK. I'll get straight to the point if that's the way you want it.

Male
Thank you.

Kathleen
It's about Dervla Collins.

Male
[Pause] Who?

Kathleen
You know exactly who I mean.

Male
Remind me.

Kathleen
The young woman from The Hub. The one you've been seeing on the sly. The one you've been shagging.

Male
Oh, fuck off, Kathleen. You don't know what you're talking about.

Kathleen
[sounds angry] Don't bullshit me. She's told me all about you.

Male
Enlighten me.

Kathleen
Dervla Collins. Eighteen years old. Lives up on Main Street with her mother Orla Collins. Dervla, long dark hair. Petite. Lonely. Vulnerable.

Is that beginning to ring any bells?

Male
I think I know who you mean but I come across a lot of young women, and older ones, at The Hub, so that's probably why I don't really know who she is.

Kathleen
You've befriended her. Looked after her. Given her money. Bought her things. All your usual signature moves. Don't look like you're insulted. Remember. I know.

Male
You're not jealous, are you, darling Kathleen?

Kathleen
Don't touch me.

[A long pause]

Male
Think you're above all this now, do you? Married to John Walsh, local businessman. Live in a big house.

Kathleen
This isn't about me and you. This is about Dervla. You need to stay away from her.

Male
Do I? I don't think you're in a position to tell me what I can and can't do.

Kathleen

I'll expose you. I don't think it will go down too well with your connections, will it?

Male
Are you threatening me?

Kathleen
No. I'm promising.

Male
How do you think your family will feel when they find out the truth about you? What you're really like? Your secret.

Kathleen
[sounding less confident] I don't care about that anymore. Maybe it's time the truth came out. I'm prepared to sacrifice my anonymity to save a young woman from going through the same thing I did. Dervla is not eighteen for another couple of months.

Male
She's legal age. Not that it interests me.

Kathleen
[makes scoffing noise] You're a fucking liar. She's a minor. You stay away from her.

Male
I think this conversation is over. I don't know what you're talking about.

Kathleen
I swear to God, if it's the last thing I do, I will expose you. I will go to court. It's bad enough I have to live with what happened to me. I am

not letting another young person go through that. Especially when she wants out and you won't let her.

Male

Oh, how very noble of you. I don't believe for one moment you'll do that because then you'll have to tell the whole truth. You may not care what people think about you. But your husband won't be impressed. Nor will your son.

Kathleen

This is nothing to do with Kian. [Fear in her voice]

Male

Oh, now that sounds like I've found a chink in your armour.

Kathleen

You leave my son out of this. [Raising her voice with barely controlled anger]

Male

[gives a derisory laugh] You seem to be forgetting something, Kathleen. [Pauses, then in a low voice] He's my son too.

Kathleen

[Angry scream. Shouting] Don't you dare say that. You don't deserve to use that word. He is no son of yours.

Male

We can always let a court of law decide that. There's such a thing as DNA testing. Not sure what John will think to that, though.
[Scuffling of furniture]
Get off me, woman! Feck's sake, Kathleen. Get a grip.

Kathleen

[Panting hard and then crying]

Male
Jesus, you've made my face bleed. What the hell is wrong with you?

Kathleen
Leave Dervla alone and get out of here.

Male
[Menacing voice] You are on thin ice. You'd better watch your step.

Kathleen
[calling out to him as if he's leaving] Feck you, Fergus! Feck you!

I played the recording once again and read through the transcript to ensure I had it down word for word.

THIRTY-ONE

Ahern pulls the collar up on his coat as he gets out of the car. It's particularly dark up at Skerries Farm. It's an isolated spot, set back and barely visible from the road. He's parked around the back of the building, reversing in so he can make a quick exit if needed. Not that he's expecting any trouble. Not tonight. But it's best to be prepared.

It's his usual meeting spot with Conor Doyle. In fact, it was Conor who suggested it. Ahern prefers to communicate over the burner phone he has, but tonight he needs to give Conor something. He's not particularly comfortable with the plan, but Denvers is insistent and it's a big payday for Ahern. He's recently upped his prices. This is a new level Denvers is going to, and the increase in fees is totally justifiable: Maureen's treatment fund is looking healthier than ever.

The weather isn't great, and it looks like it's going to rain. He could do without this meeting, but that Siobhan Regan won't take a warning. Everyone is getting twitchy.

As is usual, Ahern switches on the voice record app on his phone. He keeps the recordings stored away safely. No one knows about them, but if ever things unravel, this will be his evidence for plea bargaining. Not only that, it's good insurance against anyone blackmailing him.

Conor's transit van is already parked, and Rory can see the glow of the interior light. As he approaches the van, the door opens, and Conor hops out.

'All right there, Rory?' says Conor.

Ahern bristles at the informality of the greeting. Conor's a cocky git for sure. No respect, these youngsters. Back in the day, his mere presence on the horizon would put the fear of God into the kids. He blames the parents and schools. They've all gone soft in the head.

'Conor,' says Rory. The smell of weed is strong, clinging to the lad. 'You fecking stink. Try opening the window of the van when you're smoking that shit.'

'Now why would I want to do that? Sure, that's a waste letting it all drift off into the fresh air.' Conor grins. 'So, what's up? Need someone else following, vehicle modifications? What did you think to my last bit of artwork?'

Ahern inwardly sighs at the pathetic childlike pride Conor has about his low-level harassments. Although Ahern didn't sign off on the bottle of urine fiasco. That was Conor going free-lance and enjoying himself far too much.

'You need to stick to the script.'

'Sure, I promise. No more piss-throwing, I know.' He holds his hands up in surrender. 'So, what's it to be?'

'You're going to Mia Denvers' party, right?'

'Yeah. Me and a few others.'

Ahern nods. He's hesitant about the plan Denvers came up with. He hasn't been one hundred per cent certain he was going to even ask Conor to go through with it until this very point. There's a lot on the line if Siobhan Regan uncovers anything else. She's far too close to the truth, whether she realises it or not. He reminds himself what's at stake. He thinks of his wife's medical expenses. With that extra money, she can have all the care she needs. They can get her to America for that treatment the doctors in the US are trialling.

He swallows. Yes. He's going to go through with it. It will be the last one he'll do, though. After this, he's out. He'll have money in the bank and enough digital insurance to keep everything and everyone quiet.

He tells Conor what he needs him to do. 'Don't involve anyone else. Got it?'

It's hard to tell in the dark with only a weak moon for light, but he can see Conor looks concerned. The lad shifts on his feet. 'Sounds like shit just got serious.'

'Not entirely. Think of it as prevention rather than cure.'

Conor lights a cigarette and lifts his chin up to the sky as he blows out the smoke. 'I don't know.'

'Don't go getting cold feet now,' Ahern warns.

'It's a bit more than the usual,' says Conor. 'I don't like the sound of it.'

Ahern is ready for this. 'I'll double your money if it all goes smoothly. I don't want any feck-ups.'

'Double, you say?' Conor looks tempted, but still uncertain.

'You don't have a lot of choice,' says Ahern. 'You know I can have you arrested and banged up at a moment's notice. I'm sure you don't want a stay in Cork prison, now, do you? They'll like a good-looking lad such as yourself.'

'But what you're asking is serious shit,' says Conor. 'I might just take my chances.'

Ahern has another card up his sleeve. 'How's your mam, these days? Business going well?' Conor's mother is known to offer her personal services to locals and holidaymakers alike. 'Hope she's keeping safe.'

'You leave my mother out of this,' snaps Conor.

'And that is entirely down to you.' Ahern doesn't want to threaten the lad in this way, but he doesn't have any choice.

'OK. I'll do it,' says Conor after a while.

Ahern reaches into his pocket and passes a small plastic zip bag, no bigger than a matchbox, to Conor. 'It's in there.'

Conor takes the bag and looks at the contents through the clear plastic. 'Doesn't look much.'

'It's enough.'

'OK. Usual terms and conditions, then,' says Conor.

Ahern takes an envelope from his other pocket which he gives to Conor. Conor inspects the envelope and flicks through the euro notes.

'You'll get the other half once it's all done,' says Ahern. 'We have a deal?'

Conor holds out his hand. 'It's a deal.'

Ahern doesn't want to shake hands at all, but he does nevertheless, before walking back to his car. Once inside, he uses the hand sanitising gel from the glove box. He can't risk taking any germs back home to his wife.

He takes one last look in his rear-view mirror at Conor Doyle standing at the back of his van. Conor tips a salute with his forefinger and Ahern heaves a sigh of relief. Not long now, and all this will be over for good.

THIRTY-TWO

The week has dragged, and Freya couldn't be happier that it is
Friday night and she's going to the party at Mia Denvers' house.
Freya is glad she bought some decent clothes with her and takes
some pride in admiring herself in the mirror. She has no idea
what the fashion in Dingle is. Kian told her to dress down in
something casual, but Freya is well aware she is going to be
partying with people Kian's age and she wants to look older
than fifteen.

Her mum comes and stands in the doorway. 'You look nice,'
she says. 'Just pull the dress down a bit; it's quite short.'

Rather than get into a row with her mum, Freya wriggles
the stretchy dress down. She can pull it back up once she's out
of sight of her mother.

'Kian should be here soon,' says Freya, flicking her hair over
her shoulder and then turning around to look back at herself.
Yes, she is definitely going to pull the hem of the dress up. She
might as well be Amish otherwise. She smiles at her mum.
'Have you heard from Dad again?'

She notices her mum tense a fraction, even though Siobhan

pretends to be casual like she's not bothered. 'No. Not today,' she replies. 'Have you?'

'No. I thought he might call you at least,' says Freya. She didn't think that at all, but it distracts her mum enough that she doesn't say any more about what Freya is wearing. A text message pings in. 'Oh, that's Kian.' She picks up her bag and gives her mum a kiss on the cheek as she sidesteps through the bedroom doorway.

'I want to speak to Kian,' says her mum.

Freya rolls her eyes but she's facing the door and her mum can't see. 'What about?'

'I want to check what time you're getting home.'

'You don't have to worry; I'll be fine with Kian.' Freya hurries out the door, but her mother is hot on her heels.

Freya jumps into the passenger seat. 'Drive.'

Kian looks confused. 'I think your mam wants to speak to you.'

'No. It's you she wants.'

'Ah, Kian,' says Siobhan, coming around to his side of the car. 'I just wanted to check what time you're bringing Freya back? I'm thinking midnight.'

'Yes, sure. That's fine. I'll make sure she's back and don't worry, I'll look after her.'

'I know you will. Have fun both of you. See you at midnight, Cinderella.'

Siobhan laughs at her own joke, but Freya groans. 'Bye, Mum. Love you.'

Kian drives away and heads across town towards the harbour. 'We're meeting a couple of mates for a drink on the beach first,' he says. 'That OK with you?'

'Sure.'

Kian's friends are all very nice. They say hi to her and ask her how the week has been going. She recognises a couple of them who she met earlier in the week. Kian gives her a beer and she smiles gratefully. She'd be mortified if he'd given her a Diet Coke or some other fizzy drink. He leans over and whispers in her ear that she can't go mad with the booze. Freya smiles in acknowledgement and begins to relax.

After an hour, they bundle into Kian's car and he drives them all to Mia's house, where the party appears to be in full swing. The evening is warm and the sound of chatter and laughter mixes with the music that drifts in the night air from around the back of the house.

Freya follows Kian and his friends in through the front door of the double-fronted house with dormer windows in the roof. The hallway is vast and the property spreads both left and right. They walk through to a large open-plan kitchen and family room. The back of the house leads onto a terrace and the bifold doors are wide open so it's hard to work out where the kitchen ends and the gardens begins. There are people everywhere, and Kian and Freya squeeze their way through to the kitchen island that has been transformed from a vegetable prep area to a bar.

People are saying hello to Kian and calling out to him and his friends. Girls hug him and some kiss him in greeting. Kian turns and ushers Freya further into the party. Someone shoves a bottle in his hand and another into Freya's. Kian is introducing Freya to a girl.

He has to shout above the noise. 'This is Mia. Mia this is my cousin, Freya.'

'Hi there,' says Mia, smiling.

'Hi. Thanks for letting me come,' Freya replies, and then wishes she had said something cooler. She sounds such an idiot.

'No problem. I vaguely remember you from a few years ago.'

They smile at each other and then Mia is whisked away by a couple of other girls.

Kian says something that is drowned out by the noise but he's gesturing towards the garden and Freya tags along. She feels like a puppy dog, trotting along behind him. She is out of her depth, but at the same time wants to try to prove she's mature. She wishes her friend Sophie was with her.

'Back in a minute,' says Kian in Freya's ear. 'Wait here.'

Kian is off through the partygoers, leaving Freya on her own. It didn't take him long to ditch her and now she's standing there, not knowing where to look or what to do with her hand that isn't holding the bottle. With no pocket to stuff it into, she holds the bottle with both hands and tries to look casual.

There's a swimming pool in the back garden and a barbecue in the corner where a man is on burger and hot dog duty. His baseball cap obscures his face as he looks down at the grill. He's wearing an apron and, as he moves from behind the grill to grab some buns, Freya sees it has a muscled torso in a pair of swimming briefs printed on the front. She wants to gag. What a weirdo.

She suddenly remembers the man who had spoken to her when she was in Conor's van the other day and realises that it's the same man at the grill. Mia Denvers is his daughter. She shudders.

'Not a pretty sight, is it?'

Freya spins around and sees Conor standing there.

'Not at all,' she replies.

'He fancies himself something rotten,' says Conor. 'I saw the way he was looking at you the other day.'

'He's a creep. Why can't men grow old gracefully?' Freya thinks of her own dad and hopes he never dons an apron like that. She'd die.

'I know, right? He must be well into his fifties. And that's Mia's mother over there. Aisling Denvers.' He points to a woman standing to the side.

Aisling has striking red hair fashioned in a precision-cut bob. She's wearing linen trousers and a floaty top. To Freya's mind, the woman looks quite sophisticated. Unlike her husband.

'They don't look like a couple,' says Freya.

'Marriage of convenience,' says Conor. He takes a sip from the bottle of beer he's drinking. 'Thanks for the text message. Made for interesting reading.'

'Good.' Freya is relieved.

Conor puts his hand around Freya's arm. 'Come over here. I want you to meet my friends.'

Freya glances over to where Kian is sitting, hoping to catch his eye and send a pleading look, but he's too interested in the girls he's with. Conor is already guiding her over to the table and she reluctantly goes with him.

There is another lad and two girls sitting at the white plastic table. They look up as Conor practically plonks Freya down in an empty chair, before pulling up another for himself. 'All right, everyone,' he says. 'This is Freya.'

The others smile at her. Conor doesn't offer their names in return and Freya is too shy to ask.

'You friends with Mia?' asks the other lad.

'No. I'm here with my cousin,' says Freya.

'And I guess you're not from Ireland,' says the lad. 'That's definitely an English accent. My name's Declan, by the way.'

'I live in Brighton,' says Freya, wondering if he's heard of the place.

'Ah, sure, I know Brighton,' says Declan. 'Been there on a lads' holiday once. Nice place.'

'It's OK.'

'Who's your family?' asks one of the girls.

'The Regans. Do you know them?'

'Wait. The Regans. I know that name,' says Declan, putting his hand to his forehead as if it will help summon the answer he is looking for. 'The one who went missing, yes?'

'That's right. That's my aunt. Kathleen Walsh. She's my

mum's sister and I'm here with my cousin, Kian Walsh. Do you know him?'

'Of course, I know ya man. I'm sure the six degrees of separation is half that here.' Declan gives a laugh. 'Kian was a couple of years above me at school.'

'How do you know Conor?' asks the girl.

Conor gives a laugh. 'Ah, sure, you're not jealous, are you, Sheena?'

'Go away. Why would I be jealous about you?' scoffs Sheena, pulling a face at Conor. 'I may be fed up but I'm not hard up.'

Declan and the other girl laugh. Freya can't help giggling at the put-down.

Conor ignores Sheena's jibe and turns to Freya. 'You want something stronger?' He nods at the beer bottle she's holding and gives her one of his winks.

'I don't mind,' says Freya. She really wants to say no, but that would be embarrassing.

'Wait there. I'll be two seconds,' says Conor.

The others slip back into their conversation and Freya sits there in silence until Conor arrives with another can of Coke. He puts it down on the table. 'I've slipped some vodka in there for you,' he says.

'Thanks,' says Freya. She picks up the can and takes a sip, nearly choking on the strength of the vodka.

Sheena laughs at her and turns to Conor. 'I hope you haven't been too heavy-handed there. I'm not sure our English friend is used to alcohol.'

'Ah, she's grand, aren't you, Freya?' says Conor.

Freya feels the burn of embarrassment. 'Sure,' she says.

'What time do you have to be home?' asks Sheena.

Freya swallows an uncomfortable lump in her throat. 'No time.'

'Ooh, no time,' mimics Sheena. 'What are you, some sort of

wild child?'

Freya forces herself to laugh. 'Something like that,' she says.

'Do you take after your mam, then?' asks Sheena.

Freya is wary at the mention of her mum. 'What do you mean?'

'I hear your mam's not very popular around the town,' says Sheena.

Freya notices a tense silence around the table. 'I don't know anything about that.'

'She's been pissing off a lot of people,' says Sheena. 'Going around asking questions about Kathleen Walsh and what happened to her. Like she's some kind of private detective, that's what my mam said.'

'Leave it,' warns Conor.

'Feck off telling me what to do,' says Sheena.

Declan leans towards Freya. 'Take no notice. She's had a few drinks. Always shooting her mouth off.'

'Go feck yourself, Declan,' snaps Sheena.

Freya definitely doesn't want to be there. She wants to be any place other than the party. Especially now she knows her mum is having the piss taken out of her by everyone. For fuck's sake, why did her mum even come here and start interfering? She should have left it and Freya should have refused to come with her. She should have just turned up on her dad's doorstep.

'Look, whatever my mum does is nothing to do with me,' says Freya, hoping to rescue the situation. 'If you must know, I think she should leave it.'

Sheena raises her eyebrows, clearly surprised by what she's hearing. 'So you agree that your mam is an interfering old cow?'

Freya can see the challenge in Sheena's eyes. If Freya agrees, then she will feel disloyal to her mum; if she defends her mum, then it will cause more trouble with Sheena. Everyone is waiting for her response. Freya takes a gulp of her vodka and Coke. 'Yes, she's an interfering old cow.'

For a moment there's silence and then Sheena bursts out laughing. Everyone else around the table laughs out loud too. 'Maybe you're not such a stuck-up English fecker after all,' says Sheena as she pauses to catch her breath.

Freya politely laughs along but she feels hot and flustered. She gets up using the excuse that she needs the toilet and hurries off into the house before anyone suggests they come with her.

THIRTY-THREE

Kathleen is in her bedroom at home. Alone. She is sitting by the full-length window in the front gable of the house which overlooks the driveway. That way, she can see who is approaching the house before they've even got to the door.

She hasn't got long; she needs to upload the conversation she had with Kian's biological father. She had never wanted to confront him – that's why she has stayed silent for all these years. She has never felt the need to tell the truth. It might alleviate her guilt at keeping it a secret, but it absolutely wouldn't be of comfort to anyone else. The ripple effect would cause so much devastation for everyone involved. As for her parents, they would be horrified. They would not appreciate the dirty washing aired in public. She gives a small smile at the expression. Never had it been so appropriately assigned. God-loving and God-fearing – or rather, gossip-fearing, Kathleen had always thought.

She Airdrops the voice note from her phone to the iPad and

replays it in full, just to make sure it has all transferred correctly. Then she sends another copy to her secret email account, before wiping the phone clean of any electronic trace. It's easier and less painful, wiping digital footprints.

She looks at the small box at her feet. It's a memory box where she keeps sentimental things. Some from her own childhood, but mostly from Kian's. The first drawing he did at nursery school. His little footprints from two weeks old where she and Siobhan had painted his tiny little feet with blue poster paint and then pressed them against a piece of card. They'd done the same with his handprints. John had smiled and said it was sweet but had not been as impressed as her and her sister had. There was the little note from the tooth fairy that Kathleen had written and left under Kian's pillow when his first tooth had come out. He must have been about five then, she thinks. And Kian's school photos. His First Holy Communion photo with the little prayer book her parents had given him. Then his Confirmation photograph. He had been less enthusiastic about this and had agreed to it more out of tradition and not wanting to upset her and John, who in turn didn't want to upset their own parents.

Hasn't that been the story of Kathleen's life? Always doing the right thing – at least on the surface, where you could be judged. Behind closed doors, that's where the secrets lurk.

She digs deep into the memory box. No one looks in here. John isn't the sentimental type and Kian has no desire to revisit the *Oh my God it's so embarrassing* memorabilia of his childhood, so Kathleen has always known it is a safe place to hide her big secret. The box has a piece of card in the bottom and hidden underneath that is the envelope she has secreted away.

A car engine in the lane makes her look up through the window towards the oak gates. She's not expecting John home, but she's always on her guard. A car passes by and continues on its way, and Kathleen breathes easier again. She turns her attention back to the false bottom of the box and, catching the corner with her pink-polished fingernail, she lifts the base up and takes out the envelope. It only has two things in it.

She hasn't looked at these for a long time, and her heart picks up the pace with anticipation.

The photograph brings back so many memories. Things she knows, embedded in her mind like computer coding, but to see it again makes her brain reproduce them with such startling quality it's like she has triggered a 3D printer. She feels she can reach out and touch that face again. Twenty years ago, when they were so much younger and so much in love. She closes her eyes, and her fingers slowly retrace the jawline, stubble grazing her fingertips. She can sense the line of his nose and the sweep of his lips, remembering how they felt on hers. She recaptures that giddy feeling of being totally in love. The excitement of even thinking about seeing him and then the fizzy tummy, the fluttery heartbeat, the racing pulse. It all comes back to her. God, she loved him then.

Kathleen puts the photo to one side and then slips out the flimsy and shiny strip of paper. There are two black-and-white ultrasound images of Kian. Her surname and the date printed at the top, together with the estimated due date. John had never paid too much attention to her antenatal appointments, so when she went into labour, he simply assumed she was a couple of weeks early. In reality, she was two weeks overdue. He had questioned the discrepancy once in the delivery suite when he'd made mention of the baby not coming on the right date. The midwife had swiftly dismissed his query, reminding him that dates are only an estimate.

Kathleen lays the ultrasound on the floor alongside the photograph and, using her phone, takes a picture of each. She emails her secret account with these and sends copies to her iPad. As before, she deletes the images from her phone and then deletes the outgoing emails, confident she has covered her tracks.

A tear makes its way down her face in compassion for her seventeen-year-old self. Loaded with twenty more years of knowledge, she wants to wrap the naive and innocent Kathleen Regan up in her arms and take her away from all the pain that waits around the corner.

She slips the photograph and scan image into her handbag.

Her phone rings and makes her jump. It's the throwaway untraceable one which contains only one number in the contacts list. She accepts the call.

'Hi,' comes Dervla's voice.

'Hi. You all set for the morning?' asks Kathleen.

'Yes.'

'And what have you told your mam?'

'Exactly what you told me to say,' replies Dervla. 'That I've a job in Cork, which is the truth anyway.'

'Was she OK about you leaving this morning?'

'She was fine. I'm not sure she's that bothered. I'll be one less thing for her to worry about.'

'And the place you're staying is OK?' Kathleen rubs her forehead. She can feel a headache coming on.

'Yes. Stop worrying. I'm safely in the Travelodge in Tralee. I took the bus like you said,' replies Dervla. She pauses before continuing. 'Are you OK? You sound a bit stressed.'

'Sorry. Been a hectic day. I've had a lot to sort out,' replies Kathleen. 'Plus, my sister's surprise visit from England this weekend hasn't helped. We're out tonight. Down the pub.'

'Lucky you.'

'Not really. I could do without it, but Corin and Siobhan thought I'd like the surprise. I'm going to have to go along with it all but as soon as I can I'll be there. Just stay low.'

Dervla laughs. 'You're making it sound like some gangster movie with your "just stay low".' She mimics Kathleen's words but with an American New York accent.

Kathleen feels a rush of irritation, but she manages to check herself. 'Please be careful,' she says. 'We don't want anything going wrong now.'

THIRTY-FOUR

The party is even busier now. Freya has to shuffle her way through the kitchen out into the main hall where still more people are standing around talking. Someone is on their mobile phone and another couple sitting on the stairs are snogging each other's faces off.

There are several doors off the main entrance hall. Surely one of these must be the downstairs loo.

'There's a bathroom upstairs you can use.'

Freya turns and one of the girls in the group chatting smiles at her. She points upstairs. 'Top of the stairs. Left at the end of the hall.' She gives a quizzical look. 'Or it might be right. Anyway, I'm sure you'll find it.'

Freya mumbles a thanks and, sidestepping around the two stair-snoggers, heads up to the first floor. The upper floor of the house heads off in three directions: left, right and towards the back of the house. It reminds Freya of a hotel rather than a home.

She spots an open door and can see a light-pull dangling from the ceiling and a white tiled wall. Once inside the bathroom, she locks the door, glad to have five minutes to herself.

She uses the loo, washes her hands and then sends a Snapchat to Sophie of her reflection in the mirror, pouting with her fingers held up to the side of her face in the peace sign.

She captions it.

Bathroom party selfie!

She adds it to her story on Instagram with the hashtags #ireland #party #selfie #funtimes.

The last hashtag is a complete lie. Freya does not want to be there anymore, but it's still an hour and a half before she has to be home. The handle on the bathroom door rattles and someone bangs on the door, declaring they are desperate and can whoever is in the loo please hurry up.

Reluctantly, Freya vacates the bathroom, barely getting out before two girls bowl in.

Freya goes back through to the kitchen where she finds a clean glass and fills it from the tap with cold water before drinking it in one go. Her head is killing her. She needs to get out of this place. Freya walks out onto the terrace, deciding she'll have to find Kian and get him to take her home. She can see Conor at the table, looking at his phone. She wonders if she can sneak past without being noticed.

She's about to dodge by when he looks up. He sees her and smiles, waving in her direction, and then beckons her over.

'I thought you'd got lost,' he says when she makes her way over to the table.

'I was on the phone to my friend,' says Freya.

'I've got you another drink,' says Conor, passing her a can of Coke. 'Come and sit down.'

'Yeah. Thought you'd ditched us,' says Sheena.

Freya sits down, wondering how long a polite amount of time will be before she can leave.

Kian appears at Freya's side. 'You all right there?' he asks.

'She's grand,' says Conor.

The girl Kian was talking to earlier drapes herself over him. 'So this is your English cousin?' She waggles her fingers by way of hello at Freya, who nods and smiles in return. Then the girl is pulling on Kian's arm. 'Come on, I want to dance.'

Kian doesn't protest and off he goes.

Despite her earlier bravado in front of Sheena, Freya is beginning to wish she hadn't come to the party at all. When Kian came over, she found herself hoping he'd say it was time to get back. But judging by the way he's hooked up with that girl, he isn't going to be leaving any time soon.

As she scans the terrace, her eyes fall on Mia Denvers' father, who is tidying up the grill area now under the sharp stare of Aisling Denvers.

As if sensing she's being watched, Aisling turns around and her eyes meet Freya's. The older woman pauses, but then her gaze flicks to Conor and the rest of the group. She smiles and waves at them, before tipping her head towards the bin bag she's holding open for her husband to dump the rubbish.

'What's she like?' asks Freya.

'She's all right. Has a lot to say about most things, but then she is the local councillor,' says Declan.

Freya is distracted by Sheena and the other girl laughing wildly about something and she goes back to being on the periphery of the group as they share a joke. Freya sips her drink and checks her phone. There's a Snapchat from Sophie, who looks to be at another friend's house on a sleepover. She's in her PJs with a face mask on and poking her tongue out at the camera. Freya snaps a picture of the party with the pool in the background and captions it with *The Irish know how to party!* before sending it to Sophie. Freya feels a pang of homesickness. She wants to be there with Sophie. She wants to feel relaxed. She wants to feel safe. She doesn't know where that notion has come from, but she's out of her comfort zone here.

She takes another sip of her drink, finishing off the can.

'Want another?' asks Conor.

She shakes her head. 'No, I'm fine.'

'It's a party. Come on, you can have another,' urges Conor.

'No. Honestly, I'm fine.' Freya is far from fine. She feels sick. She gets to her feet and the ground beneath her tips. She grabs the back of the chair.

Conor puts a hand out to steady her. 'You OK?'

Freya frowns. 'I'm fine.'

'She's fine. Didn't you hear her? She's fine.' Sheena is mimicking Freya's English accent.

'I'm going to the toilet,' says Freya.

'I thought you'd just been,' says Conor.

'What are you, my keeper?' retorts Freya. Her head is pounding, and her throat is dry.

'Never you mind why a girl has to go to the bathroom, Conor Doyle,' says the girl whose name Freya still doesn't know. The girl turns to Freya. 'Here, I'll go with you.' The girl picks up her bag, which is more like a rucksack. Freya wonders what she's got in there. The bag is overflowing and a yellow sleeve of a jumper or jacket or some sort of garment is hanging out. The girl stuffs the yellow sleeve back into the bag. She squashes it down and fastens the zip before coming around to Freya and linking arms with her. 'Come on, I'll show you where to go.'

Freya doesn't tell the girl she already knows, but she's grateful of the steadying arm as they half-walk and half-stagger back into the house.

THIRTY-FIVE

'Jesus Christ, Siobhan!' Corin's eyes almost bulged from her head as I finished relaying to her what I'd found on Kathleen's iPad.

'Shh, don't be shouting now,' I said, glancing back towards the house where Niall was sitting in the living room watching the hurling on the television. Sorcha and Erin were tucked up in bed. It was getting on for nine thirty and Corin and I were sitting out on her patio, the firepit alight and blankets wrapped around our shoulders while we shared a bottle of wine. To an onlooker it would look very idyllic. But looks are deceiving.

'Have you got the photos on your phone? I want to see them.'

'They're not nice to look at,' I said, picking up my phone and finding the images.

'And what about the conversation?' Corin reached over and I placed the phone in her hand.

'There's a transcript of it on my phone. I don't want to play it out loud.'

I waited while Corin went through the photographs. I

didn't have to ask when she was looking at the bruising on Kathleen; I could see from the pained expression on her face.

'Oh, sweet mother of God,' whispered Corin. And then, with anger in her voice, 'The bastard. He wants stringing up.'

She handed me back the phone and I opened the document with the transcript. 'It's word for word,' I said, handing her the phone once again.

Corin took several minutes to read it, before looking up at me. 'He's Kian's father?'

I nodded. 'Sounds like it.'

'So, wait, how does this all tie in with Kathleen's disappearance?' She looked at the transcript again, as if the answers would appear on the screen or Siri would suddenly burst into life and solve all our problems.

'I'm not sure yet,' I said. 'If Kathleen was having an affair and John found out, I guess he had reason to cause her harm. I don't like to say it, but we can't rule him out. We've seen what he's done to Kathleen and to Kian: who's to say he didn't go too far?'

'I don't know, Siobhan, that's a bit of a stretch of the imagination.'

'Agreed, but it's possible,' I said. 'Although, she did say to me she had to get proof of something that would bring some important people down. So maybe something went wrong there.'

'And who are these people?' asked Corin.

'Obviously, it could be Kian's biological father – Fergus Denvers.'

'I guess so.' Corin took a sip of her wine. 'And where does Dervla come into all this?'

'Kathleen was helping her to get away. Orla Collins said she had a job in Cork. She didn't know what Dervla was getting away from, but it sounds like the same sort of thing that happened to Kathleen.'

'What... grooming?' Corin hesitated as she said the word.

I nodded. 'Exactly what I mean. What if Denvers wasn't the love of her life, or what she thought he was at the time? He was clearly taken with younger women. Older teens, to be exact. Over the age of consent, so he stayed on the right side of the law, legally, if not morally.'

'Fecking hell,' muttered Corin. 'If you're right, we are in way over our heads here.'

'I know and that's why I'm trying to stir things up a bit.' I sipped my wine and looked out to the end of the garden where a wire fence was barely visible in daytime and practically invisible at dusk, like now. It gave the illusion that Corin's garden continued on into the hillside beyond.

'That's a very dangerous game you're playing, Siobhan. I don't like it at all. You need to go to the guards.'

'The guards? Who do you mean? I don't know what to make of Finn and, even if he is genuinely helping me, he doesn't have any authority, not senior authority. And before you say Rory Ahern, I don't trust him either. He's definitely been acting strange and trying to stop me getting to the bottom of all this.'

'Where do you go, then?' asked Corin.

'Higher than Ahern. Higher than somewhere local,' I said. 'I need to go out of area for this.'

'Shit, Siobhan, this is not good,' said Corin. 'When are you going to do that?'

'I feel like I'm walking in Kathleen's shoes, but I need to get more evidence. I have bits and pieces, but I need to link it all together,' I said. 'Tomorrow, I'm going to talk to him.' I jabbed my finger at the phone screen with the transcript. 'I'm going to put the cat among the pigeons and see what happens. I've already spoken to Rory Ahern. I've wound John Walsh up. And now I'm going to start on him.'

'I don't think you should be doing that at all. You should go to a different Garda station, sure, but just give them what you've got and let them investigate.'

I shook my head. 'No. I want more evidence. I don't trust anyone right now.'

We spent the next twenty minutes or so going back over everything and arguing for and against going to the guards now or later. Corin was adamant I shouldn't stir up any more trouble, but I was equally adamant I needed to.

'Whatever you do, please be careful,' said Corin. 'I don't want a repeat of... well, you know.' She didn't have to say what she was referring to; we both knew she was thinking of Kathleen. Corin sighed. 'Do you think she's still alive?' she asked softly.

It was a few moments before I could answer. 'I want to believe she is, but I don't honestly know. I thought she would have been in touch by now if she was.' A tear found its way from the corner of my eye. 'But I have to hold on to the possibility that she's out there and, for whatever reason, can't get in touch. Maybe she doesn't think it's safe enough.'

'Which is why you're intent on pursuing this,' stated Corin.

'Partly. I suppose if we're doing a deep dive into the psychology of all this, it's primarily out of concern and worry about Kathleen,' I said. 'But also partly to prove something to myself.'

Corin frowned. 'Like what?'

'That I'm still a good journalist,' I confessed, feeling almost embarrassed at the need for validation.

'You don't need to prove that,' said Corin.

I appreciated the unflinching faith she had in me. 'Maybe not to you, but to myself.' I took another sip of wine, the alcohol helping me express myself properly. 'I've been so wrapped up in being a good mum and a good wife that I forgot to be me. And, yes, I know that sounds self-indulgent bollocks, but I miss the old me that went out to work and got stuck into worthwhile stories. I miss having that self-belief and confidence.'

Corin nodded. 'And you think you'll get that back if you can solve Kathleen's disappearance?'

'I don't know, but I need to try.'

'And at what price?'

'What do you mean?'

'Is it going to cost you your marriage?' asked Corin. 'Can you not have both?'

I looked down into my near-empty glass as my old familiar foe of guilt rocked up. I could feel the tears prick my eyes. 'I can't fix my marriage until I've fixed my past.'

'Now, that's the bit that sounds bollocks to me,' said Corin. 'From what I can gather, you're using Kathleen's disappearance as an excuse to ignore your marriage. For feck's sake, Siobhan, that should be your priority, not your career and not Kathleen.'

I looked up in stunned silence. Had she really just demoted Kathleen's disappearance from top spot on the priority list?

'Don't be looking at me like that either,' said Corin. 'You said yourself that Kathleen chose to leave. She's also chosen not to get in touch. That's not your responsibility. That's down to her.'

'But I made promises to her,' I said.

'Things that you've told me but haven't told Danny,' said Corin. 'Can't you hear yourself? You're worried about breaking your promise of silence you made to Kathleen. You haven't told Danny the truth, but you've told me. You've already broken your promise.'

'But you're different.'

'I'm not at all. In fact, if anyone deserves the truth it's your husband, and I don't understand why you're prepared to put your marriage on the line over a promise that doesn't mean anything. Danny deserves to know everything.'

A silence descended as I weighed up Corin's words. I had never been so conflicted in my life.

Corin spoke again; this time her voice was softer. 'Look, Kathleen didn't put you first when she laid all that at your door,' she began. 'Let's just say she's OK. She's started a new life somewhere. Yeah?'

'OK,' I said, wondering where Corin was going with this.

'She's safe and living her best life, right? Well, she hasn't thought about you, me, our parents or even Kian in all this. She hasn't made contact to let us know she's fine. And that thought pisses me off.'

'Agreed,' I consented. 'But what if she's not fine?'

'If something bad has happened, then why are you keeping quiet? It's not helping her in any way. All it's doing is destroying your marriage.'

'I should have told him from the start about Kathleen coming to see me and then me meeting her with the money a few days after she disappeared.' My words were mumbled into my chest. I was ashamed of myself.

'Yes, and then he would have probably been cross for a while, but he would have understood,' said Corin. 'Now you have to deal with that, but worse, you have to try to fix the trust that's been broken.'

'It might be too late,' I said, tears falling freely that I didn't try to check.

Corin came over to sit beside me. 'Oh, Siobhan, it's not too late. That boy loves you. He worships the ground you walk on – we've all known that from day one – but he's hurting because you were shutting him out.'

'I'm such an idiot,' I said, leaning into my sister and taking the comfort she extended.

She kissed the top of my head. 'You're not at all. Please speak to Danny. What have you got to lose?'

She was right, I had nothing to lose. As it stood, I had

already lost it. 'Thank you,' I said, sitting up and wiping my face with the cuff of my cardigan.

'Trust me, it will be OK,' said Corin. 'And in the meantime, we will do everything we can to try to find out what happened to Kathleen. But you don't have to prove yourself to anyone. All this talk about finding yourself.' She air-quoted the phrase. 'It's bollocks. You can go and be a journalist again. No one, particularly not your husband, would stand in your way. You don't need to prove yourself to anyone and that includes yourself. If you're doing this, do it for our family's peace of mind.'

I nodded. 'Fuck. When did you get so wise, Corin? You're the baby of the family. I'm supposed to dish out the advice.' I gave her a playful tap on the arm. She gave me a gentle nudge with her shoulder in return.

The back door opened, and Niall came out onto the patio. 'The girls are fast asleep, and the game is over,' he said, stretching his hands in the air. 'I'm going to turn in for the night now.'

'I should go to bed too,' said Corin. 'I have to be up early tomorrow to do the shopping. Mam starts getting anxious if I don't turn up with it by eleven o'clock.'

I squeezed Corin's hand. 'I know you do a lot for them,' I said. 'And I'm grateful.'

She shrugged. 'It's no big deal.' Corin got to her feet. 'I hope you don't have to wait up too long for Freya.'

'I've said midnight. I'm sure Kian will bring her back on time.' I stood up and, after giving Niall a hug goodnight, I went over to the annexe, where I made myself a cup of tea and tried to find something on Netflix to keep me occupied.

I only half-concentrated on the TV show as I mulled over my conversation with Corin.

She was absolutely right. I needed to tell Danny the truth. I owed him that. After that I could only hope he'd forgive me. I wasn't sure how I was going to pay the money back to our savings account, but I'd find a way, even if it meant taking a part-time job somewhere. I'd work in a pub or wait on tables, anything to make up for it. The more I thought about it, the more I knew it was right. I couldn't keep my promise to Kathleen anymore, and technically I'd already broken it by telling Corin. Danny didn't deserve to be shut out.

All the time I was thinking it over, I was keeping an ear out for the sound of Kian's car bringing Freya back.

As the hands of the clock crept towards twelve, I became increasingly unsettled. I didn't know what it was, but I had a feeling Freya wasn't going to be home on time. By five past twelve, my anxiety was making me twitchy. It was only five minutes, I reasoned. They might have stopped for something, or if they were getting a taxi maybe it was late picking them up.

Ten minutes later and I could feel myself getting annoyed. It was irresponsible of them not to be back in time or let me know they were going to be late. I sent Freya an iMessage asking where she was. I hit send and, after a few moments, the message turned green. *Sent as a text message.*

I hated that as I had no way of knowing if it had been delivered or read. Over the next ten minutes I sent two more text messages.

By twelve thirty I'd had enough and decided I'd call her. If it embarrassed her, then, tough.

The call didn't ring but went straight to voicemail.

'Fuck's sake, Freya,' I said out loud. She always had her phone charged when she went out. It wasn't like her not to. In fact, she often took a power bank with her. I found Kian's number in my contact list and phoned him straight away, reminding myself not to fly off the handle at him immediately. I was to keep calm until I found out why he hadn't brought Freya home on time. There might be a logical explanation. The phone rang out to voicemail, which kicked off another swear-fest from me. 'Answer the bloody phone,' I said, as I called again. Voicemail a second time. 'Kian, it's me, Siobhan. Is everything all right? Freya was supposed to be home at twelve. Call me so I know what's happening.' I had to force myself not to sound too pissed off but irritated enough so they knew I was being serious.

I sent a text message as backup. This one went through as an iMessage, which was reassuring, although I had no idea if he'd read it.

Why didn't I find out where the fucking party was? I could borrow Corin's car and drive down there.

I looked out of the window, hoping that I could manifest them appearing. There were no lights on over at Corin's house and I imagined they were all fast asleep in bed by now. Oh to have small kids. Life was less of a worry then. At least you knew where they were and had some control over life. The bigger the kids, the bigger the worry. Whoever came out with that pearl of wisdom was one hundred per cent on the money.

By one o'clock, with still no word from either of them, my anger had morphed to panic. This wasn't like Freya at all. And as for Kian, why the hell couldn't he look at his phone and call me?

I was debating whether to wake Corin or call Finn when the sound of a car pulling onto the drive and the sweep of the headlights had me hopping to my feet. Now I wanted to throttle them for making me worry so much. Jesus, I'd give them what for.

I swung the door open and folded my arms across my chest, but as the light from the annexe shone across the driveway and the driver's door opened, I realised it wasn't Kian or Freya, but Finn. My eyes swept across the car, expecting the two of them to hop out of the back, but there was no sign of either of them.

I looked at Finn. His face was serious, his eyes dark and his mouth unsmiling.

I tried to speak, to form words, but nothing came out.

'Siobhan,' said Finn, coming to stand in front of me. He held my arms as if ready to catch me. 'I need to talk to you. About Freya.' He guided me back into the annexe and sat me down on the sofa, holding my hands in his. 'Freya's gone missing from the party,' he said.

I frowned. What was he saying? Freya was missing? No, that wasn't right. 'She's with Kian,' I heard myself say.

Finn shook his head gently. 'She's gone missing from the party. She's not with Kian.'

I closed my eyes, trying to take it in. 'What do you mean? How is she missing from the party? I don't understand.'

'She went to the loo and never came back. No one knows where she is or if she's with anyone. We've got people out looking for her now.'

I looked at him in confusion. 'A search party?'

'Unofficial at the moment. Kian is beside himself. He's out there too. Refused to come with me. Blaming himself, like.'

'Oh... oh...' I couldn't form words. My brain wasn't working. 'Shit.' I got to my feet. Paced the room, my head in my hands. 'No. Please, Finn. It's not true. Please. Oh God.'

Finn was on his feet, holding me to him. 'Shh, now. She's probably just wandered off somewhere or tried to come home. We mustn't jump the gun. I'm sure she'll be found in no time. Probably gone off down the beach with some of the others. You know what kids are like. You know what we were like.'

I forced myself to calm down. This headless-chicken panic mode was not conducive to the situation. I took several deep steadying breaths. 'OK,' I said. 'I'm OK now. Wait a second.' More deep breathing and I fought to control the turmoil threatening to overwhelm my body and mind. I released a long slow breath and focused on Finn. 'I'm all right. I promise.'

'Good. That's it, Siobhan. Stay calm,' said Finn, his eyes

fixed on mine. 'Now, as I said, I'm sure she's just gone off, like teenagers do, without giving anyone else a second thought but...'

'There's always a but,' I said, wrapping my arms around my body.

'Is there anything you need to tell me?'

'Like what?'

'Like, all this business about Kathleen. Has anyone said anything or threatened you in any way?'

'Fuck,' I gasped. 'You think someone's done something to her to get back at me, don't you?' A wailing noise leaped from my throat at the thought. 'No. Finn. No. Please. No.'

'Siobhan,' said Finn, his voice sterner. 'I'm only asking. We've no evidence to suggest that, I'm simply covering all bases. I need to you keep your shit together now.'

More deep breathing. More convincing myself I needed to calm down. Finn was right. I was not helping matters at all. 'Erm... maybe. I don't know.'

'You need to tell me everything,' he said.

'We haven't got time. I need to find my daughter,' I replied. 'I can't sit here and chat to you like nothing is happening. I need to be out there. It needs to be an official search, not a load of kids from a party wandering around town, half-heartedly looking for her.'

'For feck's sake, Siobhan,' said Finn.

I stopped as a thought occurred to me. 'How did you know she was missing?' I asked. 'Who called you? And why didn't anyone call me?'

'Kian called me,' said Finn, without hesitation. 'He's out there trying to find her and thought I could help. He didn't want to worry you or get Freya into trouble for sneaking off, or whatever it is she's done, or get a bollocking from you.'

It made sense what he was saying and, of course, I wanted to believe him. I had to believe him because right then, he was all I had. 'Sorry,' I said. The fog of panic was lifting and although I was terrified for the safety of Freya, I needed to be doing something proactive. 'Here's what we will do. We'll go and look for her. You and me. I'll leave the door unlocked in case she makes her way home. I'll leave a note telling her to call me.'

'Good idea. If you're sure.'

'Positive. I can't sit here and do nothing. I'll message Corin. I don't want to wake her, not yet. Only if it's an emergency,' I said, feeling better now I was in some sort of control. 'If we can't find her in the next half an hour, we'll go and talk to the kids at the party. Whose party was she at?'

'Mia Denvers's.'

I thought my heart would stop beating there and then. 'Mia Denvers?' I repeated. 'Aisling and Fergus Denvers?'

Finn nodded. 'That's right. Why?'

'Fuck. Fuck. Fuck.' I almost shouted the words. 'Get in the car. I'll explain as we go.'

THIRTY-SIX

'You're going to have to trust me on this,' I said, as Finn sped into Dingle town. 'Someone has taken Freya to get at me because I'm getting close to the truth. In fact, I'm so close I'm within touching distance, and all this is going to blow up in their faces.'

I took out my phone and sent a text message to Nicole.

> Freya is missing. I need your help. I think she's in danger. Do you know where she is? Please help me.

'You're going to have to stop talking in riddles and give me some details,' said Finn. 'What's your theory?'

I looked down at my hands and twiddled the wedding ring on my finger. I wished Danny was there.

'It's more than a theory,' I said, getting out of the car.

Finn followed me, after getting a torch from the back of his car that was far superior to the pathetic one I'd grabbed from under the sink in the annexe earlier. We made our way over to the harbour and he scanned the area in front of us. The place was empty.

'So, let's hear it then,' said Finn.

'Something happened to Kathleen when she was younger,' I said. I was way past the point of keeping secrets now. All of a sudden I didn't care about trying to resurrect my journalistic career. I didn't care Kathleen had asked me not to tell her story. Even Danny and our marriage were relegated to second place. If finding Freya safe and unharmed was the price I was going to have to pay, then I would do so in a heartbeat. I turned to Finn. 'Kathleen was groomed when she was a teenager, although at the time she wouldn't have called it that. I don't know if we even knew what it was then, but she had an affair with a married man. Got pregnant by him but ended up marrying John Walsh.'

Finn let out a low whistle. 'Holy Mary, Mother of God. I was not expecting that.' He ran his hand down his face. 'Who was the married man?'

'I'll get to that,' I said. 'Kathleen carried on as if John was the father because he didn't know any different. Fast forward to now, working at The Hub, Kathleen comes across another young woman, teenager, just like she was, who is having an affair with a married man.'

'The young woman being Dervla Collins,' said Finn.

'You know?'

'It's a guess. I'd been told that Kathleen was close to Dervla. When we were investigating Kathleen's disappearance, Sharon from The Hub told us that.'

'This bit is pure speculation on my part, but that's what I think happened. Kathleen wanted to help her escape and was going to expose the man.' We had reached the far side of the harbour and there was no sign of anyone about.

'We should go back to the car and have a drive around the town,' said Finn. 'We can call in a couple of pubs that she might have gone in. There are a few that let the youngsters in even though they're not supposed to. I can go in and ask around.'

I felt slightly reassured having Finn with me, but the help-lessness and feeling of panic were lurking below the surface. It was all I could do to stop my mind from racing to some very dark places.

'I wished I'd known Freya was going to a party at the Denvers' place,' I said.

'Why's that?'

'Because the married guy who is Kian's real father is Fergus Denvers.'

Finn stopped in his tracks. 'What the feck?'

'I know. I was like that, but I've got a recording of Kathleen arguing with him. She saved it. It was her security, if you like. Her proof, and now I have that proof. There's no way he wants that to come out and he is trying to stop me.'

'Wait. You think Denvers has something to do with Freya being missing?' Finn gave me a sceptical look.

'I do, as a matter of fact. He has everything to lose. His wife's a politician, for God's sake.'

We got into the car and Finn started the engine. 'So, is it Denvers who has been having an affair with Dervla?'

'Yes. Can you imagine the scandal if that got out? And I reckon Rory Ahern knows all about it but they're old mates and Ahern has been covering for him. He's as good as threatened me this week. Now can you understand why I was suspicious of you?'

'Jesus Christ, Siobhan. I don't know. That's making a lot of assumptions, and you've no proof about Ahern.'

'I've asked Orla Collins to try to get in touch with Dervla and get her to ring me. If I can get her to make a statement, or at least confirm this to me, I can take them both down.'

Finn didn't answer and I took that as his disapproval, but I didn't care. With every passing thought, I was more and more certain about my theory.

We drove along the road and Finn turned off onto a side street, pulling up outside a pub.

'What are we doing here? It's way past closing time.'

Finn gave me an old-fashioned look. 'Closing time yes, but lock-in, no. You've been living in England far too long if you've forgotten about the lock-ins. Now, wait here. I'll go in and ask.' He came out a minute later and shook his head at me, before getting back into the car. 'They're going to call me if they hear anything,' he said. 'There are a couple more pubs I can try.'

'Thanks,' I said, checking my phone for what seemed like the hundredth time. No messages from Freya or Kian.

'How does this all tie in with Kathleen?' he asked. 'What do you think happened to her?'

I swallowed a lump in my throat. 'I think she was going to expose Denvers. Either he paid her off and she's done what everyone says she's done – you know, started a new life – or he did something to her.' I exchanged a look with Finn. 'By that I mean something bad. He's killed her.'

I could hardly believe I was saying those words, voicing such thoughts, but weirdly I felt numb to it. Whatever had happened to Kathleen, I couldn't change that now; but my daughter was out there somewhere in danger and at risk. I still had time to change that. At least I hoped I did.

The next two pubs were the same. No one had seen Freya and I couldn't stop myself from crying a little. Finn hugged me and told me that they would soon have to make it official and bring in the big guns.

'We need to go to the Denvers' house,' I said. 'Talk to people there. Talk to Denvers. I'll fucking kneecap him if I have to, but he's got to talk.'

Finn drove over to the Denvers' house and we pulled up onto the drive to the backdrop of music and a heavy base beat. The party was clearly still in full swing.

'Just go easy now,' said Finn, as we got out the car. 'No

interrogation. We ask around to see if anyone's seen or heard where Freya is. Leave me to talk to Aisling and Fergus Denvers. The most important thing is to find Freya. Then we can see what we'll do about Denvers. Keep our cards close to our chest, yeah?'

'I can't guarantee anything,' I said honestly. 'I don't care what you say, I'm talking to Denvers before I leave here tonight.'

Finn gave a roll of his eyes but didn't say anything and we walked around to the garden, via the side gate.

There weren't as many youngsters there as I had been expecting and I wondered if some of them had thinned out already. I checked my watch. It was gone two o'clock in the morning now. I cast my gaze around the garden and pool area, searching the faces, looking for Freya, hoping she'd come back here from wherever she'd gone. But none of them were my daughter. A few of the youngsters looked up or over at me but their interest didn't last.

Finn and I made our way around the grounds, stopping at the different groups of kids and asking if they'd seen Freya. I had a photo of her on my phone, which I held out for them to see in case it jogged their memories. I'd forwarded a copy of the photograph to Finn, and he was doing the same. We met back at the terrace, with the same result. Nothing. No one remembered seeing her, let alone if she'd left.

'Where are Aisling and Fergus?' I asked.

'Must be in the house. Let's see if we can find them,' said Finn, heading over towards the open bifold doors.

There were fewer people in the house and Aisling Denvers was milling around the room with a black bin liner in one hand, gathering up empty beer cans and bottles. She looked up as we approached her. 'Sure, have you ever seen a mess like it?' she said. 'Now, what are you both doing here? Is it a formal visit? If next door has complained to you about the music, I've already had the kids turn it down.'

Finn held up his hand to stop her. 'It's not a formal visit... yet.'

This had Aisling's attention. She straightened up and walked over to the kitchen area, putting the bag of recycling down by the bin, and took off the yellow rubber gloves she was wearing. 'Come through to the study.'

We followed her out of the kitchen and across the entrance hall to a room on the left and took a seat on the sofa as indicated by Aisling while she sat at her desk. She looked expectantly at us.

'Siobhan's daughter, Freya, was here earlier with Kian Walsh,' began Finn. 'But at some point this evening, Freya's gone missing. We were simply trying to find her before we make it official.'

'Oh, missing? So sorry. I don't mean to be rude,' said Aisling. 'But I'm not sure I can help you. I don't think I know your daughter. She was definitely here earlier?'

'Yes. With my nephew,' I said.

'And I take it you've spoken to him?'

'Of course,' I said, feeling irritated that she was asking such obvious questions.

'Kian's out there looking for her now. I've spoken to some of the other kids, but no one knows where she's gone,' said Finn. 'Obviously, a story like this, where there's a connection to you and your home, is bound to draw some attention. I wanted a chance to speak to you first, give you the heads up, like.'

'Thank you. I appreciate that,' said Aisling. 'And I'm really sorry I can't help you.'

'What about your husband?' I asked. 'Is he about? I'd really like to speak to him too.'

'Fergus? Actually, I don't know where he is,' replied Aisling, with a frown. 'He was here earlier. He was on burger duties. I suppose he could have slipped upstairs to bed. I'll go and check. Wait here.'

I felt like I was back at school, being told what to do by one of the nuns. Aisling Denvers exuded authority. She didn't appear to be a woman who would take no for an answer; if she told you to do something, you did it.

'That's a bit weird, isn't it?' I whispered to Finn. 'She doesn't know where he is and it's their daughter's party.'

'Let's not jump to conclusions.'

'I don't like this at all,' I said. I took out my phone and tried to ring Freya again but, as every time before, it went straight to voicemail. I had a message from Kian, and I read it out to Finn. *'I'm so sorry, Siobhan. One minute she was there, the next she was gone. I'm still out looking for her.'*

'He feels pretty bad,' said Finn. 'Especially after what happened to his own mother.'

I wanted to say so he should but also knew it would be wrong for me to lay the blame at his door. I knew what that was like. I sent back a message telling him not to worry and we would contact him as soon as we knew anything. My stomach churned as another wave of fear and panic welled up inside me. I was going to have to tell Danny soon. He had the right to know. I dreaded to think how he'd take the news.

Aisling bustled back into the study. 'As I thought, my husband is fast asleep in bed. And no, I'm not going to wake him, if that's what you were going to ask.'

'But my daughter is missing,' I said, wondering if I could barge past Aisling and wake Denvers up myself.

'I appreciate that,' said Aisling. 'But my husband has taken a sleeping tablet, so there's no way I'd be able to wake him. Anyway, I'm sure your daughter was still here when he went upstairs, so he won't be able to help you.'

'Thank you, Mrs Denvers,' said Finn, placing a hand on my shoulder. 'When your husband does wake up, if he remembers anything, perhaps you can call us.'

'Of course.'

'I think it's time we made Freya's disappearance official. I'll be in touch again, no doubt,' said Finn.

'No doubt,' replied Aisling.

I followed Finn out of the house and back to the car.

'I have to go to Ahern,' said Finn. 'He's next in the chain of command. I'll also put a call in to Area. We have to do things by the book now.'

'I need to tell Danny,' I said.

'Sure. Do that now and I'll get hold of Ahern.'

My hands trembled as I located Danny's number. I was on the brink of tears already, with no idea how I was going to break the news to him and what sort of reaction there would be.

THIRTY-SEVEN

Ahern treads softly down the stairs and out of the house. It's two thirty in the morning and he doesn't want to wake Maureen. He goes out to the car and checks the GoPro he attached behind the grill earlier is still in place. He switches it on before getting into his car and heading off.

He drives out through Dingle, past the station. He's not going there at all. He has arranged a meeting. It's risky. They didn't want to meet him at first, but he's persuaded them to come. They are beginning to panic as the net closes in, hence the late-night call to him demanding he sort things out. He needs to cover himself now, in case things go wrong. He's not going down alone, that's for sure.

Soon, he's pulling off the main road and driving down the track to Skerries Cottage. As he steers the car around the back of the tumbledown property, he smiles to himself.

She's already here. She took the bait, all right.

He makes sure he leaves his headlights on long enough that she turns and squints, holding her hand up to shield her eyes. She makes an impatient gesture for him to turn them off, but he switches to side lights.

Ahern gets out of the car and walks over to her.

'Jesus Christ, Ahern,' scolds Aisling Denvers. 'Are you trying to burn my retinas out?'

'Sorry, didn't realise.'

She looks up at Skerries Cottage. 'No guests yet then, I take it?'

'Soon,' he replies. 'It's all in hand.'

'Good. I've had your bloody Finn Casey and that Siobhan Martin at my house looking for the girl. They wanted to speak to Fergus.'

'I know. Finn called me. Siobhan has made an official missing person's report.'

'That could be a problem. Make sure you deal with it as we agreed,' snaps Aisling.

'Of course,' replies Ahern tersely. 'A word of warning. Siobhan knows way more than we ever thought.'

Aisling's eyes narrow. 'How much more?'

'She knows about Fergus and Kathleen.'

Aisling takes a breath. 'That was over twenty years ago. Without Kathleen Walsh there's no proof and, even if she was here, it's her word against Fergus's. Not that I need that kind of attention from the press.'

'It's not just that,' interrupts Ahern. 'She knows about Dervla, or at least she suspects. It won't be long before she knows everything. Once one of them comes forward, there will be others and there will be nothing either of us can do. It will be a runaway train.'

'I know that,' retorts Aisling, clearly agitated. 'I am aware of the Me Too movement.' She paces around.

'We need to call a halt to what's planned for tonight. It's too risky,' says Ahern. 'I can arrange to find the girl on the beach. You know, too pissed to know what she's doing.'

Aisling looks at him in surprise. 'You'll do no such thing,' she says. 'By carrying this out, we will be making sure Siobhan stops digging. We have to keep the girl long enough to scare the bloody life out of her mother so she gets the message. We can't be handing her back after a couple of hours.'

'I don't like this plan of yours,' says Ahern. 'I told you that from the start.'

'Well, it's too late to be getting cold feet now. It's time to be decisive and strike hard. No more of your pussyfooting around.'

'That might solve today's problem, but what about the next time it happens?' asks Ahern.

'Short of shooting my stupid fecking husband, you mean?'

Ahern is sure Aisling is not joking about that. He is fully aware that the Denvers' marriage is purely one of convenience. Fergus had the connections that Aisling never had, to get her into politics. Fergus also had – still had – an eye for the ladies, especially the younger ones. It was something Aisling had discovered very early on in her relationship with Fergus, and her ambitions had allowed her to overlook it, for the most part.

It didn't come to a head until Denvers took it too far a few years ago and the girl's parents had threatened to go to the papers if they weren't compensated fully. Aisling, however, had other ideas about a trade-off, and enlisted the help of her long-standing friend, Rory Ahern, to apply pressure in exchange for a not-insubstantial sum of money. Before Rory knew it, he was on her payroll. He may have come off it, but what with Maureen getting ill and rising medical bills, it had been a mutually beneficial allegiance.

Aisling Denvers looks Ahern dead in the eye. 'Fergus is becoming a liability, and I won't allow that. I won't let anyone bring me down, not after all the work I've put into my career. Once this is done, you're going to arrange for that husband of mine to have an accident.'

THIRTY-EIGHT

Kathleen hadn't meant to argue with her sisters earlier at the pub, but she'd let the drink get the better of her. She hated the fact she had used Siobhan as a decoy, but sending the text message about needing help would throw the guards off. It would muddy the waters and they wouldn't know which direction to take their enquiries. She hopes that Siobhan will forgive her, because she's surely going to get a lot of flak over it. 'Are you all set?' Kathleen asks Dervla.

It's been two days since Kathleen left in the middle of the night. She and Dervla have been staying in a caravan in a holiday park. She'd chosen it because the 'holiday park' consisted of ten caravans in a farmer's field with no amenities and certainly no CCTV. She booked it online under Dervla's name, using a secret credit card she had obtained without John's knowledge.

Booking online didn't come without risks, but no one would be looking for Dervla and, although the Garda could eventually find out she had a credit card, Kathleen was certain they wouldn't go to all that trouble. If they were going to look at her bank information for some kind of paper trail, then they would use the bank account that John was aware of.

Kathleen also made sure she didn't use the home computer or her phone to book the caravan. She used her secret iPad. She'd purposefully left her phone at home before she'd gone out to the pub so it would look like she had forgotten it. The fact that John had never wanted CCTV or a doorbell camera made it easier for her, as there would be no definite proof one way or the other. All she had to do was avoid the main roads where she could get picked up on someone's camera, and walk to the caravan park. It was five miles away and tramping down the narrow lanes in the dark wasn't ideal. Just as well she kept herself in good condition: she had made it safely to the accommodation.

Kathleen has been checking the news for the past two days, and there has been no national mention of her being missing. In the run-up to this escape, Kathleen has been dropping hints to her friends that all was not well in her marriage. She hoped this would be drip-fed back to the Garda as they built up a picture of her home life.

After leaving the caravan park they caught a bus to Tralee, and there they met Siobhan, who handed over the cash. After that, they'd taken the train to Cork.

Now, on day three of her disappearance, they are in the flat above the pub where Dervla has a job.

'I can't believe you managed to do all this for me,' says Dervla. 'I can't believe I've finally got away from Dingle and that bastard.' The relief is too much for Dervla and she sits down on the sofa and begins to cry.

Kathleen is at her side. She puts her arm around Dervla and holds her close as the young woman finally releases all the emotions she's been harbouring for the past year. Kathleen wants to cry too. She's done it. She's saved someone from him.

She has a deep sense of redemption. She's finally managed to atone for her inability to help herself.

Eventually, Dervla's tears dry and she looks gratefully up at Kathleen. 'Thank you,' she whispers.

Kathleen smiles. 'You don't have to thank me.'

'I would still be there if it wasn't for you.' Dervla sniffs and wipes her tears with the back of her hand. 'What are you going to do now?'

'I'll go back to Dingle, once I've made my statement to the guards here in Cork.' Kathleen doesn't trust Rory Ahern. She needs to make a full statement about what happened to her at a Garda station with no connections to her hometown.

'I'm hungry,' says Dervla, sprawling out across the sofa. 'What's for tea?'

Kathleen hesitates at the question. Dervla reminds her of Kian when he was younger.

'I'll need to get something. What do you fancy?'

'Pizza?' suggests Dervla after a moment's thought.

It wouldn't be Kathleen's first choice, but it's easy and will save her having to cook. She's tired and longs to get to bed. Tomorrow she's got to face John and her family.

'I'll nip out to the shop now,' says Kathleen. 'Any particular topping?'

After what seems an age, Dervla makes up her mind and asks for garlic bread too. 'I'm going to have a shower while you're out,' she says. 'I need to wash my hair. It's manky.'

The weather isn't so great and, looking up at the sky, Kathleen sees the clouds are grey. Much like her mood. She thought she'd feel a sense of relief once she was away from Dingle and Dervla was safe, but that sense is absent. She comforts herself with the thought that maybe it's because she still has to make a formal statement about her past and hand over the evidence she's gathered, and then there'll be the ordeal of facing John.

She wonders now if it was wise to have walked out in the

dead of the night, abandoning The Hub and the people who rely on her there. Not to mention her parents, who have no doubt been climbing the walls at her disappearance. The guilt she feels is immense. Perhaps she should have been upfront with everyone. But if she had, there's a chance she wouldn't have been able to get Dervla to safety. After all, she couldn't trust Rory Ahern, or anyone remotely connected to him in the Garda. No, she was right doing it this way. At least, she hopes so.

Annoyed at her own doubts, Kathleen pushes the thoughts from her head. She's at the shop now and, five minutes later, emerges with a carrier bag of food and snacks, together with a bottle of Coke. She will do a big shop tomorrow before she leaves so Dervla has enough to keep her going for a few days. After that she'll be starting work in the pub and be able to have her meals there – that was the arrangement Kathleen had made with the landlord.

Kathleen had been lucky when she and Dervla had taken a day trip to Cork a month ago to look for accommodation and a job. The bar job had been advertised in the pub window and Kathleen had posed as Dervla's mother but loitered in the background while Dervla spoke to the landlord. It was sorted there and then.

As she walks along the road, something makes Kathleen turn around. She has a feeling of being watched. Someone close behind her. But no one is acting suspiciously. Everyone is going about their business, paying her no attention. She tries to shrug off the feeling and puts it down to being tired and on edge.

The feeling remains and Kathleen stops to look in a shop window, but really she's trying to spot a reflection of someone watching her. She sighs. She's getting paranoid. It's ridiculous.

All the same, she's glad when she turns the corner and the pub is in sight. The door to the flat above is at the back, down an alleyway. It smells of beer and piss. Kathleen rummages in her handbag, looking for her phone but can't find it. She usually texts Dervla to open the door. It's a small safety precaution they agreed upon but, annoyingly, it looks like Kathleen's left it indoors. She'll have to knock and call through the door instead. She's about to climb the metal staircase up to the door of the flat when she has an awful sense of danger.

She spins around and lets out a cry of alarm.

John is standing there, his gaze fixed on her and his arms folded. 'Hello, Kathleen,' he says, in a faux-pleasant voice.

Kathleen's heart pounds so hard, she's sure it's going to burst out of her chest. She momentarily thinks about fleeing up to the flat but doesn't want John to find Dervla up there. Her brain is offering her multiple solutions, all in a couple of seconds. Should she walk on by? Will he let her? Should she turn and run? He'll chase her. Someone will see. They'll call the guards.

It's as if he can read her mind and, in those two precious seconds of indecision, he moves close to her and catches her arm in his big hand. His finger almost touches his thumb, squeezing her flesh tightly through her cardigan.

'How did you find me?' she stammers.

He smirks. 'Well, it was simple and rather ingenious of me,' he says. 'All I had to do was put a little tracker inside that card you have of St Joseph. You know, the one your mam gave you. The one in that little plastic wallet? I know it's in the bottom of the inside pocket. You'd only notice it in there if you took the card out, and I know you never do that.'

Kathleen wants to cry. After all the trouble she went to, she never thought he'd do something like that. She has sorely under-estimated her husband. 'Why? Why did you do that?'

John tuts. 'We need to talk, but not here in the street.' Still holding her arm, he forces her towards the alleyway. Kathleen sees the tip of the bonnet poking out. 'Get in the car,' he orders.

'No,' she says, trying to pull against him.

'For feck's sake, Kathleen. Get in the fecking car. We need to talk. Do you know what trouble you've caused back home? Everyone is looking for you. Everyone. Your parents are worried sick and your sisters... Jesus, it's a whole fecking circus for you. Now, get in. I don't want to talk out here in the street.'

'You want to talk?' She's wary. She doesn't know if she can trust him.

'I haven't come all this way for nothing,' he snaps. 'Get in the fecking car.'

Kathleen has a sense of Dervla watching. John doesn't know she's brought Dervla with her, she's sure of that. He mustn't know. She has to keep the young woman safe and doesn't want John to decide to go up to the flat. Maybe she can take John away from here if she gets in the car.

'OK. OK,' she says. 'I'll get in the car, but can you let go of my arm? You're hurting me.'

John loosens his grip but still hangs on to her and walks her around to the passenger door. He only releases his hold once she's in the passenger seat.

'Don't try anything stupid,' he says, slamming the door and stalking around the front of the car to the other side.

Kathleen glances up to the flat and can see Dervla at the window, watching them. There's a look of terror on her face. She's scared and doesn't know what to do. Kathleen locks eyes with her, willing her not to break cover. To stay in the flat. She gives the slightest shake of her head, warning Dervla not to try to come to her rescue.

Then John is in the car and Kathleen averts her gaze and looks instead at the windscreen. The locks clonk into place, and Kathleen knows she can't get out now, even if she tried. Another wave of fear hits her and a tear leaks from the corner of her eye.

THIRTY-NINE

I sat in the back of the car with Danny beside me while Niall drove us to Dingle, having picked Danny up from Shannon Airport. I had managed to get hold of Danny and he was on the first flight out of Heathrow. Niall had insisted on collecting him and Corin had also come along. The girls had been deposited with Niall's mother to keep them away from all the comings and goings and conversations they didn't need to hear.

Finn had reported Freya's disappearance to Ahern and a full police search was underway although, at present, Ahern had said it was low-key as it was more than likely Freya was sleeping off a hangover somewhere. I hadn't been impressed by this rather dismissive assumption, but Finn had assured me I had to let the guards do things their way now.

I'd seen Kian last night and he had been beside himself with worry. He didn't stop apologising and I could see the whole thing was spinning him out. It was bringing back memories of Kathleen's disappearance. I had to take the weight of that responsibility. I had been party to that, and I was at fault. Once Freya was found, I owed Kian an explanation; whether he'd forgive me, I didn't know.

It was getting on for midday and, after the initial outburst on the phone when I had told him that Freya was missing, Danny had barely spoken to me. The tension in the car was like a pressurised capsule and I fully expected us to implode any minute. I would rather he was angry and shouting at me. Questioning my decision to let Freya go to the party after everything that had happened. I deserved that. I deserved a complete and utter bollocking. I'd fucked up, taken my eye off the ball, and this had happened.

But Danny wasn't going ballistic. His stony, cold silence was so much worse than any outburst of anger.

Tears slid down my face as I looked out of the window, feeling nothing but utter despair.

'You should have stayed in Dingle,' said Danny, his voice as sharp as a boning knife. 'You should be there looking for her now. Stop feeling sorry for yourself.'

I wiped the tears from my eyes, hurt by his words, which sliced at my heart. 'I've looked everywhere,' I said in my defence, while at the same time feeling I had no right to defend myself. I was wholly responsible for this, and I should shoulder the guilt I deserved. 'The—'

Niall cut in. 'The guards don't want us there right now. They told us to come and get you. Siobhan has been up all night. She's exhausted.'

Bless Niall. His words were spoken softly, as they always were, but they were also firm. An unspoken warning to Danny to go easy on me. I saw Niall flick a look to Danny in the rear-view mirror, holding his gaze. Unspoken communication passing between the two men.

Danny looked away first, his head turning to the window where, like me, he was probably looking, but not seeing. All he could think about was Freya. I knew all too well that feeling of complete despair and agony at the situation.

We finally got back to Corin and Niall's house. 'I'll put the kettle on,' said Corin, while Niall said he'd phone Finn to see if he could get an update.

Danny followed me into the annexe and dumped his overnight bag on the sofa. 'Do your parents know?' he asked.

I nodded. 'Yeah. I told them this morning. Didn't want them to find out from someone else.'

'How did they take it?'

'I only spoke to my mam. She was somewhere between cross and worried.' I didn't add that my dad would probably be pointing the finger at me, saying stuff like history repeating itself and why did I let Freya go and why didn't I pick her up. All the things I was thinking myself.

'I need a fucking drink,' said Danny.

'Coffee. I haven't got anything stronger.'

'Coffee will be fine. I need a clear head as I don't intend sitting here on my arse all day waiting for the guards to plod around with no sense of urgency.'

I made Danny a coffee, black, no sugar, the way he liked it. I couldn't stomach drinking anything. I hadn't eaten all morning, but I had zero appetite. 'I'm so sorry,' I said, feeling the need to say something to try to break the godawful tension between us. 'If I'd have known... I wished I hadn't let her go. I wished I hadn't even come here. I'm so scared, Danny. Like, really scared. Losing Kathleen is one thing, but I can't bear the thought—'

'Stop,' he interrupted. 'Stop talking like that.' He put the coffee down on the table and came over to me. We stood there looking at each other and I'm sure my own pain was reflected in his eyes. He moved his hands, as if he was going to hold me, put them down and then, changing his mind again, pulled me towards him.

This small act of human kindness, some affection from my husband, the man I had known since I was a teenager and still very much loved, was enough to trigger the tears again. They came in big uncontrollable sobs.

At one point I realised Danny was crying too. I wrapped my arms around him, and we clung together as if our lives depended on it. I wanted to curl up into a ball, fall into a coma, and only wake up when this nightmare was over, when my daughter was home and safe and the three of us were together.

A knock at the door had us pulling apart. Danny opened it and Niall stepped in.

'Just spoken to Finn; they're widening the search outside of Dingle. Calling in some extra officers and some of the locals are organising a search party. Everyone is pulling together to try to find her.'

I noted the words: try to find her. No reassurances. No promises. My knees buckled and I sank onto the sofa as my body began to shake uncontrollably. That was not like me at all. I did not react like that. I was strong. In control. But at that very moment, I had never felt any weaker or less effective.

'I'm coming to help look for her,' said Danny.

Niall gave a sympathetic look. 'Finn said to ask you both to stay here.'

'Fuck that,' said Danny. 'If you think I'm sitting around all day on my arse while my daughter is missing, then you can think again.'

'Sure, I get that,' said Niall. 'But Finn said Ahern is coming over. He wants to speak to you both. So, sit tight, eh?' He gave Danny's arm a firm but friendly double tap. 'Do ya want anything, now?'

'No. We're OK,' said Danny. He looked at his watch. 'If Ahern's not here in half an hour, I'm off. He can come find me if he wants me that badly.'

Niall nodded. 'Come over to the house if you want. Corin's going to wait in. I'm going off looking.'

Danny nodded. 'Niall,' he said, as his brother-in-law reached the door. 'Thanks.'

Niall gave a chin-lift in acknowledgement and left.

'Fuck. Fuck. Fuck,' said Danny in exasperation, each expletive louder than the other. He ran both hands through his hair, then interlocked his fingers behind his head as he paced the small living room. 'Fuck!' He completed several more circuits of the room before sitting down next to me. He took my hands, encouraging me to turn towards him. 'Siobhan, you need to tell me everything – and when I say everything, I mean absolutely every fucking minute detail. Got it?'

I knew I had to tell him everything and he listened patiently as I went through it all, from the night Kathleen disappeared to going to Tralee and meeting her with the money I'd switched from our savings to my personal account and everything I'd found out since I was here, right up to Freya going missing. He only interrupted to ask a few questions to clarify details.

'Now you know as much as me,' I said. 'I'm so sorry, Danny. I promised Kathleen I wouldn't say anything. If I told you, you'd be in an untenable position yourself. You'd have to choose between backing me up or lying for me.'

'How very noble of you,' he said.

His comment hurt but I was in no position to argue. 'I am sorry, despite what you think,' I said.

He let out a sigh. 'I'm sorry, Siobhan. That was shitty of me.' He held his head in his hands, his elbows propped on his knees. 'I get it, but I still wish you'd told me. You should have trusted me. You should know I would have walked over hot coals if you'd asked me to.'

I noted the past tense in his words. I had messed up more than I could ever imagine.

'It wasn't a lack of trust,' I said. 'I trust you with my life, but I had made a promise to Kathleen, and I had a different kind of trust that I couldn't break. And like I said, I didn't want to put you in a difficult position.'

'You should have let me be the judge of that.'

'I know that now.'

Before he could answer, there was another knock at the door. 'Ahern, no doubt,' said Danny, getting to his feet. 'Just so you know, I'm taking no bullshit from that man.' He opened the door and, sure enough, Sergeant Rory Ahern was there.

'Danny,' said Ahern.

Danny opened the door wider and Ahern came in, removing his hat as he did so. I got to my feet and was surprised when Finn followed his superior in.

'Why aren't you out looking for my daughter?' asked Danny, looking at his old schoolfriend.

Ahern cleared his throat. 'We have other officers out there doing that,' he said. 'We need to go over the events of last night in more detail. And events leading up to her disappearance.'

'That's not important right now,' I said. 'We need to be out there looking for Freya. All that can wait until afterwards.'

Ahern was unperturbed. 'Finn tells me you suspect Fergus Denvers to be involved in the disappearance of your daughter.' He ran the rim of his hat between his fingers.

I looked at Finn, who wouldn't meet my gaze but mumbled something about being sorry and he had to tell Ahern. 'We need a clear picture of everything,' he finished.

'I don't know for sure, but if it relates back to Kathleen going missing and what happened to her and to Dervla Collins, then I think you're the one who should be looking for Denvers and questioning him.'

'Oh, we will. It's our job. Not yours,' said Ahern. 'I need to hear it from you now, that's all. May I?' He indicated the sofa.

'Look, this is going to take far too long,' said Danny impatiently.

'As I said, we need a clear picture of everything,' said

Ahern, sitting down and unzipping his jacket. He took his notebook and pen from his pocket and looked up at me expectantly.

'This is a fucking joke,' muttered Danny.

Ahern shot him a look but said nothing.

I sat down in the chair opposite and relayed once again everything I knew or thought I knew. Finn had taken the seat next to Ahern, but Danny remained on his feet the whole time. The tension radiated from him, and I knew he must have been exerting the utmost self-control.

It was nearly an hour later when Ahern finally put his notebook away, seemingly satisfied he'd got all the information he needed or that I knew.

'Thank you for this,' he said, getting to his feet.

'I take it you've spoken to Fergus Denvers,' I asked. 'You are going to speak to him, aren't you?'

'Yes. In good time. These are very serious allegations, and we need to do this properly,' said Ahern. 'You don't need to worry about any of this now though. I have it all in hand.'

I didn't like the way he said that. It brought back too many memories of Kathleen saying she didn't trust Ahern and that was why she was going to Cork to make a statement.

'Right, well, if that's all,' I said, getting to my feet.

Ahern and Finn rose simultaneously. 'Finn will be around tomorrow to take a formal statement,' said Ahern.

'Never mind all that,' said Danny. 'Can you get back to some real police work and find my daughter?'

'As soon as we have any news, we'll be in touch,' said Ahern. 'And if Freya comes back, can you let us know straight away so we can call off the search. We're putting a lot of resources into this and it all costs money.'

Danny stood in the doorway, watching them leave, his hands in his pockets. Someone who didn't know him would think he looked casual and calm, but I could see the tension in his shoulders and the back of his neck. Once Ahern and Finn had left, he slammed the door shut.

'Cheeky fuckers,' he seethed. He hooked up his jacket. 'Did you see the way Finn couldn't even look at us? I tell you, if something happens to Freya because of their incompetence, I'm going to sue their fucking arses off. In the meantime, I'm off to find our daughter. I don't trust those idiots.'

FORTY

Freya stirs from a deep sleep. She can't quite open her eyes yet. Her mind is struggling to drag itself into the conscious world, but her body is aching. Her shoulders are sore, and her back is painful. The mattress she's lying on is so uncomfortable. And there's that smell seeping into her nostrils. She can't identify it, but it's stale and musty.

She finally manages to open her eyes and it takes a while for her to bring anything into focus. Through a bleary haze, streaks of daylight fall across her vision. She's aware of a blanket over her, but there's no pillow.

Her brain is rapidly computing her surroundings. She is not in the annexe at Aunty Corin's house. She is in a room she doesn't recognise. She manages to get herself into a sitting position, but her head is killing her. It feels as if a vice has been placed either side of her temples and it's being tightened every time she moves. She feels queasy and her mouth is parched. The mattress is on bare floorboards and the blanket is an old grey scratchy thing that smells of wet washing. There's a faint whiff of stale cigarettes on the fabric.

It's only as she turns her head towards the light that she realises the window is, in fact, boarded up.

Her brain moves up another level of consciousness and a wave of fear surges through her. Frantically, she pushes the cover away from her and at the same time visually and mentally checks herself over. She's fully clothed. She's still wearing her underwear. Nothing has been ripped. There are no visible bruises or marks. She concentrates. She can't feel any pain down there between her legs. Freya blows out a long breath of relief and tries to remember what happened last night.

She went to the party with Kian. She remembers sitting at a table and talking to his friends. She can't quite put faces to them, although she knows they were two girls and two boys. Was one of them being mean to her? She really can't remember the details; she just has a sensation of one of the girls saying things to her. It's all hazy and unspecific. Did she get drunk? And where was Kian?

As she's thinking, she hears rain begin to splatter against the windowpane. She looks for her phone. She needs to ring Kian to get her from wherever she is. Her mind is now beginning to make sense of the conscious world and she looks at the boarded-up window again with a clear head. She takes in the dirty mattress she's sitting on, and the bucket in the corner of the room.

Shit. She's in some bloody squat. She needs to get home. She wants her mum. Where the fuck is her phone? She's got to get hold of Kian. Maybe he's in a different room. Did they come here to party?

A wave of nausea hits and for a moment she thinks she's going to be sick, but it passes, leaving her feeling cold and shivery.

She crawls off the mattress and manages to get to her feet. Her legs are like jelly, and she stumbles to the door. She pulls on the handle, but the door won't open. She tries again, this time harder. She tries a third time.

She stares at the door. It's jammed. Surely, that's all it is.

'Kian!' she calls out as she tries yet again to open the door. 'Kian! It's Freya. I'm stuck in this room. Kian! Are you there?' She stands still, listening for any sound. Maybe he's asleep in another room. She slams the palm of her hand against the door, then thumps it with her closed fist. No response. 'Kian! This isn't funny. Get me out of here!' She kicks at the door. She thumps it again. Now she's hammering and kicking at the same time. Yelling for Kian to let her out. She starts shouting for help. For anyone to hear her.

But no one comes.

She's got to get out of that room, but how? She rushes over to the window, stumbling on the mattress. She peers through a gap in the boards and can see the rugged hillside beyond. She angles herself to look to the left and the right, to look downwards and upwards. There is nothing there other than fucking grass, rocks and boulders.

She remembers her bag. Where is it? She spots it at the end of the mattress. Her phone's in there. She can ring her mum and she can come and get her out of here. Freya can put on her locations setting and her mum can do that Find My iPhone thing. She rummages in her bag. Where the fuck is her phone? She tips her bag upside down, emptying the contents onto the floorboards. The bag is only a small shoulder bag but still she delves her hand inside, in case the phone has somehow got stuck. But there's no sign of her mobile. She pats her pockets. She pulls up the blanket, in case it's caught up. The phone is not there.

The panic comes again. This time in tidal wave proportions.

Freya doesn't know where she is, why she's there or what happened. But she does know she's in danger. She begins to cry. She needs to get out of here. But how? She wants her mum. Her dad. She wants to be back in Brighton, where everything is familiar. Where she's happy. Where she's safe.

FORTY-ONE

THEN

'Where are we going?' asks Kathleen as she realises John is driving out of the city.

'We're going home,' says John.

'What? I thought you wanted to talk.' Panic surges through her and Kathleen struggles to keep it contained. 'You never said anything about going home.'

'A bit like you never said anything about leaving,' replies John. His voice is calm, over-friendly, and charming – just like he is with clients and business associates. But Kathleen knows this is the prelude to John launching his attack and getting exactly what he wants. She knows his modus operandi.

'Why did you put a tracker in my bag?' she asks, suddenly knowing she needs all the answers. She has an awful feeling about what he has planned for her, and she doesn't think any of it is good.

'I knew you were up to something,' he said. 'I had, how shall we say... complaints. Complaints about what you were encouraging others to do. Complaints about what you were threatening to do.'

Kathleen gives a sharp intake of breath. How much did John know? Did he know about the conversation she'd recorded? No, he couldn't. Denvers would never have told him, surely not. 'I still don't get why you put a tracker in my bag.'

'Because I knew you were up to something, I just didn't know what,' admits John. 'I thought you were planning on running away with another man.'

She gives a derisory snort. 'As if I'd want to do that after being married to you all this time. I'd sooner live the life of a spinster.'

She doesn't see the hand shoot out. The backhanded slap John delivers catches her full in the face, smashing her bottom lip into her teeth. Kathleen lets out a cry of pain and puts her hand to her mouth.

'Shut the feck up,' he shouts at her. 'I took you in when you got pregnant. I married you. I didn't have to, but I did. You should be grateful for what I did for you.'

Kathleen can taste blood. When she dabs at her mouth, her fingertips come away red. She knows for certain the conversation John wanted is only going to be one-sided. He's going to dish out her punishment. He's not going to let her speak.

And now she's trapped in the car with him, with no way of escaping. Her only consolation is that every mile they cover towards Dingle is a mile further away from Dervla. It's keeping Dervla safe for now.

Kathleen is glad she hasn't got her phone with her because that means Dervla can't call her. The poor child must be wondering where the hell Kathleen is. Dervla probably thinks Kathleen has walked out on her. As soon as she can, Kathleen will call her and explain what's happened, but she can't do that while John is with her.

It's less than two and a half hours from Dingle to Cork, but as they approach their house John doesn't slow down. He carries on driving, right past the turning for the lane.

'Where are we going?' asks Kathleen. Her lip is sore and swollen from where he struck her.

John glances over at her. 'Shut up.'

She sees his fingers flex around the steering wheel and so she sits back in her seat, not wanting to give him any cause to lash out at her again. The panic she'd kept at bay rises a notch and her stomach gives a roll of anxiety. Where the hell *are* they going?

They drive out along the Slea Head Drive towards Fahan and Kathleen is out of ideas as to their destination. It's only when John turns off the road and onto a narrow, rutted dirt track that Kathleen knows exactly where he is taking her. Nestled against the backdrop of the hills beyond, Skerries Cottage awaits them.

'Why are we here?' Kathleen asks. She's never liked this place and hasn't been up here for years. John inherited it when his parents died. There was something about the stone cottage standing alone on the hillside, looking out on the distant horizon, that made Kathleen uneasy. It wasn't a welcoming home at all. Even when it was lived in, it had an eerie quality about it. The fact that rumours ran rife about it being haunted from years back didn't help. Fortunately, John had never wanted to undertake a renovation of the place. He preferred their modern house nearer the town, which everybody could admire and be impressed at how far the lad from Fahan had come.

John ignores Kathleen and pulls up around the back of the place. Kathleen notices the door is ajar, as if someone has recently been here. As John gets out of the car, Kathleen knows this is possibly her only chance of getting away. She has no idea what is about to happen, but all her senses tell her it's bad. The moment John closes his door, Kathleen yanks on her door handle and launches herself out of the vehicle. The second her feet touch the ground, she's running as fast as she can around the side of the cottage.

She can hear John shout at her to stop, but she ignores him. If she can get to the end of the drive and out onto the main road, she might be able to flag down a passing car. But John is fast. Faster than her. She can hear his feet pounding along the track, which is littered with patches of weeds and grass. She extends her stride; she has to get away. She has only just cleared the second corner when his hand clamps down on her shoulder, snatching her backwards, throwing her off balance. She crashes to the ground.

Kathleen is crying. She tries to get up, but John has her pinned face down. His body is across hers and she cannot move. He is pulling her arm, wrenching it up behind her back. Kathleen screams in pain.

'Stop fecking fighting,' he growls. 'You stupid bitch.'

'You're hurting me. John! Please!' She stops moving. Stops resisting. After a couple of seconds, she feels the pressure release on her body and arm.

'Get up, woman,' orders John, holding her arm behind her back. He uses his other hand to help her up. Then he turns her around and roughly pushes her in the back towards the rear of the cottage. 'Get inside.'

'I don't want to,' she protests. 'Can't we talk out here?'

'And have you run off again? I don't think so.'

They get to the back door and Kathleen comes to a halt. 'I don't want to go in there.'

'Do as you're fecking well told.'

'No.'

The slap is hard and nearly knocks her off her feet. But she was braced for it this time. She knows she mustn't go into Skerries Cottage. The second slap sends her head the other way. She feels like a pinball, slamming from one side to the other. But she stands her ground.

Next thing Kathleen knows, she's struggling to breathe. He has his hand gripped around her neck. The pressure on her windpipe is immense, restricting the air supply. She panics. Tries to grab at his hand, to pull him away. She feels light-headed. She's going to pass out. And then he releases his grip, and her legs give way. He catches hold of her.

'Love, honour and obey, Kathleen,' he snarls into her ear. 'Remember the promises you made in church. Now stop fighting me and get in the fecking house.'

She's frightened now. John has never done that to her before. Sure, he's been physical with her a few times, but it's only in the last couple of years that it's got bad. But nearly strangling her? Never. She enters the cottage and the damp, musty smell, combined with a stale urine aroma, assaults her nostrils. She hasn't been in this kitchen in nearly twenty years, not since John's father died. His mother died when John was ten. She takes in the mess in the kitchen as she staggers through the room. There are some broken crockery pieces on the draining board which she's certain have been there since her father-in-law died.

'Upstairs,' orders John, giving her a poke in the back.

Kathleen hesitates. 'Please, John. Let's go somewhere else to talk.'

John sighs. 'Just do it, Kathleen.'

At the top of the stairs he tells her to go into the back bedroom. Kathleen doesn't think she's ever been up here. The window has been boarded up, but there are sufficient gaps between the planks of wood to allow shafts of light to shine through. The room has peeling blue wallpaper that hangs limply from the plaster. There are areas where part of the wall has come completely away, revealing the rotting lathes behind it. Water has obviously got in from the roof at one stage, as there is a big damp patch on the ceiling. The fireplace is full of beer cans and bottles and there's a mattress on the floor under the window.

'Sit down there,' says John.

'I'm not sitting on that. It's filthy.' Kathleen looks at the stains and dirt on the fabric. There's a rip at one end and a spring is poking through.

'Do it.' John gives her a shove. Kathleen staggers back and ends up falling onto the mattress anyway. 'Now, I've got a few things to do. You can wait here. When I come back we're going to have a serious talk.'

'For God's sake, John, you can't leave me here!' Kathleen goes to stand, but John takes a menacing step towards her. He's towering over her and she's too frightened to move.

'You need time to think about what you've been doing behind my back,' he says. He goes over to a built-in cupboard beside the fireplace and takes a book out. He thrusts it at her. It's the Holy Bible. 'This used to be mine. My father used to make me read this when I had disappointed him, when I had sinned. I think you need to be reminded. Matthew three, verse two.'

With that he leaves the room, and she hears the door lock behind him.

Kathleen ignores the Bible and rushes over to the door, pulling on the handle, shouting for John to let her out. He doesn't reply. She can hear his feet on the stairs as he descends. She screams louder but he ignores her.

The sound of a car engine starting has Kathleen rushing over to the boarded-up window. Through one of the gaps, she angles her head and can see the lower half of John's car. The wheels turn and the car moves out of sight. He's left her here with the stupid fucking Bible! Has he gone mad? She has to get out before he comes back.

FORTY-TWO

'I'm going with you,' I said, as Danny zipped up his jacket.

'You should stay here,' he replied.

'I can't. Like you, I need to do something,' I said. 'I don't want to be on my own.'

Danny stopped and looked at me. 'Why's that?'

'I don't feel safe. But more than that, I need to find Freya. I don't trust anyone, especially now Ahern knows everything, thanks to Finn.'

'Finn?' Danny frowned.

'I confided in him. He's told Ahern.'

'And Ahern is mates with Denvers,' said Danny, filling in the blanks. 'You think there's some kind of cover-up going on?'

I nodded. My eyes filled with tears. 'It's been going on for years. Probably even before Kathleen. Certainly after her. Dervla wouldn't be the first one in over twenty years. Not for someone like Denvers.'

'He was always a bit of a creep,' said Danny. 'Real smooth, like. The women seemed to love him.'

'It couldn't have been kept hidden all this time without a cover-up,' I said. 'Can you imagine if something like that got out? He'd be ruined and everyone around him. His wife, for a start. And if Ahern has been helping him then he'd be in deep shit too.'

'Kathleen had proof with the transcript, enough to bring both Fergus and Aisling down,' said Danny.

'And if she didn't have anything on Ahern, maybe she was relying on Denvers naming him, you know, to try and save his own skin.'

'The whole fucking lot of them are corrupt,' said Danny. 'But you know what?'

'What?'

'All this is secondary. This can wait until after we've found Freya.'

I nodded. 'I know.'

'Right, let's get going.'

A movement outside caught my eye. Through the window I could see Corin coming across from her house. I opened the door before she got there. 'What's up?' I asked.

She gave me an apologetic look. 'They just turned up,' she said quietly, indicating behind her with a jerk of the head.

Jesus, just what I needed. My parents.

My mother bustled past Corin. 'Oh, Siobhan, we had to come. We couldn't sit at home on our own with no one telling us anything. We've tried contacting Rory, but he's busy searching for Freya.' She stopped in her tracks as Danny appeared behind me. 'Oh, Danny. I didn't know you were here.'

'Hello, Marie,' he said, and then to my father as he came to stand beside my mother. 'Séamus.'

'Danny, lad,' said my dad. 'I'm sorry about this. I told Siobhan to stop her meddling. One missing daughter is enough for this family. But she wouldn't leave it, would she?' He glared at me. 'Always dancing to her own tune, that one, and look what good it's done.'

'With all due respect, Séamus,' said Danny, stepping in

front of me. 'Why don't you shut the fuck up. Leave Siobhan alone for once. This is not the time to have yet another swipe at her. Freya is missing and the last thing we need is you coming around here lambasting your own daughter and detailing your perceived shortcomings of her.'

There was a stunned silence. I exchanged a look with Corin, who silently mouthed the words 'Jesus Christ.' No one ever spoke to my father like that.

I looked at my mother, who was just as dumbstruck. My father wasn't faring much better. It was like he was having to check he'd really heard correctly. And then, to my utter surprise, he nodded, as if agreeing with Danny.

'Of course,' he said briskly. 'You're right. This is not the time.' He stopped short at an apology.

'You're welcome to come in and wait,' said Danny, as if he'd greeted my parents at the door civilly. 'But Siobhan and I are going out to look for our daughter.' He felt for my hand and held it tightly.

'Why don't you come back over to mine?' said Corin, touching our mother's arm. 'It's more comfortable. Dad?'

'Séamus?' Mam looked at my father. I hated the way she always deferred to him, but I guessed it was too late to hold out any hope that she might one day take control.

'Yes. We'll do that,' said my father. He went to go but paused and looked back at Danny. 'Keep us up to date.' I thought for a moment he was going to say something to me, but he turned and went back towards Corin's house. I didn't have time to analyse the gesture.

We left the annexe as Niall was coming across the drive.

'Danny!' he called out, holding aloft his car keys. 'Take my car.' He tossed the keys over and Danny caught them.

'Thanks, Niall.'

'I'm going to join the lads down at the harbour. Kian's there waiting for us,' said Niall. 'We're going out to The Banks and the lighthouse to look. I'll take Corin's car.'

'I get the pleasure of sitting with Mum and Dad,' said Corin with a sigh. She gave me a hug. 'Don't give up,' she whispered.

I returned the hug before jumping in the car with Danny, who already had the engine running.

'Sorry about that back there,' he said. 'I'll apologise to your dad later.' He drove out onto the main road.

'Oh, don't apologise,' I said. 'It's about time someone put him in his place. I actually think there was a glimmer of respect in his eyes after that.'

Danny shrugged. 'I don't really give a fuck. I just need to find Freya.'

I closed my eyes as I thought of Freya and willed with all my might that she was OK. That she knew we were looking for her. *Stay alive. Please, Freya, stay alive. Do whatever it takes, just stay alive.* I repeated the words over and over again in my head. I wasn't giving up on her. We'd find her. I would not stop until she was safely in our arms where she belonged.

<h1 style="text-align:center">FORTY-THREE</h1>

Freya is curled up in a ball on the mattress. She's been crying on and off for what seems like forever. She has no idea why she's been locked in this room. She has had some hazy flashbacks to the party, and something about going to the toilet and disjointed recollections of one of the girls coming with her keep replaying in her mind, frame by frame. She thinks they are significant, but her brain hasn't been able to make sense of the chain of events.

She's dreaming of being in a car. Sitting in the back with another girl who she doesn't know but feels comfortable with. She can't see who is driving, but she is laughing with the girl. The next thing is a sense of danger. She can hear the ocean and she and the girl are walking into a building. Freya looks behind her at the car that has brought them to this house.

The person gets out of the driver's side.

Freya lets out a cry. She sits upright. Panic ripping through her. Sweat pools above her top lip. Her heart is racing, and she gasps for breath. She's scared. Her dream – her nightmare – was so vivid. It takes a moment for her to remember where she is and then it comes crashing back in technicolour. It's not a nightmare. It's a memory. She's remembering more and more of that night.

She looks towards the window and realises it's dark outside. It must be another night. How long was she asleep for? Is this Saturday night? No one has come. She's desperate for a wee and knows she's going to have to use the bucket in the corner. There's a toilet roll beside the bucket.

This is so humiliating. So embarrassing. But she needs to relieve herself.

She crawls over to the corner, crying as she squats over the bucket.

When she's finished she crawls back across to the mattress and takes a sip of the water that was left for her. The bottle is nearly empty, and she wonders if anyone is coming back for her.

She resumes her earlier foetal position and wonders what her mum is thinking. She will be going mad with worry. Freya wishes she'd never argued with her mum. She shouldn't have been a stroppy teenager and she shouldn't have gone to the party.

Another memory comes to her. It's of being in the toilet with a girl who had been sitting with them at the table. She gave Freya a sip of her drink while they were standing there, talking about another girl who had also been sitting with them. And that boy. Conor. God, why had Freya ever got involved with him? What was she thinking? She should have stayed away from that lot. And Kian, where had he been? She frowns, forcing herself back to the party. He was with a girl, that's right. He said he wouldn't be long, and she'd looked over at one point. Kian and a girl were in a deep clench, snogging each other's faces off. No wonder he hadn't been there to make sure she was OK.

But the girl in the bathroom with her, who had given her the water, seemed so nice and friendly. Not like the other girl at the table.

Freya knows, without a doubt, her drink must have been spiked. It's the only explanation. The girl who took her to the toilet spiked the water she'd offered Freya.

But why?

And who was she?

Freya has a sudden attack of panic as she remembers the PSHE lessons at school where they were told about human trafficking. Fuck. Is that happening to her? The tears come again. And eventually a groggy, dream-filled sleep comes too.

Freya is woken by the sound of footsteps on the stairs. She sits up and listens. She holds her head as pain shoots through it. Another headache. Another deep sleep. She looks at the bottle of water and tries to remember if the seal had been broken or not. The sound of a creak of the stair confirms someone is definitely coming. Her heart jumps with excitement. She's going to be rescued. She leaps to her feet and is about to rush over to the door when something stops her. There's another set of footsteps on the stairs. These ones are heavier than the first set. She suddenly feels fear.

She doesn't know why, but she throws herself back down on the mattress, trying to regulate her breathing as she pulls the cover up over her face and then places her arm across her eyes, so whoever it is can't tell if she's awake or not. Her instinct to survive is strong and it's telling her not to let them know she's awake.

She hears the key turn in the lock and the brief scrape on the floor as it is pushed open.

'Check on her,' says a voice. Male. Older. She doesn't recognise it.

'Sure,' comes a young female voice.

Freya senses the girl come over to her and kneel. She feels her arm being moved and hair is pushed from her face. Freya wants to cry. She's sure her eyelids are flickering, giving the game away, but the girl says nothing. Freya opens her eyes a fraction and she is met by the clear green eyes of the girl. All at once, the memory rushes back. It's the girl who took her to the toilets at the party.

'Is she breathing?' asks the man. 'For feck's sake. I could do without this fecking drama.'

The girl mimes *shh* and briefly puts her finger to her lips, before brushing Freya's hair back over her face and replacing her arm. 'She's breathing all right,' says the girl. 'Best let her sleep. She'll be fine.'

'Here, leave a fresh bottle of water for her.'

Freya hears the man roll a bottle across the floor and wonders why he doesn't come into the room. 'Make sure you wipe it down. Don't want any fingerprints on the bottle.'

'Ah, that's why you're wearing gloves and won't come into the room,' says the girl. 'Frightened you're going to leave some DNA.'

'Don't get smart with me.'

'Is this bottle laced as well?' she asks.

Freya is sure the girl is asking these questions to let her know not to drink the water.

'What do you think?'

'I wouldn't expect anything less from you, Sergeant Ahern,' says the girl.

Freya is sure her breath just hitched in her throat. Ahern? That's the man who was at her grandparents' house, she's sure of it.

'Shut the feck up,' snaps Ahern. 'You're getting far too big for your boots. I can easily have you stay here and keep her company.'

The girl faffs with the mattress and then gets to her feet. 'Sorry.'

'So you should be. Now, let's go.'

'Yeah. I don't like this place,' says the girl. 'Never mind Skerries Cottage, it should be called Scary Cottage.'

Freya commits the name to memory. She hears the door close and then, as it's locked from the outside, she hears the girl speak again. 'How long are you keeping her here for?'

'You ask a lot of questions,' says Ahern.

'Just wondered. I assumed the search party would be up here soon.'

'You leave that with me. She won't be here when they come searching for her.'

The voices are fading, and Freya sits up, gasping for air. What the fuck are they going to do with her? Was the girl trying to warn her? But how on earth is she going to get out of here?

Her throat is dry and she wishes she could drink the water, but there's no way she's touching the stuff. She thinks for a moment and then unscrews the cap, before pouring some of it into the pee bucket. If they come back, she can pretend she's drunk some. Let them think she's out of it and then, if she gets a chance, she can make a run for it. It's not much of a plan, but it's the best option she's got right now.

FORTY-FOUR

We had searched all afternoon and long into the evening. It was as if the heavens were sharing my despair and turmoil and the angels themselves were crying. The rain got heavier and heavier until, eventually, the guards had called off the search, promising to resume at first light. They'd so far searched Dingle, the harbour, and the beach. Tomorrow they would gradually widen their search, fanning out from the town.

Danny and I had reluctantly returned to the annexe, and I was relieved to find out from Corin that Niall had taken our parents' home earlier in the evening. I couldn't face them right now. I was emotionally exhausted.

Corin had cooked a shepherd's pie and left it on the work-top, and even though neither Danny nor I had the mind for eating, we both agreed we should try to keep our energy levels up as we'd need them tomorrow.

'I just don't know where else to look,' I said, poking the mashed potato with my fork. 'All around town and beyond. I mean, where else could she be?'

'Someone must have taken her in a car,' said Danny. 'And

that someone managed to get her out of the party without a fuss, so we have to assume she went willingly, or she was drugged.'

I gasped at the suggestion, even though it had been lurking in the back of my mind all afternoon. I wanted to cry, but I think my brain was blocking that neurological pathway. Either that or I literally did not have any tears left, only a massive, ragged hole in my heart.

I was on the brink of some sort of hysterical episode of despair, but if I let that consume me then I'd be wasting time and energy dealing with the fallout. I had to keep Freya at the front and centre of my every waking thought.

Danny pushed his plate away, the food half-eaten. 'If she's not in Dingle and not in the immediate area, where would she be?' He was thinking out loud.

'Some place where no one goes or would happen across her,' I said.

'So, we have the beehive houses along at Fahan,' said Danny. 'We could try them.'

'But how could they leave her there and be sure she wouldn't escape?' I asked.

'Tie her up, I guess.'

I shuddered at the thought of Freya bound up with tape or rope or even chains. 'It would be somewhere where no one could hear her, unless she's gagged,' I said.

'Actually, I don't think it will be the beehives,' said Danny. 'Too obvious.'

I picked up my phone and sent yet another message to Nicole's number.

> Please, Nicole. Freya is still missing. Please help us. Can you think of anywhere she might be? Do you know anything? Anything at all? I don't care about anything other than getting her back safely.

'We'll try there anyway,' said Danny, almost having a

conversation with himself. 'We'll do that now. I don't give a shit about the weather.'

We drove out along Slea Head Drive and I looked out at the choppy waters of the Atlantic Ocean. Night was falling and as I switched my gaze to the other side of the road, to the houses and buildings we passed, everything was laid out in different shades of grey. Every driveway we passed, I looked up, my eyes searching for any sign of our daughter. I looked at the houses, wondering if she was in there, being held against her will. I couldn't imagine she was anywhere by choice now. It had been too long. She would have come home by now. Of that I was certain.

The hillside became less populated with buildings the further away from town Danny steered the car.

We got to Dún Beag Fort Visitors Centre where, on the other side of the road, a small stone prehistoric fort that had been unearthed in the 1970s was set. It was only accessible via a small footpath that was, of course, closed at this hour. It was open daily so if anyone was hiding out there, they'd soon be discovered.

'How far do you want to go?' asked Danny.

I looked back at the visitors' centre, with the Famine Cottages beyond it. Again, not a place someone could access easily or hide out for any length of time. 'Let's go as far as the beehive place,' I said. 'We can start again there in the morning. It's too dark now, I don't think we're going to just come across her on the path.'

'I'm speaking to Ahern tomorrow and insisting they start going house to house,' said Danny. 'If he doesn't agree, I'm going higher.'

I could see his hands gripping the steering wheel so tightly his knuckles were turning white. I wanted to reassure him it was going to be OK, but how could I when I was starting to have doubts myself?

The beehive huts where you could also pet lambs came into sight and Danny pulled over into the parking space. 'Is this where the van followed you to?' he asked.

'Yes. Right here; he reversed and then drove off.'

He got out and stood at the wall, looking out to sea. I went and stood beside him. Neither of us bothered about the rain that was still coming down, albeit more of a drizzle now. I looked up at him and saw a tear trickle down his cheek. He breathed in deeply through his nose and swiped at the tear, but it was no use. It was only replaced by another and then another. Until he was crying without even trying to stop. I slipped my arm around his waist and rested my other hand on his chest.

'It's OK to cry,' I said softly.

'I just want her found,' he said before a sob caught in his throat. He bowed his head. 'I swear to God, Siobhan, I'll do anything to get her back safely.'

'I know. I know,' I said.

He turned and dropped his head against mine and I held him tight as he cried like I'd never seen him cry before. And I had never felt so guilty as I did in that moment. I should not have let her go out. I should not have brought her here with me. I should not have come to look for Kathleen. Not if this was the price I was going to have to pay.

FORTY-FIVE

THEN

Kathleen's fingernails are broken and the skin at the tips of her fingers is sore and bleeding. Try as she might, she cannot get the boards off the window. There's a tree outside and she had some small hope she'd be able to get across onto it and make her way down to the ground, but that only ever happens in fiction or on TV. The reality is she's locked in this room and there is no escape.

She really needs a wee, but she doesn't want to use the bucket in the corner. That is so dehumanising. She still can't believe he's done this to her. What does he hope to achieve by it?

Tears of anger, frustration and fear track their way down her face. She doesn't wipe them away; she lets them fall freely. She wonders if Dervla is all right. It's now five hours since John kidnapped her. The word sounds dramatic, but that's what he's done and now he's holding her hostage. What the hell has happened to him and why is he doing this? He's unhinged.

Kathleen is tired. She wants to sleep but she doesn't want to lie down on the mattress. She rests her hands behind her, and her fingers brush the Bible. She picks it up. What did John say to her? Matthew three, verse two. She finds the chapter and scans down to the second verse.

Repent, for the kingdom of heaven has come near.

Repent? He wants her to say sorry, to regret, to atone for what she's done. For leaving him? She guesses that bit kind of makes sense, but the rest of the verse... She gives an involuntary shiver. She knew John's dad had been strict with him and, like her own, God was king, in all literal and metaphorical ways. John's father had often quoted the Bible at him, John had told her he was made to recite the Hail Mary in front of his father for however many times his father saw fit. John had always been scornful of such punishment and berated his late father for being a tyrant and yet, John was now doing it himself.

She blew out a breath, wondering how many Hail Marys John was going to make her say. Siobhan had been right when she called him Father John.

It's sometime later when John returns to the room. There's a calmness about him that makes Kathleen wary. She fully expected him to come storming in, but he's totally composed and in control.

'Right, this is what is going to happen,' he says, standing in front of her. 'You're going to come home and all this nonsense of you leaving me is to be forgotten. I'm prepared to forgive and forget.'

She looks at him in utter confusion. 'You want me to come home?' she repeats, unable to believe she heard him correctly.

'Yes,' he replies as if she's asked the most stupid question in the world. 'Come home now and we will forget all about this. Blessed are the merciful.'

Kathleen can't go home yet. She's got to make a statement in

Cork about Denvers and Ahern. 'John, you don't seem to understand,' she says. 'I can't.'

'What are you talking about, woman? Of course you can.'

She wonders if she can get out of here and somehow get back to Cork, if John will track her down again.

'Look, before I come home, there's something I need to do. You have to let me go back to Cork, just for a day, then I'll come home.'

'What do you mean?'

'It's simple. I need to do something important first.'

'What's so important that you need to go back there?' John's eyes narrow.

'I have to make a statement about something that happened to me when I was younger and that is happening to another girl now,' says Kathleen.

'What do you mean, something that happened to you?'

'I don't want to talk about it now.'

'Is it to do with Denvers?'

Kathleen freezes. 'Denvers?'

'Yes, don't think I don't know,' says John. 'I've known for a long time. Your dirty little secret. Your affair with a married man.'

'And you never said anything. Why?' She doesn't understand why he's being so flippant about it. She thought he'd go mad.

'What was the point? It was over by the time we were serious and then when you got pregnant with Kian, I knew you wouldn't be going back to him.' He gives her a self-satisfied smile. 'I knew you were a bit easy before I married you. That's why I went out with you. But my father was right. You were an easy lay.'

Kathleen shakes her head. Anger spikes in her. 'I wasn't easy,' she spits at him. 'I was taken advantage of. I was groomed by Denvers.'

John laughs out loud. '*Groomed?* What the feck are you talking about?'

'Denvers groomed me from when I was at school. He waited until I was seventeen to sleep with me so it would be legal. I wasn't easy!' She shouts the last sentence.

'Oh, come on, Kathleen. You're rewriting history.'

'You bastard.'

'Shame you got yourself pregnant, though. I could have done without marrying you at such a young age.'

She flies at him, her rage uncontrollable. 'You bastard!' she shouts. 'You stupid fucking bastard. I didn't get myself pregnant.'

He catches her flailing arms. 'Oh sorry, I got you pregnant. I didn't hear you complaining.'

'You didn't get me pregnant,' she shouts at the top of her voice. 'It wasn't you!' And then she laughs out loud at the stunned look on his face. 'No, you didn't get me pregnant. In fact, I think all these years you've being firing blanks.' She wants to hurt him now. Get her own back. Punish him as revenge for all the years of pain and hurt, physical and emotional, that she's had to take from him. 'Why do you think we never had any more children? You couldn't have any.'

'What are you talking about?' His hands grip her wrists tighter.

She doesn't care. 'You're not Kian's father. There's no one to carry on the Walsh family name you're so proud of,' she says, barely recognising her own voice. Such is the venom, she can almost taste it. 'I was pregnant by Denvers.'

'Bitch,' he grabs her by the throat. Both hands are around her neck. He's squeezing and squeezing. Kathleen tries to pull his hands away, but she can't. She can't breathe. He's going to kill her.

FORTY-SIX

Freya doesn't fall back to sleep after Ahern and the girl have gone. She's too wired. Her headache is clearing, and her thoughts are starting to become sharper. This is good but it's also bad, as the reality of her situation hits her hard. She has to keep it together though. She has to be alert in case they come back in the night for her, and she doesn't hear them.

God, the mattress is uncomfortable and the smell in the room is strong. The bucket isn't helping matters.

She gets to her feet and walks back and forth from one side of the room to the other. Her legs are cramping, and she needs to stretch them. If only she could have a drink. As she reaches the mattress, she doesn't see the edge is rucked up a bit. She catches her foot underneath it and falls onto the blanket.

'Shit.' That was her toe. 'Stupid fucking mattress,' she mutters and, in her frustration, smacks her hand down onto the edge. 'Ow!' Her hand hits something hard. What the hell is that? She lifts up the edge of the mattress where there's a lump.

Her eyes are going to pop out of her head. She can't believe what she's looking at. It's a mobile phone.

She suddenly remembers the girl fiddling with the mattress

when she was kneeling in front of her. She must have put it there.

'Oh my fucking God,' says Freya out loud, and then corrects herself. 'Thank you, God!' Her hands shake as she grapples with the phone. It's not switched on. It's an Android phone and she's not familiar with how to use it.

She's so intent on working out how to switch the phone on that she almost misses the sound of the car engine pulling up outside and the crunch of wheels on the stones. It's not one car. It's two.

Freya freezes for a moment as she processes what is happening. She springs into action, rushing to the window and craning her neck to look through the gap in the boards. The second vehicle has its headlights on, and the first car is bathed in a bright white glow.

A figure gets out of the first car.

Male. Tall. She thinks back to the man at her grandparents' house. The same man who came to visit her earlier. Rory Ahern. It's him. She's sure it is.

He's talking loudly. Confident no one will hear him. She looks towards the second vehicle and can see it's a white van. She feels a wave of sickness as the driver gets out. It's Conor.

He looks up towards the window and Freya throws herself to the side and out of sight. At that moment the phone springs to life and the screen glows white.

Her mum. She has to call her mum. Fuuuck! What is the number? She knows it. Her mum's had the same number since forever: 07475. No. Wait. Is that right?

Freya tries to recite the number out loud. 'Oh, seven, four, eight, four. Shit.' She can't remember. Her mind is blank. She can hardly breathe. She's trying to catch her breath. Panic is setting in. She hears the door downstairs being scraped open. They're coming for her. She's not going to be able to call her mum. 'Oh, seven, four, seven, five. Four, four two.' Her fingers fly over the keypad and the last three numbers are a blur as she hits the call button.

She can hear them talking downstairs. She can't make out what they are saying. She backs as far into the corner of the room as she can. Or maybe she should stand behind the door and try to run out. Yes. She'll do that. Frantically, she arranges the blanket, trying to make it resemble some kind of human form. It looks nothing like a person, but it might just buy her some time. Or should she pretend to be unconscious? What the hell should she do? She's crying with fear and panic.

The phone is ringing. She presses it to her ear. Pick up. Pick up. Mum. Please pick up. It continues to ring. She can hear Ahern's feet on the stairs now. The phone goes to voicemail.

Hello, you've reached Siobhan Martin's number. Sorry I can't take your call. Please leave a message and your number and I'll get back to you. Thanks!

Jesus! Shut up. Freya wants the recording to end. There's the beep to leave the message. Hurry up! She wills the beep to be over.

'Mum, it's me. Freya. I'm at a house. Scary Cottage or something. Ahern is here with Conor. Help me please, they've come to get me.' She is whispering and hopes to God her mum can understand her. The key is turning in the lock and Freya cuts the call before stuffing the phone into her sock. She dives onto the mattress with her back to the door and closes her eyes.

FORTY-SEVEN

'My phone!' I sat bolt upright on the sofa. My phone. Where the hell was my phone? Danny, lying right next to me, was awake and sitting up immediately. Neither of us had wanted to go to bed last night. We didn't think we would sleep so we had sat on the sofa, cuddled up together. Trying to cling onto a small thread of hope that was getting thinner and weaker by the hour.

'Where is it?' said Danny, jumping to his feet.

I must have fallen asleep with it in my hand, but I could hear it right next to me. I leaped up and grabbed the cushions, throwing them to the floor with no regard for where they landed. Danny yanked the seat cushion off and there was my phone. I snatched it up, but it had stopped ringing.

'It's gone to voicemail. I can't cut in on the call.'

'Who is it?'

'I can't tell yet.' I wanted to cry. What if it was Freya?

'Give it here.' Danny swiped the phone from my hands.

I couldn't keep still as he patiently waited for the phone to take the message. 'It takes a minute before we can access it,' he said. 'But I can check the missed call list. Here we go. I've no idea whose number this is.'

'Let me see.' He held the phone for me to look at. 'It might be Nicole,' I said, barely able to contain my panic. 'I messaged her. She might be calling me back at last.'

'Right, sit down. I'm accessing the voicemail now,' said Danny.

We perched on the edge of the sofa. I had to stuff my hands in my mouth. I wanted to scream. Cry. Yell. I don't know what I wanted to do.

You have one new message. Today at three-twenty-two a.m.

'God's sake,' I muttered.

And then we heard it. Our darling precious beautiful daughter. My heart almost burst from my chest with relief but as I listened to her message complete and utter desperation took its place.

'Scary Cottage? Where the fuck is that?' Danny looks at me. He plays the message again. 'Why do I know that name?'

'I don't know. I don't know,' I said. My mind was blank. I felt I should know it too. 'Skerries. Scary Skerries.' I looked up at Danny. 'She means Skerries Cottage. It's John Walsh's parents' old home. The one just past the beehive houses at Fahan. Oh God, we were there earlier. We were so close.'

Danny was moving before I'd even finished my sentence. 'Come on. We're going there now. Call Finn. Call Niall. Call anyone you can think of.'

We were in the car and screeching out of the driveway within seconds. Good job it was the middle of the night and there were no cars about. Danny tore around the twisty road like some sort of rally driver. I fastened my seat belt and, with one hand gripping the dash to steady myself, I rang Finn.

'Siobhan,' came his sleepy voice. 'What's up?'

'I don't have time to explain, but Freya is up at Skerries Cottage. The Walsh's old place at Fahan. Ahern is there with Conor. They're going to get Freya.'

'Oh, thank God for that,' said Finn. 'That's great news.'

'NO!' I shouted the word down the phone. 'It's not. They are holding her up there. They're involved. I don't know how, but she's in danger from them. Please, Finn, ring whoever you need to and get up there. We're on our way now. Hurry!' I ended the call as Danny overcooked a corner and the car slammed into the wall of someone's driveway. He didn't stop. Just straightened the car and sped on his way.

'Try calling the number back,' said Danny.

I was ahead of him there. The phone rang but didn't answer. 'She's not picking up,' I said, as more panic took hold.

'Maybe she hasn't got access to the phone anymore,' said Danny.

I tried another time, but it rang out a second time.

'Ring Niall,' ordered Danny. 'We're going to be there in five minutes. I'm not waiting for anyone. Tell him to get there ASAP.'

This time I made sure I was clear about Freya being in danger and it was probably the first time I'd ever heard any urgency in Niall's voice as he promised he'd be there with some of the lads. Who the fuck they were I didn't know and didn't care, but the cavalry were on their way.

'We're coming, Freya,' I said through tears of anguish. 'We're coming, darling.' I repeated it over and over again. It was the only way to stop myself from going insane. 'We're coming. We're coming. Stay alive, Freya. Do whatever it takes but stay alive.'

FORTY-EIGHT

'I'll wait here. You go and get her,' orders Ahern.

'I don't know if I can carry her on my own,' says Conor.

'Go away. A fine young man like you. Anyway, she shouldn't be totally out of it. That last lot of sedative wasn't so strong.'

Freya goes along with expectations and groans as if she's been disturbed from a deep sleep. She moves slightly.

'Hey, Freya,' says Conor. His voice is close, and he jiggles her shoulder with his hand. 'Time to wake up.'

Freya rolls over and pretends to focus. She genuinely lets out a small cry of alarm as a balaclava-covered face looms over her. She shuffles back away from Conor as if she doesn't know who he is. She thanks her lucky stars that she took GCSE Drama. Her teacher always said she had a gift for acting. Now she's going to have to give an Oscar-winning performance.

'It's OK. I'm not going to hurt you,' says Conor through the balaclava. 'We're just taking you somewhere more comfortable.'

'Shut up,' snaps Ahern from the doorway. 'She doesn't need to know anything.'

Conor reaches out and grabs hold of her arm. 'Get up.'

Freya does as she's told, pretending to be unsteady on her feet. 'Please don't hurt me,' she says. That part's not acting.

'Do as you're told, and you won't get hurt,' says Ahern.

'Can't you help me here?' asks Conor.

'Just do it,' retorts Ahern.

Conor loops Freya's arm over his shoulder, keeping it in place with one hand. His other hand snakes around her waist to hold her upright. She goes along with it. The last thing she wants is for him to carry her, as he might see the phone in her sock. She can smell stale cigarette smoke on his clothes and there's a hint of body odour, but she's not sure if that's her or him.

Side by side, she staggers downstairs with Conor, who curses regularly at the awkwardness of it and moans at Ahern for not helping him.

They are outside now and Freya takes in big gulps of fresh air. The headlights on the van have been switched off, but the sidelights are on and illuminate the ground enough that she can see where they are going. Ahern is at the van, and he slides the side door open with a gloved hand.

Freya is trying to weigh up the best time to make a break for it. She pulls her arm away from Conor's shoulder.

'It's hurting me,' she says, and is relieved when Conor lets her hand go and removes his other hand from her waist. There's nowhere she can run, though. She has Ahern in front of her and Conor behind her. She slows her pace and pretends to stagger. She has seen the one hope she has of getting away. She puts her hand out to the boot of Ahern's car to steady herself.

'Jesus, take your hand off the car,' says Ahern. 'Get her off there.'

Conor pulls her away and Rory strides over, using his sleeve to rub Freya's handprint from his car. 'Get her in the van.'

Freya walks on before Conor has a chance to hold her. She sidesteps around Ahern and, as she reaches the end of his car, she darts around the back so fast it takes a moment for either of them to realise what she's doing. She's quick on her feet and glad she wore her white trainers. She races down the side of the van, praying to God she beats Conor to the end.

She fully expects to run straight into him as he comes from the other side, but he's not there. She doesn't look back.

She can hear Ahern shouting at Conor to catch the bitch, but this just drives her on even more. The ground is uneven and she stumbles but keeps her balance. The driveway slopes downwards and the momentum gives her even more speed. She's at the end of the driveway and out onto the road.

Freya hesitates. Which way? She has no idea where she is. The sea is ahead of her, which must be south. She turns left. East. Please let it be in the direction of Dingle.

She hears an engine. It's the van, she's sure. There's more than one engine noise. She can't work out if it's a car or a van. She rounds the bend; her lungs are burning, and her legs are already protesting at the sudden exertion. She overestimated her recovery from being drugged for two days. She feels light-headed and a stitch is already coming in her side.

The road is lit up ahead of her. For a moment she thinks a car is coming towards her, but then she realises, it's behind her. Gaining on her. The van swerves in front of her, screeching to a halt. The side door slides open, and a hand comes out.

'Get in!'

It's not Ahern. It's a girl. She's wearing a yellow jacket. Freya shakes her head. No. She's the girl from the party. The one who brought her here. 'Get in!' repeats the girl. 'I'm trying to help you. Conor is too. Get the fuck in.'

Freya looks back. There's another car coming at speed. It has to be Ahern. Something tells her being caught by Ahern is far worse than getting into the van with the girl. She has no choice but to grab the girl's hand. The moment she's yanked in,

Conor floors the accelerator and they are speeding away before the girl has time to shut the door.

Freya is gasping for air as the girl throws herself onto the floor beside her. 'Jesus. You took your time.'

'Who are you?' asks Freya. 'I don't understand what's going on.'

'My name's Nicole,' said the girl. 'We're taking you home.'

Freya wants to cry with relief. 'Are you really?'

'Of course we fucking are,' comes Conor's voice from the front of the van. He looks around and grins at her. 'We may be a bit rough around the edges but we're not hardened criminals. Drugging and kidnapping, that's serious shit. Besides, this will be my ticket out of here. Away from those crooked bastards.'

'Conor! Watch out!' yells Nicole.

Freya watches Conor turn his head back to the road. Two headlights are coming straight at them at speed. There's nowhere to go. Conor swings to the left, the van crunching against the wall and bumping over the grass verge. The oncoming car veers to the right, but it's too tight a space and the vehicles come together with an almighty crunch.

Momentum flings Freya and Nicole forward and they hit the seats in the front of the van.

For several seconds, Freya is stunned. She can hear the constant blare of a car horn. She can hear voices and shouting. She's tangled up with Nicole against the front seat. Freya moves her arms and then her legs. She's sore and she hurts but she doesn't think anything is broken. She looks at Nicole. There's a nasty gash on her head which is bleeding.

The car horn is still blaring. Somehow Freya manages to roll over and untangle herself from Nicole. She can hear car doors opening and more voices. 'Conor,' she croaks. 'Conor.' She hauls herself up on her knees and then to her feet. Conor is slumped over the steering wheel. She pulls him back and then lets out a scream.

One side of his face is completely smashed in from the impact with the steering wheel and his eyes are wide open, staring at nothing.

The door to the driver's side of the van opens. Freya backs away. She can't let Ahern get her. She's got to get her and Nicole out of here somehow.

At first she thinks she's imagining the voice. That the universe has answered her prayers. It can't be.

'You need to call an ambulance,' the voice is saying. 'Siobhan, call a fucking ambulance. I'm going up to Skerries.'

Freya moves forward to the front of the van. 'Dad,' she says. He doesn't hear her. He's looking back over his shoulder. He's about to get down from the van. 'Dad!' she screams, louder. And then louder again. 'Dad! It's me!'

There's a silence. He looks up. He says her name. 'Freya. Oh, sweet Mary Mother of God.' The shock has made him go full-on Irish. Freya laughs at the ridiculousness of it. She doesn't think she's ever heard her dad revert to a strong west coast accent before. She laughs harder and louder. Hysterically. 'Wait there!' he shouts. Within seconds the side door is open, and Freya launches herself into her father's arms.

FORTY-NINE

Danny and I spent the night in the hospital at Freya's bedside. She had been taken by ambulance and, after a thorough check-over, the doctors had said she was OK, but they would like to keep her in for observation. We didn't argue with that, but we were not about to let her out of our sight that night and had sat on either side of her bed in the most uncomfortable plastic seats ever invented. It didn't matter though. Our daughter was safe and unharmed.

The following morning, once Freya had eaten some breakfast, and I knew Danny was going to be sitting with her, I took ten minutes to go and find Nicole. She was in a different room along the corridor.

'Hey,' I said, poking my head around the door. 'Can I come in?'

She was sitting up in bed, eating toast. She had a bandage around her head but, other than that, no other visible signs of injury. 'How's Freya?' she asked.

'She's good. A couple of bumps and bruises, but she's going to be OK.' I sat on the chair next to the bed. 'Thank you, Nicole. Thank you for saving her.'

'You shouldn't be thanking me. I should be saying sorry to you.' Nicole looked down at her toast.

I wanted to forgive Nicole for her part in kidnapping Freya, I really did, but I needed an explanation, not an apology. 'What made you do it?' I asked. 'It wasn't a spur-of-the-moment bad choice thing. It was premeditated. I thought you wanted to help me. It doesn't make sense.'

Nicole continued to look down at her plate. I waited. I couldn't move on without knowing what had gone through her mind. 'Please, Nicole, I need to know.'

'Conor told me what Ahern wanted him to do,' said Nicole at last. 'Conor came to see me. He was freaking out about it. Said he didn't want to go along with it. Kidnapping and drugging a fifteen-year-old girl was way out of his comfort zone.'

'Really?'

She looked up and met my eyes. 'Yeah. As it happens, it was,' she said. 'Conor was not a criminal. Not like that. I'm not saying he was a saint, but it was low-level stuff. Selling a bit of weed to his mates. Making deliveries for people without asking questions. I know he followed you in the van that time, but he wouldn't have done anything to you. He was only trying to scare you off.'

'What made him agree to the kidnap, then?' I asked.

'Ahern said if he didn't, something might happen to Conor's mother.'

'What?'

'Yeah. She had clients, if you like. She...'

'Was a prostitute,' I suggested.

'If that's what you want to call her. But whatever, she was Conor's mum and he wanted to protect her.'

I tamped down my knee-jerk reaction to that bit of information, rejecting the tags of prostitute and kidnapper. They were a mother and son who, for reasons I didn't know, had turned to extreme measures to survive – a product of a broken society, perhaps?

I still wasn't satisfied though. 'If that's the case, what made him help Freya?'

'We planned it together,' said Nicole. This time there was a flicker of pride in her eyes as she looked up at me. 'We were both very much aware we were being used by Ahern and Aisling Denvers. They were getting us to do their dirty work and it would only get worse. If we did this, we would be in too deep.'

'Why didn't you go to Finn?' I asked. 'He would have helped you.'

'We didn't know if we could trust him.' Nicole took a sip of her water. 'We went along with what Ahern told us to do and we always planned to escape with Freya. We forgot to tell her that bit and she made a run for it herself.'

'She thought it was her only chance,' I said.

'I was already hiding in Conor's van when he drove up there,' continued Nicole. 'Ahern was going to move Freya because he knew the search would be widened the next day. Conor was supposed to take her to the lighthouse. Ahern had a key. He said after that he'd let her go. Conor didn't believe him though. Well, he didn't believe Aisling Denvers would let her go.'

A chill ran through my bones at the implications of the last sentence. I couldn't bring myself to contemplate that outcome. 'So you and Conor hatched a plan?' I asked.

'Yeah. We were going to drive straight back to your sister's house. To you.'

Tears filled my eyes. I wasn't sure why I was crying, but the thought they were planning to bring my daughter home set off all kinds of emotions I couldn't even begin to understand. 'Thank you,' I whispered.

'We figured you'd protect us. They wouldn't dare touch us

if you were involved. If you knew the whole truth.' A big tear plopped from Nicole's eye. 'Whatever they had planned, we thought we'd end up the same way.' She sniffed. 'I think the guards are coming to talk to me today.'

'Yeah, I expect they are. They're going to take statements from all of us. Tell them the truth and it will be OK. I promise you. You're as much a victim in this as Freya, Kathleen, Dervla and Conor.'

'Conor didn't deserve to die. Not like that. He had a shit life and an even shittier end.' She began to cry again.

'I'm sorry about Conor,' I said, and I genuinely meant it. Nicole was right, he didn't deserve to die like that.

I had such a mix of emotions about everything. I still didn't know what had happened to Kathleen, but I took some comfort that I had saved one of her girls, for want of a better phrase. Whatever the future held for Nicole, I was going to make sure I was there for her and help her in some way to make a better life for herself. That would be my legacy for my sister.

'Look, I need to go back to see Freya. The doctor is coming around this morning and I'm hoping she'll be released,' I said. 'I'll come and see you before I go.'

'Will you?'

She looked so young and vulnerable sitting there in the hospital bed that almost swallowed her tiny frame up. My heart went out to her. 'I promise. And when all this is over, I'm still going to be there for you.'

'Thank you,' she whispered.

As I left the room, the guard sitting outside nodded down the corridor. I looked over and there was Finn coming towards me.

'You're early,' I said. 'Official or unofficial visit?'

'Both. But I'll do the unofficial visit first. How's Freya?'

'She's sitting up and eating breakfast, which is a good sign,' I said.

'I wanted to let you and Danny know the latest developments,' said Finn.

'Come on down to Freya's room.'

Danny greeted Finn with a handshake and, giving Freya a kiss, he stepped out into the corridor to hear what Finn had to say.

'So, we've arrested Aisling Denvers initially for conspiracy to kidnap and perverting the course of justice,' said Finn. 'And I'm sure there will be more relating to what her husband has been up to. Fergus Denvers is also under arrest. Same charges plus grooming, statutory rape, coercion. We've also arrested Ahern.'

'Wow,' I said. 'Those are big arrests.'

'Sure is. The good thing about it, Ahern is willing to deal. Turns out, he's been safeguarding himself for this day. Recorded every interaction he had with Aisling and Fergus Denvers and with Conor Doyle. It's gold. We couldn't ask for any more evidence if we tried.'

'Is he going to get off with everything?' I asked.

'No. Not at all. He'll be going to prison for sure. I feel sorry for his wife, Maureen,' said Finn. 'You know she suffers with ME. Every euro Ahern made from this partnership with Aisling, he was putting away so he could take his wife to America for treatment. He was planning on going soon.'

'Is that supposed to make us feel sorry for him?' asked Danny.

'Not for him, but maybe for her,' replied Finn.

'How long has Ahern been doing all this?' I asked. 'Has he said anything about Kathleen?'

'We haven't got down to specifics yet,' said Finn. 'I did ask about Kathleen, of course. He said he didn't know what happened to her.'

'I don't know if that's good or bad,' I said.

'As soon as we find out, we'll let you know,' reassured Finn. 'I'm sorry I haven't got any answers for you yet.'

'What sort of woman is Aisling Denvers?' I asked. 'How could she cover up for her husband? She's got a daughter of her own. It's unbelievable.'

'Sadly, she prized her career over and above everything else,' said Finn. 'That's why she wasn't very happy when you came stirring things up again. God knows why she thought kidnapping Freya was a good idea. She was desperate and thought it would scare you off.'

'Like a warning?' said Danny.

'Yeah, exactly that,' said Finn. 'She said she had never planned to harm Freya. It was all to save her own arse.'

'She clearly doesn't know my wife,' said Danny, putting an arm around me. 'Of course I wish Freya hadn't been caught up in all this, but how many more young women would have fallen victim to Fergus?'

'Thank you for coming to see us,' I said to Finn. 'And thank you for everything you've done.'

'Just doing my job,' said Finn. 'We need you to stick around for a few more days. Official statements and all that. Is that OK?'

'Yes, that's fine,' I said. 'I'm going to try to have some normal family time. After all this, we have a lot of healing to do.'

Finn nodded. 'That's good. I hope it all goes smoothly.' He looked from me to Danny, and I thought for a moment he was going to say something, but he just gave a small smile, before heading off to Nicole's room.

'He's always had a thing for you,' said Danny, his eyes fixed on the door to Nicole's room.

I was glad he wasn't looking at me as I felt a small flush of guilt rise up my chest to my neck. 'Well, I'm not interested,' I said. 'I like Finn, but that's all.'

Danny turned to face me. 'I'm glad to hear that.'

'Danny,' I began. 'I need to say something before we go back in to Freya.'

'I'm listening.' There was an unexpected softness to his voice and that alone nearly brought me to tears before I'd even begun to speak.

'I can't tell you how utterly sorry I am for all this,' I said, looking down at the floor. 'I have never been so scared in all my life. When Freya went missing...' My voice broke as the emotions of the last twenty-four hours surfaced.

'I know,' Danny said. 'I felt the same. I don't know how I managed to function, to be honest. Panic was only a breath away.'

'I mean it when I say I'm sorry. I'm more sorry than I can ever say.' I wiped away the tears that were putting in an unexpected appearance.

'I know you're sorry,' he said. 'You don't have to apologise. I'm sorry for being so angry with you. I know you wouldn't intentionally put Freya in any danger. Please, Siobhan, I don't hold you responsible.'

I cried harder at his kindness and understanding. 'I'm also sorry for not telling you everything from the start.' When he didn't reply, I forced myself to look up to him.

The pain was clear on his face. 'That's a harder one to swallow,' he said. 'It hurts a lot to think you didn't trust me. That you lied to me.'

'I know,' I whispered. I tried not to cry. Self-pity was not an attractive feature in anyone. I'd save my tears and heartbreak for when I was alone. 'At first I didn't tell you because of my loyalty to Kathleen. But it wasn't only that. I thought if you didn't know how much I was involved, then you wouldn't be drawn into the lie.'

'I always knew there was something you weren't telling me,' he said.

'I promise I'll pay the money back to the savings,' I began.

'It's not about the money,' said Danny. 'I don't care about a single penny of that. It was because you refused to tell me what you were doing in Tralee, withdrawing money that night. It was obvious there was so much more going on, but you wouldn't tell me. That's why I couldn't stay. I couldn't stay with someone who didn't trust me.'

'I can't change what I did,' I said. 'If I could, I absolutely would. I could tell you I was scared, that it was misplaced loyalty, I thought I was doing the right thing, but at the end of the day, I chose not to tell you. And then the lie got too big, too quickly, and I didn't know how to come back from it.'

We stood in silence. I had no idea what else I could say or do. Was this where our marriage was going to end – in a hospital corridor? How apt. I wondered if there was an ICU for broken hearts.

'What are you going to do about Kathleen?' Danny asked.

'There's nothing more to do,' I said. 'I don't know if I'll ever find out what happened to her. What I do know is I can't use any more time or energy looking for her when I have a daughter who needs me. Freya isn't going to get over this in just a few days. She'll need my help, and I'm going to be there for her.'

'You're a good mum,' said Danny.

'She's going to need you too,' I said.

'I'm not planning on going anywhere. I'll be here for her.'

'Was there ever any doubt? You're a good dad,' I said.

Danny stuffed his hands into the pockets of his trousers. 'Well, aren't we the mutual appreciation society?'

I gave a small laugh. 'Aren't we just.'

He took his hands from his pockets and reached for my hands. 'I want to be a good husband too.'

My heart skipped a beat at his words. 'You are already.'

'What you said just now about family healing,' began Danny. 'I'm hoping that includes us.'

I thought my heart really was going to stop that time. Danny wanted to give us, give me, another chance. I wasn't sure I deserved it, but I wasn't going to pass up the chance either. 'Oh God. I so want it to,' I said.

'It may not happen overnight, but I'm not ready to give up on us,' he said, pulling me into his arms. 'It's always been you, Siobhan. Only you.'

My heart bounced in my chest at his words. 'Danny,' was all I managed to say as relief engulfed me.

'I've missed you, Siobhan. I'm not very good on my own.'

'I'm no good either,' I said. I put my hand to his face. I loved this man with every fibre of my being, and I wasn't sure how we were going to navigate the future, but I knew this awful experience had brought our love back to the surface where it should be. 'I love you, Danny Martin. Always have. Always will.'

A smile spread across his face. 'I love you too.'

That's all I wanted to hear. As I held my husband tightly, I mentally let Kathleen slip from my grasp. I would have to learn to live without knowing what had happened to her. She would always be in my heart, but my future was Danny and Freya.

FIFTY

The water is a translucent blue, tinged with shades of turquoise and topped with white as the waves crest and rush up to the shore. There's a gentle hum of conversation interspersed with laughter and distant shrieks of holidaymakers enjoying swimming and frolicking in the ocean. She stretches out a foot from the sun lounger, her pink-painted toenails stark against the golden sand, which is warm on the surface but cooler underneath. She's got quite a tan since she's been here. Who'd have thought a girl from Dingle would be lazing on an Indonesian beach?

She reaches out for the cocktail – a mix of orange and pinks – which she sips from the straw. She could lie here all day. In fact, that's exactly what she has been doing. It's her day off from working in the laundry room of a local hotel. God, she would have never imagined she'd be washing and pressing sheets to earn some money, but here she is. Here in Bali, she has enjoyed over seven months of anonymity. Here she can be Orla Collins, and no one knows any better, and nor do they care. That's the best bit of all. No one here asks questions about home. They just want you to come in, do your shift and that's it.

She thinks back to Ireland and the day she escaped. She had needed to get Dervla and herself somewhere safe. Somewhere far away. All the time Aisling and Fergus Denvers were unchallenged, she and Dervla would be a risk. Aisling was a facilitator. By protecting her precious career with the help of Ahern, Aisling was enabling her husband to carry on with his despicable actions.

Kathleen has come a long way since leaving; not only physically, but mentally as well. No one to answer to now. No one to intimidate her. No one to tell her what to do. No one to make her feel scared. But she knows the time has come to go home. It's safe to go back now. She's been biding her time, waiting for the right moment when the danger has passed.

She looks at the Irish newspaper and the story of Fergus Denvers being charged for grooming. His wife, Aisling Denvers, charged with conspiracy to kidnap, perverting the course of justice, along with several other offences. Sergeant Rory Ahern has racked up a whole host of offences, the main one being kidnapping.

Kathleen has spoken with the Serious Crime Team on the phone and has agreed to give a full statement about everything that happened to her. She's arranged for legal representation for when she goes home – a solicitor from Cork. She still doesn't trust anyone in authority from Dingle, or even Kerry, for that matter.

And now it's all official, there in black and white, she thinks of Fergus Denvers in particular. She was expecting to feel something for the man she once loved but is surprised there is little or no emotion. Maybe pity for him. He was a pathetic man really, and she's glad she can look back on her past and have no guilt. It's taken time to get to this point, but she feels happy in herself for the first time in a long while. Now she can go back and face her community and her family. Most of all she can face Kian. She had never wanted to tell him what she had gone through when she was younger. She didn't want Kian to know his life had begun from a place of control and manipulation. She didn't want her feelings of shame to be reflected in his own perception of himself.

Despite knowing it wasn't her fault, the shame still lingered. If Kian had known, he would only have seen a victim, and she didn't want her son to see her like that. Now though, after distance and time, she knows she's a survivor, and soon to be victor. That's the mother she wants her son to see. And now he can. Kathleen thinks back to that night in Dingle when John had almost strangled her.

She had lost consciousness. She really thought she was about to die, but he had released her for some reason. When she came around, John was standing over her with the Bible open in his hands. She had curled up in a ball, frightened he was going to attack her again and this time kill her. But he had just looked at her with utter disdain.

'John chapter one, verse nine,' he had said, thrusting the Bible towards her. 'Read it. Out loud.'

With a shaking voice, Kathleen had done as she was told. 'If we confess our sins, he is faithful and just and will forgive us our sins and purify us from all unrighteousness.'

'Repent and I will forgive you,' he said. 'I'll let you leave and by leave, I mean leave Dingle and never come back.'

And she had done that. There in that squalid room, she'd said sorry to him. He'd made her pray with him, and then he'd let her go on one condition: that she never came back and never made contact with Kian.

'All the time you're silent, then Kian is safe,' he'd warned. 'Don't cross me now, Kathleen.'

She'd had no doubt John was deadly serious. He'd sooner live a lie than let anyone know he'd been duped into thinking

Kian was his son for the past twenty years. So, she'd agreed. What choice did she have?

But now the tide has turned, and she feels stronger than she'd ever thought possible. She can go back home and reclaim her life – no, not reclaim, rebuild. She'll rebuild her life free of lies and deceit. She'll have the life she deserved, with her son.

The Serious Crime Team have assured her they are taking John's threats against Kian seriously and have already questioned him about historic and more recent incidents of domestic abuse. She realises now, like all bullies when their power of control is removed, John is nothing but a gutless coward. This will be another battle where she will reign victorious. Kathleen folds the newspaper in half and drops it into her bag. She'll read it again later. Right now, she has something to do.

She looks up and sees Dervla heading down the beach towards her. Dervla waves and Kathleen smiles. The young woman has come a long way herself since escaping Dingle. Kathleen doesn't regret what happened and how they ended up here. How could she? They've both got their lives back, or something of a life anyway. Her only regret about leaving Dingle was her family, and Kian especially. But now it's time to put things right.

'Are you ready?' asks Dervla.

'Yes. Are you?'

Dervla nods. 'It's the right time to do this.' She sits down next to Kathleen, who takes her phone from her bag and calls up a number. She passes it to Dervla, who waits for her mam to answer.

'Hey, Mam,' she says. 'Thought I'd let you know that I'm coming home next week.'

Kathleen waits while mother and daughter speak. It sounds like the conversation is going well. Mother and daughter have some work to do on their relationship, but Kathleen has high hopes for them.

Dervla ends the call and passes the phone to Kathleen. 'Your turn now.'

Her hand shakes a little as she selects the contact in her phone. It connects, rings and is answered in the space of a few seconds.

'Hello, Siobhan Martin speaking.'

Kathleen pauses, emotion catching her words at the sound of her sister's voice. 'Hello, Siobhan Martin, this is Kathleen Regan speaking.'

There's an audible gasp from the other end of the line. 'Kathleen?' The word is whispered.

'I'm coming home,' says Kathleen, through unexpected tears. 'I'm coming home.'

A LETTER FROM THE AUTHOR

Huge thanks for reading *The Missing Wife*. I hope you were hooked on Siobhan's journey. If you want to join other readers in hearing all about my new releases and bonus content, you can sign up for my newsletter!

www.stormpublishing.co/sue-fortin

If you enjoyed this book and could spare a few moments to leave a review that would be hugely appreciated. Even a short review can make all the difference in encouraging a reader to discover my books for the first time. Thank you so much!

I do hope you enjoyed reading about Siobhan and her sisters. I love writing about families. I'm one of four siblings and I have four children myself, which is probably why I find the whole family dynamics fascinating.

Family can evoke such strong emotions and can bring out both the worst and the best in us. They can provide the safety net which allows us to say or do things we wouldn't necessarily do 'in public' good or bad and, equally, they can provide the source for us to do things which would be considered out of character.

I thoroughly enjoyed bringing all these elements and more into the lives of the Regan sisters. It's been great to see how far Siobhan would go to protect her sister and during the writing process I often stopped and asked myself what would I do? To be honest, I'm not sure of my boundaries – hopefully I won't have to put myself to the test.

Thanks again for being part of this amazing journey with me and I hope you'll stay in touch – I have so many more stories and ideas to entertain you with!

Sue x

www.suefortin.com

facebook.com/suefortinauthor
x.com/suefortin1
instagram.com/sue_fortin_author
tiktok.com/@suefortin_author

ACKNOWLEDGEMENTS

I couldn't write a book about sisters without acknowledging my own sisters, whether we are bound by biology or by kinship. Your sisterhood is the thing that keeps me sane, listens to my woes, shares in my highs, makes me laugh and cheerleads me across the many finish lines in life. You know who you are, and you are all wonderful!

It's a lovely feeling getting to the end of a book; it brings a sense of accomplishment. But I would never get my manuscript into any decent shape without the amazing and insightful input from my brilliant editors at Storm. Thank you!

As always, much gratitude to my agent, Hattie, for being at the end of an email or Zoom call and for the reassuring knowledge that you're simply about if needed.

www.ingramcontent.com/pod-product-compliance
Lightning Source LLC
Chambersburg PA
CBHW011127190726
48289CB00012B/2941